Cassandra

Books by Kerry Greenwood

The Delphic Women Novels
Medea
Cassandra
Electra

The Phryne Fisher Series
Cocaine Blues
Flying Too High
Murder on the Ballarat Train
Death at Victoria Dock
The Green Mill Murder
Blood and Circuses
Ruddy Gore
Urn Burial
Raisins and Almonds
Death Before Wicket
Away With the Fairies
Murder in Montparnasse
The Castlemaine Murders
Queen of the Flowers
Death by Water
Murder in the Dark
Murder on a Midsummer Night
Dead Man's Chest
Unnatural Habits
Murder and Mendelssohn

The Corinna Chapman Series
Earthly Delights
Heavenly Pleasures
Devil's Food
Trick or Treat
Forbidden Fruit
Cooking the Books

Short Story Anthology
A Question of Death:
An Illustrated Phryne Fisher Anthology

Other Novels
Out of the Black Land

Cassandra

A Delphic Woman Novel

Kerry Greenwood

Poisoned Pen Press

Poisoned Pen Press
6962 E. First Ave., Ste. 103
Scottsdale, AZ 85251
www.poisonedpenpress.com
info@poisonedpenpress.com

Printed in the United States of America

This book is for Richard Revill. Fox.

Acknowledgments

With thanks to David Greagg, Jenny Pausacker, Susan Tonkin, Stuart Reeh, Edward Jarrett, Sarah Jane Reeh, Andrea Walker, Vanessa Craigie, Themetrula Gardner, Irene Kazantzidis, and Danny Spooner.

Cast List

TROJANS

Aegyptus	a shipmaster
Aeneas	son of Aphrodite
Anchises	father of Aeneas
Andromache	wife of **Hector** and mother of **Astyanax**
Astyanax	son of **Andromache** and **Hector**
Briseis	Trojan woman captured by **Achilles** and claimed by **Agamemnon**
Bashti	an Egyptian woman
Cassandra	daughter of **Priam** and **Hecube** and priestess of Apollo
Cerasus	son of **Priam**
Clea	a Trojan woman
Cycne	an Achaean ex-slave, now a Trojan girl
Dardanus	first king of Troy
Deiphobos	son of **Priam**
Dion	fisherman and priest of Poseidon
Eirene	'peace,' a Trojan girl
Eleni	twin brother of **Cassandra**, priest of Apollo
Erecthi	son of **Priam**
Ethipi	a shipmaster
Eumides	a trader, Trojan slave in Mycenae
Ganymede	a Trojan prince kidnapped by Zeus

Hector	son of **Priam**, captain of the city, 'bulwark of the city'
Hecube	the Queen
Idume	priest of Adonis
Iris	a Trojan girl
Lani	a woman of Troy
Maeles	fisherman and priest of Poseidon
Maeron	a Trojan boy
Mysion	priest of Apollo
Nyssa	the twins' nurse
Oenone	wife of **Pariki**, mother of **Corythus**
Pandarus	Trojan hero
Pariki	son of **Priam**
Perseis	mistress of maidens
Polites	son of **Priam**
Polyxena	daughter of **Priam**, sister of **Cassandra**
Psyche	an archer of Troy
Priam	the King, 'the ransomed one'
Sarpedon	a hero of Troy
Sirianthis	a soldier of Troy
Státhi	a mou or cat, Egyptian beast, friend of **Hector**
Theones	a shipmaster
Tithone	the healer, priestess of the Mother
Tros	second king of Troy, the holy city of Ilium

AMAZONS

Aigleia	'eagle-eyed'
Charis	
Eris	'strife'
Hippia	'horse-woman'
Myrine	
Penthesileia	leader of the Amazons, daughter of **Ares**
Tydia	

ACHAEANS (also called **ARGIVES**)

Achilles	son of **Thetis**, leader of the Myrmidons
Agamemnon	son of **Atreas** of Mycenae
Arias	a hero
Arion	of Telamon, 'dolphin-rider,' a bard
Atreidae	collective title for the brothers **Agamemnon** and **Menelaus**
Calchas	high priest of Apollo
Castor and **Polydeuces**	twin brothers of **Elene**
Clytemnestra	daughter of **Zeus** and **Leda**, half-sister of **Elene**, married to **Agamemnon**
Dikaos	lord of Tiryns
Diomedes	a hero of Aetolia
Elene	daughter of **Zeus** and **Leda**, most beautiful woman in the world, married to **Menelaus**
Elis	a woman of Mycenae
Hermaphroditus	a nymph who had her wish granted
Iphigenia	daughter of **Agamemnon**, sacrificed for a wind at Aulis
Menelaus	brother of **Agamemnon**, prince of Sparta and husband of **Elene**
Menon	apprentice to the bard **Arion**
Neoloptolemus	son of **Achilles** by **Deidama**, born after Achilles left Sciros where he had hidden among the girls
Nestor	the 'honey voiced' old man, went with the Argonauts and then to Troy
Odysseus	prince of Ithaca, called Kokkinos 'red-head'
Palamedes	of Euboea, father of **Chryseis** and lover of **Yrses,** responsible for bringing **Odysseus** to the Trojans **Patrocles** lover of **Achilles**, killed by **Hector**
Perseus	founder of Mycenae, demigod
Philoctetes	an archer, marooned and retrieved on prophecy of **Eleni** of Troy

Pithias	a goatherd of Mycenae
Talthybius	herald of the Arrgives
Telamon	married the kidnapped **Hesione**, princess of Troy
Thersites	an Achaean soldier
Tyndareus	king of Sparta, foster father **Elene**
Talthybius	herald of the Arrgives

HEALERS

Achis	a Kritian healer
Asius	a healer
Chryseis	daughter of **Palameses**, wife of **Diomenes**
Diomenes	priest of Asclepius, also called **Chryse** 'the golden'
Glaucus	master of Epidavros, priest of Asclepius
Itarnes	a healer and **Diomenes'** best friend
Lapith	a Corinthian healer
Macaon	the surgeon, son of **Glaucus**
Podilarius	the physician, son of **Glaucus**
Telops	a healer
Thorion	a healer
Tiraes	an old man

PATIENTS (or SUPPLIANTS)

Cleone	an Achaean woman
Milanion	a soldier
Myrses	lover of **Palamedes**
Päis	a pregnant woman
Pilis	man of Kokkinades

Notes on the House of Atreus

First was TANTALUS, son of Zeus, who liked offending gods. Stole nectar and ambrosia and sold it to men. Tattled about Olympus. He cooked and served up his son PELOPS to Zeus, who took offense, and sent him to stand in crystal water but never be able to drink to be in biting range of apples and never eat. Zeus resurrected PELOPS, replacing his cooked shoulder with an ivory one.

Pelops, king of Phrygia inherited mischievous tendencies. Courted Hippodemia, princess of Pisa. Her father challenged each suitor to a chariot race which he always won. She got tired of this and sawed the royal axle half through. Wheel fell off, Pelops won, and killed Oenomaus. Hippodemia married Pelops and bore Thyestes and Atreus.

Atreus married Aerope but she fell in love with Thyestes and bore him two children, which Atreus cooked and served up to his brother at a reconciliation supper. *AT THIS POINT THE GODS CURSED THE HOUSE OF ATREUS AND ONE CANNOT BLAME THEM.*

Subsequently, Atreus's sons were Menelaus of Mycenae who married Elene, and Agamemnon, who married Elene's mortal sister Clytemnestra and sacrificed his own daughter, Iphigenia, at Aulis for wind to Troy. Subsequently Clytemnestra took up with Aegisthis, Agamemnon's nephew, incestuous child of Thyestes and his own daughter, born as a revenger for his father, and they killed Agamemnon when he came home from Troy.

Gods

ACHAEAN

Aphrodite	of Cyprus, 'the Stranger,' goddess of erotic love, also known as Ishtar
Apollo	the Archer, 'Sun Bright,' Sun God, patron of Asclepius the Healer
Ares	god of war
Artemis	the virgin hunter
Asclepius	son of **Apollo**, patron of medicine
Athene	Pronaea the virgin, his sister
Attis	the castrated god
Boreas	god to the north wind
Clotho	the Spinner, **Lachesis** the Measurer and **Athropos** who cuts the thread of life; the Spinners, the Fates

Demeter	the mother goddess
Eos	goddess of dawn
Erinyes	'the kindly ones,' 'the revengers of blood,' the Furies, **Tisiphone, Alecko,** and **Mageara**
Hephaestus	smith of the gods
Hera	wife of **Zeus**
Hermes	the Messenger and guide of the gods
Hygeia	daughter of **Asclepius**
Hypnos	god of trance
Morpheus	lord of sleep, brother of **Thanatos**
Pan	'ageless' lord of forests and goats
Pluton	'the rich one,' a title of **Hades**, god of the underworld and ruler of the dead
Poseidon	'Earth Shaker', 'Blue-Haired,' god of the sea
Selene	goddess of the moon
Thanatos	'dark angel,' lord of death
Zeus	the Father

TROJAN

The Lady Gaia	Mistress of Animals, Snake Lady, one of the Three Women, **Maiden**, **Mother** and **Crone**, who rule all female principles and breeding, mating, healing, growing, and nurture. Her black aspect is **Hecate**, Destroying Mother, goddess of war
The Lord Dionysius	male principle who rules wine, writing, and intelligence, also madness, sex, and sacrifice
Apollo	Sun God, aspect of **Dionysius**
Adonis	the dead god, god of rebirth; known in Egypt as **Osiris** or **Tammuz**

HORSES

Banthos	horse of Glaucus
Pyla	horse of Diomenes

Prologue

Aphrodite yawned. She stretched, the mossy garment slipping down over her perfect breasts and pearly arms, sighed, and shook back her silky hair, long and golden. Olympus, home of the gods, basked under honeyed sunlight.

Even perfection can become tedious.

'My Lord,' she called, 'Sun God and brother, shall we play a game?'

'What game, lady?' asked Apollo, lounging at the foot of the throne of the gods. 'And what is the wager?'

'A golden apple, one of the Hesperides' from the tree at the end of the world. A mortal sent it to you, but I stole it,' she smiled. Apollo returned the gaze levelly, blue eyes staring into grey, and the goddess of love faltered a little.

'You have a regard for mortals,' she challenged. 'You guard them and teach them and they amuse you. Let us play a game with mortals—for the apple. My power against yours, my Lord.'

'Your thesis?' asked the woman, Demeter, Earth Mother.

'That love is stronger than death,' said Aphrodite. 'That there is nothing, nothing which even the gods can inflict upon humans, that will have victory over love.'

'Sentiment,' snorted Athene, Mistress of Battles. 'Men are foolish, clumsy, and ruled by lust and greed. Except for my own city, the realm and cities of Achaea are brutal and stupid.'

'Your city, Athens, is as brutal and stupid as the rest,' rumbled the Sea God, Poseidon. 'And Mycenae, ruled by Agamemnon, yes,

and Tiryns and Argos, are blood-soaked and cursed. Even my greatest storms could not wash the taint of brother murder from them. Even worse is Troy, the holy city Ilium, where an upstart king banished my worship from the walls. I am minded to the destruction of Troy, my lords.'

'Then let it be Troy,' said Aphrodite eagerly. 'We shall play out our wager between Achaea and Troy; that should be a testing enough ordeal for our game. If you lose, I keep the apple. Come now, my Lord Apollo—you may have first choice in creating your creature. Will you wager?'

Apollo looked at the apple, gleaming in the immortal hand, and nodded.

He sat down on the edge of the Pool of Beginnings and breathed on the water, which misted and then cleared. A picture began to form.

'I shall have an Achaean, since you support Troy,' he commented. 'A child, since we must train him all his life. A peasant, I think, they are stronger.'

Green hills and bright sun formed in the mirror-pool, idly stirred by Apollo's breath. 'A beautiful boy,' he continued, 'but one who does not know his beauty. A priest healer, Lady Aphrodite, not a warrior. Warriors die too easily, and if he was killed in battle I might lose my bet. Where are you, little one, favoured of Apollo?' he asked, stirring the mirror. 'Come, come to me, my gage, my plaything. There.' His finger stabbed into the pool and ripples ran out silver and sparkling. 'The perfect one. His name Diomenes, but they will call him Chryse, the Golden One.'

'Too late,' gloated Aphrodite. 'Thanatos, the God of Death, has him. Try again, Lord Apollo. Your plaything is dead.'

'Not yet.' Apollo cupped his hands around his smiling mouth and called. Something swam up to the surface of the pool; an angel in cloudy draperies, cradling a sleeping boy in his arms.

'Mine,' said Apollo. 'Diomenes is mine.'

'Drop your prey, good dog,' taunted Aphrodite. 'Snarl, dog!'

Death inclined his hemlock-crowned head with dignity and swooped down into the picture again, delivering Diomenes into the arms of Death's brother, bay-crowned Morpheus, who is called Sleep. The boy shifted unhappily, writhed in pain, and held out his arms to Death, and the gods laughed merrily.

'There,' said Apollo. 'He will grow up in the temple, my temple, worshipping me. Who will give me aid? Poseidon, my Lord Zeus?'

'I will give him no gifts,' said Poseidon. 'He will fear the sea. And until Troy is fallen, my Lord Sun God, I will not help you.'

'He must worship without belief,' said Zeus the Father. 'You have an advantage, my son; your puppet is male and the Achaeans do not recognise the importance of women, who they call slaves and vessels for seed, of no more significance than a fertile field. Therefore, I will give him an independent mind, but that is all. I do not like these games,' added the Lord Father Zeus, walking away. 'Mortals were not created solely for your amusement, my son.'

Apollo did not reply but bent his head, the dark hair falling over the marble-smooth shoulders, hiding his face and his bright, disturbing eyes. There was a short silence, in which Aphrodite and Queen Hera exchanged glances.

Apollo stirred the surface a little, watching the child Diomenes settle into sleep. The pool showed the interior of a white temple and the stature of the healer Apollo, whose son is Asclepius the physician, made of ivory and gold. He drew in a breath, snuffing the savour of burnt meat. Divine nostrils flared. When he spoke, his voice was rich with satisfaction. 'Diomenes will meet your puppet, Lady Aphrodite, but all your sweet scents and fluttering doves will not be able to seduce him. If he loves her, it will not last. Because this is a doomed love; as doomed as a god can make it. Many things are stronger than love, the frailest force in the universe. Chryse Diomenes will sicken under the burden of death and blood and war; and he will leave her there, at the gates of Troy, as the towers flame like oil-lamps and are quenched with blood.'

'Troy will fall,' said Poseidon hungrily. 'I will wash out their presumption with bitter water as salt as unnumbered tears.'

Aphrodite, in her moss green draperies, sat down on the edge of the pool and breathed on the water. It revealed a large city built of grey stone. Many ships were in the harbour, and banners flew from the highest point.

'*In the palace of Troy, which shall not fall if I can prevent it,*' *said Aphrodite, stroking a silver-feathered dove, '*she is being born. My maiden. Cassandra the twin, understanding all, seeing all. No god will be able to hide from her! I give her clear sight and a strong heart. She will meet your Diomenes, Lord Apollo, your golden Chryse, and she will not falter, and neither will he. They will endure though the city falls into destruction, because love is stronger in despair. Nothing will part them; they will be one flesh. Join with me, mother and queen! Hera, Demeter, behold your daughter.*'

*They looked into the Pool of Beginnings, where a golden-haired child and her brother toddled fearlessly into a temple and snakes wreathed them. Demeter Earth Mother put out her hand, palm down, her arm and hand twined about with never-fading flowers. '*Daughter Cassandra,*' she said, '*be wise and strong. Trust in yourself.*'

*Hera, queen of the gods, breathed divine life into the small figure. '*Daughter Cassandra,*' she said, '*you have dominion and the power of command. But beware of men, little princess. Beware of the beguilements of the Lord of the Sun. For that is what you intend, is it not?*' she challenged Apollo. '*You intend to seduce her from the Mother to your worship, Sun God?*'

'*Of course,*' agreed Apollo. '*She will be my maiden, then maiden no longer—and she will fail, Lady of Mortal Love. No human can be more steadfast than the gods. I will test her, Aphrodite of Cyprus, and she will fail. Her loves will fall from her like leaves from a tree, leaving her naked to men's cruelty and men's lust. No love will be left in her when she meets my creature Diomenes, and he will have no love left to give. Your wager is lost,*' he smiled his three-cornered smile, breathtakingly beautiful.

'*Humans cannot be as enduring as trees,*' Demeter was uneasy. '*What game is this, played without rules? Poor healer, poor princess! If you persist in this, my lord, I will oppose you. The power of Earth is great and it is ancient—far older than your petty male worship of ideas and words. I will assist her, I warn you, if you intend to cheat.*'

'What about Troy?' Poseidon breathed on the water and black ships swept across the troubled sea. 'Troy can stand against any siege. How then, shall it fall and I be avenged?'

'That is another matter,' said Athene uneasily, 'in which the Father Zeus has an interest. Leave to me the fall of Troy, and the punishment of blasphemers.'

'And the maiden Cassandra and this poor healer-priest Diomenes?' asked Demeter. 'Shall they be caught up in these great events and tortured and twisted, all for the sake of a wager? Have you no pity?'

'For the sake of the golden apple,' said Apollo to Aphrodite, 'I oppose my Chryse Diomenes to your Cassandra, Princess of Troy. I will prove that your light power, frail love, easily broken, is no match for thought and philosophy and war; I will prove that men will trade all the happiness in the world for a handful of ashes. The golden apple is mine.'

He snatched it out of Aphrodite's hand, then dropped it as if it stung his fingers. She had warmed it with the heat of her eyes and it shone white hot, sizzling on the marble floor. 'Not yet,' said the goddess of love. 'You have not won yet.'

Chapter One

Cassandra

It was a black vision. Sand under my feet, the ocean roaring, the flames biting at the sky as the holy city of Ilium was consumed. Achaean voices in the night; harsh, triumphant, trumpets braying the death of Troy.

It was not a vision. I smelt sweat, grease, salt, men, and burning. Always the burning, the reek of wood and flesh which soured my nostrils and seared my throat. I have no refuge. I am unarmed. I will not be here. I will not hear. I will not see. I will not feel.

◇◇◇

When we were three, they took us, my twin brother and me, to the house of the Mother, the cave under Troy where Gaia the goddess dwelt, pregnant with life. I am told that we are identical, Cassandra and Eleni, both small, square children with the golden hair of the house of Tros.

We were not afraid, because we were never afraid when we were together. Nyssa, our nurse, led us to the entrance of the cave, and I remember hearing her voice quaver as she said, 'Go in, now, and don't be scared.' We wondered that Nyssa was frightened.

We could see nothing to fear. We joined hands in case there should be something interesting in the dark which one of us might miss and toddled forward into the grateful dark. Both Eleni and I have always had sensitive eyes which cannot bear strong sunlight.

It was not black, in the womb of the earth mother. A little light leaked in from the open door and more through cracks in the beehive brick which made the dome. The floor was dry and sandy.

The walls were decorated with frescoes of dancers and bulls and we were fascinated. Eleni pointed and said, 'Bull,' and we toddled over to touch the picture, tracing the proud horned head and the curves of the elegant acrobats, the bull-leapers, coloured ochre for male and white for female. In the centre of the womb rose the phallus of Dionysius the god, erect, pointing skyward, and when we ran out of bulls we sat down with our backs against it, beginning to be bored.

There was a slither in the sand and two snakes came out of some hole and inched towards us. We were delighted. We had never been allowed to play with the house snakes, and these were much bigger than the rat killers that lived under every house altar. They were as fat as my arm, mottled a beautiful green and brown like the gauze on our Lady Mother's veil that came, she said, from so far away.

The snakes paused, flicked the air with their forked tongues, and inched towards us. Eleni and I held our breath, afraid that we might scare them. They moved in a fascinating way, leaving v-shaped patterns in the dust. Although we could hear a scrape of scales, they seemed to flow, without effort, and the patterns rippled as they moved. They seemed to be creatures entirely divine, unearthly, purposeful.

They split up and approached us. I stared into the dark, hoping that they would come closer. Eleni whispered, 'Pretty,' and reached out his hands. They came closer, one snake for each twin, and rose up from the ground, so that we were looking for a moment straight into the serpents' eyes.

There was something there, we both felt it: intelligence or will. Slowly, as though they did not want to startle us, the heads swayed to left and right, and we giggled as the flickering tongues touched first one ear and then the other.

The snakes withdrew. We were sorry. Then an old woman and a young man came in, looked at us, and went out again. The woman was ancient. Her hair floated like a white cloud, she was bent and toothless and leaned on a staff. The young man glowed with life. He had a fierce, wild face and he grinned at us with white teeth. He carried a vine staff in one strong brown hand and he was wreathed with vine leaves.

It was the first time we had seen the gods. Mother Gaia as crone and Lord Dionysius in all his dangerous joy.

We cried when they left and Nyssa rushed in with two priests and took us into the temple.

I remember it chiefly because they gave us honey. We had never tasted such sweetness before.

◇◇◇

The Lady Queen Hecube was our mother and the Lord King Priam was our father. They were magnificent, golden, and distant as clouds. Nyssa looked after us, the royal twins. She was fat and skilled and loving. Her eyes were black, as was her hair, and her skin was like the sea foam at the water's edge, where it is pale brown and crinkly. She was an Achaean and she taught us her language, as well as our own and the words for the gods, which were in an old and holy tongue. Nyssa's only child had died, and when we were born the Lady Hecube had given us into her arms. She loved us as if we were her own.

Eleni and I were quick—or so Nyssa said—and we liked words and names. We would play word games between ourselves, learning the dangerous lesson that words can be used to cloak thoughts as well as reveal them.

'What is Achaean for the father god?' eight-year-old Eleni would ask me as we lay down for our compulsory sleep in the heat of the day.

'Zeus, the Sky Father, Compeller of Clouds,' I rolled the title over my tongue.

'And the Trojan?'

'Dionysius, Vine-Clad. What is the Achaean for the mother?'

'Hera. I think.'

'Yes. And our mother?'

'Gaia, mother of all. But Cassandra, there is another lady other Achaeans have. Nyssa told me when you were out with the herb gatherers. What were you looking for in the marsh, anyway?'

'Roots of comfrey, for wounds. What did Nyssa say?' I settled more comfortably into the curve of my twin's side. He was not interested in herb, and I was. It was the first time we had not both been occupied in learning the same thing and he was a little jealous. So was I, of him, for getting any new stories out of Nyssa.

'Artemis.'

'Well, what does she do?'

'She's a virgin and she hunts things. Her priestesses are virgins, too.'

This struck me as odd. 'Why? What special virtue lies in virginity? Are they barren?'

I was working with the healers and they were all women, as it was well known that women keep the secrets of birth and death. Are not the sisters Clotho, Lachesis, and Athropos the spinners of fate? Clotho spins the thread of life, Lachesis measures it, and Athropos cuts it. Maiden, mother, and crone; no state is good in itself. They all have their season and their power.

'I don't know, twin. That was all Nyssa said.'

I rolled over and idly examined our room. The sky blue paint was peeling away from the plaster where the ceiling joined the painted fresco of tritons and sea-creatures. Poseidon Earth-Shaker had originally painted in one corner, blowing a conch, but he had been painted over when Laomedon the king had banished the god from the city of Tros. You could still see the outline of a broad-chested man with blue hair under the later fishes.

'Do you want to be a virgin all your life?' asked Eleni and I pulled a handful of his corn-coloured hair.

'You know I don't. I want to marry you.'

He laughed and said, 'Even to follow a goddess?' I thought about this. 'I don't know,' I said. Eleni turned to me and I saw his blue-green eyes glint in the cool light. 'I would not be a virgin to follow any lady,' he said. He kissed me lovingly. His mouth tasted of green herbs, fresh and unripe.

'It will be six years before we can marry,' I said wistfully. 'When we are fourteen.'

'We shall go up to the temple,' said Eleni, his arm around me.

I sighed on his breath, 'And tell the Lady Gaia and the Lord Dionysius. I will have a purple chiton and a himation of gold.'

'I will have a purple tunic and a mantle of gold,' he kissed me again.

'Because we are the royal twins.'

'And the snakes gave us the gift of prophecy.'

'And they will bless us,' I stroked Eleni's neck, where the hair sprung rough from the nape.

'They will marry us to each other,' he whispered into my ear, making me shiver pleasantly.

'As Pharoah marries his sister,'

'As Pharoah marries her brother,'

'And we will be together for ever and ever,'

'And death shall not sever us.'

Strophe and antistrophe, this was litany. We loved each other with a pure love which was all encompassing. If Eleni loved something, then I loved it also. We kissed with eight-year-old passion which had nothing of the flesh in it, and fell asleep, as we always did, with our arms around each other, Eleni's head and mine on the one pillow, each mimicking (Nyssa said) the attitude of the other.

We dreamed, and this is what we dreamed: the coming of a new god, a flesh-eating demon, who ate up Troy and belched fire. We woke screaming.

'Demon! I saw a demon!' Eleni grabbed wildly for comfort and I seized him tightly, witless with shock. We clutched each other close and found a little comfort in our embrace. 'Dreadful,' I panted. 'He's coming to eat us!'

'And there were shades, grey ghosts—did you see them?'

We shuddered strongly. We had been taught that the dead, after remaining for three days until they are properly burned, go on to join the gods in the meadow playground where it never snows and wind never blows, to lie down with their loved ones in sweet grass and sleep or wake as they like, with the proud horses of the City of Horses beside them. Never to return, impossible to summon, no longer concerned with us, to be properly mourned and with all suitable ritual to be dismissed to their deserved rest in the fields of heaven. But Eleni and I, with one mind and sight, had seen grey shadows like men and women, draped in shadowy cloth, wandering mindless through grey streets, lost to their earth and their former selves, with no memory.

'Their lovers,' he choked, and began to cry, and our tears mingled and rolled down into our hair, 'they passed each other and never knew that they loved.'

'The children,' I said, crying freely, 'the children and the mothers not touching, not knowing...'

We cried together, speaking the vision for the first time. Previously they had been playful, funny, charming things, scenes of places far away, and sharing them in our minds had been enough. Now we were seriously disturbed and words gave us structure and took away some of the horror.

'A demon god, on a throne, lord of demons, an eater of people,' my twin sobbed into my breast.

'Blood on his jowl and on his hands, dripping,' I shook with terror and disgust.

'Smoke from the burning of dead animals and men all around him; he snuffed it as though it smelt sweet as incense,' whispered Eleni.

'Horrible,' I agreed. 'He's coming to eat Troy.'

'Yes. We are his sacrifice—that's what it means—the soldiers are coming to make a burned offering of Troy to their demon.'

'The soldiers. I saw them. Bronze men. They shone in the sun.'

'Glittering. Their helmets are made in the shapes of beasts.'

'Beast men, with a beast god.'

Open-mouthed, Eleni and I kissed. Salt with tears, the kiss was harsh, bitter as the embrace of the shipwrecked we sometimes found on the shore, arms around each other, dying mouth locked to mouth.

We slept again after a little while. We did not dream again and we did not tell anyone about the vision, not at the time. It seemed too strange, too horrible. We should have gone to the temple and told the priest of Apollo about it. He sent the dream, straight and wounding as an arrow, poisoning our sleep and stirring our passion.

We were woken by Hector, calling us to come down to the harbour with him. We dragged on our tunics and found our sandals and ran past Nyssa, who was telling us to wash our faces, and scaled Hector like a wall.

He laughed—we could feel his bass laugh through his embrace—and perched us one on each shoulder. We were high up and perfectly safe—Hector would never let us fall—and we grabbed a handful of his coarse, pale hair as we jolted down the steep street which led to the Scamander Gate. We crossed the Place of Strangers' Gods and Hector set us down while he mounted his horse, then we scrambled up and clung to him, one each side, like the monkeys that Theones the shipmaster had brought back from the coasts of the strange land where the men were black and the forests yielded gold. Hector's eyes were grey and they twinkled. He never teased and he always let us come with him.

'What was wrong with you, twins?' he asked, hugging Eleni closer as he seemed likely to fall off. 'I heard you crying.'

Eleni looked at me round the bulk of our brother's torso. I shook my head. I did not want to tell. 'Just a bad dream,' said Eleni. 'We had a bad dream. Where are we going?'

'Down to the harbour—two ships have come in from Kriti. Wine for the king, finest olive oil for the perfumers, and…' he paused, smiling.

'Honey for the twins!' we chorused, greedily.

Our brother Hector was as tall as a tree, as strong as a bull, massive and gentle. He could throw a spear further than anyone else, tame the wildest horse with words and touch, leap like a deer and fight like a lion. What foe, what demon, could overcome Hector our brother?

He was our best source of stories. Hector knew everything.

The first story I remember he told us, we must have been four or five years old. We were lying on the flat roof of the palace. The palace is a rambling, three-storeyed building, the finest in Troy. It occupies the highest point. The Achaeans would call it an acropolis. When we came here from the Island, we built flat roofs, and although the newer houses have sloping roofs which drain better, the palace is the oldest building in Troy.

Hector was lying on his cloak, the purple himation of the prince of Ilium. All the royal house were dressed in purple, derived from boiling murex shells. We were not allowed to go down by the dyers because of the dreadful smell, so it became a fascinating and forbidden place, and we went there when we could, although Nyssa always knew because of the stink and because our feet were dyed by contact with the running gutters. Then he scrubbed us with soapleaf and pumice stone and scolded all the while.

We never minded Nyssa scolding. We learned a lot of new words. The only way she could effectively punish us was to separate us—we were proof against spanking and words ran off us like water off a turtle's shell. But when separated we cried so lamentably, and above all so loudly, that she always relented after about an hour and put us back together again. Whereupon we would cease crying instantly and embrace and then think of something even more wicked to do. Poor Nyssa—we led her a trying life.

Eleni and I were lying on either side of Hector, resting our chins on his chest. He was broad-shouldered, our brother, and we liked the way the muscles moved under his skin when he breathed. He was as golden as a lion, with a mane of bright hair and a bristly golden beard as thick as twigs at the roots. His hands were big, with golden hair on the back, which I liked to tug at, and his arms were massive and bound with gold bracelets. He wore a pale green tunic of the cloth which came out of Egypt and was called linen. They make it out of reeds.

He had laid aside the pot of ink which he always wore on his neck, with the scribe's pen in it, and the scroll of Egyptian papyrus to make notes on. Our brother made notes about everything. He was the arranger of the city, the king—our father's right hand. Hector knew to bale how much wool we had sold to Phrygia, how much amber and tin bought from Caria, and how much pottery and how many necklaces from Achaea down to the last and tiniest bead. He knew how many horses were in any of the king's herds, their breeding, their increase, and their value as chariot horses or plough beasts. Hector had at his little finger's end more knowledge of the people of Troy, their trades, their occupations, and their private lives than all of the Priam's sons who sailed and traded across the Pillars of Heracles and up and down the shoreless sea.

They said in the city that he had numbered the winds and counted the tides and they laughed at him, though carefully and out of earshot. They might curse his name and his family all the way back to Dardanus, as they searched a hold for a forgotten ingot or accounted for a lost sheep eaten by wolves the previous winter, but they trusted him, and he was very strong, a mighty warrior when there was cause. Was it not Hector Cuirass of Troy who had led a charge against the Mycenaean pirates who had landed and sacked a village, killing them to the last man?

Lying on Hector's chest was his cat, a creature called Státhi, ash, because of the colour of his fur. He was a gift from a grateful priestess in the Nile delta, from a place called Bubastis. We did not ask what she was grateful for and Hector never told us. Státhi was the first cat we had ever seen in the fur. He was about the same size as a small dog, though dogs were terrified of him, and he had thick, deep velvety fur, ash-coloured and barred with black like burned wood. His eyes were leaf green and cool. Hector had been given him as a small cub, and had carried him in his tunic against his heart for the length of the voyage, afraid that such a small creature might die of cold. Thereafter Státhi considered Hector the only human worth noticing—I think he thought our brother was a large furless cat—and was distant with all others, if not hostile. Once Eleni and I had pulled his tail and been swiftly punished for our impudence with a hand each sliced across with talons as sharp as a hawk's. We had not noticed that Státhi had claws—he kept them concealed in his paws—and we were much astonished and had howled. Hector had not been sympathetic.

'Státhi is a divine creature, the servant of a goddess,' he had reproved us. 'You must expect to be hurt if you provoke him.'

Státhi had never seemed like a servant to us. He had a royal, arrogant leisure in all his movements. When the palace dogs attacked him in a body, barking at this strange new creature, he called upon his lady and she doubled his size, endowing him with eyes that glowed like embers and teeth of strongest ivory. She had also given him a scream which rose from a growl to a shriek, a voice that summoned all within hearing to the rescue.

Not that he needed rescue. The dogs, thoroughly unnerved, decided that there were other things that urgently needed their attention and thereafter left him severely alone. He still occasionally slapped an intrusive nose with his thorned paw, just to remind them that a goddess' friend was present, and they always retreated, howling. Státhi would sometimes allow a caress from someone other than Hector, and Eleni and I loved to stroke his velvety fur. But he would endure the caress rather than enjoy it, and when he was tired of the touch he would turn and bite, hard. The city called him 'Hector's shadow' because, unless he had important business in the palace kitchens, he was always at the prince's heels, an aloof and mystical being, interested in everything, following his own purposes.

Hector had once found him in the goddess' shrine, seated with his tail wrapped around his paws, staring into the eyes of the sacred serpents, who also sat coiled and apart. Divine creatures recognise each other's divinity.

'Tell us a story,' we begged, keeping a wary eye on Státhi, who might scratch if we disturbed him. Hector stared up at the starry sky. It was summer and hot in the palace below. It was cooler on the roof, where there is always a breeze.

'I've been unloading ships all day,' he said sleepily. 'What sort of story?'

'About us.'

'About Troy.'

Hector sighed—our chins rose and fell with his breath—and said, 'Do you see those stars? The shape like a square, over there?'

'We see them,' said Eleni, speaking for both of us.

'Once in the Troad, before this city was built, there was a king who had a beautiful child.'

Státhi, liking the sound of Hector's voice, settled down into a crouch. We snuggled closer to our brother's sides and wrapped the folds of his cloak around us all.

'The child's name was Ganymede,' said Hector. Like his hair, his voice was golden, slightly husky and sweet on the ear. 'The child was so beautiful that the god himself wanted him as a lover, so he sent an eagle down to the house of Tros and the eagle of the gods took the child up into the air, high as the sky, and brought him to the god. There he was much beloved, until the god's other lover, a daughter of the goddess, grew jealous. Then the father, to save the child, lifted him higher into the cosmos and placed him among the stars. They call him Aquarius, the water-bearer.'

'And is he happy?' I asked. 'Wouldn't he rather be a prince of Troy like you? Didn't his mother and father cry for him?'

'They gave Tros and his wife two great horses—the mother and father of the horse herds of Troy.'

'But they were horses, not a son,' said Eleni, echoing thought.

'Gods will not be denied, twins,' said Hector gently. 'When a god requires a life, then it cannot be denied. All people can do is make the best bargain they can.'

'Could an eagle come and carry us off?' Eleni asked anxiously. Everyone told us that we were beautiful, and we were twins, too—that might attract a god's notice. Hector laughed so much that he jolted us off his chest. He hugged us close and sat up, groaning, much to the displeasure of Státhi.

'An eagle could not possibly carry you off,' he said, rubbing at his chest where our chins had rested. 'You are much too heavy for one poor eagle.'

We were comforted by this and all four of us drifted off to sleep.

Chapter Two

Diomenes

I was six when I died.

I heard Glaucus, Master of Epidavros, talking to my father, their voices blurring in the gloom. My eyes were dimming. I could no longer feel my hands or feet. I was beyond the awful pain which had burned through my insides. I floated for a little, listening.

'The boy has eaten nightshade berries,' the master commented evenly. 'They are lethal. There is nothing we can do. The boy will die.'

'Is there no god to whom I can sacrifice?'

My father sounded desperate. The Carian woman, my mother, had died when I was born. I was his only son. If I had been in my body I would have wept as my father did, but I was floating like a feather, and feathers cannot weep.

'A white kid to Apollo,' said the master kindly. I know now that he was certain of my fate and was just giving my father a task, so that he should not have to stay and watch me die—poisoning is an unsightly death to watch. 'Apollo can do anything.'

Footsteps sounded on the marble floor as my father ran out. The body was gathered up into the master's arms. He laid it gently on a carved bench, composed the limbs decently, and sat down to watch it die.

Thanatos came for me. Out of a light more golden and beautiful than ever sun shone in Achaea, came a glorious man, clad in streamers of cloth like clouds. He touched me and I reached up both arms to clasp around his neck. Warmth and a sweet scent like spring seemed to infuse me.

'Little brother,' said Thanatos, god of death, 'you are young to die, but you are welcome. Look down. There is your body.'

From the sky I looked down, while he held me carefully. There was a pale boy with golden hair. His face was twisted ugly. He writhed and groaned. Next to him sat master Glaucus. Around him flowed a warm, rich energy, following the contours of his strong hand, his bony shoulder, his bearded head. He glanced up and spoke, as though he could see us.

'Farewell, little brother,' he said gravely, 'if it is your time.'

I nodded. I was joyful in the embrace of Thanatos the angel and I did not want to go back to that whimpering thing on the bed. I snuggled closer, into the cloud-soft drapery, and whispered, 'let us go, Lord.'

A great voice spoke, though I could not understand what it said. Thanatos sank gently, cradling me close. The voice spoke again and Thanatos kissed me, his lips printing a warm mark on my forehead. Cloud-dark and crowned with bay leaves, Death leaned down towards my body.

I cried because I did not want to leave him; he was so glowing and soft. He said, 'I will see you again, little brother, never fear,' and swept me down to my body again.

I did not want to be there. I screamed so hard for Thanatos to come back that the master gave me a strong infusion of poppy syrup. I slept, finding sleep almost as gentle an angel as Death.

Since then, I have never been afraid of death. I know him to be a benign deity, who gathers the fallen into his arms. I was so young when I died that I had not had a chance to be afraid; now I doubt I ever will be.

That does not mean that I do not fight him when I have to. We have a good understanding, Thanatos the bright angel and I. I save all that can be saved; he comforts all that cannot.

I told the master of Epidavros all about Thanatos and Morpheus when I awoke the next day, cured even though I had swallowed a handful of nightshade berries (I had seen ravens eating them, so I thought they were edible). He listened politely until I told him that Death had kissed me. He exclaimed at that and showed me my face in a silver mirror. I had never seen my own face before. My forehead was pale and high. I have brown eyes, the golden hair that made the boys call me 'Chryse,' and a long nose which my father said resembled my mother's. I smiled into the mirror, interested, because the boy in the mirror smiled when I smiled.

But Glaucus, the master of the temple, was looking at my forehead. It was marked. There was a double line, a scar like a burn without puckering, the silvery mark of Death's lips.

My father did not want to leave me at the Temple of Asclepius, but the master gave him such presents—a young woman from Corinth as wife, two farm workers, half a flock of goats, and a slip of the sacred olive tree, which bears more fruit than any other—that he left me with the master to learn to be a healer.

I remember that they washed me in the lustral basin, gave me a clean tunic, and cut a lock of my hair. Then they took me to the temple and the priests blew the sacred trumpets and lit incense before Asclepius. There was singing all about me. It was not a miracle—Death is the only god I have ever seen—but as I stood there in the cool carved temple with the morning sun spilling in through the columns, one of the temple snakes came out of its hole, flicked its forked tongue at me, flowed across the altar, and coiled up between my hands.

I was so small that I could only just reach both hands and my chin onto the altar, so I was eye to eye with the snake. It looked at me in the way of its kind, unemotionally, then rose a little to flick its tongue at each hand. Then it lost interest and coiled up again in a patch of sun.

I thought it was interesting, but it did not impress me as the angel had done. Behind me, I heard the assembled priests gasp. The snake belongs to the Mother, of course, Earth, the mother of all men, but the house snakes in the temple belong to Apollo the Archer, who bestowed the gift of healing Asclepius and his followers. Master Glaucus embraced me as I came down the steps and told me that I had been greatly favoured.

I was sleepy and hungry and overawed by the great temple and all the people. The master seemed as tall as a pillar, his white hair flowing, his white beard curling around like tree roots. His face was all bones, his nose like the prow of a ship, his eyes as black as midnight and as sharp as a needle. He picked me up, wrapped in his mantle, and I fell asleep on his shoulder.

He took me into his own house, to be educated with his own sons and other pupils. I was much younger than they were—they were young men and I was a child—so instead of oppressing me they adopted me as 'Death's Little Brother.' Macaon and his brother, Podilarius, taught me riding and dicing and how to play the lyre. I was a complete failure at hunting, as I hated killing things, but they did not despise me, saying instead, 'Here is Aslepius' tender plant, healer of wounds.'

Though I could not hunt, I could sing. We sang a lot. Beautiful, delicate harmonies praising the god in the temple, and rough Phrygian and Achaean drinking songs for the tavern. I never sang the war songs, saying my voice was not suited to blood and death and heroes.

The temple of Asclepius was not a sad place. People died there, it is true, but many people were born there and most of our patients lived. Some were touched by the god. Some were mad. The god sends dreams to those who sleep in his temples, and from the dreams our wisest priests could sometimes unravel the knot which had tangled sanity.

From the direction of the rising sun, the suppliants came along the white road. They were always thirsty and dusty when they came into the first temple. I used to sit in one of the cypress trees and watch the procession trailing towards us, the rich on horses or in litters carried by slaves, the poor limping along on crutches, attended only by anxious daughters or wives.

Rich or poor, they received the same treatment and care from us; otherwise the god would have been angered. The Bright

One dealt healing and peace, but if offended, fired arrows of pestilence and death.

The suppliants travelled in groups, as there were bandits on the road, and timed their arrival for dawn. If they arrived later than that, they would have to wait until the next day to sleep with the god, although we dealt with urgent wounds and broken bones on the spot. The first temple was built to receive them, to feed them broth with soothing herbs and to wash off the stains of travel. I asked my master why they could only come in at dawn, while we came and went from the sacred precinct all the time. He smiled and said that the ways of a god were not to be questioned by men, adding, 'We are healing their minds, Chryse, not just their bodies. Know thyself. All the stages of this treatment have a purpose and a reason, tried over many years. One thing that cannot ever be hurried is the undermind, the mind which must be convinced that it can be healthy. You are Hermes psychopomp today. As you are a guide, do you know the ways of the passages?'

'Yes, Master Glaucus,' I nodded. I had wandered through and played in all of the maze of tunnels which connected the dormiton of the god, the cool paved underground chamber where the suppliants slept, to the dazzling surface. They slept in the tholos, in the womb of the Mother, and waited for the god to send them a dream which would reveal the root of their disease and give us a clue to their treatment. Sometimes dreams were perfectly clear—a certain herb or treatment would be revealed to the suppliant. More commonly the dream would be rich with symbolism, obscure, requiring the wise priests to sit and talk for days with the dreamer before they could find out the core and seed of their illness. As Hermes, I took the seekers by the hand, one by one, and led them through the tunnels and mazes underground, where various priests in the masks of gods spoke to them out of the darkness.

Master Glaucus said, 'Today, instead of just waiting for the suppliants to come to the tunnel, you shall stay with them from the beginning. Then you may see how the god reveals himself to mean. How many herbs do you know now, Chryse?'

'One hundred and three, Master, and most of the combinations,' I said proudly.

'What treatment would you give a woman of thirty suffering from yellow jaundice and dropsy, boy?'

'Hot water baths, Master, and infusions of vervain and dog's grass in barley broth.'

'Why would you give barley?'

'It soothes, Master. Also it is good with vervain, they complement each other.'

'Why not use rue for the jaundice?'

'Master, rue is cold and wet and her complaint is also cold and wet. She needs hot dry herbs.'

'Barley is hot and wet, boy.'

'Yes, Master, but combined with vervain it is drying and stimulates excretion of liquids.'

'Good, very good. What herb is in your wreath?'

'Vervain, Master.' I reached up to touch the spray of leaves which encircled my head and confined my hair. I was already clad in the psychopomp's purple tunic and golden harness.

'Why do you wear vervain?'

'It is the divine herb, Master, revealed to Asclepius by the god himself.'

'Tell me of the four humours.'

It was getting on to dawn. A small cold wind sprang up. In the light of the flammifer on the temple gate, my master as tall as a tree. I could not see his face, but his voice was gentle.

'The four humours are sanguine, which is hot and wet; bilious, which is cold and dry; choleric, which is hot and dry; and phlegmatic, which is cold and wet. As above, so below, Master, they are the four elements, air, fire, water, and earth.'

'Good. As we walk, tell me how to reduce a broken nose.'

I fell in at his side and took his hand. Like those of all physicians, his nails were short and his hands were always clean. To be otherwise would be like leaving blood or matter on a temple floor—displeasing to the god.

'Master, one washes the blood away and feels the cheekbones and jaw for breaks.'

'How do you detect a break?'

'Master, it feels soggy.'

The shadows of the cypress trees which grew all through the temples were black as ink, and their aromatic scent was all about me. As I tried to match my pace to master's stride, the owls of the lady hooted a warning about the coming day.

'Then the suppliant should drink a soothing infusion of poppy, vervain, and marshleaf. If there are no other breaks, I would take two rolls of bandage and gently push the nose back into line from inside the nostrils, then leave the bandages in place for three days until the nose begins to heal.'

'What warnings for this treatment?'

'Er…oh, yes, Master, the suppliant must not lie down on his back to sleep, but on his side or front, in case blood fills his throat and he chokes.'

'Your are a good pupil, little Golden One.'

I trotted faster to keep up with him and said, 'I have good masters, Lord.'

'Here we are. Now, Chryse, you will accompany the suppliants all the way to the dormiton and tholos. After that, you may come and see me and we will talk again. Do not interject with questions,' he added, smiling at me, 'but save them for me when you have seen all there is to see.'

I nodded and he patted my shoulder and left me.

There were seven people waiting in the reception temple. They were tired and dusty and priests were serving them with the sleepy broth, composed of chicken's flesh and onions, sage, rue, and vervain, comfrey, barley, and poppy. It nourished those who had fainted on the road and soothed the over-stretched nerves of the anxious.

When I entered the temple the priest saw me and hurried over to order me out. 'The master told me to follow the suppliant,' I protested.

He cast me a harried look and muttered, 'You cannot be seen here dressed like that! Put this cloak on, boy. The psychopomp must not be visible until the cavern entrance.'

I wrapped and pinned the himation, which covered my purple tunic, and sat down against the wall as unobtrusively as I could. I had noticed that if I concentrated hard on not being seen, people's eyes skated over me. Besides, the patients were concerned with their own ills.

There were four men and three women. Milanion, a soldier, with a spear point lodged in his jaw. Cleones, a woman with dropsy, swelled and uncomfortable, her skin so stretched that it seemed about to split. A pregnant girl who could not be delivered, panting and red faced with the effort of staying upright and conscious, her arms cradling her swollen belly. Mindful that no one was allowed to die or be born in the sacred precinct, I knew that the attendants would carry her out of the tholos as soon as her labour became productive.

A child of perhaps four in the arms of his mother, whimpering in a strange monotonous voice. He had fallen down a cliff chasing a goat and hit his head. Now he was blind. His mother would lie down with the god and dream for him.

There was a man seeking help for impotence, a woman hoping to be cured of barrenness, and an Achaean with a bandaged foot, which had been broken and healed without setting properly, so that he could hardly walk. A bony man of perhaps forty clutched his belly, complaining that he could not digest his food anymore and that his insides had rebelled against him.

As Eos, the goddess of the dawn, trailed her golden draperies over the horizon, the suppliants began to talk, encouraged by the seven listening priests. I watched, secure as a mouse in a mouse hole, as the suppliants talked and the appropriate priest found the right patient.

Milanion spoke confidently to Telops, who had been a soldier, when he would not have been comfortable with Achis, the slender Kritian. The pregnant girl held out a sweating hand to Achis, however, recognising something essentially female and understanding in him. The barren woman leaned into Thorion's shoulder, comforted by his bulk and strength, while the impotent man spoke quickly to Asius the eunuch, Attis Priest. Lapith the Corinthian spoke to the dropsical woman in her own dialect while the club-footed Itarnes was seized by the wounded Achaean.

The temple was a babble of voices and I could only hear snatches of the conversations.

'I got it at the battle of the deep valley,' the soldier was saying. 'Near enough to killed me. There my brothers died and my father and uncle. I am the only one left of my grandfather's kin.'

'I was given to him by my uncle, for my father is dead,' the pregnant girl gasped to Achis. 'I hate him. He has said that he will kill me if I bear him a girl. I wish I were dead. I have been so long in labour that my bones are racked. I want to die.'

'Death cannot be what life is, little sister,' said Achis gently. 'The cup of death is empty and in life there is always hope.'

She began to cry. Achis gave her some more broth and his shoulder to rest her head.

'It catches me here,' said the bilious man, 'especially after a feast. I must have offended some god—but I've made offerings before them all, and nothing does me any good.'

'We were ambushed and we had to run,' the Achaean said to Itarnes, 'across the stream and up the ridge. We were hiding under a brow of stone when a boulder fell and crushed my foot. I couldn't scream. It was the hardest thing I have ever done. The scouts would have heard a fly rubbing its wings together. I did not make a sound, not then, and not when my brothers hauled me across the rough ground. By the time we got home, my foot was a mass of broken bones and nothing to be done. I am less than a man, I dare not marry lest my children bear club feet too. I healed, though it would have been better if I died.'

'I am a man with grown sons, all of them clean and handsome' said Itarnes, exhibiting his deformed foot. 'And there was a hero with a swollen foot, worse damaged than you. His name was Oedipus.'

'And look what happened to him,' said the patient sourly. 'Killed his father. Married his mother. Spent the rest of his life wandering blind until he finally died in Theseus' territory and caused a war.'

'Come now, how many wars have you caused?' Itarnes asked, and the suppliant laughed, almost against his will.

'He will sell me,' mourned the barren woman to Thorion. 'My only chance is to have a child, a son. I love him, and am so afraid! He will sell me to the Corinthians, who know not the Mother, or to the barbarians from Caria.'

'Or to the pygmies, who will make you a goddess,' murmured Thorion, 'or to the Massagetae who will teach you to ride a horse and fire a bow. A terrible fate, little sister, to be given to the Amazons who fight like men or to the Tauraeans who eat human flesh.'

This did not seem to be a comforting statement and I wondered why Thorion had made it. The woman burst into tears and Thorion continued, 'Or to the Trojans who are masters of horse, to live in windy Ilium of the tall towers and scatter grain before the triple goddess. Or to the Hittites, to worship the pillar of the sun and eat porridge. Or to the Phoenicians, to sail on their well-found ships and visit many ports, bargaining for tin as far as the Cloudy Islands, or down the coast of Africa to trade for gold with men as black as night, so far away that the stars are strange. You spirit is in fetters, little sister. The world is wide. Why are you so afraid of it?'

The woman wept loudly. The impotent man was saying to Asius, 'I was given her as a present. My wife is old and has borne many sons. This new girl is a slave and so beautiful—black as a serpent and lithe like a willow. I wanted her, I lay down with her, she was willing, and then—nothing. She laughed at me and I beat her and now she is sullen and my wife is angry with me. I am old and my seed is dry within me. I am as impotent as you, Attis Priest. Sex makes a man. Like this, I am a woman, helpless, laughable, useless.'

'There are more things that make a man than his sex,' said Asius.

I listened carefully, trying to sieve meaning out of what sounded like common gossip, to be heard in every agora in any village. Just so had my elders talked when I came with my father to sell goats and cheese in our own village. It was the speech of the women at the market stalls, discussing pregnancy and birth and death and the best lichen brew for dyeing cloth. It was the talk of old men sitting on benches in the shade drinking watered wine and talking, endlessly talking, about old battles and lost heroes and the ways of the neighbours. I could not see the sense in it but I had been ordered to accompany the suppliants and I would never have disobeyed Master Glaucus.

After hours of this conversation, the suppliants were taken, one by one, into the temple next door, where they were stripped of their clothes and jewelry, bathed with lychnis and warm water and clad in the white robes of those who go to meet the god. I went with the pregnant girl Païs, horrified by the distension of her belly, which curved out abruptly from slim legs and narrow hips. There was no shame in nakedness before the god and his priests, although the Achaeans required such modesty of their women that we often received suppliants who had concealed some disease of childbearing so long out of shame that they were incurable except by the god himself. Most of them died. At least at the temple they died without pain, possessed by the sleep of Hypnos the dreamer.

Païs was carried in Achis' arms to the entrance of the temple. I stripped off my cloak behind a laurel bush, straightened my wreath, and came forward to take her hand.

'I am your guide, Lady,' I said giving her the honorific for all women—Pronaea, the Mistress, whom the Athenians call Palla Athene. Her hand was strong in mine, sweating and hot. 'Can you walk?'

She leaned on Achis a little and then straightened, her back arched against her burden, walking on her heels with her free hand cradling her belly. 'I will walk,' she said proudly. 'I will thus die sooner. I want to die.'

I drew her gently forward into the dark and the dazzling brightness faded as we paced along a dry, sandy incline. We turned the first corner and the light was cut off. Her hand clutched mine.

'Do not let me go!' she cried, and I held tight, saying, 'Lady, I will not let you go.'

First turn to the left and the first god. Ares, god of war in his golden mask appeared and Païs gasped. 'Hatred butchers in the heart,' said the god and vanished. I led her on, slowly, second to the right and the next god. Aphrodite, goddess of love, masked, scented with jasmine, stroked the suppliant's cheek. 'Love is stronger than death,' she said. Païs sobbed. Further into the soft dark and another goddess; Artemis the virgin, masked and angry; 'You betrayed me!' she cried and I felt Païs flinch. Zeus appeared and said nothing, only laid a heavy hand on her shoulder, and Demeter, pregnant with Spring, whispered, 'Don't be afraid, little daughter.' Hera, the crowned queen, bent her head in acknowledgement, then we were past into the cavern, Païs sobbing and stumbling behind me, Hermes the guide of the spirits, psychopomp, in purple and gold.

She lay down in her place and I covered her with a blanket made of the finest white lamb's wool. Achis, who had come the direct way and was waiting for her, sat down at her head and she slept. There was only one more god for her to meet and it was Apollo, the Sun God, who would come in her dream.

My next suppliant was the old soldier, Milanion, whose hand was cold and calloused in mine. He started when Ares loomed out of the dark. 'Your comrades are dead,' said the god in a great voice. 'Dead and gone, resting in the Elysian fields or paid the toll to Charon. You cannot call them back, warrior.' Then we went on, past Aphrodite, who smiled; Hera, who frowned; Artemis, who seized his wrist and hissed, 'Release my warriors, old man, they are my huntsmen now!'; and Zeus, who extended a shadowy hand and laid it on his head. 'Live,' said the god. I led Milanion down into the cavern and delivered him to sleep. He had not said a word.

I went back to the direct tunnel to the surface and took the barren woman by the hand. Her skin was chill and dry. She did not speak and never altered, although Ares ignored her, Aphrodite slapped her, and Demeter the Mother sprinkled her with pollen, honey scented in the dusty darkness.

The others had all been led through the night back passages to their sleeping places. I carried the only light, a pearly bead of flame in my oil lamp. Usually I went back to the surface once my task was done—I did not really like the dark—but I had been ordered to watch. I sat down by the wall and cradled my little light.

Each sleeper lay outstretched, head to the north, feet to the south. Each attendant priest sat at the sleeper's head, listening to whatever words might fall from their lips as they dreamed. I wondered whether I would see a god, one perhaps as splendid as Thanatos had been when I was so young.

I saw no god. I heard the sleepers muttering. The Achaean with the broken foot began to scream, a hoarse, sobbing cry of mortal pain. It seemed to go on for years. I nudged his attendant, my friend Itarnes.

'It's all right, little brother,' he whispered. 'That is the scream he has been keeping inside all these years. He needed to release it.'

'Won't he wake the others?'

Itarnes smiled and shook his head. He was right. Everyone was concerned with their own inner torments.

A priest in the mask of Demeter approached Païs, knelt, and ran his hands up her thighs, so that she parted them. I could not see what he was doing. My friend explained. 'The baby is twisted in the womb and cannot be born. We can move it into the right position and thus she will be lighter of her son.'

'Then why send her here to lie down in the dark?'

He hushed me with a finger on my lips. 'To give the gods a chance to intervene. The gods are benign, but they need means to their hand and we are their instruments. Hush, little brother. You are here to watch.'

I watched. I saw Milanion's finger scratching at his jaw, where the spear point was immovably fixed in the hinge of the bone.

I had examined him myself. The injury had partially locked the jaw and no force would have removed the metal. Now he was so relaxed by poppy-laced broth and the holy sleep that he was clawing a slit in the skin and removing the spear point with his own fingers.

A priest in the mask of Apollo lay down next to the barren woman. In her sleep, she moaned, an animal noise full of desire, and pulled at the robe, dragging the priest on top of her. I do not know who it was, the mask covers the whole head. Should she have opened her drugged eyes she would have seen the golden face of the god looming over her, a man's body caught in her arms. I watched in astonishment as the suppliant's robe was pushed aside and the bodies joined. The barren woman cried aloud in what sounded like triumph.

Itarnes laid a whole hand over my mouth, sensing that I was about to say something unwise and far too loud.

'While he is in that mask he is the god,' he hissed. 'Sit down, Chryse!' When I struggled, he said coldly, 'Diomenes!' At the sound of my real name I sat still and listened. 'He is the god and she needs a child. It may be that there is no fault in her, but that her husband is barren. However good the soil, it needs fertile seed. The god will give her a child. Will you behave if I let you go?'

I nodded and he released me. I was shocked and said nastily, 'What of the impotent man? Do we mate with him, too?'

'No need. His impotence is in his mind. The mind is our province, little brother. There. The birth is imminent.'

Païs' cries had changed. She was panting. Shudders were running up and down her body. Her legs twitched. Two attendants lifted her gently onto a stretcher and carried her up the direct path to the outside world. They moved at a brisk jog trot and I followed them, blinking and crying in the sudden sunlight. They laid Païs in the cool temple of women and her attendant priest Achis caught the baby as it emerged, blue and red and ugly, on a burst of blood. I felt ill.

He then wiped the creature clean and tied and severed a throbbing blue cable which attached it to the girl's body. There seemed to be blood everywhere. It was the first birth I had seen and after the revelation that there were no gods, it was too much for me. I sat down suddenly and closed my eyes.

I heard a thin wail and Achis' voice crooning 'There, there, little man! Mother,' he urged gently, 'here is your son.'

Païs gave a tired laugh. I heard the swish of a cloth on the marble floor. The slaves were cleaning up, as a mess is distasteful to the god. Achis hauled me to my feet and I was led outside.

'Overcome by the mystery, little brother?' he asked lightly, smiling. He knew what went on in the fraudulent dark. I hated him, violently and suddenly. I shook off his hand and ran, tears streaming down my face, into the temple and slid, falling in an ungainly heap at my master's feet.

I did not look up but held onto a fold of his robe as the whole story tumbled out—the soldier removing the spear point and the barren woman mating with the priest in her sleep and the Achaean screaming. He heard it all, in grave silence. Then he raised me to my feet and dusted down my tunic.

'Was it possible to remove that piece of metal from Milanion's face?'

'No, Master.'

'Why not?'

'It was too firmly fixed, Master, and the muscles had contracted.'

'So the only way it could be removed was to make him sleep.'

'Yes,' I agreed dubiously. 'But we could have just drugged him.'

'Yes, we could. Then where would have been the story?'

'The story, Master?'

'If consulting a god is as easy as ordering a wheel fixed, would men believe in it enough for it to work?'

'I don't know, Master.'

'Would the Achaean have screamed in any other place?'

'No, Master.'

'And the barren woman, would she have accepted a lover?'

'No, Master.'

'And the birthing woman—would she ever have allowed a man to touch her?'

'Probably no, Master.'

'Well, then. We need to heal, Chryse. It is our great task.'

'But, Master...' I grabbed a fold of the dark robe, 'Master, there are no gods.'

'You saw a god yourself, once, little brother.'

'That was Death, Master. There are no gods but Death, then,' I said mulishly. He smiled at me and patted my shoulder.

'Every Asclepid knows that, Chryse,' he said sadly.

◇◇◇

'You have saved him from death and removed him from belief,' commented Poseidon. 'And your maiden is in love with her twin brother. I don't understand how those two can ever come together. Meanwhile, what about my revenge? Is Troy to stand?'

'Troy will fall,' said Apollo absently, staring down into the water at Diomenes asleep in the temple. 'Have patience, Sea God.'

'Troy will not fall' said Aphrodite with equal certainty. 'See how brave she is, how beautiful! Your puppet will surely love my daughter Cassandra as soon as he sets eyes on her.'

'Then he shall not set eyes on her. There is another he shall see first,' chuckled Apollo.

Chapter Three

Cassandra

I was not supposed to see the mystery called childbirth until I had become one of the Mother's maidens with my first bleeding of sacrifice blood. But I teased my teacher Tithone so incessantly that she set me fifteen pectoral herbs to learn perfectly and said that after I had managed a broken bone all by myself, I could come to watch Clea give birth. She was expected to do so very soon.

I was twelve and convinced I knew everything.

I spent a week annoying my twin by insisting on haunting the exercise field, where the young men practised fighting and the maidens shot their bows. Eleni only stopped complaining when Hector gave him spear-throwing lessons along with Polites, our brother, who was four years older. This was an honour and Eleni stripped and took to the field with as much pride as any Trojan warrior. I giggled at the contrast between slim fifteen-year-old Polites, with his long oiled thighs under the war skirt, Hector as tall as a tree, and little Eleni with his stumpy ungrown shape. However, I did it privately and behind my hand.

I was waiting for someone to hurt themselves. Childbirth is the great female mystery and I was eager to see it. I was not a nice child.

I sat watching the warriors, instructed by Hector, practising with the spear. Our Trojan spear is shorter than the common, but heavier, with a barbed bronze head. It is used for stabbing at close quarters and can be thrown a long distance with a spear thrower, a longish piece of wood with a crook at the end. This is a Trojan skill and takes learning, but it can cast a spear three times the distance that an unassisted man can throw it.

I wriggled into a more comfortable seat with my back against the sun-warmed wall of the temple of Apollo, the sun god aspect of the Lord Dionysius. He rules prophecy, so he was my god. I felt very comfortable in his temple but was always on the brink of falling asleep when there and I wanted to watch. I pinched my wrist and sat up straighter.

The maidens, a flutter of coloured tunics, were further away, near the little hill, between the city and the river Scamander. I could see a purple tunic among the pale green, ochre, and rose. It was probably Andromache, our playmate and destined wife of our brother Hector. She resembled Eleni and me, being pale skinned with dark golden hair and the grey eyes which marked the god-touched, although she had not shown any sign of prophecy or skill in healing. In fact, she had no interest in healing but was good at arms. The elders thought that she might be protected by War, him whom the Argives call 'Ares'. The Amazon Myrine, who was of course War's child, trained Andromache especially hard, stating that she of all the maidens would need to know how to fight.

Even at ten Andromache was tall and strong. I could hear Myrine shouting at her to keep her wrist tensed against the pluck of the string and scolding her for allowing it to skin her inner arm. Andromache drew and loosed again. She would not cry. Andromache never cried.

Then I heard a cry and a thud. Instantly I was up and running for the centre of the field, where two young men had been wrestling.

I ducked past Eleni, who was leaning on his spear, circumnavigated Hector and slid to a halt next to the fallen, whom I recognised as Sirianthis. He was a hapless boy, always hurting himself. I could have guessed that my first broken bone would be Siri. His mother put it down to her having spent most of her pregnancy tripping over things. He was a pleasant boy, though, and everyone liked him. He tried very hard and never minded the other boys laughing at him.

He was lying on the ground, curled around his injury, clutching his upper arm and trying not to cry. I recognized the strange fish hook shape of his body on the dusty ground and said, 'Siri, I need a broken bone. All you've done is dislocated your arm.'

'Sorry,' he panted. 'It hurts. Can you fix it, Cassandra?'

'Of course, but if you had to hurt yourself couldn't you have broken something? I don't know if Tithone will think that this counts. I'll get Hector. It will be all right in a moment, Siri, I promise. Who are you?' I asked the other boy.

He turned a shocked face up to me and said, 'Maeron, lady. I didn't mean to hurt him.'

I ignored this. 'Go and get your tunic, lie him on his back with the tunic rolled up between his shoulder blades while I fetch my brother.'

Hector, who was about to cast the spear, put it down again and followed me to where Siri lay whimpering. The stretched-out position strained all his displaced sinews, those strings which knit a muscle together. Hector leaned down and stroked the hair from the boy's sweating face.

'It will stop hurting soon, little brother,' he said soothingly. 'Maeron, sit beside him and hold him still while I pull. No, grab the other shoulder and brace yourself.'

'Hector, Hector, let me,' I begged, hauling on his elbow. 'Thithone said I had to do this before I can see the mystery.'

Hector looked at me sternly. 'A warrior must not be left unattended because of the healer's private purposes,' he said. 'But you may give me orders, Cassandra, if you do so right away.'

When my brother called me Cassandra like that he was seriously displeased and I quaked. But I knew the procedure and ordered, 'Take his wrist in your hand, brother, and put your foot under his arm pit. Now pull gently until the arm goes back into the socket.'

I had seen this several times. It was always fascinating. As Hector pulled on the arm, the shoulder joint moved under my hand, from an ugly displaced lump to the shape of the boy's proper shoulder. All medicine, said Tithone, was restoring the body to its proper shape and condition. There was a click, Siri bit back a cry, and Hector laid the restored arm across the boy's chest.

Hector looked at me. I remembered what remained to be done. 'Wriggle your fingers, Siri,' I ordered. 'Can you feel your hand?'

'Yes, Princess. Thank you.' Maeron was holding Siri close and I perceived that they were lovers. I blushed to think that I had just ordered poor Maeron about as though he was a dog when he must have been worried about Siri. And Hector was angry with me. This healing was more difficult than it looked. It involved people, and mere knowledge of methods of healing did not begin to cover it.

'Now, Cassandra, what next?' asked Hector. Luckily, I knew.

'I bandage his arm to his side and send him off the field to rest, taking broth and marshleaf infusion to soothe the inflammation, and he is not to move his shoulder for three days. I can apply oil of mint to cool the joint and reduce the swelling and he must be watched for fever,' I parroted, making a bandage from Maeron's tunic. Hector bent his head in approval I watched Maeron help his friend to his feet and they limped off the field, passing into the city through the Scamander Gate, which was nearest to Siri's house.

'Now, Cassandra, we must talk. Or rather, you will talk to me while Eleni goes with Polites to practise the use of the spear thrower.'

Eleni went, glancing back at me in compassion. Hector was very seldom angry with us but when he was he did not rage or slap. Rather he was sad and measured and his every word sank into the heart and stung like a thorn.

'Oh, Hector, I am so sorry…' I began.

Instead of hugging me, he asked gravely, 'Why are you sorry?'

'I shouldn't have thought of Siri as a…task I had to do in order to see childbirth. I'm fond of Siri, but I treated him like a…thing.'

'You want to be a healer, don't you?'

'Yes.'

'Then you must know that all your patients are people and you have to love them. Not all the time, Cassandra, and not for ever. But while they are in your care then they must have your whole heart. Otherwise you will never heal them.'

'But Hector…' I ventured closer to him and took his hand, 'that can't be right.'

'Why not?' He was relenting enough to argue and I felt instantly better. We began to walk back towards the city of Troy. The walls shone white in the morning, the walls, the height of three men, built by Hereacles the hero in recompense for his massacre of my grandfather and his sons.

'The best healer of these sorts of injuries is Myrine the Amazon,' I stated.

'Yes,' Hector agreed.

'But Myrine is rough,' I protested. 'She grabs and heaves and swears at them, curses them for foolish men, closes wounds with her fingers, pressing hard enough to make them cry out, and then she curses them again for weaklings and children.'

'She tended me when I fought that boar,' said Hector. 'Her harsh words recalled my courage and her hands were skilled and strong.' I saw the scar down the outside of his thigh where the tusks had sliced his flesh. 'She sucked out the dirt and poisonous saliva with her own mouth, swearing by Hecate that I was the clumsiest hunter she had ever met. Can you doubt that she loved me then?'

I thought about this, reviewing what I had seen of Myrine the Amazon. It seemed unlikely but it was true. She did love her patients. I nodded.

'Go then, little vulture,' said Hector, patting me. 'Tell Tithone you have replaced a dislocated shoulder and beg her, from me, to consider this equivalent to the task she set you.'

To salve my conscience, I went first to the small house in the first circle where Siri lived. His mother greeted me and gave me a small clay bird as a present for tending her accident-prone son, and I went off to find Tithone in a very guilty state.

I told her what had happened and she listened without a word. Then of all things, she laughed, a bright and joyous laugh, almost like a girl's. It came strangely from Tithone's aged face, and I was disconcerted.

'Aren't you angry with me, Lady?' I asked. She hugged me to her bony bosom.

'Ah, little daughter, more years away than you can count I did the same thing and my brother called me a vulture too. You will be a fine healer, Cassandra, if you keep the great warrior's advice in mind. You may not like your patients, or approve of them, or let them become close to you. But while they are yours, you must love them. Hmm. Your lord brother is a fine man, a fine man. Troy is fortunate in its captain. How was Siri?'

She just assumed that I had been to see him. She was always right, Tithone my teacher. I liked her anyway.

'He is a little feverish. I gave him poppy broth and his mother has oil of mint for the swelling. I will go and see him tomorrow.'

'I'll send someone tonight. The condition of the young changes faster than with adults. They heal faster, but they also deteriorate faster and they die quicker. Remember that.'

'Yes, Lady.'

'Recite the pectoral herbs,' she said and I brightened. This meant that she had accepted Siris's dislocation as my broken bone.

'Coltsfoot, mint, squillis, marshleaf, red poppy, thyme, vervain, comfrey, yarrow, sundew, ivy, hyssop, lungleaf, blackthorn bar, elecampagne,' I announced.

'How are they used?'

'For a cough in the chest which bubbles, Lady, an infusion of elecampagne, coltsfoot, lungleaf, and thyme but not poppy.'

'Why not?'

'It stops a cough, Lady, so that the person can't spit out the fluid.'

'Good. For a dry cough?'

'Lady, honey and red poppy, marshleaf and sundew.'

'Good. Why do you use thyme?'

'Lady, it cools a fever and makes the lungleaf work better.'

'Good. Does marshleaf affect the cough?'

'No, Lady, it just soothes the insides.'

'Good. Now, Cassandra, tell Nyssa that you will be away for a while, collect your mantle, and meet me at Clea's house.'

I did not wait to thank her, but ran out of her house into the steep street. Eleni had returned from the field and was ready to console me, but I was alight with purpose and threw myself into his arms, laughing.

'You recover fast,' he said suspiciously. 'Wasn't Hector angry? Ouch! Take care, twin!'

'Eleni, are you hurt?' I drew away and felt him over anxiously. There were hot spots in his muscles, discerned with my fingers, but he did not seem to have broken anything.

'It's nothing,' he said grandly. 'Hector says that all warriors have sore muscles after exercise.'

I clipped his ears affectionately and gathered up my mantle, the warmest one for winter. 'Tithone's taking me to see Clea give birth,' I said to Nyssa. 'She said to tell you I'd be missing for a while.'

Nyssa did not share my excitement. She kissed me sadly and when she drew away I saw that she was crying.

'Oh, Nyssa!' I said, conscience struck. 'I won't be long. I promise.'

'It's not that, Princess. You are growing up. Soon you will leave me.'

'Never,' objected Eleni, hugging her from the left side as I embraced her from the right. 'We'll never leave you!'

When I left he was comforting Nyssa by loudly and childishly demanding instant attention, a bath and massage for his battle fatigue. I love my twin very much.

◇◇◇

Clea was seventeen. This was, Tithone had previously informed me, her first child. Her husband was a tall, strong Trojan and she was a delicate-boned Phrygian woman, so time and care would be needed to deliver her safely.

Naturally, I was familiar with the methods by which women receive the seed of men which grows in the womb. When I came to leave the maidens, I would sit as every other woman in the city had to sit, with a band of plaited horse-hair around my head in the Place of Maidens. There I would stay until a stranger dropped a golden token of the Mother into my lap and took my hand, saying, 'In the name of Gaia.' Because I was a princess of the royal house, no arrangements with suitable boys could be made. I would have to lie down with a complete stranger, preferably a visitor to the city. We knew that the Maiden would infallibly be angry with the man who took one of the handmaids away. She would be even angrier with one who stole a princess. Therefore the foreigner. The lovers were always masked with the face of Dionysius, Lord of the Trojans. One such man would lead me away and by means of his phallus I would leave my allegiance to the Maiden and join my fate to the Mother.

I could not wait. The kisses and stroking hands of my fellow maidens were sweet, but they did not satisfy me. Some of them would never leave the Maiden; they had no wish to encounter the phallus of the Lord. Myrine the Amazon was one of these. Until I left the maidens I could not marry my brother and twin Eleni, my dearest love. Time moved too slowly for me.

Clea was sitting, bent double, clutching her belly and moaning. Tithone came into the small house in the second circle and announced briskly, 'The blessing of the Mother upon this place.' Then she proceeded to order Clea's neighbours to sweep her house clean while we moved Clea into the street to strip and wash her over the earthenware trap in the drain. The smaller houses in the circle did not have elaborate plumbing, as the palace and the large houses further up did. Still, they all had water piped from the triple spring which flowed at the very highest point in the city and they all had a privy which opened into the main sewer and was flushed with water—Priam had ordered all who built houses to see that this was so. Cities in such godless places as Achaea, Tithone said, had not discovered that filth and excrement breeds plagues in the miasma that surrounds them, polluting the air and poisoning the people, bringing swift vengeance from the god Apollo, who loathes such irreligious behaviour.

Troy never had a plague.

Clea's belly, which had ridden high, seemed to have changed shape. As we washed her with salty water and then with fresh infusions of hyssop, her neighbours cleaned her house, untying every knotted cord. We smoothed back Clea's hair and doused her three times with cool water to which soapleaf had been added. Passers-by touched her reverently on the belly. Touching a woman so close to the female mystery is supposed to bring good luck.

After that we led her back inside her house. Tithone began the incantations of the goddess, a long, long chant which I knew very imperfectly. As acolyte, I wrapped Clea in a red chiton and combed her long hair so that never a tangle remained.

I knew that Clea's husband was in the temple of the Mother and would remain there, dedicated to prayer, while Clea was in labour. If she lived, he would be garlanded by the priests and sent down the hill from the temple with rejoicing. If she died, he would remain there in mourning for a moon from waning to waning, eating only barley bread and speaking to no one. Unless he did this, he could never marry again.

If the baby died, the temple would take both of them for the same period, expiating the Mother's wrath and despair at the loss of her child.

I began to wonder if I really wanted to attend childbirth, but there was no turning back. The chant had begun, the woman was in labour, and I was acolyte and forbidden to look away, leave, or be sick.

Tithone paused between cantos of the chant and began to talk to Clea. She was sweating and in pain. I had not realised that childbirth was painful. I thought it was a joy to bring a new creature into the world. Now I saw Clea was crying and her clutch on my hand was desperate.

Tithone laid a hand on her belly and asked gently, 'How long since the brine came, Clea?'

'It was the time of the hottest sun,' gasped Clea. 'I hurt!'

'Ah,' said Tithone. It was two watches since then—almost half a day. It seemed a long time to me. 'The child in the womb lies in brine like sea water, Cassandra,' she said to me. 'When it is ready to be born the sea water drains away and the child struggles to break free. Lay your hand, here.'

I did so and felt a strange pulsing under the drum-tight skin.

'A live thing wants to be free and reach the light,' said Tithone, 'but it will take its time. What I must do, daughter, is continue to chant and you must massage her back, here and here'—Tithone always knew where it hurt—'and talk to her.'

'I hurt!' gasped Clea again. I laid both palms to the place indicated by my teacher and felt Clea's pain. It struck through my vitals and I gasped.

I had such a bond with Eleni. If he hurt, so did I—that is how I had known that his battle bruises were not serious. This was different. It was as though the Mother had decided to let me know how childbirth felt, though my own body was as yet unripe. My own unformed breast ached. My untouched womb contracted like a fist. I slid down until I was embracing the labouring woman as she sat on a backless chair, my face between her shoulder blades, my belly against her back. The muscles were as hard as rock under my fingers.

Tithone had been watching me; I think she knew that this might happen. She did not break off the chant, but touched me briefly on the head as though she was blessing me.

A creature was struggling to be born: a live thing, with consciousness of a vague sort, but with appallingly fierce drive and will. It did not care if it tore its mother apart in the birth; all its force was set on breaking free of the confining prison of the womb and I had to help it. Unconsciously, I embraced Clea closer, and began to breathe in her rhythm. Our hearts beat as one. When she groaned, so did I. When a contraction ripped her, it tore me also. Under my hands with the god-sight, I saw the little animal twist and claw with hands that had all their nails.

For the first watch it was only pain. I found later that Eleni in Nyssa's arms writhed in agony and nearly frightened her to death until she sent to Tithone and found out what I was doing. Thereafter she told Eleni that this was what his mother had borne to birth him, which subdued him for days.

Pain, after a while, transcends hurt. Clea was washed with waves, which I translated, once I had the trick of it, into force and pressure. It was not the same pain as a burn or a broken bone, which hurts differently, treated or untreated. This was more like an internal qualm which signifies that one has eaten too many unripe berries and the body is trying to be rid of the poison. Yet it was not that, for the woman was bearing the pain gladly, in order to be lighter of her burden and to bring alive to the goddess a new person.

At the point when I thought I might die of this pain, I looked imploringly at my teacher. She did not pause in her chant, but made a gesture which seemed to gather something up into a ball. I groaned through another contraction until I realised what she meant.

It was all one, birth and death and life. At that realization I got the trick of translating pain into pressure and I got my mind back, so that I could consider what I was doing.

Troy is ruled by the tides. They dictate when Hector's ships can leave and when they can come in. They wash the beaches clean and bring fish and wrecks to our shores. The moon is mistress of the tides. They wax and wane as she becomes the maiden, mother and crone, vanishing to renew herself in the dark time we call the Night of Hunted Things. This birth was tidal: each new wave washed us further up as the sea-creature wriggled to be free and Clea strove to make her body into something from which it could escape.

Wash and crash, I conjured tides. I could hear the chant, though Tithone sounded very tired now. I called up the moon-dragged waters, salt and relentless, and felt the baby writhe under my hands. Clea cried out—it was then that I noticed she had been silent for a long time—and Tithone knelt between her legs.

With a wriggle and a flash and a cry of triumph from Clea and from me, the baby was born into Tithone's hands. There was an instant intoxicating sense of lightness and freedom, which could have come from either Clea or from the baby. I relinquished Clea into her neighbour's embrace and knelt next to my teacher. So small a thing, so perfect, smeared with blood and grease and opening its mouth to scream.

Tithone laid the baby in a dish full of warm salt water, still attached to its mother by a cord of marvellous complexity the colour of lapis lazuli and coral. No Egyptian worker could have made a twisted enamel so beautiful.

We lifted her and laid her on her own bed, the red cloth swathing her hips tightly. Tithone took her flint knife and a skein of white thread. She tied the cord and cut it, washing the baby clean of blood and grease. Clea panted and was delivered of a pad of flesh, then sagged back into her attendant's arms.

It was a girl child, a fact which would add to the rejoicing. It was well known that the women of Troy, well skilled and strong, were sought in marriage by many men of the west kingdoms and commanded respect. I marvelled at the small hand which clutched my finger. The newborn opened dark blue eyes. She looked at me coolly, a creature well pleased with the outcome of its struggle, a warrior resting from battle.

Tithone took the baby up and carried her over to Clea, who lay exhausted, battered, and bruised. Blood was still seeping from her loins. She bared a breast for the baby and winced, then laughed, as the hungry mouth clamped shut.

'Go,' Tithone ordered the boy who had been sitting outside the door for the whole day and the whole night. 'Tell the Mother that there is a new girl child in Troy and tell Clea's man that both of them are well.'

The boy, who was apprenticed to the priest of Dionysius, sprang to his feet and ran. I heard his hard bare feet striking the cobbles. It was almost dawn. My knees were sore and I was stiff as a plank, but I was intoxicated with joy. Tithone joined me at the doorway as the sun began to rise in splendour and a cool wind sprang up. The sky was a sea of god and rose.

'That is the mystery of birth, little daughter,' she croaked, laying a hard hand on my shoulder. 'Are you glad to have it?'

'It is a terrible mystery,' I heard myself saying, 'but yes, teacher. I am glad.'

Behind us, in the house, Clea's baby began to cry. I felt a jolt in my womb and put down a hand to investigate it. I brought back a palm marked with blood. I had joined the Maidens.

Chapter Four

Diomenes

I hid for two days when I discovered that there were no gods. The master left me alone, ordering my friend Itarnes to bring me soup and bread. He tried to talk to me but I did not want to talk and eventually he went away.

I sat on my sleeping mat in my cell and thought. Sometimes I had to hold my head in both hands because it felt as though my skull was bursting. This was the first serious check my belief in the world had ever had. It was only when I tasted mistletoe in my broth that I realised that Master Glaucus was treating me for hysteria.

There were no gods in Epidavros—only Death. All healers come to terms with Death—we must understand and accept him, or give up and die in our turn. I had seen death. I had held the hands of an old man while he was dying. I had seen the body slacken, the throat relax, the hand grow heavy and loose in mine as the breath escaped and the soul took flight. I had seen no god then, not even Thanatos.

But the old man had seen a god. I remembered this and sat up. The old man had seen Ares, the war god, leading a company of his old comrades in a charge; he said he was swept up in the rush of their onset, and in saying that the death-rattle had started in his throat. 'Onward!' he had cried with his last breath, calling his old friends, long dead, by their names.

My head drooped again into my hands. The man was old and probably mad; his mind had gone. There were no gods populating the dark of the temple's most sacred place, only priests in masks, persuading men to accept healing by mimes and tricks. I thought of the man with the pain in his belly, told by the god to forgo roasted meat and wine and honey for his soul's sake. I thought of the statue of Asclepius, seated in his carved chair, with the snakes in his hands and his dog at his feet, ivory and gold, flickering in the lamplight. I thought of the temple snake flicking his tongue at my hands and the master telling me that I had been greatly honoured, and I heard myself laugh bitterly.

Someone had come in. I did not look up.

'There are no gods,' said the master's voice.

'No,' I replied.

'Foolish boy,' he reproved. 'They are all around you. Not as men would like to see them, in men's bodies, subject to men's lusts and greed, walking about the world granting each petty wish. They are in the earth, Chryse, in the sky, in the wind, in the fire and water and in breath. You will find that the gods are reliable, he continued as I stared at him, 'if you do not rely on them for small things.'

'For life and death, Master?'

'They are small things to the gods. When we are gone'—he waved his hand at the temple and the walls of Epidavros—'when we little men are dead and forgotten, the earth will go on. The sky will arch overhead, the moon will wax and wane, and unknown women will give birth to men who have never heard our names. The world is old, Chryse. It will get much older before the end. And you will find, Diomenes my son,' he pulled me to my feet and into his strong embrace, 'that you have more power than you know in these hands of yours, and that, too, comes from the gods. Now. You have spent enough time thinking?'

It was a good question. I felt suddenly that if I had not spent enough time, I had spent all the time that I had. I nodded and he kissed me, his beard bristling my cheek.

'Wash your face, pack a spare tunic, and meet me in the herb store. Wear your most comfortable sandals.'

'Why, Master? Where are we going?'

'Wandering,' he said, and swept out.

I gathered my belongings, including a comb made of the cypress wood of the temple trees, an oil flask, a wine flask, and my dagger. It was a present from a grateful patient, sharp as a razor and decorated with a strange Egyptian beast like a small lion without a mane, stalking ducks in reeds which Asius Attis Priest called lotus. I washed my face as I had been told, rolled my goods into a suitable bundle tied about with thongs so that I could carry it on my back, and ran to the herb store.

The master was not there. Itarnes told me that he had bidden me to watch the healing of the child who had fallen down the cliff. Apparently it had just been revealed to the mother who had slept for him in the temple that the child's sight might well be restored. Revealed to the mother! More fraud! However, I had spent enough time thinking and my thoughts were not comforting.

I staggered a little as I turned and Itarnes supported me. He was barrel chested, very strong, and smelt agreeably of olives.

'You've been on too low a diet lately for all this running, little brother,' he said. 'Lean on me, now.'

'Itarnes, I'm sorry...' I began. His good-natured, ugly face turned to me. I noticed that he had dark brown eyes, alight with kindness. I felt ashamed for snubbing him.

'It's nothing, little brother. When I found out I punched a temple wall and refused to wash for a week.'

'Why did you refuse to wash?' We passed the row of pine trees and came into the place in front of the main temple. It was bright daylight and the air smelt resinous and fresh. I had been inside too long.

'If cleanliness is pleasing to a god and there are no gods, then why wash?'

I laughed. He had a valid point. 'Master Glaucus would say that cleanliness promotes health,' I said slyly. He clipped me lightly over the ear.

'Health is a god,' he said, making a pun on the title of Hygeia, female patron of medicine and daughter of Asclepius. 'Come on, Chryse. And remember, this insight is for the priests alone. If men did not believe in gods, what would heal them? To the temple, Chryse. Macaon is going to operate. This will be fascinating. The child is blind from a skull fracture. The bone is depressed, it appears.'

'Depressed?'

'The skull, little brother, is like a pot. It protects the brain like a hard shell protects a tortoise. If a sharp blow strikes a pot, what happens?'

'It breaks.'

'Yes. Now surround the pot with a goatskin, shrunken to fit it closely. Strike the pot and break it. What happens?'

'The broken piece is retained by the skin,' I said slowly, thinking it out. 'But it presses inward.'

'Fill the pot with cheese and there you have it. The cheese will be dented by the pressure of the broken piece. Now how do you mend it?'

'If it was a pot I would put my hand in and push the broken piece out.'

'Very good, little brother, but you cannot touch the cheese.'

'I don't know. I can't imagine. Pressing on the piece would drive it in further. How?'

'You will see. Wait now, we should get you something to eat. Sit down here and I'll fetch something—shall we say bread and cheese?'

We both laughed. I noticed that my voice was shaky and I was suddenly ravenous. Itarnes lowered me into a seat not too far from the altar of the temple and bustled away.

The woman was seated in front of the altar with the child on her lap. The priest of Hypnos the Dreamer was talking to the child in a low monotonous murmur. The child's unfocused eyes were open, but it obviously did not see. The woman was sitting very still. Hypnos Priest took a sharp pin from his belt and stuck it into the child's hand, and there was no squeal of pain. He nodded and stood back.

Macaon approached, carrying a strange object. I had seen something like it before. I ransacked my memory and found it. It was a screw, such as the farmers use to break up rocks. It was made of bronze, suspended in a triangle of wood, small enough to hold in one hand.

Itarnes returned with bread and cheese and I ate hungrily, watching as Macaon fitted the triangle and began to turn the screw forcefully into the child's head. It was a horrible sight, unnatural and cruel.

'He must be in agony!' I exclaimed with my mouth full. 'Why doesn't he cry?'

'Hypnos is with the suppliant,' said Itarnes. 'He dreams and feels nothing. In any case the skull is not very sensitive. There— see—the screw is fixed. Now the lever.'

Macaon operated a lever at the side of his triangle and lifted the fracture. When he saw the skin tugging, he fitted a bolt across the lever and removed it. The priest Hypnos knelt by the child and began to ask him questions. The child replied in an eerie voice, such as is heard in sleep.

'Where are you?'

'In the temple,' said the child.

'What can you see?' came the soft, insinuating voice.

'Asclepius.'

'What colour is he?'

'Gold and white.'

Itarnes gasped. I said, spattering crumbs, 'It is a memory. He has seen the temple before.'

I spoke too loudly, or perhaps the priest was listening for dissent. He held up a coin before the blind child's eyes.

'What is this?'

'Round gold thing,' said the child mechanically. A peasant's child, he would never have seen golden coins.

'What is the picture on it?'

'A bird.'

That silenced me. There might be no gods, but there were healer priests who could restore sight. I had finished my bread and cheese and felt altogether more real. I was also very impressed.

Macaon ordered that the child was to stay very still for several weeks while the break healed. Still with Hypnos, he had not cried or even blinked. His mother carried him out of the temple, weeping with relief.

I returned to the herb store and found my master sorting medicinal herbs and arguing with Polidarius.

'I can't stay here all the time,' he was saying. 'Healers must travel or how are they to learn? The temple will do very well without me. This is not a long journey—I shall be away perhaps a month. I must go to Tiryns and Mycenae, and maybe then to Corinth. They say that there is a plague in the villages and that will spread unless it is checked. I know I could send you or one of the others and I do not doubt your skill. But I grow stale in this sacred place. Ah, Chryse. Was the child healed?'

'Yes, Master. He did not even cry. What is this dream of Hypnos?'

'It works on some—the young and those willing to trust. In that sleep there is no pain, none at all. The child was completely in the hands of Hypnos Priest. If he had ordered, the boy would have seen demons or felt that he was flying. Hypnos Priest will instruct you when you are older. It is not a skill to be given to the immature. Are you ready to go?'

I drew a deep breath. 'Yes, Master.'

'Good. My son tells me that you are a good rider. Go choose yourself a horse, then, and order mine made ready. We shall sleep tonight in Kokkinades. West, a day's easy ride.'

Itarnes escorted me to the stables. The master's horse was called Banthos, the dappled one. He was a proud beast, prone to snap at an importunate hand, but smooth as a husked chestnut and trained to have an easy, comfortable gait. I told the slave to saddle the master's horse, then I walked to the end of the stables and patted noses, looking for my favourite.

She was a little mare. I called her Pyla because she came from Pylos, an offering to the temple from a merchant cured of an itch which had maddened him enough to consider suicide. He had left without his itch (poultices of fresh marshleaf, dock, and lychnis and infusions of valerian and comfrey) and had delivered three colts a month later. Pyla was the colour of good Kriti honey, with an affectionate nature and an especial craving for hawthorn flowers. She was young and strong and used to me. Not perhaps a well-bred horse, but broad in the beam and accustomed to mountains. I found her head gear and saddled her, slinging my rolled cloak across her willing back.

Then I led her and Banthos out into the sunlight. The master came, still arguing with Polidarius, and mounted, settling his robes. Itarnes hugged me and I returned the embrace. 'Good fortune and the gods be with you,' he said, grinning.

I mounted Pyla and trotted at the master's side out of the gates of the temple of Asclepius and into the road.

Though I had been on this road before, I had been six and I did not remember it well. When we came out to the north, the road split, one part going west to Tiryns, the other east to the town of Epidavros. I had often gone east with the other apprentices, seeking taverns to sing and drink wine in. But I had never gone west and I had always wondered where the road led.

Now I was going to find out. I was thirteen years old and I was out in the world again.

◇◇◇

The world was wide and scented with resin and dust. It was autumn, I realised. All the trees in the temple are evergreen; it takes concentration to notice the changing of the seasons.

Pyla trotted politely at the side of the master's horse. For a few hours we travelled in silence, but it was a pleasant silence and I had a lot to look at. The grapes were ripening well, it seemed, the plump purple patches almost too heavy for the vines. I recalled being a child who tended the goats and lay a whole day in the thyme-scented grass, looking at the shadows of the mountains and making beasts and faces out of clouds. I thought of the small Chryse with pity. He was so ignorant of the world and of men.

We came into Kokkinades at an easy pace and found no one about in the agora, which was odd. It still lacked several hours until sunset and usually the marketplace of such villages has a cast of inhabitants fully as well known a satyr-play. The old men on benches by the shady side of the square, market women arguing with customers and proclaiming the merits of their cheese or their weaving, and maidens passing to the well for water with amphorae on head or hip.

But in the main square of this village there was no one. I shivered.

'Men of Kokkinades!' called Master Glaucus in a loud voice.

I did not hear anything, but the master went to the house on the far side of the square and wrenched open a door. It was a stone house with two windows. I felt sure that it must belong to the chief family of Kokkinades.

He looked inside, stepped back, and stood silent for a moment. I wanted to look inside but he pushed me roughly away.

'Chryse,' he said slowly, 'take the horses and walk out along the road, to the west. When you are 500 paces away, stop and call out in a loud voice that a healer has come.' Master Glaucus' own voice was taut with some strong emotion.

'Yes, Master. What do I do then?'

'Wait. I will not be long. Take my cloak, boy, I will have to burn this tunic. Go on, Chryse!'

Puzzled, I walked both horses, who were restive because they had expected to be fed and stabled in the village, 500 paces along the white road. The slopes of the hills were covered in poppies, I remember, and I saw seven varieties of thyme and a sun-coloured butterfly. I felt very foolish when I reached the prescribed place, but I had my orders. Tethering Banthos and Pyla to a convenient olive tree, I cupped my hands and called to the silent hills, 'A healer has come!' I waited, then repeated it.

Since I could not see anyone, I sat down and took a drink of water—our water skin would need replenishing soon—and ate a broken piece of barley bread which I found in the ration-bag. I wondered what had happened to Kokkinades. I could not see any sign of bandit attack; no arrows, no spear marks or blood, and the houses had not been broken into or damaged. Bandits usually set villages on fire after they left. I would have assumed that the people were all away on some festival—the Dionysiad was near—if it had not been for that strained note in my master's speech.

I heard a rustle and leapt to my feet. A woman came climbing down the bank to the road, carrying a small baby and towing another two children behind her. She stopped when she saw me.

'Are you a healer?' she asked suspiciously.

'I'm an acolyte, Lady,' I said politely. 'Master Glaucus is in the village and will presently be here.'

'In the village? Then he is lost. Kokkinades is doomed. Some god has been offended and he has struck us with a plague. Apollo. It must be Apollo.'

'Are you…' I was about to say 'the only survivor' but changed my phrasing hurriedly, 'alone, Lady?'

'No, the others have gone to sacrifice to Apollo to ask him to take off the curse. It must have been that bull. It was prideful of us to sacrifice a bull.'

'Are you well, Lady?' With my new-found knowledge of the non-existence of gods I could not enter into the argument. She made a holy sign with her free hand and said, 'Thanks be to all the gods, yes, I and the children are well. Though what we will do or where we will go, I do not know.'

I could not think of a reply to that so I said, 'Leave it to the gods, Lady.'

In this way I arrived at hypocrisy and started on my journey towards becoming a man. My master came up at this moment, heard my declaration, and did not even smile.

'Woman, where are all the people of Kokkinades?' He sounded angry. The woman recoiled and pointed down the road, where I knew that the village of Irion stood. I had been born there.

'At the temple of Apollo of the roads,' she said shakily. 'It is not an hour's walk, Lord.'

Glaucus grabbed Banthos' rein, untied him, and leapt onto his back. I followed hastily and we galloped away.

'Master, what has happened to the village?' I screamed through the dust and the beat of hoofs.

'Their own stupidity has happened to them. By the gods, if there were gods, Diomenes, they would despair of men.'

'Why?' I asked, choking on a mouthful of dust.

He did not reply. I drove my heels into Pyla's flank, urging her to keep up, but we failed to match the speed of Banthos and had to follow in his dust cloud. Inevitably, we dropped behind. I tucked my feet into Pyla's belly ban, my soles against her silky hide. I could not see a thing (and perhaps neither could Pyla) but thus attached, I could not fall off.

I wondered what the men of Kokkinades had done to make Master Glaucus so angry.

As the dust settled, I rubbed my eyes and saw that we had arrived at a small and badly maintained temple of Apollo Pathfinder. Thirty people were gathered outside. My master had dropped Banthos' rein and was striding into the building. I leapt down, tethered the beasts, and followed on his heels.

This temple had only one priest and he was very old. His beard was white and curled to his waist and his head was entirely bald.

One look at him told me that he had lost his wits. He was mumbling prayers, all confused, marrying bits of harvest prayers to the petition of rain, mispronouncing the words so that I could only pick out phrases occasionally. This sometimes happens to old men who have outlived their time. Usually some pectoral ailment carries them off to merciful death at the end of the next winter.

The sacrifice had been made—a kid—but this priest could not intercede with Apollo for his people.

Master Glaucus put the priest gently aside and said loudly, 'Are you men of Kokkinades?'

There was a murmur of agreement. A stout, middle-aged man stepped forward and said, 'The men of Kokkinades hear you. Who are you, Lord?'

'I am Glaucus, Master of Epidavros.' They stepped back a pace at this and bowed. I looked at their faces. They were labouring men and farmers, weather beaten and gnarled like old olive roots by longs years of hard work in the fields. They did not resemble each other at all except for the eyes. They all had the same expression. They were all terrified.

'Ten years ago,' said the master slowly and loudly, so that those outside could hear, 'an oracle from Epidavros told you that your well was cursed, and ordered you to dig another higher up the hill. The god also ordered you to clean your houses, wash your clothes, and dig new privies on the lower side of the village. Did you obey?'

'Yes, Lord. We would not disobey an oracle,' said the stout man.

'I came into Kokkinades to find the houses full of dead children. So I thought about your village and how this could have happened. How could such simple people have offended a powerful god?'

'It was the bull,' said another man. 'I told you, Pilis. We should not have sacrificed the bull.'

'It was the oracle of Apollo!' roared my master. 'In Kokkinades there is a well which lies lower than the drain from the market place. From the look of it that is where you have been getting all your water. Is this true?'

'Yes, Lord. The new well was too far from the village,' said Pilis timidly, 'so we opened the old one again.'

'Apollo has cursed you. You have two choices. You can move—all of you—to Tiryns, or you can obey the oracle. Apollo Sun God is not to be denied. He does not speak to many and his words are to be instantly obeyed if he deigns to speak to men. But if you decide to go to Tiryns you must wait here for a month—at this temple—and not go on until there is no sick person amongst you. Choose, men of Kokkinades. I will wait for you outside. Who is related to this priest?'

'He is my grandfather, Lord,' said Pylis.

Glaucus took the old man's hand and placed it in his grandson's.

'Look after him. It is because of the disobedience of the village that he is god struck.'

Glaucus swept out. He was magnificent. He could appear dignified while wearing only his tunic, stained with sweat. He stalked over to the horses and stood patting Banthos' nose and whispering to him. I got close enough to hear what he was saying.

'Men,' said my master, 'are the most idiotic pernicious animals to ever crawl on the earth. Why do you tolerate them, Lord Apollo?'

I was surprised to hear him call on the gods, in whom I knew he did not believe. However, I had enough sense to stay silent and occupy myself by grazing Pyla along the verge, where some dry but edible grass had been missed by the temple goats.

The villagers were engaged in a debate which would certainly occupy them for at least the whole night and probably the next day. The master gave Banthos a final caress and said over his shoulder, 'Find a dry spot for us, boy, and preferably some water—but go up the hill for it, never down. Then light a small fire and boil the water.'

'Master, I have no cooking gear at all. How…?'

'The priest lives there.' Glaucus pointed impatiently. 'He will not grudge us a pot. He'll never need it again.'

Entering the small hovel, I found a bronze cauldron. I hauled it out and scrubbed it with sand, then dragged it up the hill to where I had heard a stream. It looked clean, but I rinsed the pot and carried out my master's orders. He would not let me come with him to tend the women and children in their camp further down the hill, so I rubbed down the horses and sat huddled over my small fire, feeling very alone and isolated in the night, with the men of Kokkinades' voices and the hooting of lady's owls my only distraction.

A watch later the master came back, ate some bread, gave me the empty cauldron to refill. He lay down naked on his cloak to sleep, having discarded his tunic ten paces from our camp. I heard him groan as he turned over.

'Are they very ill, Master?'

'Yes. Ten have died so far. All the children will die, I think at least those under three. Tomorrow we shall look for fresh vervain and hyssop.'

'We have some dried, Master.'

'We had, but I used it all. And the herbs which grow in the place are suited to the diseases of the place and the people. Tomorrow, Chryse, we will discuss the doctrine of signatures. And tomorrow these morons will have decided what to do and we can leave.'

'But Master, what about the women and children?'

'There is nothing I can do for them but to persuade or daunt their dim-witted men to obey the oracle. It was a sensible oracle, that one, and would have saved their lives.'

'A sensible oracle, Master?'

'Yes, I composed it myself. Go to sleep, Diomenes.'

Chapter Five

Cassandra

Nyssa was right. I was growing up.

Ordinarily, I would have moved from my Nyssa's house to the Temple of the Maidens, where the Trojan women were taught rituals, songs, herbs, and skills which they might not have learned from their own mothers. This includes spinning, carding, weaving, dyeing, embroidery—we are famous for the beauty of our textiles—and some house-making, metal smithing and tiling. After a few years in the temple, the maidens specialise in whatever it is that they are best at. We are the well-skilled maidens, we Trojan women, and men come to marry us from all over the world, even the Achaeans who dislike our customs and say we are too free. Men come seeking Trojan wives from as far as the Black Mountains on the borders of Caria, where the language is utterly strange.

Those who have no skills are still valued, because we are also, they say, the most beautiful women in the world.

Some, of course, never marry. They stay with the maidens to teach or carry on their own trade or become priestesses of the Maiden. A few go every year from Troy to wander with the Amazons, the women who fight like men. Our friend Androm-ache would have gone with them if she had not been promised to Hector.

For the fate of the women of the royal house is stricter than that of the common people. We must marry where we are given, if there is a political reason. No other women in Troy are so constrained. Others can make their own marriage agreement with their new husband. The daughters of Priam must go where we are sent. Our reward is peace for the city of Troy and for that we would do anything.

Still, it has its advantages. Because I was a princess, and also a royal twin, I was allowed to stay with my brother Eleni and Nyssa our nurse for longer than the others.

At night, in our common bed, Eleni and I discovered new things about ourselves. I was growing breasts. Eleni, in the course of a year after I had seen Clea's child born, had grown tall and slim, and there were other developments, with which we played and gave each other pleasure.

I remember the surprise I got when after handling the papyrus-root phallus, it spurted seed. It smelt of wormwood. I was afraid I had hurt Eleni, but his skin was flushed and he gasped with pleasure. I reached the same delight when Eleni's exploring fingers happened upon the thing which the Trojans call the goddess' pearl. The pleasure was so strong that I felt that my bones had been filled with honey.

Sweet Eleni, sweet twin, so close to me that we were one flesh. But never one flesh in truth. We knew that I was still a maiden and must remain so until the sacrifice to Gaia, otherwise the goddess would curse both of us. Our seed would wither, our bones ache, our sight dim, and the children of such an unholy union would fail in the womb and die untimely. We knew that if Eleni made full union with any woman before he had cut his hair for the father Dionysius and made the sacrifice of wine and honey in his temple he would sprout disfiguring seed and no one would marry him. We ended our nights locked in each other's arms, flushed and sticky but still technically virgins. Oh my own Eleni. His face on our pillow in the morning light was so young, unlined and pure, his hair lapping my shoulder, his mouth open against my breast.

I was twelve before I found out that I could not marry him. Nyssa told me. We were sorting wheat seeds, a peaceful occupation, sitting in the shade under the vine. The vine leaves made patterns on the marble floor, dark green outlined in gold. We were discarding the dried, darkened or broken seeds and spilling the good plump ones through our fingers to winnow out the bits of leaf. I remember how it poured with a rustle into the basket at our feet.

'You will become a healer, little Cassandra,' Nyssa cooed. 'You have a quick eye.'

She could sieve seed faster than me; her eye for imperfections was as bright as an eagle's for prey.

'I think so,' I agreed sleepily.

'You know that you cannot marry your brother, Cassandra,' she said quietly.

It took a moment for the implications to sink in, then I sat up straight and grasped at the sliding tray.

'I can't? Nyssa, I have always meant to marry Eleni! He wants to marry me!'

'Yes, my pet, my lamb, but he can't.'

'They do in Egypt,' I objected. 'In Egypt brothers always marry sisters. The word for lover is sister. Aegyptus the sea captain told me.'

'That is Egypt,' she said, taking the tray out of my shaking hands. 'This is Troy. You are Priam's daughter, and you must marry where he directs. You cannot marry your brother. You may be given to anyone with whom your father needs to cement an alliance. That is the fate of the daughters of the king. You have always known that, my lambkin.'

'I…but Nyssa, no, we are twins, we are the royal twins, it is different for us!'

'Not that different, my golden one. You cannot marry your brother. I know that you have not broken your maidenhoods, you would not do that. But you are growing up, Cassandra, my bud, my flower, my little lamb. You must find your skills and then leave the Maiden for the Mother and when you do that you must live apart from Eleni.'

'You're wrong,' I said insolently. Her brown wrinkled face contracted into a grimace that looked like pain. 'I am a princess of the royal house of Priam and I shall do as I like. I shall marry my brother Eleni and no one shall stop me. No one.'

I achieved a dignified exit, stalking out of the courtyard into the street, my new long tunic swishing behind me. Then I took to my heels and ran, half blind with fury, for Tithone in the lower quarter.

I reached her street, skidded around the corner and ran into her house without even stopping, as is proper, at the threshold. Tithone was combing her hair. It was dark hair stippled with silver and it spilled around me as I buried my head in her lap and sobbed out the story.

To my horror, it was true. I could not marry my twin.

'But in Egypt...' I sobbed, clinging to the idea that somewhere there was justice. Tithone shook her head. The herb-scented hair lashed my wet eyes.

'No, little daughter, it cannot be. Come. I will show you why. You will not speak until we are out of the house we are to visit, is that clear? Not one word, Princess.'

Tithone called me 'Princess' when she was most solemn and usually most angry. I nodded. My world was falling to pieces.

Tithone bound up her hair. The common people thought that there was magic in her hair, and charms made from it were sold in the markets. She found this dryly amusing but took care that no one had a chance to cut a stray piece of it by binding it close to her head and wearing a veil. When I asked her why, she said, 'If it is a charm it must be rare.'

I walked behind her, muffling my wet face in a fold of my cloak. We descended the city, out into the ramshackle town which surrounded Troy.

It had grown up largely because the city had expanded beyond its walls. Hector said it also harboured people who did not like the city's rules but who required the protection of the house of

Tros and holiness of Ilium. Eleni and me—oh, Eleni my lost love!—had always been forbidden to come there, so naturally we had haunted the place, relishing the strange smells and weird gods and odd languages. There we had learned three phrases in Phrygian and lots of disconnected words, mostly obscene, in a babble of different tongues. Low Town was always interesting. Most of the sailors lived there. It was our favourite part of Troy.

Near the altar to the strangers' gods we turned left, diving down a narrow alleyway redolent of rotting garbage and sewage. Tithone had often told Hecube, the queen, that unless Low Town was cleansed we would have a plague. In the autumn sun it stank, and flies rose from the unpaved gutter in the centre of the alley.

'Blessing upon the house,' said Tithone, entering a hut made of reeds and driftwood. It was dark inside. I could make out a woman and a baby, and someone else stirring in the blackness. The woman was hushing a newborn, which cried with an incessant grating voice which set my teeth on edge.

'Revered one,' said the mother, 'you are welcome.'

'Fire Lady of the Goddess,' said a man's voice. 'You are welcome to the hearth.'

Tithone did not even mention my presence, but took the baby out of the mother's arms and carried it into the street. I followed her.

In the street she unwrapped the baby and showed it to me. It was dreadfully deformed.

Ten days old, perhaps. The face was a mask of horror, without eyes, the skull monstrously huge, the arms and legs missing. I bit my lip and did not say a word.

'It will die,' she said matter-of-factly. 'Now, hear the mother's tale.'

We went back into the hut and the woman hushed the monster against her breast and asked, 'What of the baby, Revered One, Mistress of the Pillar?'

She was awarding Tithone some of the titles of Isis, the Lady of the Egyptians. From her accent, delicately slurred, I took her to be a true Egyptian, not one of the Peoples of the Sea who have settled on the Nile delta and who still speak Danaan.

'He will die in three days,' Tithone said without emphasis. 'The gods will take him home. You must spend a month in the Temple of the Mother and then you will be cleansed.'

'We offended the gods,' the woman wailed, and her husband came and held her tightly. 'We offended them by leaving the River Land and coming here.'

'Why did you leave?' asked Tithone. The young man answered, stumbling in his speech as though he had lately learned our language.

'Isis knows that we are sister and brother, and loved each other from our one birth.' They were twins! I bit my lip harder. 'Bashti and I came down the river and there were the People of the Sea. We left our father because he had sold Bashti to one of the Danaans, curse them with many curses! They caught us and forced my sister, my spouse, then left her for dead, like prey. Me they blinded. She brought us here to windy Ilium, then lay with me after it was clear that she had not conceived a monster of those beast-men. But their seed has corrupted her blood. I hear the wrongness in the child's cry. I have felt its wrong-formed body. We are cursed. Better she had left me to die in Egypt.'

'Better I had died there under their hands,' said the woman bitterly.

'No. Death is never better, daughter,' said Tithone gently. 'Wait till this child dies and you are cleansed, then go and lie in the temple of Dionysius and you will conceive a child who will be clean and whole. You, man, must only lie with your wife when she is pregnant. Thus will the curse be removed. How do you live, daughter?'

'We are weavers,' she said, hope beginning to dawn in her voice. I could not see her face. 'We have skill to make the finest linen, the pleated gauze that the Pharaohs wear—they call it woven air. But we cannot afford flax fine enough for good cloth.'

'Come up into the city when the child dies,' said Tithone. 'Come to me and I will talk to the mistress of the weavers and she will find you a stone house. Such skill is valued in Troy. Blessings be upon you,' and she went out.

I followed her until we were standing on the bank of Scamander, the river of Troy. Flax and papyrus reeds lined the edge, piping with the bird's cries.

'It was not the Danaan's? I asked in a voice as small as the birds'.

'No, daughter.'

'But I could do that—lie down with the god and only lie with Eleni when I was pregnant—could I not do that?'

'Healers must deal with the situation as it is, daughter. Could I tell them that their love was cursed, that the corruption in the woman's blood was the closeness of her birth to her husband? I would merely have given them both up to death by despair. Their love is the only thing they still have left to them after such long and painful voyaging. This way, they will not conceive any more monsters and can stay with each other. But you, Princess, are not yet compromised. And even if you were'—she knew me well, Tithone my mistress—'even if this night you and Eleni defied the most solemn edicts of the gods of Troy, I would not allow it to continue. After cleansing on barley bread and water for three moon, you would go to the maidens and Eleni to the youths, and you would not see him again until after both of you were safely married to someone else. I could mention to your father, Priam the Lord King, that an Achaean marriage might keep the peace a generation more. Do you want me to do that?'

'No,' I whispered.

My heart was breaking.

Suddenly a god was with me—Apollo the Archer. Sunlight blinded me; heat burned my skin. He was tall, beautiful beyond belief, golden as molten gold from the furnace. He laid one hand on my breast and I melted in his fire. His voice spoke not in my ears but in my head and reverberated in my womb, which contracted into a knot. Something like a finger penetrated me. 'You are mine, Cassandra,' said the great voice. 'My ears and eyes in Troy, my woman, my bride. I will lie with you and fill you with my fire. I am yours and you are mine, Princess.'

Sweet, sweet, piercing sweet, the touch of the god. I opened my eyes and he was gone, but there was a scent of honeysuckle in the filthy street. I trembled as I stood and Tithone bore me up. I leaned on her stringy shoulder, blinded by the light.

'Which god?' she asked, and I heard myself say, 'Apollo.' Tithone grunted.

'Go back to your twin, most favoured of Priam's daughters,' she said. 'Talk to him. Explain.'

I don't remember walking back to Nyssa's house, but about an hour later I found myself lying beside Eleni in the afternoon heat, trying to explain.

He stared at me and we embraced with desperate closeness. We clung for an hour, not consoled by the touch of skin on skin. We would never be lovers. I was the daughter of Priam and the bride of Apollo. Eleni and I could not evade our destiny. If we broke all the laws of the gods and of Troy we would only bring forth monsters.

Then a vision came to Eleni, which I shared. He had flung himself over onto his back, out of my arms, and a golden woman appeared, lying beside him. My twin's eyes widened. She was beautiful beyond compare, glowing with life. Her hair hung down and brushed his breast and left delicate scorched lines where it touched. She laid both hands on his shoulders as she leaned over to kiss his mouth. I heard his breathing shorten and his pulse raced in the wrist I held in my hands.

'Mine,' said the woman. 'Eleni, you are my husband, the creature of my heart.' I was suddenly reminded of someone, a mortal woman like myself. The bones of the face and the way she framed words; the curve of the mouth and the way her hair hung down as though it flowed like water. I could not catch the resemblance. Eleni was transfigured. He was as beautiful as the goddess. She reached up and unpinned the chiton. Naked, she was perfect. Eleni gasped something and held out his arms. Ishtar the goddess knelt over my brother and her smooth flank and thigh touched mine, the golden skin as hot as metal. For a moment she towered over us, Eleni supine and me clutching him from the side. Then she bent and kissed him; once on the mouth, once on the belly, once on the phallus.

Then, as I lay and could not breathe, she sank down on my brother, engulfing in her sheath the phallus I could never have. I watched as it vanished. Eleni cried as if in pain and stiffened until I thought his back would break. Once, twice, the phallus slipped into the sheath. Then she said, 'You will lie with me again, Eleni the Trojan—not with your twin, but with me,' and she vanished.

Eleni threw himself into my arms and kissed my mouth and I had barely touched him when he reached his climax and sank onto my breast to weep as if his heart was broken.

Thus in tears we discovered that the love of the gods is shattering for the mortals whom they favour. We wished that we had been born apart and unrelated, and that we had never attracted divine attention.

But we knew as we wept that we were fated.

That night we lay down with Hector on the roof of the palace. Alexandratos, our brother, whom we called Pariki, the purse, after the shepherd's bag he always carried, was sitting with his back against the bull's horns which crowned the roof.

Pariki was eighteen, a vague and dreamy youth, with a streak of cruelty. Eleni and I did not like him; he had nasty fingers which tweaked and tickled when no one was watching. Luckily he was about to leave on a trading mission to Sparta and Corinth. Pariki had the grey eyes of the god-touched and long golden hair which he was very proud of, arraying it across his smooth shoulders. The only skill he had so far envinced was the Dionysiac one of making love; at this his repute was very high. This did not concern Eleni and me and one of the most satisfying moments of our childhood had been the contrivance which spilled oak gall distillate on Pariki's pretty head. It had dyed his hair black for some months. We reckoned it worth the spanking we had got from Hector for wasting his Egyptian ink. Typically, Pariki would never say that he liked Hector's stories, but he often happened to be on the roof when we came there to hear them.

Andromache had joined us that night. She was twelve, too, taller than me, and we were glad that she was there because Hector knew all about what had happened to us and we did not want to talk about it. Because Andromache worshipped our brother and would be married to him in spring, we yielded the place on his left side, nearest his heart, to her. Eleni lay behind me and Státhi reposed in his customary place on the warrior's chest.

I was meanly pleased that Státhi did not treat Andromache any better than the rest of us. He scratched her just as hard if she tried to touch him. Since Státhi slept every night with Hector we wondered what he would do to the maiden when she came to the warrior's bed.

Then I saw how Eleni looked at Andromache and nothing seemed funny anymore. The face and form of the woman in the vision had seemed familiar; now I knew. The goddess had taken Andromache's form to seduce my brother. He was in love with her.

And she was in love with Hector, Bulwark of Troy, eldest son of Priam.

It was the first time the gods had played games with us. We were desperately vulnerable and hurt.

Andromache snuggled into Hector's shoulder and demanded a story.

'What story, children?' he asked amiably. 'Gods?'

Eleni and I shuddered. 'Not gods.'

Hector's face changed; he had noticed our reaction. 'Andromache shall choose,' he said gently. 'Come closer, twins, you are cold.' His chest was bare and his flesh was dry and warm. I rubbed my face against his shoulder, feeling the thick pad of muscle over the bone. His arm encompassed Eleni and me and his hand closed on my brother's arm, comfortingly tight.

'Heroes,' said Andromache. Hector chuckled. 'Which hero, little maiden?' he asked 'Perseus? Theseus?'

'No, Theseus is a cheat,' said Andromache, who had strong opinions on honour. Myrine said that she thought like an Amazon, which was a great compliment from Myrine. 'Heracles.'

'Ah, well. There are many stories about Heracles.' Hector sat up a little, his back against our rolled cloak, causing Státhi to slide down his chest, make a short, disgusted exclamation and leave red furrows in his wake. Hector rearranged us with Státhi on his lap and began in his storyteller's voice.

'Once there was a great hero who came to Troy to seek horses from Laomedon, our grandfather, king of Troy.'

We had heard this story before but we liked hearing stories again. The first hearing you are too excited and long for the resolution; the second time you can pay attention to the story. Andromache wrapped herself around Hector while Eleni and I, desolate in the wake of the shattering of our marriage and our encounters with the god, embraced closely, his belly against my back and my face buried in Hector's chest.

'They will call me Hector Sibling Coat if you get any closer,' he commented. 'Now, to the story. Laomedon was the fifth king, descendant of Dardanus who received the divine horses in exchange for his son Ganymede. Laomedon inherited the herd; all subsequent kings had bred them wisely and they were the best horses in the world.'

'They are still the best horses in the world,' declared Andromache. She was a better rider than any of us—probably better than any Trojan warrior. She seemed to have an instinctive understanding with her mount. I had seen her leap onto the shaggy back of a wild stallion, a lord of horses, just brought in from the summer pastures, and tame him into willingness, if not submission, on one wild ride. I could ride adequately, as could Eleni, and our brother Hector could drive a two-horse chariot with as much ease as a child drives a wooden toy. We had always wondered if part of his charm for Andromache was that he had promised to allow her to drive his own prized chariot pair, whom no other hand was allowed to touch.

'True,' Hector agreed. 'Heracles was the son of the Achaean father god, Zeus, the stern one, compeller of the clouds, and Alchmene, a Danaan woman from the Tiryns, which is girded with walls. He came with six ships through the straights which we thus call the Pillars of Heracles and arrived at a time when Laomedon had broken his bargain with Poseidon.'

'What was the bargain?' I asked ritually.

'Laomedon had offered six of his horses to Poseidon if he would build the walls of Troy. Then he could not bear to part with the horses and Poseidon sent a sea monster so ravenous that it bit the keels out of boats and swallowed the fisherman whole. Heracles' companions were Telamon and Iolas and the men of Tiryns. They say there was an oracle…'

Hector paused, then went on. 'The oracle commanded that the Princess Hesione, daughter of the king and sister of our father, King Priam, be chained on the shore for the monster, and that this sacrifice would appease Poseidon Blue-Haired, whom Laomedon had cast from the city.'

For some reason, Hector was troubled. Andromache squeaked as his arms tightened about her and drew her closer. We in Troy did not sacrifice living things. Our gods did not like such sacrifices. Only the barbarian Achaeans burnt dead flesh and spilled blood before their cruel gods. We gave seed and flowers and garments and gold to the gods of Troy, and honey and wine; only once a year did a creature die for the gods. That was the bull which was sacrificed to Dionysius, at the festival which marked the turning of winter to spring. We garlanded the perfect bull with flowers and brought him from his stall to die for the season. Then we ate his flesh and drank his blood mingled with wine which made the whole city drunk, giving our fleshly worship to the god of increase and wine. The Dionysiad lasted for three days and even the maidens of the goddess and the man-loving priests of Adonis danced and coupled in the squares, for a god must have his due.

Hector continued, 'The hero sailed into the bay and saw the princess chained to Scaean Gate where the oak tree grows.

Telamon seized Hesione and Heracles bargained with the sea monster began to rise beneath the Achaean ship. It was bigger than the ship and angry because it was baulked of its prey. Its head came out of the water and it grabbed the mast, snapping it and chewing the sail. Laomedon promised horses if the hero could kill the monster.

'Heracles bound on his bronze armour and his helmet and took his spear and his sword, and as the monster's head came around leapt full into its mouth. The Achaeans wailed as its teeth snapped shut over him and it dived beneath the surface again. But Telamon had Hesione and wanted her, though he had made no bargain for the king's daughter.

'In the waters of the bay, the Trojans saw the monster writhing and twisting. It was the length of three ships, as broad in the middle as two, and it roared fearfully, so loud that the guards on the Scaean Gate covered their ears. The Achaeans began to mourn for their hero, wailing and beating their breasts, when the monster gave a convulsive jerk and Heracles the Hero hacked his way out of its belly, so that it spewed its guts and stranded, dying messily in the shallows.

'Later it took all of our fleet to drag it into the deep water so that the tide could bear it away.

'Heracles came alive out of the monster and walked, dripping scales and fishy blood, up the steep streets to the palace to demand his promised price. The Achaeans and the Princess Hesione followed him. Laomedon the horse-lover refused him his reward, breaking solemn oaths sworn by the gods. Standing in the throne room with his sons all about him, he defied the hero and bade him begone with insulting words. Heracles was possessed of battle fury.'

'What's battle fury?' Eleni interrupted.

'He lost his mind, all knowledge of himself, and killed everyone standing,' said Hector. 'He killed the king and all but one of his sons. His sword moved like a reaping hook, cutting down the youth of Ilium. They ran and he pursued the royal house of Tros, breaking down the walls, pulling stone from stone and killing when he found them, with sword and spear and hands and teeth. Stones bounced off him, spears could not pierce him, swords broke on his invulnerable body. Then the Princess Hesione caught the remaining child—Podarkes swift-foot, who had run for his life—and held him to her breast and defied Heracles to kill him. Heracles, servant of women, could not touch her. He ransomed the child for her gold-embroidered veil, the maidens veil which girls wore at that time. Thus Hesione's body, freely offered, appeased the hero and he lay down with her in the rubble among the bodies of her brothers. It is said that although he was mired with blood and stronger than the sea, he did not hurt her as he lay with her. Heracles, goddess-brought, was sworn not to harm women.

'Hesione ordered that horses should be brought and given to the hero, and gold to Telamon and the men of wall-girt Tiryns. This was done. Hesione gave the child, whom she named Priamos, one who is ransomed, to Lykke the wolf-woman to raise, ordering her to take him into the mountains. She appointed the eldest princess to rule until Priamos returned. That Priamos is our father, the Lord King Priam the old.'

'What happened to Hesione?' asked Andromache. Hector did not answer immediately, but stroked a living hand down the girl's side and kissed her on the mouth. Behind me Eleni muttered. I turned and kissed him, afraid he would make some unfortunate comment.

It was the first time that I did not know for certain what Eleni would do.

Hector said regretfully, 'Telamon kidnapped her. Heracles, possessed by remorse for his murders, re-built the walls, as you see them now. While the hero was hauling stone, Telamon of Tiryns stole Hesione, Princess of Troy, and sailed away with her.

'The princess sent word that we should not pursue her; she had no wish to start a war with the barbarians. Heracles finished the walls and went home. There, possessed of that same fury, he killed his own children and was set twelve labours, the labours that made him a god.'

'And Hesione?' asked Pariki's voice, stilted as though he spoke though clenched teeth.

'She lived with Telamon for the rest of her life and had many sons,' said Hector. 'It is an old tale, brother.'

'It is an insult which has not been avenged,' said Pariki. He stalked away. We heard his sandals slap against the stone steps of the palace staircase.

For some reason Hector would tell no further tales that night. He held us close, as though he feared to lose us.

Chapter Six

Diomenes

The master was right, of course. In the night most of the children of Kokkinades died.

Next morning the village had reached its decision. They would go to Tiryns after their one moon's rest at the temple. We mounted and rode away, hearing behind us the wailing of women and the thudding of hoes into the dry, uncultivated ground. Kokkinades had paid a price for disobeying the gods, and they were burying it.

Master Glaucus did not speak for three or four miles, until the noise of mourning had died away. Then he said, 'Diomenes, do not say that there are no gods. That place was god struck. No other explanation would ever satisfy men. Do you understand?'

'No, Master.'

'Men will never accept that any stroke of fortune is their own doing. Never. Women will do so, but they are instinctive, incapable of thought and animal. Men must be daunted and only the gods can daunt them.'

'Not even the gods daunted Kokkinades, Master. They disobeyed the oracle and opened the old well.'

'Against stupidity the gods themselves contend in vain, my son. Tell me what herb is sovereign against affections of the lungs. Which herb do you always use, no matter what the combination?'

'Lungleaf, Master.'

'Why is it called that?'

'Because the leaves are shaped like lungs.'

'And which herb do you use as the basis for all kidney treatments?'

'Marshleaf, Master.'

'What do its leaves look like?'

'Kidneys, Master.'

'And for sexual diseases?'

'Mandrake root, Master.'

'Which looks like?'

'A phallus, Master.'

'The gods designed the herbs to feed and heal all things, Chryse, and in doing so they marked each one with either a colour or shape to tell us what part to use for what ailment. What's the best cure for a nettle sting?'

'A dock leaf.'

'And where does dock grow?'

'Next to nettle.'

'Indeed. Now,' he dismounted and picked a small, bright pink flower, 'what's this, Chryse?'

I looked carefully at the shrub, then at the shape of the blunt-toothed leaves and squarish, silky flower. I sniffed and smelt a familiar scent.

'It looks and smells like meadow wound leaf, Master, but the plant is too tall and the flower is the wrong colour.'

'Heracles gave it to men,' the master began, looking up suddenly as a rider approached. He stared, then walked forward two paces and held out his arms.

'Heracles, Master?' I prompted.

'Sired on the virgin Alcmene just over the ridge,' said a beautiful voice. 'Taken to Thebes after he strangled two huge blue serpents in his cradle. Who talks of the hero on this misfortunate road?'

'Arion,' exclaimed my master, and the two men embraced in a swirl of robes. They kissed like old friends, beard to beard.

'What brings you here?' asked Glaucus. 'My dear Arion, how good to see you.'

'And what has dragged you out of your temple, Asclepius-Priest?' laughed Arion. 'I thought you safely imprisoned these ten years, minding the god and everyone's business.'

'Rogue,' commented Glaucus. He pulled the other man around to face me and said, 'This is Arion the great singer, Dolphin-Rider. This is Diomenes called Chryse, my acolyte, God-Touched. He has just found out that there are no gods, and we are journeying to show him that there are.'

'Where to?' Arion took my hand and smiled into my face. He had the darkest and brightest eyes I had ever seen and black hair which straggled down over his rich, dusty, singing robes like ropes. He and my master were alike: beak-nosed, bearded, and authoritative. Glaucus was heavier and his hair was white; Arion was thin and wiry and had only two stripes of white in his harsh black hair. Badger-Haired Arion; I had heard of him. I had sung several of his tavern songs and one lyrical invocation of Selene, the goddess of the moon. I had also considered him mythical.

Something of what I was thinking must have come to Arion, because he pulled me into an embrace and laid my hand over his heart. It beat strongly.

'Golden One, I am alive and I am quite definitely Arion,' he chuckled. 'Did you say where you are going, Glaucus? My memory is not what it was.'

'Tiryns, then Mycenae. Where are you bound?'

'Mycenae for the great truce. We can travel together. If you wanted the boy to see the greatest princes, they will all be there. Odysseus of the nimble wits, it's his idea. He has a lot of ideas.'

'What is his idea?' I asked, freeing myself.

'There is a maiden called Elene. She is the most beautiful woman in the world,' said the bard solemnly. 'All the princes of the Danaans were ready to kill each other for her. Now it seems that King Odysseus of Ithaca has found a solution. There is to be a league of Elene's suitors, who will all swear to defend her father's choice, and to war against those who try to steal her.

For she has been stolen before and now must be safely married before she brings the whole world to ruin.'

'Have you seen her?' I asked.

Arion grew still. 'I have seen her. She is the most beautiful woman in the world. You shall see her too, little healer, and judge for yourself. But beware your heart or she will steal it and eat it. I interrupted your lesson, Glaucus. What were you saying about Heracles?'

'This is Heracles' wound leaf, ignorant singer of the Achaeans,' said Glaucus. 'It grows only from here to Tiryns and is used for all wounds, ulcers, and oozing scars. It is hot and dry, boy, so take care to use it only on wet wounds. It dries up blood.'

'Take a supply,' advised the bard. 'There will be blood enough before Elene is given away.'

We rode on a little. I had done as the bard advised and garnered two handfuls of Heracles' herb. I was just wondering what the most beautiful woman would look like when Arion slowed and called, 'Here is the tomb of the warring brothers. Have you heard the tale, little healer?'

'No, Lord,' I stared at a pyramid of rock, covered with bronze shields which had tarnished to the thinness of skin. It was clearly very old.

'Ignorant singer, eh, brother?' he eyed Glaucus. 'Would you like to hear it?'

'Oh, yes, Lord. I love stories and I have not heard that one before.'

Arion slowed his patient horse to a walk and began to sing. His voice was rich, clear and ringing. It cast a spell like Hypnos Priest. No listener ever heard Arion Dolpin-rider unmoved.

'The brothers Akrisos and Proitos, closer their love than roots clings to vine,' he began.

Pyla carried me—I could not have been said to be riding—at the bard's side as he told of the father who denied his daughter Danae marriage and locked her in a high tower until the god came to her in a shower of gold and she conceived Perseus the hero. Proitos brought the giants, the Cyclopes, to build him high-walled Tiryns, then quarrelled in turn with the god Dionysius, and his daughters were driven mad. The brothers lost or gave away their cities, Argos and Tiryns, but it did not save them from their dreadful fate.

By the time the song wound down we were treading the dusty path up into the mountains and Arion touched my cheek.

'Look there, Healer Priest,' he said, turning my entranced face into the sunset. 'There are the walls built by the giants.'

I had not known that anyone could build so high. Occupying the whole of a shoulder of cliff thrust out into a chasm, Tiryns of the high walls glowed in the sunset. I gasped and Arion chuckled.

'You are a good listener, Chryse, so I'll give you some advice. Do not mention the prince in Tiryns. One of the mysteries, that is.'

'What is?' I asked, still amazed at my first sight of the city.

'There is no prince of Tiryns,' he said. 'Since Heracles' days it has changed hands twenty times and always for bad fortune. At the moment it is held for Argos by Dikaos, the just one, until a rightful prince shall be found. If I was that prince, I would give my inheritance to Boreas the north wind and leave for somewhere nice and distant; Libya, say, or Africa. I tell no tales of Heracles in Tiryns, boy. Here lived the coward Eurystheus who speaks to a hero from inside a grain amphora is not to be emulated.' He laughed. 'Come then, brother,' he said to Glaucus. 'It grows cold in these mountains at night. Let us see what welcome unlucky Tiryns can give two wandering healers and a straying bard.'

The welcome was warm. Arion, it appeared, was well known. The guard on duty on the wall over the keystone gate crowned with gods cried out, 'The famed singer! Arion Dolphin-Rider has come! Welcome, Master. Who travels with you?'

'Glaucus the healer, Master of Epidavros, and his acolyte Chryse God-Touched,' roared Arion. 'You did not used to shut this gate so early!'

'Come inside,' said the guard. The gate creaked open and we rode inside. It shut behind us with a clang. Tiryns had bronze gates, hollow cast and fitted over stone lintels and posts. Not even the Cyclopes who had built them could have forced those doors. I had a small internal qualm as they shut. I wondered whether they kept friends in as well as they kept enemies out.

'What's happening, eh?' demanded Arion of the gate guards, who were fully clad in breastplates and helmets. 'We saw no enemies on the road.'

'The Lord Dikaos ordered it, Lord,' said the soldier nervously. 'Ah, here he comes,' and he abandoned us to return to the wall.

Dikaos, lord of Tiryns, was slim, young, and dressed in a very coarse chiton which barely reached his knees. He wore no jewellery of rank and no crown. Only his haughty, intelligent face made him look any different from a peasant's son. He had heard how unlucky it was to be prince of Tiryns and evidently wanted to make sure that he was never mistaken for one.

'Arion,' he said coolly, and then bowed the knee to my master to the precise depth indicated by courtly custom. 'Master of Epidavros. We are honoured. Particularly at the moment.'

'Why?' asked Arion bluntly. I noticed that he used exactly the same manner and form of speech to everyone, from me to the soldier to the lord of Tiryns. Being a bard, he was not accorded any rank and he gave respect to no one who hadn't earned it. He took my hand as I fell back, overawed by the city. 'What is going on, Dikaos?' he demanded. 'Are you expecting an army?'

'No, we already have one,' said Dikaos. 'Without warning and under the shield of darkness, Menelaus and Agamemnon brought Elene here. They meant to go on to Mycenae this morning, but the wretched girl is sick. She is weeping in pain and none of our herb-women can ease her. I have shut my gates against the army of suitors who will roar through the plain of Argos as soon as they find out where she is, and I do not know what bitter rain will fall on unlucky Tiryns. Already the old men are recalling Heracles throwing his brother Iphicles off the battlements and recounting the sins of Eurystheus, may he be cursed and all his line and his remote descendants wherever they are.'

'What is the matter with the lady?' I asked. At the sound of my voice the lord of Tiryns looked down and his taut face softened.

'Thank all the gods,' he said. 'A healer who is not yet a man. Is he good, Master Glaucus?' he asked, taking my hand in his. 'Can he be trusted?'

'In all things,' said my master gravely, and I flushed with pride. 'He is Diomenes of the healing hands, but he is not yet come into his full power. What ails the maiden?'

'If she was my child I would say it was pure temper,' Dikaos snapped. 'But now she really does seem ill. If she dies here, I am a dead man and my city will be sacked. Yet even you, Master, would not be able to see her without one of the Atreidae, either Agamemnon or Menelaus, being present, and this girl will not allow. They will all accept Diomenes, I hope.'

We had crossed a wide courtyard and come to the door of a great house. The walls were of stone, the windows high and narrow and the roof steeply pitched. It loomed and it made me nervous. I had never seen a hall of this size and so much high-piled stone oppressed my spirit. Dikaos still had hold of my hand. A slave opened the studded door and the lord of Tiryns led us into a large hall furnished with benches, then into a smaller room hung with colourful tapestries. The bedchamber smelt musty and was airless and cold. Dikaos finally released his hold and I sat down gingerly on the edge of a large, saddle-sprung bed. I jumped up again as it gave under my weight. I was used to sleeping on the tiled floor of my temple. Dikaos did not even smile.

'This is my own house, lords. Please sit down and refresh yourselves—attend the guests, bring washing water and bread and wine at once'—he called and there was a scurrying of feet as slaves dived to obey him—'then I shall bring you to the kings and perhaps this can be solved without bloodshed. You, little Asclepid, have you your healer's tunic?'

I nodded. Dikaos shut the door of our room and we heard him hurry away.

'Chryse,' said my master, 'be very careful with this maiden. Do not touch her if you can help. There will be a woman with her—talk to her first. She will tell you what is wrong. Then speak to the other maiden, the one supplied by Tiryns. Between the two stories you may be able to diagnose Elene's illness. Now, you must clear your mind of all other things. You must wash yourself clean of any speck of impurity and we will give you bread and wine. Then you will go to the kings and we will accompany you. The woman will take you to the maiden Elene. Take the bag of herbs. There will be water and a fire to prepare an infusion. What are the hysteria herbs?'

'Mistletoe, Master, rosemary to clear the wits, thyme to soothe the brain, poppy for the pain.'

'Good. Here is water. Scrub yourself clean.'

A slave had brought a cauldron of hot water. I stripped and washed all over with soapy lychnis leaf and rinsed myself clean, half-listening to Arion and my master discussing the army of suitors which had set all Achaea by the ears.

'Locusts,' said the old singer. 'They have drunk rivers dry and eaten crops off the ground, and behind them famine flies on her ragged brown wings. The men of Pelops' land have gone mad. It amuses some god, no doubt, to drive a nation insane over one maiden, it makes a good son, Glaucus, but is it reasonable?'

'Is she so beautiful?' asked my master, as I allowed a slave to dry my feet and fit on my sandals. I stood up and the man dropped my healer's tunic, made of the finest Egyptian flax and embroidered with gold, over my head. He combed my hair and bound it with a golden fillet. I sat down with my master and Arion fed me bread soaked in wine, one piece at a time, and told me about Elene.

'She is the daughter of Zeus and a woman called Leda, to whom he came in the shape of a swan,' he said. 'She was stolen by Theseus, old though he was, and her brothers Castor and Polydeuces brought her back to Sparta, to her foster father. Another mouthful, Chryse. Poor Tyndareus' court was overrun by all the youth of Pelops bawling for her hand—and, of course, the rest of her. She is indeed the reincarnation of Aphrodite on earth. I have never seen such beauty. Menelaus, brother of Agamemnon was chosen and took her though he has not lain with her yet. He has been made heir of Sparta by Elene's father, a step up from being a mere prince of Argos. Here, a little more—this is good wine, Chryse. But until Menelaus gets Elene to golden Mycenae where the league will be sworn, she can still be stolen. That is why Dikaos' hair is greying rapidly and why you must heal the girl and let her husband take her away. There. That's enough. Good. Not a spot on the tunic. As white and innocent as a new shorn lamb. Look, Glaucus.'

My master inspected me, took my right hand and looked at the nails, put our bag of herbs into my arms, and we went out of the room, under the keystone arches which stiffened the building like ribs, into the great hall.

There were four men seated on a dais at the end of the hall. Smoke rose in a column through the roof from a great hearth in the middle of the floor. Bronze and gold gleamed through the fumes.

'Healers of Epidavros, Diomenes and Master Glaucus, and I, Arion the Singer,' announced Arion as we walked toward them. 'We bring you greetings.' In a lower tone he added to me, 'Agamemnon, Lord of Golden Mycenae, Castor and Polydeuces the brothers of Elene, Menelaus the husband, Prince of Sparta.'

They sat ranked like gods, huge and imposing in their armour. The brothers were identical twins, big men with muscles which crossed and interlocked as they moved. Menelaus was tall and running to fat, a jovial man with a smiling mouth and a beard which curled like a fleece. Agamemnon, Lord of Men, was huge, broad as a door, his breastplate gleaming and his massive arms and hands jingling and heavy with gold. He fixed his eyes on me and said loudly, 'Come here, Asclepid.' I approached and he leaned down and peered into my face, his hand engulfing my neck. He smelt of grease, wine, and smoke. His beard was streaked mutton fat, his teeth were broken, and his breath was foul, but I did not recoil. He closed his hand a little and my heels were lifted off the floor. I kept my eyes on him and tried not to choke.

'Brave,' he laughed, patting me on the shoulder and setting me down again. Menelaus ran a hand down my side to my buttock, poked me in the belly and said, 'Young.' He smiled, the smile never reaching his eyes.

I looked at the wrestler and the boxer. Their cold gaze fixed on me for a moment, then dismissed me.

'Enough.' Arion was front of me. 'Leave playing, my lords. Will the boy do for your bride, Prince, or shall we find more mannerly company?'

I trembled at this tone, but Menelaus laughed. He had a rich, deep laugh.

'Ay, let him see her. You, Arion, have you any song of Heracles?' he asked, with a spiteful glance at Dikaos.

'Heracles the hero, Lord, has been my especial study.'

Arion snapped his fingers and a slave handed him his lyre. I heard him begin to sing of the disgraceful behaviour of King Eurystheus as I was conducted out of the great hall, up a flight of stairs, and into an antechamber.

The woman sitting on a stool was old—I would judge her to have been Elene's nurse. She also gave me a raking stare, then smiled.

'She is weeping yet, Asclepid,' she told me. 'She fell into a fury, then into this despondency. Her head hurts and her limbs ache and she cannot travel. She has dismissed us all and screams if we enter the room. I have left a brazier burning and boiled water in the ewer beside it. Go in, healer, and see what you can do.'

'What ails her?' I asked.

'She is the most beautiful woman in the world and no one loves her,' said the woman.

'Where is the maiden of Tiryns?' I asked, recalling my instructions. 'I wish to speak with her.' The old woman shooed in a sullen girl and shut the door.

'Are you a healer?' asked the girl. I nodded, trying to look as grave as my master. 'Tell me, maiden, what ails the Lady Elene?'

She shrugged. 'Just temper. She cried and wailed and beat her breasts and said she wanted to die. Since then she has been crying and wailing. She will not eat and cannot sleep and neither can we, for worry that she will bring a siege down on us.'

'Get some good red wine and a young chicken with which you will make a barley broth, and do it quickly,' I snapped. 'Take this lump of poppy. Go to my Mater Glaucus and say that I need poppy syrup with honey and wait until he has made it, then bring all three things to me at once and with the greatest speed.'

'As you order, Master, but if I behaved like that my father would have beaten me.'

'Quickly,' I said and pushed her out.

'I will keep the door until you call,' said the nurse. 'No one shall come down. Do what my lady wills, boy. She is in desperate need. Go in Asclepid.'

I entered a large room, rich with tapestries. It was furnished with a huge curtained bed, in the middle of which was a humped shaped which whimpered.

I paused. I had heard that sound before. Wounded men cry in that manner, knowing that they are dying. This was not an hysterical fit such as maidens have. I sat down next to her and found a hand. It was slim and brown and clung to my fingers.

'Tell me your sorrow, Lady,' I said.

She started at the unknown voice and the hand left clinging and slid up to my face, tugging at my hair, and tracing my cheek and jaw with a touch as light as cobwebs. I captured the hand again and urged, 'Sit up, Lady, and speak with me. I am Diomenes the Asclepid, God-Touched, a healer priest.'

She wriggled into a sitting position and exclaimed, 'You're a boy,' and I first caught sight of the most beautiful woman in the world.

They have sung of Elene that she was pale with blue eyes, but that is not true. She was dark, with eyes like trout pools and hair like chestnut and a mouth the colour of autumn berries or the red poppy flower. Her skin was olive with a dusting of hair like gold. She might have been a little taller than me, not goddess' stature as poets have sung. It was impossible to describe her; no one feature was special, but altogether she was astonishing, even divine. With her hair dishevelled and torn and her eyes red with tears she was still beautiful enough to take my breath.

'Oh, don't,' she wailed. 'Not you too!'

'Lady?'

'No one looks at me. They look at this,' she took a handful of the chestnut hair, 'or this' she dragged her hands down her perfect cheeks, 'or this,' she tore aside her tunic and revealed her body, lovely and symmetrical in every curve. 'Not me, not Elene!'

I began to see what she meant. I was flooded with pity for her. I caught both of her hands in mine and looked into her eyes.

'I can see you,' I said. 'Elene.'

'They stole me when I was twelve,' she wailed. 'Men with their filthy mouths, their dirty hands. Theseus threw me flat and raped me, his loins all dabbled with my blood. He laughed at my scream of pain; he grinned as if he had done something clever, as though he had stolen something. Then I was rescued and auctioned to Menelaus, another old man. I will never be alone and no man will ever love me and I will never be able to lie with the one want, never, never, never. I am cursed. I wish that I was dead. They guard me as though I was a treasure, only to use me themselves, to own me.'

'Lady, they can own your body, but they cannot own your mind,' I observed. She looked at me properly for the first time and took a breath, though tears flowed down her cheeks.

'That is true,' she said quietly. 'Diomenes God-Touched. When did you meet a god?'

'When I was six, in the temple.'

'I wish the god had never lain with my mother or that she had been barren,' she said. Her voice was clear and delicate in tone, like a moth's wing striking a thin glass vessel.

I said calmly, 'There are no gods but Death.'

'Mad, you're mad. How can there be no gods?'

'Death is a god. I have seen him. He kissed me, here on my forehead.' She traced the scar of Thanatos' lips under my hair. 'But he is the only god, Lady. I come from the Temple of Asclepius and I know.'

Elene stared at me, straight into my eyes. I gazed back. Her eyes were brown flecked with spots of gold, deep enough to drown in. 'And my mother?'

'Lay with someone, Lady, but it was a man she lay with.'

'And I?'

'You are beautiful beyond all reckoning and men desire to own you, as though beauty can be owned.'

'They will own me. They have possession of me. I cannot run away. If I did the next man who saw me would claim me. I will always be owned by someone.'

'They can own your body, Lady, but so can sickness, so can sleep, so can pregnancy. Your body is not important. Only you can know what you are thinking. Inside your head you are always alone. If you do not speak you cannot be condemned. We god-touched keep our own council, Lady.'

'I hate them,' she said, not passionately but coldly. 'Their greasy bodies and their dirty hands. I will never be theirs, never.'

'You need not be theirs,' I said. Thus I might have spoken to a bird in a cage, and it was false, all false, the counsel of a child or a slave, but I had to say something. I had to comfort her. If it had pleased her she might have spilled my blood to bathe in or stripped my skin for a garment. I loved her so much that I would have instantly died for her. Greatly daring, I leaned forward and just touched her lips with mine.

She took my hand and looked at it. It was clean with short nails. She laid it upon her breast. Instinctively, my fingers cupped the curve and pinched the nipple. Her eyes flicked over me, assessing something.

Elene knotted her hand in my hair and dragged my mouth down to hers. Her kiss tasted of salt, then of herself. She pulled my robe off and her hands found my phallus that rose to meet her. Then for the first time I lay down in a woman's arms, her body slick with sweat and tears still falling from her almond eyes, and I was inside her. I almost swooned with pleasure. She sucked at my mouth as though to extract my soul.

It was too sudden and sweet to last long. My seed sprang in her womb, but she would not let me go. She locked her flanks around me and held me fast, whispering, 'I will give myself away, Diomenes, once in my life, to one who wants me, one who has not bought me. One man shall say of Elene that she was kind, she was generous, she loved me. Do you love me?' she asked and I said, 'I love you,' into her throat, and kissed the breasts which pressed against me. Then we began to move again, dizzy with desire, the flowery musky scent rising from her body, until I cried aloud with a pleasure that was close to pain, and heard her stifle another such cry in my hair.

I knew I must not fall asleep and I rose from her arms with immeasurable reluctance. It occurred to me that I had done enough to be cut to pieces just by kissing her mouth. Menelaus would kill both of us if he saw us lying in each other's arms, my cheek against Elene's breast.

So I kissed her again and rose, sluiced my body down with boiled water and put back my healer's tunic, and covered the maiden with her robe. She was so still that I thought she might have fainted, but her heart beat under my hand which cupped her breast.

'Diomenes,' she murmured. 'Do you love me?'

'I love you,' I said gently, 'Elene of Sparta, wife of Menelaus.'

She sat up at that, a hand raised to slap. I sat still and she did not hit me. Nor did she cry again. Her face set and she took several deep breaths. No one ever said that Elene lacked courage. I went to the door and took in the wine, the poppy, and the broth.

'If you eat this, most lovely of all women, I will tell you a secret,' I said, and placed the bowl on her lap and the spoon in her hand. 'It is a secret which will relieve you of all the attentions of old men,' I added. She ate the soup, slowly at first and then quickly as her body told her that it was hungry. 'It is true that you may not bestow yourself as you wish, Lady, except this once and with someone whose life you now hold in your hands. But in this flask is syrup of the red poppy which brings sleep. When you run out, every healer in the country can make it. In this bottle is enough to send four strong men to sleep for the whole night. It is three days journey to Mycenae, Lady. The syrup cannot be detected in honeyed wine.'

She made a grab for the flask, but I swung it out of reach. I had something else to say.

'I will never forget you, Lady. You are the first woman to lie with me. I love you. But you must send him to sleep, Elene, not kill him; and you must eat and sleep and live or I cannot bear my life, Princess of Sparta. Your word, Lady.'

She was so beautiful that my eyes were greedy for her. Every curve, every bone, was perfect in its place. She was not like the maiden Galatea whom the sculptor made, because no stone could ever convey the smoothness of her skin, the delicate flush of rose upon her cheek, the scented hollow of her throat, the tracery of blue veins along the inside of her wrist.

She crossed both hands on her heart and said, 'I swear, Diomenes, Asclepid, I swear that I will not kill and I swear that I will live. Tell me you love me.'

'I love you,' I said, and she let me rise.

At the door, she caught me in a close embrace and kissed my mouth until I was nearly overcome, then she pushed me roughly away. I staggered as I left the room and the old woman laughed.

'Did she slap you? I heard no screams.'

'No, just pushed me. She has eaten the broth and I have left her some syrup.'

'What was her ailment?'

'Fatigue and fever,' I said at a venture.

I walked the cold corridor behind a house slave until I came to the room. Neither Arion nor my master was there, for which I was very thankful. I could hear shouts and breaking pots from the great hall and Arion's voice bawling a tavern song about a woman who could take nine lovers a night. I pulled off my robe and fell into the embrace of my cloak, exalted with the knowledge of the flesh and cold with knowing that I would never lie with Elene again.

◇◇◇

Apollo lounged against the balustrade of the Pool of Mortal Loves, a smug smile turning up the corners of his perfect mouth.

'By your own works are you vested, Aphrodite the Stranger,' his voice flowed like honey. 'I have given your darling, your most beautiful mortal Elene, to my Diomenes. He will never love another.'

Aphrodite bit her lip, drawing a strand of her golden hair over her marble-smooth shoulder.

'You have wrought well,' commented Zeus hungrily. 'Never have I seen such perfection in mortal form. She is as beautiful as a goddess—more beautiful than some,' he added under his breath. Hera shot him a ferocious look and he hurried on, 'Is the wager won, then? Your princess of Troy can never equal Elene. And the Sun God has caught his mortal very young—such things remain for the rest of a mortal life, which is not long. I think you've lost, Lady.'

Aphrodite clutched the golden apple to her rounded breast.

'Cassandra has yet to meet a lover. Men are fickle, Lord and Father. Women, you will find, are not. She must not fall in love—not yet. Not until she meets Diomenes.'

'She will fall in love,' said Apollo, his voice smooth as oil. 'And with no fickle mortal, Lady Aphrodite. Sicken her for human love as you will. Divine love does not fail. Your princess will love me—my maiden, my favoured one. And beside my love, the love of a god, no mortal can compare.'

'We shall see,' snorted the goddess of love.

Chapter Seven

Cassandra

We had always known about the future, Eleni and I.

When we were children it was small things—pictures. Sometimes flat and static like the frescoes, sometimes moving, as though we were watching through a window. One time we saw a strange grey animal twice the size of a horse, barrel bellied and comic, rolling into the water with a great splash, and it was not until I heard Aegyptus the sea captain describe a creature he called a 'river horse' that I knew that it was a living animal and not a dream. Occasionally we caught sight of people we knew; we once saw Myrine the Amazon with her sisters sitting around a fire in a wood and eating roasted venison, and told Nyssa before Myrine came back to Troy that she had a new deerhide jerkin embroidered with black and white things which turned out to be porcupine quills. We saw, and heard, Aegyptus suggesting to his crew in the strongest terms that if they did not get up off their overfed Trojan arses and wear ship they would never get home to the exceptionally unchaste wives who awaited them in several ports. Once we had a vision, brief but alarming, of Hector in bronze armour casting a spear which went through a warrior in strange garments and pinned him to the ground.

We went, every evening, to dine with our parents. Nyssa dressed us in clean garments and brushed our hair, over our serious objections. Often we were asked what we had seen and until we learned about tact we had often revealed things which the city would rather had stayed hidden. We had seen one of the ships dumping fish guts into the Scamander, for instance, an act forbidden by Priam. We had seen our brother Pariki slap a maiden who did not fancy him and had described in minute detail his assault on her and how she had broken a terra cotta pot over his head and sent him reeling into the street. We wondered while we were telling this why the whole palace was laughing. Mostly our glimpses into the future were minor and sometimes we had difficulty separating present from past. We had revealed with excitement that the fleet had found a whale stranded on the beach, which had happened before we were born. At another time, however, we had seen a herd of horses being brought in, among them a pure white mare, which, we said, would be the mother of chariot horses. This mare came in the next season and Hector claimed her. She foaled his two chariot horses, so closely matched that no one could tell them apart.

Occasionally, the dreadful dream would come back and we would wake, crying and appalled. Beast men in bronze sacked and destroyed, raped and murdered, and the steep streets of Ilium ran red. We saw the Scamander choked with floating bodies. This dream we told, but to Hector only. The palace was too full of people for us to reveal anything which might cause panic. Hector listened, grew grave, and made us promise not to tell anyone. We didn't. We preferred not to think about it.

We did not want to remember that, as far as we knew, we had never been wrong.

Every evening, one of the sons of Priam would call for us and we would walk decorously up to the palace and take our seats on benches near the royal thrones.

If it was Hector we could usually persuade him to carry us.

All the children born from the dedications to the Lord Dionysius were sons and daughters of Priam the King. Any maiden who bore her first child from her sacrifice to Gaia had to give it to the king. This discouraged anyone tempting the gods by arranging that a future husband would present himself in the Place of Maidens. The children were given to such as Nyssa to be raised and they had the same rank as Hector or Pariki. Children like Andromache who came to be married also lived in or by the means of the palace and held the honorary rank of children of Priam. My Lord King Priam had five children by my mother Hecube, the Queen, three by other wives and some fifty sons and thirty daughters who issued from the loins of the god.

'Twins,' said Priam consideringly. We looked up. He was terribly old, that Priamos who had been ransomed by a princess. His beard was white and hung down his chest and his hair was like snow. His eyes had been blue but now had faded. He put out his hand and we kissed it.

'You have the gift, God-Touched,' said our father the king. 'Pariki your brother is leaving Troy to go to Sparta. Do you see anything of his voyage?'

'We saw it before,' I said eagerly. 'A beautiful woman kissed him on the mouth.'

'A beautiful woman?' asked the queen. 'That is not unusual.' Pariki grinned and there was a general laugh.

'A goddess,' said Eleni.

The hall groaned. In some sense, we could hear what they were thinking. It was like Pariki, they thought, to go to Sparta and be kissed by a goddess while the rest of the sailors got dysentery drinking dockside wine. I looked at the queen, my mother. She wore a chiton of pale blue, the rarest and most difficult colour, and her wrists were knobbed with age and heavy with golden bracelets, her fingers weighed down with rings. She took my hand and said, 'You are still with the Maiden, Cassandra?' I nodded. 'And Tithone tells me that you will be a good healer. You have found your skill. There are strangers coming next week. Would you and Andromache like to leave the Maiden and join the Mother then?'

'My Lady, I…' I glanced desperately at Eleni. 'I do not wish to marry yet, not until I am a healer.'

'Do you wish to join the Temple of the Maiden?' she asked, meaning to ask if I was a lover of women. I did not know what to answer.

'Lady, I cannot decide.' I faltered, trying to hear what Eleni was saying to our father the king.

'Then I will decide. In eight days, Cassandra, daughter of Priam, you will sit in the Place of the Maidens. Then you will live here in the palace. Your twin will live here too,' she added, noticing the desperate clutch of Eleni's fingers on mine, behind our backs.

The king said some something to Eleni and then we were allowed to go. We walked slowly back to our bench, then crept away under Pariki's knowing smile. I did not need a gift for prophecy to tell us that it was Pariki who had told our parents of our forbidden closeness.

That night we kissed and kissed and made love within our laws and fell asleep only when the sun glared over the walls.

But it felt different. Since the goddess had come in Andromache's shape, Eleni's love was not inclined to me, not the love of his body I had possessed before, though I could still please him.

In the next eight days we clung close yet were not close. We ate little and slept less. Nyssa scolded Eleni and made him chicken broth and told him that the love of women was different from that of a sister. Tithone dosed me with poppy and mistletoe and explained that the love of a man was different from the love of a brother. I did not listen. I would go to the Mother and Eleni would lie down with a masked priestess in the temple of Dionysius the Father, and things would never, never be safe again.

Perhaps it was worse for Eleni. I had no lover now except the god, whereas Andromache existed and loved Hector and could never be his.

I was lying in bed with Eleni's head on my shoulder and we were watching the sun come up on the sacrifice day. We had run out of tears.

'I see a vision,' I said suddenly. 'Eleni, I smell burning, and I see a warrior in gold armour—who would make armour out of gold?—lying dead, his enemy laughing and you taking... can you see?'

'Yes,' he said eagerly, 'I'm taking a woman dressed in a saffron chiton by the hand. Turn around, I can't see your face...turn around, maiden...'

I had already recognised her. Andromache, grown up, tall, smiling. I could not imagine how this could happen. Eleni still could not see her face.

'Turn, maiden, fair woman,' he whispered, then clenched his fist. 'Oh, no, has it gone for you too, twin?' I nodded. 'Did you see her face?' I shook my head. I knew who it was by her shape and her colouring, I did not need to see her face. But I did not tell Eleni.

Nyssa had plaited horsehair bands for us both. She dressed us and brushed our hair and we did not exclaim because then she would cry and so would we. We walked to the Place of Maidens, I kissed Nyssa and she hugged me. Then I laid one hand on my brother's face, cupping his cheek in my hand. He did the same for me; it had always been our greeting as children. We did not kiss.

Our minds had always been one until the gods intervened between us. For a moment, we regained our oneness. I knew Eleni, and he knew me, far closer than any coupling. He was inside me. I was inside him. No lover would ever be as close to me as my twin. Nothing was lost. Just everything.

Our hands dropped simultaneously. I walked into the garden which is called the Place of Maidens, and Eleni and Nyssa climbed further up the street to the Temple of Dionysius. I could hear Nyssa crying as she went, but my eyes were dry.

The garden was bright with flowers and the coloured tunics of the maidens and surrounded with scented hollows under the bay trees. I sat down with my hands in my lap, noticing that Nyssa had dressed me in a pure white chiton. Several voices greeted me but I said nothing. I felt achingly empty. I hoped the stranger would come soon and not hurt me too badly. But it scarcely mattered if he did. I was halved like a fruit. Part of me had been cut away.

Perhaps an hour later a golden coin dropped into my lap and a deep voice said, 'In the name of Gaia.' Obediently I rose and the stranger took my hand.

He was tall and dark. The mask covered his face. His black hair flowed across broad bare shoulders. I noticed that one lock had been carefully braided and a blue bead bobbed at the end. He was no Achaean; maybe an Egyptian. I did not know if I should speak to him but I tried a greeting in that language. He shook his head. As we crossed the Place of Maidens I tried three other phrases, but at each one the blue bead danced. Perhaps he was mute. The god had found me a stranger who would take the curse of the Maiden without a word between us.

We came to the dark hollow and I lay down, as I had been taught. He knelt and took off my chiton. I closed my eyes. Involuntarily, my body stiffened. I was afraid.

Hands caressed me, stroking along and down. He smelt of olive oil and a spicy aroma which I had never smelt before. The hands slid between my thighs as Eleni's had often done and I felt some response. I sighed and so did the stranger.

I could hear rustling in the other hollows, then a short, cut-off scream of pain. I grew frightened again and the hands soothed me. With my eyes shut tight, I reached for the stranger's body and drew him close, caressing him as I had caressed my brother, almost managing to think that it was Eleni, though the stranger's chest was deep and the shoulders massive and the hair on his body was as coarse as wire. I found the phallus and shrank again. Impossible. I would be torn to pieces by this stranger and even Tithone would never heal me.

Again, the hands, and a gentle murmur from the mouth behind the mask. The clever fingers probed and explored and my excitement grew more intense. Tremors began to run along my body.

The stranger judged that the sacrifice was ready. One strong hand was laid over my mouth—this was prescribed for the avatars of Dionysius, so that the other maidens would not be terrified—and something butted the hollow which I had denied my brother. I braced my shoulders against the ground and it struck again, sending strange reverberations through my body. The hands caressed me briefly, calloused hand. I released the breath I was holding and then my scream was smothered.

Something was inside me, very strong, a live thing, a body joined to mine. The torn veil stung and bled. But the stranger was inside me and holding me tightly and my arms went around his neck and my legs around his waist. It hurt. The veil had ripped. The stranger seemed possessed. He thrust like a mating beast, his hip bones thudding into my thighs. I was afraid and in pain. I called for Eleni. For a despairing moment I was utterly lost. Then I found him.

In a strange double vision, Eleni and I lay inside a masked woman who held us close; at the same time as he reached his ritual climax, I felt our body glow and burn and the stranger's seed fountained inside us.

So I had not lost Eleni. When I opened my eyes, I was surprised to see the stranger lying on my breast instead of the masked woman.

The stranger got up. I found my chiton and pulled it on. My thighs were dripping with blood which made a huge patch on the white cloth. He helped me to my feet and led me into the sunlight. At the door of the temple a priest took the horsehair band and crowned me with flowers. I knelt down before the statue of the Mother and said the ritual prayers. I cut a lock of my hair and laid it before the image, sore and a little shocked. I had not realised how strong men were. The stranger with the blue bead went into the temple to be purified.

Andromache was waiting for me as I limped out of the temple into the street. She was pale and there was more blood on her tunic than mine.

'Can you walk?' she asked. I nodded.

'Yes, but I'm not going to. Nyssa is coming for me,' I said. 'She is coming now.' I could feel her loving, fussy presence coming closer. 'They are bringing a litter; sit down with me, Andromache.'

'So it isn't true,' she said, looking at my tunic patched with blood. 'You didn't lie with your brother.'

'Did you think I had?' I felt too tired and bruised to take offense. Andromache had always said exactly what she thought and no one had been able to persuade her that this was not necessarily a good idea.

'It was talked about,' she said.

'Who lay with you?' I asked. 'Did it hurt?'

'A huge man in a tunic. I think he was a noble—he was wearing a lot of gold bracelets. Yes. It hurt. I hate him. He hurt me. I'm still bleeding. I would never have done this if…if…'

'You had known what it was like?'

Her lips tightened and she lifted her chin. 'Yes.'

'Well, then. It is a sacrifice well-made, but I think we had better call Tithone.' I had forgotten my own wound, which had already stopped bleeding. I was no more bruised than I had been wrestling with Eleni. Healing has always been able to make me forget my own hurt. It is a great blessing.

Nyssa came and had us carried to her house, where Tithone was waiting. She washed our lacerations, told us that she had seen worse and anointed us with cooling lotion. I noted the amount of wound herb and comfrey she was slathering onto Andromache. She did not stop bleeding until Tithone applied a styptic made of pounded tree bark.

Hector came to the door while Tithone was busy in the inner room. He embraced me gently, as though I might break and asked, 'Is she…'

'She's all right,' I said. 'Really.'

'And you, Lady?' he gave me the honorific for a grown woman and I was immediately flattered.

'I'm almost recovered.'

Hector's glance strayed to my white tunic. He noticed the bloodstain and sighed with what sounded like relief.

'I've spoken to the Lord King,' he said. 'I told him that Pariki lied when he said you and your twin were lovers and it seems that I told the truth. Pariki has gone to Sparta. Priam says that you may stay together until tomorrow. That is the best I can do for you, Cassandra.'

I did not run into his arms as I once would have done, but I was very grateful. Tithone came out of the inner room and said briskly. 'Andromache is coming home with me and since you are here, you can carry her, warrior.'

'Carry her? How is she? Poor little maiden...'

'Just a flesh wound,' grinned Tithone. 'Maiden no more. This sacrifice was in your honour, Prince. Go in. Pick her up. Gently. And come along. Cassandra, I am very proud of you,' she added, as she preceded my brother Hector out of the door and into the street. He followed, carrying Andromache as though she weighed no more than a feather. She laid her head on his shoulder and closed her eyes. I have never seen a face so expressive of trust and love.

Eleni and I put ourselves to bed early. We had a lot to talk about.

'I felt you,' he said excitedly. 'It hurt, he was hurting you, but it was part of my pleasure, you felt me, didn't you?'

'Yes. I was in pain and he was frightening me. He was so rough and urgent, look, I'm bruised.'

Eleni inspected my bruises, kissed them, and very gently slid his fingers inside, careful of the raw edge of the wound. He lay down with his face on my belly. I could smell the sweet scent of his hair as I stroked his head.

'What about you, Eleni?'

'There was a woman in a mask, she smelt stale, old, but she stroked me and then she knelt over me...like...like the goddess did. I was trying to find the goddess when I found you, twin. I felt your hurt.' He stroked the outraged flesh again. 'I felt something break and bleed and I screamed, as though he was inside me, yet I was inside her. Did I comfort you, twin?'

'Yes,' I said, 'Eleni, my golden one. I wasn't alone.'

He thought about this, covering my bruises with his warm hands.

'I will always be there when you lie down with a man,' he said quietly. 'Though I may never lie with you again.'

'And I will always be there when you lie with a woman,' I agreed, 'though I may never lie with you again.'

'Until we die we will never be alone,' he intoned our ritual, and I completed it, drawing him up to lie beside me, our heads on the same pillow for the last time.

'And only death will sever us.'

Chapter Eight

Diomenes

I woke. Someone was kissing me. A beard scratched my chin. I returned the kiss in confusion and opened my eyes.

Arion the singer hauled me to my feet and laughed at my expression.

'Come along, God-Touched,' he whispered. 'Early morning's best for travellers, especially if there is an army approaching. Should the apprentice sleep while the master wakes?'

My Master Glaucus was not only awake but dressed and ready to go. I pulled on my cloak, bundled my healer's tunic into my belongings, and washed my face. Arion gave me a cup of red wine and a piece of bread and bade me hurry and be silent.

Glaucus was listening at the open doorway. Cool light was leaking in through the bowslits and under the keystones. We took up our baggage and carried it carefully through the corridor and down the stairs. Dikaos was standing at the gate, under the gods who ruled Tiryns.

'Fare well, little Asclepid,' he said gravely. 'Good fortune on the road and come safe to your destination.' This was the formal dismissal of a king to a subject and it was perfectly proper, but there was an extra stiffness in the spare man, as though he was reluctantly acknowledging that I had done an immoral but terribly useful task for him. Still dazed with sleep, I answered as custom required and they let the three of us out of Tiryns and into the grey light of dawn.

My master looked unwell, but Arion was bursting with rude health. Something was amusing him immensely. His beard was waggling as he formed words under his breath. He did not speak, however, until we had climbed up onto the ridge and descended into the valley to the north, which would take us by goat track to Mycenae. The litter carrying Elene and her maidens, with its escort of soldiers, and the Atreidae would have to take the road. Three days to Mycenae before I could see her once more. I did not expect to lie with her ever again. I just wanted to see her, from a distance, a slave not worthy to touch her hand.

I lost myself in dreams of Elene.

Then I was nudged hard and nearly fell off Pyla. Arion declared in his robust voice, 'I have a boast, Asclepid. I have kissed the lips of one who kissed the lips of the most beautiful woman in the world.'

I gaped in astonishment. I came back to the present. We were in a dark valley full of stones the size of chariots, barren and cold, cut off from the sunlight. I was suddenly afraid. What would they do to me, my master and this singer? I had broken the first vow of the Asclepidae, never to enter the house of a woman-patient and lie with her. My master must be angry; he had cared for me and loved me and I had betrayed him. And this singer, this strong-voiced man with no fear of rank; would he not trumpet Elene's and my sweet and sacred love as a shame and a raucous tavern song over the length of the land of the Argives?

I put both hands over my face and wanted to die.

'So it is true,' said my master thoughtfully. 'Arion, I apologise for calling you an obscene-minded wretch whose music was all below his girdle.'

'I forgive you. Boy, is it true?'

I nodded, wordless. I heard Arion draw in a deep breath.

'When we reach the top of the hill and can be overheard only by gods,' he said, 'you must tell us all about it, little Asclepid. We might have to run if this is known. We will have all the world trying to tear us apart from sheer envy. I might tear you apart myself. We will have to run fast.'

'Very fast,' agreed my master. 'You always said that Libya was interesting, Arion.'

'Not Libya. Not far enough. Africa. Or the Hittite kingdoms. They say that they use a different form of music altogether. I may become anxious to study it.'

I set Pyla at the hill at a gallop, anxious to confess everything. At the top, I turned her and Arion scanned the horizon carefully. It was going to be a beautiful day to die. The sun was warm and the sky was a blue cap over the hills. Nothing was moving anywhere, not even birds.

'All right, Chryse, my son,' my master was not angry but there was a double line of pain between his browns. 'Tell us all.'

I stumbled through a detailed account of everything that had happened, from the questioning of the two servants through Elene's death-anticipating despair, to the transcendent moment when she pulled my mouth down to hers. I described her body, the feel of her skin, the scent of her hair. Arion's eyes glowed like coals. I told them about the woman who had kept the door and how Elene had dismissed me with a kiss and a shove, and how I loved her more than I could say.

'And I regret nothing, Master,' I said defiantly. 'Nothing. I could not have done otherwise if I was to die now for it. Kill me and I will still love Elene until a draught of the Styx takes my memory and I wander in wealthy Pluton's realm as a voiceless shade. I will yearn for her all my life.'

'The woman who kept the door—she was Elene's nurse?' asked my master. 'Arion, your songs will live forever and you are a great and glorious bard.'

'What? I mean, I thank you, brother, for your esteemed opinions, but...'

'The tavern songs you pollute noble halls with, they all talk about the nurse as the accomplice of the lover. One who keeps the mistress' secrets closer than her own.'

'Certainly,' agreed the bard. 'Does anyone else know?'

'The Lady Elene,' I said solemnly. 'And I think Dikaos suspected something.'

'Yes, that was a rather stilted farewell,' Arion was tugging his beard. 'But he will say nothing. He is appointed by the Atreidae, their adherent, and this would make them a laughing stock in every tavern in the Peloponnese. The brothers Agamemnon Lord of Men and Menelaus Prince of Sparta and both those brutes smother one girl with guards only to have her fall into the arms of a healer of Asclepius who is not yet a man? I could make a very funny song about it.'

'But you won't,' said Master Glaucus. Arion guffawed.

'No, I won't. I want to make many more songs and for that I need my full complement of arms and legs, my guts in my belly rather than spilled on the mountain side, my tongue residing in my mouth, and my head firmly on my shoulders.'

'Master,' I laid my hand on his sleeve, 'have I done a great wrong? I have broken my vows.'

'Wrong, Chryse? No. Fate, perhaps, brought us here into the lady's influence. You told us what she said. Women are unreasoning creatures, she would not have cared about the danger.'

I did not think that my Lady Elene was irrational. She had fought against her caged despair and accepted my solution with speed and intelligence. Everything she had said had been logical and true. There was only truth and love between the most beautiful woman in the world and Diomenes the healer. However, I did not argue with my master. It was still in the hands of fate to whether we would all die.

Then we had an omen.

Out of nowhere came two doves, the favourites of Aphrodite goddess of love. They were silver in the sunlight. No other birds were in the sky. They circled us three times, then came down to rest on my outstretched hands.

Holding my breath, I brought my hands together and they touched beaks and cooed.

Then, while we stared, they took flight together and in a moment they were gone. I could still feel the grip of their delicate claws on my fingers. One silvery grey feather caught and lodged in my hair.

'We are answered,' said Arion quietly. We mounted our horses and rode on for Mycenae.

◇◇◇

We camped that night in the mountains. The nearest village was Irion, where I had been born. My master sent me there to buy food and to speak to my father.

I found him in the tavern, drinking red wine and laughing. He had grown old. I had thought of him as tall and strong. Now I was almost his height and his hair was grey. He was stooped with hard labour, his hands gnarled like olive roots. He did not know me.

I came to his side and said, 'Father,' but he stared and did not speak. Then he brushed aside my hair and found the scar on my forehead. He gathered me into his arms and shouted, 'Chryse! How is it with you? Are you alone?'

'I am travelling with my master, but he is in the mountains talking to the god, father. He sent you this.' It was a gold piece. My father took it and declared to the tavern, 'Here is my son who is a healer priest.' The tavern grinned at me and I sat down. 'I cannot stay, father. Is all well with you?'

'Well? Very well. The Corinthian woman my wife has given me four sons and two daughters, and they are healthy and beautiful. I bless the day you met with Death, Chryse.' A small boy came to my father's knee and whined to be picked up. My father hoisted him and said, 'Here is your brother, Chryse. Give him a healer's blessing.'

I felt utterly alien and alone. Once all I had to look forward to was a life spent with the goats, my only dissipation the occasional bowl of wine at a festival, my only pride my strong sons and perhaps some skill. They might say of me, I had thought while I watched the clouds, that Diomenes was good with the animals or skilled at the harvest. Now I was a priest who had lain with Elene, princess of Sparta, and knew the mysteries of life and death.

I would have given anything, just at that moment, to be Diomenes the goatherd again.

However, I laid my hand on the child's head and blessed him. Then I collected bread and some roasted meat, a large cloth of cheese and, thinking of Arion, three flasks of the best red wine. They would not let me pay.

As I left, I heard the talk break out again. I suppose it was something that I conferred honour on my father by existing.

I walked to Pyla and rode slowly away from my village. No. I rode slowly away from Irion, a village like any other for a wandering healer whose home is in a god who does not exist.

The camp looked cosy in the firelight and I could hear Arion singing, not in his loud carry-to-the-end-of-the-hall-and-into-the-kitchen-to-amuse-the-slaves voice, but softly and to himself. He was singing,

> *Elene of Sparta was fair as the morning,*
> *Bright as the goddess of dawn.*

He saw me coming and added,

> *Dangerous as an army with well-sharpened spears,*
> *Against whom no breastplate of bronze would repel*
> *The arrow that pierces the armoured heart.*

I put down the food, broke the seal on the first wine flask, and put it into his hand without speaking.

I could not bear to say anything of my father and of Irion. The bard swilled a mouthful and sang,

> *It would be sweet to come home,*
> *Sweet to return to the hearth and the home,*
> *But time and distance change the seeker*
> *And changes the thing sought.*
> *The river crossed on another day*
> *Is always another river.*

'Why do they call you Dolphin-Rider, Arion?' I asked, desperately seeking something which would take my mind off Elene and my lost home.

'Ah, well. I was ravelling, gathering songs, singing in great halls, a famed singer,' he began with a grin of teeth through the black beard.

Master Glaucus cut a piece of meat, salted it, and said dryly, 'Famed singer because you sing so much of your own fame.'

'Of course,' responded Arion. 'If I didn't nobody might—not a risk any bard can afford to take. I had taken passage with a crew of what turned out to be Ionian pirates. They offered me a choice—jump or be pushed. I thought that it would be better to jump so I told them that I would sing a last song and then leap into the sea. It was all the fault of the Taureans, who gave me so much gold that I could not hide it all on my body and those thieving Ionians had discovered it. So, they were all delighted to hear a song from the most famed singer in Achaea. I put on my singing robes, climbed up on the poop and sang my last song—oh, it would have broken your heart to hear me!—and then I leapt.

'It was cold water and disagreeably deep and I cannot swim, especially not with my robes and all that gold I had bound round my waist. I surfaced and lay as still as I could and then something butted me, hard, and pushed me forward. Then it swam around and did it again and I thought that a monster was about to make a meal of me. Finally the creature lost patience with my slowness and dragged me over its back—here are the marks of its teeth still on my arm.' He stripped back his sleeve and I saw a row of pinpoint dots, white against the brown skin. 'It was a dolphin, creature of Dionysius, which carried me all the way to Tarentum and then shoved me ashore, breaking a couple of ribs with its nose. I crawled up the beach and into the Temple of Dionysius where the priests dried me out and cared for me. I gave them all my gold to make an image of the dolphin.

'Then I travelled to the court, to wait for those pirates to appear. The king asked them for an account of my death and they made rather a good story of the terrible storm which had swept me overboard minus, of course, my golden baggage. The sight of their faces when I walked from behind the throne in my salt-stained singing robes was wonderful.'

'What happened to them?' I asked.

'I expect they were executed,' said Arion carelessly. 'That king was touchy on the subject, having been a pirate himself. Come now, let a bard eat and tell me of Elene of Sparta and how she felt, lying under you in the tapestried bed of the lord of Tiryns.' He grinned at me, wine running down to join the crumbs in his beard.

It was too much for the end of a long day. I walked away from the fire and climbed a tree. I think I chewed bark long after they were asleep, thinking of the beautiful and despairing Elene, of how much I loved her, and how these gross men would never understand the delicacy and purity of what happened between the princess of Sparta and me. Finally I fell asleep myself and dreamed mercifully of nothing at all.

I do not know what my master said to Arion Dolphin-Rider, but we accomplished the rest of the journey without mention of Elene.

We came to Midea of the mountain about the last watch of the day. I could hear wailing and lamenting, the voices of men reproaching the gods for stealing one of their brothers.

We came gently up the last slope. A huge man was wiping tears from his grimy face with a dirty hand. He must have been bigger than Agamemnon, Lord of Men, and Agamemnon was the biggest man I had ever seen before.

'Healer!' he said and grabbed my master by the sleeve. 'In there!'

Glaucus did not dismount but rode Banthos through the partially finished gate and into what would become the acropolis of Midea. The air was full of wailing and stone dust.

The crowd stood around a massive shape which groaned. Glaucus rode the horse into the mob and Arion and I leapt down, shouting, 'Make way for the healer! Glaucus, Master of

Epidavros, comes! Make way!' We managed to clear the people away so that my master could see his patient.

He was big enough to be the brother of the man at the gate. 'Cyclopes,' whispered Arion. 'I've never seen them before. Look at the size of him! No wonder they build wide doorways.'

The Cyclope was clutching at his chest and Glaucus took hold of his hands in both of his and commanded, 'Chryse, get me water, bandages, and make some more poppy syrup. Arion, find the lord of this place and announce our coming, stable the horses, and find us some food. Now, friend,' he said, using his healer's voice, in which infinite trust could be reposed, 'I am going to pull your hands apart and you are going to take a deep breath and help me.'

I did as he ordered. A slave girl brought water in a big cauldron and I set it over a smelter's fire to boil. Nothing but boiled water must touch a wound. Then I melted the remains of the poppy carefully in a small pot, adding honey and hot water to make syrup. The patient stared for a long moment into Glaucus' eyes, then allowed the healer to drag the protecting arms back.

He had a sucking wound in his chest.

This means death, because the membrane which holds the lungs in place has been pierced and the vital essence is not being delivered to the heart. Glaucus clapped the palm of his hand over the wound and called to me, 'Bring a pad of clean linen, Chryse, dipped in honey.'

I brought it and my master laid it over the wound. The dreadful sucking noise ceased, sealed by the honey. This would not save the Cyclope's life. We bandaged his chest and fed him poppy syrup, which went down, so that at least his stomach had not been too damaged.

We allowed his fellows to carry him with great care to sit against the most complete wall. They rigged a shelter over him and two of these monsters came to sit beside him and hold his hand. It was very touching. They were so huge and so gentle. From what they said, it appeared that a load-bearing beam had broken, and the shattered end had gone into their comrade's chest. Poor giant.

Arion had located the kitchen, the stables, and lastly the lord of Midea. He was a small and fussy man, an ally of Argos and Mycenae. I never heard his name.

He came busting into the yard where the Cyclope lay dying and demanded, 'Why aren't you working?'

The first giant rose slowly to his feet and gripped the shoulder of the lord of Midea. It and the man came up into the air until they were a good yard above the ground. No word was said. Then the giant put the lord down again and resumed his place at his brother's side.

'Come, my Lord of Midea, we must leave them to their mourning,' said Arion. 'And we have been long on the road and need washing water and food.'

'Yes, yes, of course,' said Midea's lord, recalled to his sacred duties as host. 'Slaves, attend on the gentlemen at once. We are not really prepared for visitors,' he apologised, leading Arion and me out of the yard towards a small house. 'Once the walls are finished, we shall have a proper ceremony, and then Agamemnon King of Men and his brother Menelaus will decide who is to be lord—although I expect that I shall be. They gave me the task of building. Heavy responsibility.' He opened a door. 'This will shelter you tonight, sirs. Are you the bard Arion Dolphin-Rider? Could you sing for us, do you think?'

'Not while that poor giant lies dying,' said Arion. 'Have you no respect?' The small man looked shocked. 'It is not as though they are people,' he said stiffly. 'They are giants.'

'Yes, they are giants and no, Master, I beg to be excused. All this dust has ruined my voice.' The lord of Midea left in a huff and Arion chuckled softly, then spat. 'It is a great pity, Chryse,' he said off-handedly, 'that most of the world is ruled by idiots.'

I took second watch by the giant. The honey plaster had sealed the wound, but clearly he was bleeding inside. There was nothing to be done but sit down and watch him die. But as my master says, 'If there is nothing else to be done then we must do that.'

His brother sat at my other side. I changed the cloths which steamed off the body in the height of his fever and gave him sips of boiled water which had Heracles' wound herb steeped in it.

Finally, he opened his eyes. They were black, like an animal's eyes, but there was an animate spark behind them. He lifted one hand with a huge effort and stroked my hair. *'Kala'* (pretty), he said. His hand was as heavy as a sack of wool. He fumbled with something which hung at his neck until his brother removed it and gave it to me. It was a broken coin; I could not see what decorated it, but it looked very old. I tied the thong around my throat. The giant smiled at me, a childish smile from his huge, ugly face. 'Pretty,' he said again and died.

The hand slid down onto my shoulder and I had to use all my strength to place it reverently on his chest.

His brother gave a great howl of misery which summoned all the others. Their footsteps thudded on the earth like hammers. I crouched and dodged as they locked arms and began to dance around the corpse, chanting unknown blessings in an incomprehensible tongue.

I slid away before I could be trampled and came into the small room where Arion sat up, listening. I saw his eyes gleam in the dark.

'Is the giant dead?' he asked.

'He is dead. The others are dancing.'

'I left you some food, Chryse,' said my master. 'Wash carefully; you have come from the great mystery which is death.'

'Not for you, perhaps. Wash anyway. How did he die?'

'Peacefully, Master.' I found that the lord of Midea had provided roast meat, wheat bread, and grapes. 'He gave me this,' I remembered the coin and detached it. Arion held it close to the lamp.

'Hmm. Very old, Asclepid, and probably valuable. Wear it. You have the blessing of the Cyclopes and that does not come easily.'

'It was my master who cared for him.' I held out the coin. 'He should have it.'

'No, Chryse, it is yours,' said my master. 'I feel that you may have more need of it than me. Yes,' he mused as he tied it around my neck again, 'far more need of it than me.'

'Hush,' hissed Arion, 'I want to hear what they are singing!'

◇◇◇

We came into Mycenae at sunset. They call it 'Mycenae of the Golden Walls,' and at that hour the whole circuit is golden. It occupies the top of a hill—not a cliff like Tiryns, but a good-sized mount. The city encircles the acropolis and the walls are huge stones such as the Cyclopes were using for building at Midea.

'Where is the way in?' I asked. It looked impregnable, monstrous, a fortress of gods. The walls were three times my height.

'Through the lion gate,' said Arion calmly. 'Up, horse.'

There were guards either side of the gate and people anxiously lining the walls. When we came up the grey road to the gates we could see a bristle of spears and hear swords drawn with a rustle; the first time I had heard that unsettling noise.

'Arion Dolphin-Rider, the Master of Epidavros and Chryse God-Touched, his apprentice,' roared the bard. 'Let us in!'

The gates were dragged back and a very nervous guard in an elaborate helmet bade us enter and be quick. He shoved the gate back and three others barred it with what looked like a whole tree.

'Have you seen anyone else on the road?' demanded a dapper person in a spotless chiton. He had red hair and was somewhat bow legged. A man who did a lot of riding, obviously. His sharp eyes were of a peculiar reddish-brown and he had the most beautiful hands, long and fine, though calloused with some hard work.

'Not a soul but we came through the mountains, from Tiryns,' said Arion. 'There we saw the fair Elene of whom great songs will be sung when I have time to write them. Why?'

'The suitors,' said the dapper person. 'Apparently there is an army of them. Do you know when my Lord Agamemnon was to set out?'

'Two days ago in the morning,' said Arion. 'He should be with you tomorrow, if all goes well. Now, what sort of welcome shall we have at Mycenae, eh?'

'A good and warm one, for we've kings and princes from all over the land of the Argives and no one to amuse them. They can't hunt because none of them dares to leave in case he is out manoeuvred by another and they are tired of gaming. Amuse them and Agamemnon will load you with gold. Already there have been…incidents.'

'Amused they shall be,' said Arion, 'for as long as your wine holds out.'

'There is enough wine here to drown in, Arion, famed singer of the Achaeans. And there is work for the healers too. We are honoured by your presence,' he added, leading the way to a large room with a brazier. He clapped hands and slaves appeared, carrying water, a basket of bread, a cloth of cheese, and many bunches of red grapes.

'We feast—yet again—at second night watch,' he said. 'If you will bring your lyre, Master Arion, you may avert a war and you will do me a great favour.'

Arion did something I have never seen him do before. He bowed.

'Who was that?' I asked, after the elegant man had gone.

'They call him *Kokkinos*, the redhead,' said Arion. 'He is also known as Odysseus of the nimble wits, King of Ithaca.'

Chapter Nine

Cassandra

I did not miss Eleni as much as I had expected to—I missed him more.

We left Nyssa in floods of tears, all of us, and moved all our belongings up to the palace. Eleni and I parted at the gate. He went to the lodgings of the Youths, I went to the Maidens. We were desolate but resigned. I felt that my life had been cut off. So did Eleni.

The part of the palace given to the daughters of the Lord Priam and the Lady Hecube was spacious, cool, and beautifully decorated. The traditional skill of Troy, brought with us from the Island, was frescoes, and in the chambers of the daughters the masons had really enjoyed themselves.

It was a colonnaded hall, with sleeping chambers opening off it at three levels. Each room was small and whitewashed, decorated with a different motif. The room into which my sister Polyxena led me was painted with seaweed and shells and an octopus issued, all legs and arms, from a crevice in the floor. Ink-black and sea-blue, it was beautiful. The room smelt of the sea and a cool, sweet fragrance. I put down my bundle of gowns on the sleeping mat and decided that at least I had a pleasant place to be miserable in.

Polyxena was ten, an intense dark child who had not yet reached womanhood. She looked at me in a way which suggested that she could see down to my bones and asked, 'Is your brother happy?'

I sought and found Eleni. His mood had lightened as mine had.

'Not happy, but not too unhappy,' I said. 'Like me.'

'And are you always alike?'

'Yes. Have you a god, Polyxena? You see very well.'

'No god,' she said. 'None. Except that I belong to them, as we all do.'

'Of course,' I agreed politely. Nevertheless she made me uneasy. There was a black shadow behind my little sister Polyxena. She seemed to be perfectly aware of it and had obviously gotten used to it. But she was an uncomfortable companion for me and I was glad when three other sisters came in and diluted her effect. They seemed unaware of Polyxena's darkness.

'Cassandra,' said Andromache, limping in to embrace me. 'Good. You've got the octopus room. You can see the sea from your window.'

'Andromache, what have you done to yourself now?' I exclaimed crossly. 'Has Myrine seen that? What scraped you? A spear?'

'A stone. They are practising stone throwing. That idiot Siri missed the target and got me. It's all right. It hardly even grazed me.'

'Let me look,' I urged and she pushed me away, then sat down and allowed me to examine a blackening stone bruise which had broken the skin.

'What do you mean, it doesn't hurt? I've got some stonecrop and comfrey ointment. Just keep still.'

'Cassandra,' said Andromache impatiently. 'There is a contest and games tomorrow, in honour of Apollo Sun God. I am going to compete. If Myrine saw the bruise she might disqualify me. If you make too much fuss, Perseis will find out and stop me from going to the field.'

'I understand,' I modified my tone. 'Just try to stay off it today and I'll bind it again for you tomorrow. What are you competing in?'

'Spear and bow,' said Andromache between her teeth. 'And I might even win.'

'So you might.' I completed the bandage. 'There.'

My sister scrambled to her feet and dropped her unusually long gown over the bandage just in time as Perseis came in.

Perseis was my lord father's cousin, a plump woman with a lot of brown hair which flowed all around her and resisted bindings, so fine that it crept out between the pins. She had patient blue eyes and a much-tried smile. She was responsible for the behaviour and continued health of all of the Maidens. This was a truly magnificent challenge and she met it with kindness and strength, only occasionally being enraged to the point of telling us that one way of ensuring our good behaviour was to dedicate us all to a suitable beast god of the Achaeans and sacrifice us in a bevy, thus securing herself some peace and quiet and a safe journey across the Argive Styx. It had been suggested to her that killing off all the daughters of Priam might attract the attentions of the Erinyes, the Achaean revengers, daughters of Chaos, but she replied that compared to the multifold irritations of caring for thirty-eight chattering girls, she would take the snake-haired ones any time. There were, she reminded us, only three of them, Tisiphone, Maegara, and Alecto.

This happened very rarely. Mostly, Perseis was sweet.

She smiled at me and embraced me, my face against her petal-soft cheek. She smelt of baking bread and incense oil.

'Cassandra, let us have a walk around the palace so that you know where everything is. Daughters, we will be nice to Cassandra for a moon. She has left her twin and lately gone to the Mother and she will be strange in such a large place with so many people. Also, she is a prophet of the Lord Sun God. I'm depending on you to make sure that she is listened to if the Lord Apollo has anything to say. She will go to Tithone the healer every day.' Gesturing to the other young women, she added, 'Cassandra, you know Andromache, who fights men. This is your sister Polyxena, your sister Eirene, Peace—never was a maid worse named, your sister Cycne, she is from an island called Ithaca and is teaching us Achaean. There, that will do for the moment. Oh, and here is Oenone.'

I had heard of Oenone, daughter, they said, of the River Scamander. Her mother was a water nymph and her father a priest. She was my brother Pariki's wife. She was water coloured too, poor girl, pale and pearly with blue eyes and ash-brown hair like seaweed, and very pregnant. I took the limp hand and she smiled at me sadly. It was clearly unhealthy for a woman to be married to my brother Pariki.

I went with Perseis to view my new home. The floor was of tesserae, blue and unfigured, which was something of a relief because everything else was decorated with dancing maidens or lolloping dolphins. The main fresco was of a ship which had attempted to kidnap the Lord Dionysius. He had been patient with the sailors, but when they threatened to kill him, suddenly the mast had burst into vine and grape and the ship had been overwhelmed. The god had ridden away on a dolphin, one of his own creatures.

As I looked at the mural, the face of the Lord Dionysius turned to me. His eyes glowed hot, his mouth opened and he sang a small stave—only five notes. My knees went weak. The music was not sweet, but wild and breathy like shepherd's pipes. Then the painted face turned back into profile and he was gone.

'Yes, he is a powerful god,' agreed Perseis, not at all disconcerted. 'Now. Here is the water closet and here is the bath.'

There were more dolphins over the tiled pool in which green water lapped, scented like the sea.

'We bathe in the afternoon, during the hottest part of the day. The chitons are collected to be washed and are returned the next day, depending on the weather. You are learning to be a healer, but there are many crafts otherwise for you to try. Cycne, for instance, is making pots, and some of the others are spinners and weavers. Try everything, Cassandra. It is never good for a woman to lack skills, however beautiful she is. We are not Argives, to value a woman only for her appearance and her fertility and discard her when she is no longer pleasing or has not borne sons. Men come from all over the world to marry us because we are well skilled. We work in the morning, bathe and sleep, and then we dine with the lord and the lady after dark. If you are lonely I can give you a maiden to sleep with. Would you like that?'

Bewildered, I shook my head. It seemed like disloyalty to Eleni to sleep with anyone else.

'No,' I said as boldly as I could. 'I will spend the rest of my life alone—as alone as I am now. I had better get used to it.'

Perseis patted me and led me back to my room.

'Now, there are few rules, mainly because if there are rules I must ensure that they are kept and I haven't time,' she smiled. 'We must live in harmony. If there is disharmony the gods are displeased. We must be clean and behave as befits the Maidens. If you lie with a lover, you must tell me where you are going and when you are coming back—and you must not be away more than a day and a night. If Tithone needs you she will tell me also. Raiders come into the bay of Troy sometimes and they carry off Trojan women because they are valuable. We have never forgotten the loss of Hesione. You must not go down to the docks alone if there are foreign ships down there. Until your royal father makes arrangements for you to marry you are a free woman, Cassandra. Tithone the healer is our healer also, and can be called if you are ill. And if you are pregnant I must know; offerings have to be made.'

I shuddered at the idea of having a lover. I had not enjoyed the man with the blue bead. The only lover I really wanted was my brother and that could not be. Perseis noticed my reaction. 'You may have cause to change your opinion,' she said, with a reminiscent smile. 'Now, why don't you get comfortable and come down for some food when the watch changes,' and she left me to the small room and the silence.

It was a good distance to the sea but I could hear it, as you can always hear the sea in windy Ilium. I listened for the voice of either the god or my brother, but no one wanted to speak to Cassandra today.

There was a chest in my room and I unpacked my belongings. A long chiton of my favourite colour, a soft dark mossy green. Two working tunics for healing dyed a rather stipply grey with a soot-based dye which I had not dissolved carefully enough. One splendidly red tunic for the festival of Dionysius and the golden wreath that went with it, Nyssa's parting present. It occurred to me that I could attend the Dionysiad this year, now that I had gone to the Mother. Those under the protection of the Maiden were always kept indoors during the three days of the festival, and the rampaging crowd outside our door had always intrigued Eleni and me.

But that would mean taking a lover and I didn't want to. I folded the red tunic and laid it at the bottom of the chest. I put the other clothes away, noticing that I had taken Eleni's sheep's wool cloak instead of mine. I buried my face in the folds, smelling his scent, which I knew as well as my own, and wept for a while. This was useless. After a while I laid the cloak on my bed and sat down to examine my chattels, trying to distract myself from the thought of my lost twin, my own sweet Eleni. What did I own? I laid them in the chest one by one. Three interesting stones with garnets in them. A small ivory creature called an 'elephant' which Aegyptus shipmaster had swapped for an ointment for piles. A carved wooden Pallathis, the guardian of the city, who is a lady holding an apple in her hands. Some people say that it is not an ordinary apple, but the fruit of the end of the world, golden and dangerous. At the beginning of the city when Dardanus followed his straying cow to the hill of Até, a prophecy said that if the image was kept safe then the city would never all. Worried about there being only one, easy to find and to steal, Dardanus ordered a thousand copies made. Every child in the city owns a Pallathis. The temple of the lady is crammed with them, all sizes and made of all sorts of different material, wood and stone and metal. One of them is the original, but no one except the priestess knows which one. Mine was the span of my hand and painted in bright colours.

Then there was my soft purple-dyed leather bag of medicines, including the sharp stone knife I carried to lance boils and clean up broken flesh. All healers carry a stone knife, as it can be cleaned by thrusting it into the fire. When it breaks we just chip another one. I had also several bandages of old clean linen, salt impregnated, for wounds, pots of ointment for burns and bruises, a bundle of soapleaf for cleansing, and I found a forgotten bunch of the flower we call driftweed, which has short squashy stems and is used for scalds and blisters. They had rotted and I dropped the bunch out of the window into the flowerbed, shaking out the bag and repacking my tools.

I had a mixture of soapleaf and oatmeal in a twist of linen for washing myself, a pot of kohl for my eyes, some salve for reddened skin, a small knife for my nails, a silver mirror, and a comb made of cypress wood. I found a tiny phial of the finest Egyptian stone called 'glass' in the bundle. It contained oil scented with spikenard, a rich exotic smell. Eleni and I had been given it for prophesying the safe return of a sailor from a long voyage. He was ten months overdue but we had insisted to his distracted wife that he was safe. We could see him, we told her, building a fire on a sandy beach and roasting a goat. He had lost the first two fingers on his left hand in the shipwreck. It was only a little picture and we could not guess where he was. We had not told his wife that he seemed to have some female company, as Nyssa had spanked us for saying something similar the week before. I smiled as I remembered her hard hand impacting on our wriggling backsides as she said, 'Prophets should see all and say very little.' However, it was with the nymph, the sailor had finally come home. He and his wife had given us the perfume, the man possibly motivated more by our tact rather than our prophetic gifts.

Nyssa had kept it, saying that it was too precious for us to spill in some game. Now it was mine.

I must have fallen asleep then, because the next thing I remember was the dream Cassandra going to the window and looking out. She cried aloud at what she saw.

The whole sea was black with ships, hundreds of ships. They brought doom and death and I screamed myself awake with the smell of smoke and burning flesh reeking in my nostrils.

Cycne was the first to reach me. She asked breathlessly, 'What does the god say?' and I mumbled something, then said, 'Nothing, nothing. The god says nothing. I just had a bad dream.'

'Then you must go to the temple tomorrow,' she said calmly. 'There the priest of Apollo will welcome you, Princess of Troy, and he will also explain your dream. Perseis told me to tell you. She forgot to mention it. You can talk to Apollo now, since you joined the Mother. It's funny, Cassandra, back in Achaea you would have to be a maiden to be a prophet of Apollo. All of the pythonesses are maidens. Here you can't be a priest of Apollo unless you have abandoned maidenhood.'

'Yes, someone was telling me that you Achaeans worship virginity.' I levered myself upright and groaned. She took my hand and said kindly, 'Come along and bathe. It's hot. Don't call me an Achaean! I'm a Trojan. I was sold as a slave, except that here there are no slaves. A prince of Troy bought me and I thought that he was going to rape me. It was his right as my purchaser and my master had kept me fettered so that no one should damage me, not even him. I was so sick after that voyage, it took a moon to get here—and I was only twelve and just a woman and he thought he could get a good price for me.'

'Slavery?' I was still muzzy with the black aftertaste of horror in my mouth. Nyssa had often mentioned slaves but I had assumed that it was a way of keeping us under some control. Now it seemed that the institution was not mythical, after all. 'The Achaens have slaves? What's a slave?'

'A slave is a human owned by another human. A slave can be raped or killed or tortured and cannot complain, and if they run away they can be burned alive.'

'That's too horrible to be true,' I declared, stripping off my tunic and sliding into the clear green water.

Cycne took off her tunic and joined me in the bath. Wordlessly, she exhibited her scarred wrists, where she had been chained for a moon, and the marks around her knees where her master had tied them together so that she should keep her virgin price. I ran a finger along the nearest wrist. It was an old scar and well healed, but I thought of the cruel friction which could so mark her delicate skin and felt sick.

'What happened then?' I asked, not knowing if I could cope with the answer. 'Did he rape you?'

'No,' said Andromache scornfully from the edge. 'It was Hector, peerless among Trojans. Of course he didn't rape her. If the poor girl hadn't been captured by barbarians she would never have feared it. He sent her here until she should find a trade. She is going to be an excellent potter and when she went to the Mother she had no veil anyway.'

'Most of us don't,' commented Perseis. 'Aren't you going to bathe, Andromache? No? Then show me what is wrong with your leg. No, that leg, the one you are limping on.' She nudged Andromache into a sitting position and seized her foot, returning to her previous topic. 'Only the daughters of Priam and Hecube seem to have a complete veil, which makes the initiation painful, poor girls. And, of course, our Amazon here, who has collided with…a stone. Hmm. Now why weren't you telling me about it, eh? Could it be the competition tomorrow? Yes. Well. If you want to compete, maiden, you will have to avoid the running races.'

'Spear and bow,' pleaded Andromache. 'I don't have to run for them. Please, Perseis.'

'If you are well enough,' said the older woman. 'And if you can stand without trouble. But not to bathe, though. And next time, Andromache, you will tell me about your injuries and not leave me to strain my wits on discovering them for myself.'

'Cassandra had a bad dream,' said Cycne, demonstrating that lack of reticence for which barbarians are famous. I kicked her under water but she evaded me. Perseis blinked.

'Did you tell her to go to the god tomorrow?' Cycne nodded. 'Well, he will know what to do. She is his, after all. Now, maidens, be good. I have a headache and I am worried about Oenone's child.'

'The child is coming?' I asked eagerly. 'Can I attend her?'

'If you will and Tithone allows. She may well die in the birthing. Such can be expected from such misery,' and Perseis clucked away. I seized on Cycne.

'What is this misery?' I demanded. 'Tell, Cycne. And I won't drown you for telling Perseis about my dream.'

'Didn't you want me to tell? It is no use trying to hide anything from Perseis—you'll discover that, Cassandra. All right,' she said hastily as I dived for her feet. 'Listen. You know that your brother Alexandratos is called "Pariki"?'

'Yes. It means "purse" and it refers to that scrip he always wears at his belt, like a shepherd.'

'Cassandra, he was a shepherd. When he was born there was a prophecy that he was to be the destruction of Troy. The Mother's priestess ordered him killed, smothered as he was born, as the healers sometimes do to children too deformed to live, sending the soul back on the birth journey to try again. But your lord father would not have it so and gave the child to a shepherd. He lived on the slopes of Mount Idus for years and years, until he came here to compete in the games and the king recognised him.'

This sounded familiar. In fact, I think that Nyssa had told us about it when it happened, but we had taken such an instant dislike to Pariki and he to us that I had forgotten it, almost on purpose. The beautiful Alexandratos; so he had been a shepherd, that lofty one who was so proud and arrogant. I giggled at the thought.

'But he had taken a wife, this Oenone, poor thing, and he treated her very badly. He beat her. He scorned her for being of lowly birth, though she is the daughter of the Scamander. They say her mother conceived of the river god by eating an almond.'

I was about to mention that this method of conception sounded very unlikely, even for a river god, when Oenone was carried in and I held my tongue.

She was stripped and lowered into the water by three Amazons, who scowled at us and bade us make ourselves useful supporting her.

'Where did you find her?' asked Perseis. 'Cassandra, attend to our sister. Eirene, run to Tithone and tell her that the daughter of the river is giving birth. Tell her to hurry. Cycne, take her legs and we can hold her up. Good.'

'We found her on the field,' said Myrine's lover Eris, a short-tempered woman with a very fast slap for annoying Trojan youths, frequently knocked them off their insolent feet. Her head was shaved and her eye as black and fierce as a wolf's. She had one breast removed, wore only a loin cloth, and was as hard muscled and strong as a tried warrior. She was the Amazon's best hunter, fearless. They said that she had killed eleven men in the tribal feuds which blew up periodically between the Amazons and the herdsmen whose flocks they sensibly diminished. Certainly eleven strings of teeth hung onto her own scarred breast. She never mated with men, not even at the Dionysiad.

'Oenone said that she was returning to the river to give birth, but it is in spate, swift flowing, and we feared that even we could not hold her long enough. However, she made us promise to lie her in water, Perseis, so we have done that. Now, little sister,' she added to Andromache, 'how is that bruise? Will you stand with us tomorrow?'

'It is nothing,' said Andromache, lifting her chin. 'I will stand with you.'

Dismissing all concern for the birthing woman, Eris knelt next to our sister and laid her hard hand over the bruise. She concentrated. Over Oenone's moaning, which was increasing in volume, I heard a distant noise like a storm, a roar of voices and a clang like many bronze bells sounding together. Just for a moment I caught a glimpse of a terrible figure, a woman in armour brandishing a spear over her head, and saw that she was standing on a pile of corpses. Blood ran from her open mouth. A bunch of severed heads was in her other hand, suspended by their hair. Thus I saw for the first time Hecate, Destroying

Mother, Goddess of the Amazons and of Battles, Sacker of Cities, Butcher of Men.

I was very frightened, but the image flicked out as soon as I had focused on it. Andromache winced, bit her lip, then stood and crouched. The bruise was diminished and use had come back into the insulted tendons.

'Thank you, sister,' she said, and the Amazons left abruptly, which is a way that Amazons have.

We fought death for our sister Oenone all night, the next day, and into the following night. She floated in the green water, wailing to be allowed to die, and Tithone would not let her. 'You have a task,' she told Oenone briskly. 'You won't evade it by dying, daughter.' Even so, dosed with all the herbs we could think of, massaged and supported, she could not deliver and she was weakening fast. Tithone summoned me from the hall, where I had been dismissed to eat. I came to her with my piece of barley bread in my hand.

'Go up to the temple,' she said. 'Ask the god. In this matter the goddess has done all that she can.'

I bolted my bread as I ran, up the steep street to the Temple of the Sun God and in through the door. I found my brother Eleni there and ran into his embrace. I had not realised how terribly bereft I had been until I felt his gentle touch and buried my face in my accustomed place beside his neck. A wave of love swept over me. Eleni had missed me as I had missed him, like a crippled woman misses her right hand.

Mysion, the priest of the Temple of the Sun God, was watching us. He was a tall thin man with delicate features who usually moved like a cat, but now he grabbed both of us and hustled us into the shrine.

'The god is calling you,' he urged. 'Kneel and speak to him!'

The shrine glowed gold with the presence of the god. Eleni and I shut our dazzled eyes and knelt, holding hands. 'Eleni and Cassandra,' we announced, 'here to learn the will of the god.'

There was a voice, although we did not hear it with our ears. 'Both is more than two,' it said. 'Go to the river god's daughter, both of you. Turn the child in the womb. You have my favour, twins. Come in three days at noon and bring the nymph's son. Run!' boomed the golden voice. 'I can only wrestle Death for a little time.'

We turned and ran. I believe that I ran most of the way with my eyes shut. We burst into the Palace of Maidens completely in defiance of the rules that no man may enter, as no woman may enter the Palace of Youths. Perseis made a place for us and we splashed into the pool.

We did not know how to proceed but the god guided us as we felt and fumbled at the entrance to the womb. There was a gasping scream and the baby emerged, spilling blood into the pool. Eleni and I caught the creature in our clasped hands, holding its head above the water. A red face contorted with fury.

Eleni and I embraced in the blood-stained pool, as the daughter of the river god was delivered at last of Pariki City-Destroyer's child. With his beloved body in my arms, I refused all evil premonitions.

Chapter Ten

Diomenes

It was a difficult audience, even for Arion.

The hall at Mycenae is very large, taking up most of the main building on the acropolis. Because the Cyclopes prefer to build in circles and spheres—I wondered if it had anything to do with their religion—it is an oval shape and fully eighty paces from one door to the other. A hole in the roof let out the smoke from a huge fire burning on the central hearth. There must have been a hundred men in that room, all drunk, chewing bones and throwing them down to start irritable snapping fights among the hunting dogs which every guest seemed to have brought.

Slaves threaded the crowd with difficulty, carrying ewers and refilling the flat wine cups which the Achaeans use. They are called kylixes and that is the only useful information I got out of my seatmate, a dour youth who glowered into his cup and muttered to himself about Argive Elene, most beautiful of women, and how she would never look at him. He seemed very hurt when I instantly agreed. After that I sampled and pushed aside some roast goat which tasted dangerously aged, drank a little diluted wine and amused myself by surveying the men who had come to settle this most dangerous of marriages.

The dais was unoccupied, but the first tables were crowded with princes jealous of their standing. There were two men fully as big as Agamemnon—it appeared that they were both called Aias. Several men were engaged in a high-pitched argument which was becoming acrimonious. Knives had been drawn. The smell of unwashed flesh, expensive scented oil, and smoke was overwhelming. I turned my gaze inward and I remembered Elene, the strength of her arms, the softness of her breasts, the scent of her hair. My reverie was not to last. Somewhere to the left, a slave went flying as a clubbed fist punished him for spilling wine on a nobleman. He fell at my feet, bleeding from the jaw.

I began to wonder if I was going to like the Achaeans. I began to wonder why anyone liked them. My master had not allowed me to help with the injuries and illnesses in the palace, saying that such brutal language was not for young ears, so I was feeling professionally slighted. Here was someone I could help.

I hauled the offending server up and felt for broken bones. The mandible was dislocated. His teeth were out of alignment and his tunic front was stained with saliva and blood. As Arion began to sing, I escorted the slave out of the hall and into the anteroom, where a distracted person began to roar at me, noticed my healer's clothes, and waved me into the kitchen.

The kitchen was as hot as a smithy. I could not operate in such conditions, so I led the man outside and sat him down on a low wall.

'Heracles went forth,' began Arion in a voice which would have silenced a bigger army than the crowd in the great hall. 'Child-Killer Heracles,/ Battle rage gone,/ pursued by the Kindly Ones,/ Heracles went forth,' he bellowed the last line and the babble of voices cut off. No one, however lofty, dared offend a bard. The populace was still laughing at Arion's ballads about a certain miserly monarch who had refused a thirsty bard sufficient wine. The man had been called 'coin arse' ever since, in reference to where Arion said he hid his money.

The slave was shivering as I turned his face into the available light from the kitchen door.

'It's all right,' I said softly, in imitation of my master's tone. 'It's not broken, just dislocated. You aren't badly hurt.'

I put one hand under his jaw and one to the side and gave a controlled blow which clicks the joint back into place. He gave a yelp, spat out a tooth, and passed a trembling hand over his face. I produced a flask of mingled poppy and wine—we had replenished our medical supplies—and made him drink it.

'Take some of this,' I said, sitting down on the wall beside him. 'Can you speak Achaean?' He looked blank so I tried Phrygian, Carian, the island speech, and then Trojan. At the sound of the words his eyes lit and he dropped to his knees and embraced my feet.

'I am Eumides the Trojan,' he whispered, the sibilants hissing through the missing teeth, 'Master.'

'I am not your master. I am the healer Chryse and I am only an acolyte. Come, sit next to me. I will explain to the cook,' I added, as he cast a fearful glance at the kitchen door. I left Eumides washing his damaged mouth with water and went to the kitchen door. The harassed man looked up at my entry.

'Your slave is hurt. I will sit with him a while,' I said arrogantly. No more than one offends bards, will anyone obstruct an asclepid if he says that things will be thus or so.

'As you say,' he mumbled. 'He's useless anyway. And an army coming, they say—what will become of us? I can't feed another army.'

'When the league is signed they will all go home,' I said soothingly, snaring a loaf of wheat bread and ladling myself a large bowl of what smelt like meat soup. I took a handful of olives and several figs and sent a kitchen slave for a jug of diluted wine. I had this meal carried out to Eumides. The soup and bread were for him, the figs and olives for me. I had not been hungry in the great hall, but now I was reminded that men must eat. He looked up at me as gratefully as a dog does, and it made me ashamed. I was uncomfortable and spoke sharply.

'You can eat if you do it slowly and try not to chew,' I instructed. 'Your jaw will be sore for several days and any side-long blow will throw it out again.'

'They beat me for not understanding their language,' he said matter of factly, 'but I will duck next time. And it was worth it to see this much food. Agamemnon Lord of Men has no provender to spare for the unfree.'

He broke the bread into the soup, and began to eat, savouring each mouthful. I watched him as the moon rose high and silvery and full. After he had cleaned the bowl I gave him a little more wine and I sat eating figs and staring out onto the walls.

'There is a strong guard,' I said idly. I could see a forest of spears.

'We expect a siege, when the suitors of Elene arrive. If the Lord Agamemnon gets here first, the nimble one may be able to stitch together a league which will make a truce possible. Otherwise, Elene will not get unravished to Sparta.'

I winced at the thought.

'You speak Trojan very well,' he commented. 'Where did you learn?'

'We learn all languages at Epidavros because all people come there,' I said, struck with how long ago and very far away that haven of peace seemed.

'You are a healer priest,' he said. 'I thank you for my healing, and for your kindness to a slave, and even more for your words in my own tongue which I never thought to hear again.'

'How long have you been here?'

'Three years. I was a sailor who was wrecked off the coast of Pelops' land. Most of the others drowned. There was a woman, but she has been married off for a long time. The Argives like Trojan women and she was a very good spinner. Ah, Healer, it is good to speak like a man again. What can I do to repay you?'

'Speak, if you are not in too much pain.'

'What shall I speak of?'

'The House of Atreus.' I knew that he needed to do something for me and I wanted to know. 'Tell me about the Atreidae.'

'Ah, long and terrible,' said the Trojan slave, 'long and full of horrors is the tale of the House of the Double Axe.'

He turned so that his back was against the wall and his voice fell into the story-teller's chant. I suddenly realised that he was quite young, maybe only a few years older than me.

'It began with Tantalus,' he said, careful of his broken teeth. 'He who stole nectar from the gods and sold it to men, Zeus' son, the mischievous gossip who told tales of the gods. He wanted to offend Zeus, so he invited him to a meal and cooked his son Pelops as the main course. It offended Zeus as he had planned. Now Tantalus spends all eternity in crystal water which withdraws as he tries to drink it, in reach of apples which fly away when he tries to bite them. His thirst is measureless, his hunger monstrous, and there he stands fast until this day for offending the king of the gods, Cloud-Compelling Zeus the Father.'

'What happened to Pelops?'

'Zeus uncooked him, except for his shoulder which had been burned off. He replaced it with an ivory one. Pelops decided to marry Hippodameia, whose father Oenomaus bested all her suitors in a chariot race. The daughter sawed through her father's axle, so that he fell and Pelops won. Then Pelops slew the father and married the daughter and they had two children, Atreus and Thyestes. Ah, the hatred between brothers! Atreus married Aerope, but she lay with Thyestes and bore him two children. Cuckoos in a nest! Atreus invited his brother to a dinner to make peace between them, and the main dish was...'

'No, no, it can't be, it is too awful.' I protested.

'Both children,' said Eumides with relish. 'Dead and roasted like suckling pigs. Thyestes ran: he is supposed to have lain with his own daughter—she was a priestess—and they say there was a child because of this incest, the cousin of the lord, Aegisthus. Atreus had two sons, Menelaus and Agamemnon, who are very close. Perhaps the taint has gone. Menelaus has married the Lady Elene—is she really the most beautiful woman in the world, Healer?'

'Yes. Go on.'

'And Agamemnon, Lord of Mycenae, married Clytemnestra, the mortal sister of Elene. He took her from her husband and

killed him, then tore her baby from her arms and dashed it by
the heels against the wall. She has had several children by him.'

'But…' I could not think of any words to express my outrage
and my Trojan was deserting me. The slave leaned against my
knee and smiled.

'Orestes, Electra, Iphigenia. Beautiful children, but with
that blood in them, the blood of the house of Atreus…' mused
Eumides the slave.

'The blood of the house of Atreus,' agreed a cool voice from
behind me, in Achaean. As I turned, Eumides leapt to his feet
and fled.

Odysseus of Ithaca sat down next to me. I heard his leather
armour creak as he settled down. He smelt of something
cold—perhaps water. He must have just bathed. 'What were
you listening to, Asclepid?'

'The history of this house,' I said. 'A terrible history, if what
Eumides told me was true.'

'Terrible and true. You speak Trojan well.'

'So do you,' I realised. He laughed softly.

'Asclepid priest, Chryse God-Touched,' he mused. 'By what
god?'

'Death, Lord.'

'Ah, yes.' He took up Eumides' abandoned cup and filled it
with wine. 'You interest me, Chryse.'

'Lord?' I was offended with him. He had scared away my
patient. And he was drinking my wine.

'You tended the slave—why?'

'Because he was injured and I am an asclepid.'

'And our god would be affronted if you did not care for all?'

'There are no gods, Lord, just Thanatos Lord of Death. My…
my own self would be offended if I did not care for those who
need me.'

'Most interesting indeed, my healer priest. Does your master
think the same?' His voice was not sweet like Arion's. It was
smooth, full and strong, a very persuasive voice. I wondered if
he was trying to trap me into saying something about my master

which he could later use against him. So I replied primly, 'That is for my master to say, Lord.'

'I'm not trying to snare you with words, Chryse. Did you think of this yourself or were you taught it?'

'Lord, I thought of it myself.'

'Hmm. Did you? A most unusual priest. Let me tell you something. I entirely agree with you. If there are gods, then they have other things to do. The interventions for good or ill that men proclaim are accident, pure accident. Or there is another view, much argued on Cnidus. If gods exist, they take notice of men once in a way, perhaps, moving them like pieces on a board. But they have no hearts to be moved; no pity, no mercy, no love, no interest in the puppet twitching of the dolls that dance to their piping.'

'There may be something in what you say, Lord,' I said, considerably astonished.

'Come then, Chryse, perhaps we will leave the philosophical speculations for when you know me better and trust me more. I am sorry that I scared your suppliant away. I did not mean to. That was his own fear, not my doing. What more would you know about the House of the Double Axe?'

'Lord, I think I know enough. Quite enough. I shall have bad dreams in this place. If you make this league, do you think that it will hold?'

He shrugged. 'I am a small lord of a very small island,' he said quietly. 'These are heroes, Chryse, big men with vast conceptions and unbounded greed. What they will make of the matter I cannot tell. Except that they have a respect for honour, considering it to be a matter to boast of. You will find that men can be compelled to behave acceptably if you give them something to boast of. That is why words must be kept and honour maintained. If this league is sealed with words, then we must keep it or die in the keeping. Otherwise the world is ruled by night, death, and chaos—and they are not comfortable companions.'

'Arion says that the world is ruled by idiots,' I ventured. He laughed loudly, throwing back his shaggy red head, and almost fell off our wall. I grabbed him as he slipped. He was slim but strong; I would have said that they were rower's muscles.

'Ah, Chryse, who can argue with a bard? Especially not that one. The difficulty, my asclepid, is not to govern people, but to make them govern themselves, and here we are dealing with men who have never ruled themselves, who have never been controlled except by circumstance. If they see a bright pretty thing, they grab for it. If they want a woman, they take her unless someone stronger and better armed can stop them. They are men of passion and courage; heroes, you know. I myself have never been a hero. In my small and poverty-stricken island we cannot afford the luxury of heroes.'

I smiled at this. His chiton was of 'woven air.' The fillet which bound his hair was of the finest water gold, set with irregular pearls. On one wrist he wore an archer's brace two handspans broad, made of the same gold, finely figured with dolphins, studded with pearls and green and blue aquamarines. His boots were of the softest kid. 'Poverty stricken' could not have been a description of Odysseus, King of Ithaca.

He saw my expression in the half dark and smiled. Odysseus had a sweet, cynical smile which forced the watcher's own lips to curve. I felt mine doing so.

'Ah, but these things are beautiful. I like to wear them, they suit me and they please me. Heroes cause waste—remember that, Chryse God-Touched, little brother of Death. Wasted cities, wasted lives, wasted love and trust and blood. Where there is a hero there is destruction and the ailing of women. A hero's harvest is a waste of thorns. What is your real name?'

'Diomenes, Lord,' I mumbled, fascinated by the gaze of his amber eyes.

'If I call you, Diomenes Asclepid, if I need you and I should call you—and I will not do so lightly—will you come?'

I was suddenly sure that I could trust him with my life. 'Yes, Lord.'

'Yes. Remember heroes, my golden one. There must be laws and words carved in stone and honour in the world or it is all wasted. And I, Odysseus of Ithaca—I cannot bear waste.'

He was gone into the semi-dark. I saw his tunic fluttering as he paced along the wall, talking to the guards in that smooth voice. I started at a touch on my knee.

'That was Odysseus,' said Eumides from the ground. 'A subtle man, unlike these barbarians.'

'And there are no barbarians in Troy?' I asked, nettled.

'No,' he said consideringly, as if it had been a fair question. 'Troy is ruled by the sons of Priam. Strange, asclepid priest, the man I miss most is the prince of the city, the bulwark of Troy: Hector. All I ever talked to him about was those missing sheepskins which vanished at the port when we were unloading. But he is Troy for me, now that I am lost to the city forever. Hector standing on the dock with his lists of cargo, calling across the water for news of the Nile, promising us new wine if we unload quickly, with grey Státhi at his side.'

'What is a Státhi?' I asked.

'Show me your knife, Healer. Yes, I thought so.' He pointed to the small, lion-like animal hunting ducks along the blade. 'That is Státhi the cat, shadow of Hector. It is an Egyptian beast. They call it bashtet or mou. It is a sacred animal, though most animals are sacred in Egypt, the most priest-ridden place in the world—I beg your pardon, asclepid. I meant no disrespect.'

'Have you been to Egypt?'

'Yes, and to Libya, to Caria, even to Africa, where we traded for gold.'

'Have you stories to tell?'

'When my jaw heals the asclepid shall hear of wondrous beasts and amazing cataracts, living waters and teeming seas.'

'Rest for tonight,' I said. 'I will talk to you tomorrow.'

Arion's songs had calmed the mob in the great hall. At the introduction of a certain village tune plucked on the lyre and accompanied by two slaves on drums, the heroes had begun an old round dance with a lot of slapping and shouting.

The noise hurt my head. I found my master in our sleeping chamber and sat down at his feet. He ruffled my hair.

'Well, Chryse? How was the feast?'

'Noisy, Master.' I leaned against his knee. 'I have repaired a dislocated jaw and the suppliant told me such fascinating and horrible stories. Master,' I asked, soothed by his touch, 'how much does it cost to buy a man?'

◇◇◇

Purchasing the slave was not very expensive. I had seven coins, pressed upon me by grateful patients, and four sufficed to buy me Eumides the sailor, the Trojan slave. I summoned him from the kitchens. Someone had hit him again. His nose was bleeding.

'Take this,' I said, giving him my remaining coins, 'and come with me.'

'Where are we going, Master?'

'Don't call me Master, I'm Chryse the asclepid,' I said crossly. We came into the smithy, where a very large sooty person brandished a huge hammer at us until he saw my healer's robe. 'An asclepid—I was about to send for you. I think it's broken,' he said extending a foot.

It is the custom in the Argive lands that a slave must pay the smith for removing the slave's collar from his neck and the bands from wrists and ankles. I had given Eumides money for this purpose but it did not look as though he was going to need it.

'Strike the bands from this man; he is freed,' I said, showing the seal of Agamemnon which was my receipt. 'Then I will look at your foot.'

Eumides did not speak or thank me. He sat down on an anvil and did not flinch as the soldering iron hissed on the fetters and they were bent away from the flesh by hands as strong as pincers. The smith offered them to him, saying the ritual words, 'Free man, rejoice! Dedicate these chains to the god Hephaestus and thank him for your deliverance,' and Eumides took the still-warm metal and stayed where he was while I sat the smith down and examined his ankle. It was swollen and badly bruised.

'How did it happen?' I asked, feeling around the arch of his huge filthy foot to find if any of the little bones were broken. His sole was as hard as a hoof.

'I was shoeing the horses of the prince of Larissa,' he said. 'Ouch! And one of them stood on my foot, may it break all of its thrice-cursed legs and those of its master. That hasn't happened since I was an apprentice. Is it broken?'

'The little toe is broken,' I said, finding a flat bandage in my bag and binding it tightly to the next toe. 'Make an infusion of these herbs with a large wine pot full of boiling water,' I added, putting a bunch of comfrey and vervain into his hand. 'Drink it three times today and tomorrow, fasting, without wine. A prayer to Asclepius and to your patron, the lame god, must be made every time you drink it. Within a week the bones will knit; keep the splint on until then. After that you must strip and wash thoroughly all over and wear a new loincloth,' I added, for of all dirty men I had ever seen this smith was the dirtiest. I could only tell that he was human because I could see his eyes, startlingly white in the dark face.

We asked the way to the temple of Hephaestus, a dark cavern under the acropolis, and there Eumides went to the altar and knelt to pray.

I did not hear what he said. He wiped one palm across his injured face and smeared the bronze slave-bands with his blood. Then he threw the fetters down with a clatter and laid one of the silver coins on the stained stone.

I wondered what his prayer was, but it is never proper to enquire into another man's converse with the gods, however much I did not believe in them. We walked out into the street.

Mycenae was anxious. We were shouldered aside by soldiers in armour and women, usually confined close to the houses in Achaea, struggled past carrying children and bundles. They were hastening to the lower city, to the gate which gave onto the mountains, in case they had to flee the army of suitors. Babies wailed and men cursed.

'In here,' grunted Eumides, catching my arm. He dragged me into a niche and we stood very close, watching the throng and tasting their fear and excitement, which burned on the tongue like copper.

Eumides the freed slave caught me in an embrace and kissed me on the mouth. The kiss of a free man, they say, is different from the kiss of a slave. I kissed him back cordially. His body was warm in my arms but there was blood in his mouth and all my love was given to Argive Elene, Princess of Sparta. I freed myself gently.

'Well, asclepid priest, I belong to you now.' He was grim. 'What will you do with me?'

'You weren't listening,' I said, so close that I was speaking into his chest. 'You are not mine or any man's. You are free and can go where you will, though not immediately because we are in a castle under siege. If you want, you can come with my master and me and Arion Dolphin-Rider to Argos, which is where I think we are going next, thence to Corinth where you can get a ship.'

He was staring at me, expressionless, his eyes dark with suspicion.

'Why did you free me? Am I to be sacrificed?'

I was so shocked that I could not answer for a moment. 'No,' I gasped. 'What? Sacrifice a man? To what god? Do you think we are barbarians?'

'Yes,' he agreed. 'I do think so. You sacrifice all manner of creatures, spilling their blood to feed your hungry beast-ghosts of gods. Why not a man?'

'No, impossible,' I stuttered. 'Never would we do such a thing. What, do you Trojans have no gods?'

'Yes, but they do not feed on entrails and they do not snuff the stench of burning flesh with pleasure. We offer beautiful things and gold and wine and honey to the gentle gods of Troy. So you do not mean to kill me? They spoke in the kitchens of the sacrifice of a free man to ensure success. Do you not want my life? Is that not why you had me freed?'

He was in earnest. Feeling for my knife, I gave the hilt into his hand, the point to my throat.

'You can kill me,' I said calmly into the wild eyes. 'I mean you no harm, Trojan.'

He stared at me for what seemed like minutes. His breath was on my face, tainted with the scent of starvation and the overlay of blood. His eyes, I noticed, were very dark, deep, and beautiful. They were filling with tears.

'Are you not afraid to die?' he whispered, letting the blade fall. 'I could have killed you then, asclepid.'

'No,' I said truthfully. 'I am Chryse the golden one, Diomenes, Asclepid, Healer Priest, Death's little brother, Thanatosfreed. I am not afraid of meeting the black angel again. He held me in his arms and was as gentle as a mother.'

'I am ashamed,' he said, and kissed me again, frantically, although it must have been an action full of the most exquisite pain.

I pushed him gently away and wiped his face. He was weeping freely, his chest heaving with sobs.

'Come, we will go to my master,' I said. 'It will be quiet there. You need rest. And then you can tell me more stories about the world, if you will. I have seen very little of the world,' I added, as I led him by the hand up to the acropolis, 'and it seems very big and dangerous to me, and very astonishing.'

I came into my master's room and watched Eumides as he stripped and washed. He was beautiful, slim, and strong, like in body to Odysseus of Ithaca. There were scars on his back from floggings and his hands had been burned and healed many times. I had never thought about slaves before. They had been in the background all of my life. They were the hands which mended, sewed, drew water, chopped wood, cultivated fields, and poured wine. I had never thought of them as men. I was much more ashamed than Eumides, the ex-slave.

He came and knelt, naked and clean, beside me where I was sitting on my master's bed. His scarred hand cupped my face.

'I thank you for my life,' he said softly. 'Unlike you, Chryse, I am afraid to die. How can I repay you?'

There was a strong sensual suggestion and he was very beautiful. I had never lain with a man, but I still loved Elene and would not forget her by obscuring her memory with any later love. I stroked the hand and held it briefly.

'Tell me of the world,' I said, and he sighed. 'But first, I will give my third best tunic which is too big for me and you shall lie down on my bed and sleep until night.'

Master Glaucus and Arion came in as Eumides was settling down and he immediately scrambled to his feet. I desperately hoped that my master would say something which would soothe the ex-slave.

'The free man?' asked my master. 'The Trojan?'

'His name is Eumides and he may travel with us to Corinth,' I put in.

Arion grinned and embraced the surprised Trojan. 'I am Arion Dolphin-Rider, famed singer, bard of the Argives,' he roared. 'You can tell me of the world, Eumides free man. A mariner by the look of you?'

Eumides nodded, dumbfounded by the bard's robust energy.

'Good. I have sailed many seas but it does a bard good to hear new tales. I would be honoured if you could bear us company to sea-bordered Corinth, should we get out of Mycenae alive. And…' he lowered his voice and looked meaningfully at me, 'You can be company for the boy. He gets into trouble if he is left to wander alone.'

I blushed and Eumides grinned.

At that moment there came a distant bellow of trumpets, brazen and tooth-grittingly toneless. Arion held up a hand to still our laughter and said, all on one long breath, 'Praises be to all of the gods of every nation and in every place and that includes Pluton, Thanatos, and Ares the Sacker of Cities. That, my friends, is the appallingly untuned fanfare which announces the arrival of Agamemnon lord of Men, his brother Menelaus, and Elene Princess of Sparta and, all other things being equal, we are saved.'

Chapter Eleven

Cassandra

Three days later we went to the temple with the baby, which was still red-faced and screamed continuously as it was carried up the steep streets of holy Ilium. It had obviously not enjoyed being born and the continued processes of life were not amusing it either. It did not like Eleni and it did not like me and we were not greatly in favour of it after it had thrown up over us.

Not 'it.' Him. Oenone had decided to call the baby Corythus—'shoal,' as in deep water hazard. We had not heard the name in Troy before and assumed that it either related to the father Pariki's outrageous treatment of his wife or had something to do with the Scamander.

Eleni was walking beside me, holding Corythus out in front of him in case he vomited again. 'Twin,' I said, 'I don't think I like babies.'

'Twin,' he said solemnly, 'neither do I and it is your turn to hold him. Why does the god want to see us?'

'I don't know. You heard him, he just said to come back after three days, bringing this creature with us, so here we are. It is not a good idea to flout gods, especially not Apollo the Archer—do you want a plague?' I was still feeling dislocated. Eleni understood instantly and gave me his hand.

But it was not the same. Not the same at all. He had spent several nights in the temple of Dionysius since we parted. I had awoken with fire creeping through my loins, images of a woman in my mind, and another face obscuring the priestess'. This told me that Eleni, my brother and twin with whom I once shared all of my life, was lying with the priestess and thinking of our sister Andromache. He probably thought that he was calling up Ishtar the goddess, an improper thing to do in Dionysius' temple anyway, but it was Andromache who possessed his desires, not me.

I did not know how he was going to react to Hector's marriage in the spring. His hand was firm and warm and that was all—truly the hand of a brother, and I had sufficient brothers. With Pariki, I had too many.

Also, the effect of Eleni's liaison was to leave me with a heavy ache in my back and a feeling of regret and vast missed opportunities.

We reached the temple. For this honour, we had put on our best purple and we paused at the antechamber to wash down Eleni's spattered tunic. The doors opened. The following crowd muttered.

The cat-smooth priest of the Archer God walked before us to the altar and we knelt as we had before, laying the baby on the floor between us. It was a beautiful temple, I thought, as I strove to control my breathing and order my mind. Golden suns blazed in the morning light. A warm wind drifted through the high windows, bringing the scent of honey and ripe apples.

I was sinking into a drowse when the god came.

The first thing I noticed was that Corythus had stopped wailing and was cooing and trying to grasp sunbeams with his hands. Mysion Apollo Priest stood tall and cried, 'The god comes!' and a great bronze bell was struck. I seemed to see the reverberations, like rainbows patterning across the stone floor, like ripples in the pools of the Scamander.

Golden fish swam up through the water and mouthed bubbles. 'Cassandra,' said the honey-laden voice, 'you will be happy,' and I gasped, because the fiery fingers had touched my lips. 'Come at noon in three weeks, daughter of Priam, well, beloved, and lie with me and mine.'

'Lord, it shall be as you say,' I faltered.

'Eleni, son of Priam,' Apollo's voice flowed into our ears, 'you shall have the woman you desire—but not yet, little son, not for a long time. Therefore, Eleni, have patience, most fortunate of the men of Troy.'

'Corythus,' said the god, as a bright sunbeam touched the child's face. 'Grow strong. Learn your own path. Leave your mother's.'

Then he was gone. We sighed and I gulped. My mouth was dry.

Someone else picked up the baby, which was a mercy, and there was shouting and exclamations and we had to drink a lot of wine. Luckily the priest had heard it all and we did not have to explain. Finally the temple emptied and Eleni and I trailed the crowd back to the palace.

'I'm afraid,' I said at last.

'Why? Cassandra, he said that I shall have…shall have…'

'I heard him. Not for a long time, he said. But he told me to go and lie with him and I'm afraid, Eleni, pay attention!'

'Why are you afraid?'

'You were there. You remember the man with the blue bead.'

'Yes, but you were there when I lay with the priestess. That felt lovely; it didn't hurt. It won't hurt with the god. He called you his beloved.'

'It's not really the pain, it's…the closeness.'

'That's the best part.' Eleni grinned, left me at the door, and wafted away, elevated by the knowledge he would possess Andromache in the end.

I threw as horrible a thought after him as I could and he did not even stagger. Eleni my brother was closed to me. He would not be there when I went to the god.

I spent three weeks trying every craft I could find and worrying. It might have been better if there had been anything I was good at. But there wasn't. My pots sagged and broke in firing. My thread was lumpy and the embroiderer took back her precious needles after I had broken one, carelessly dragging it through the cloth. My enamel was blotchy and my dye was not fast. My cooking was either burned or raw and in extreme cases both. In fact the cook was amazed—apparently no one had managed to do that before.

For me, it was easy.

I went to weapons training and found that I could shoot a good accurate arrow—but I had been able to do that since I was a child, throw a reasonable spear and ride so that I did not usually fall off. Myrine told me to stick to healing after the eight-year-olds beat me in a foot race. Tithone had deserted me. She had gone on a journey to see her sister healers, at a convocation held somewhere in a forest in Caria, and I was not allowed to tend people without her. The other maidens chattered incessantly about the great honour bestowed on me and speculated, giggling, about what making love to a god would be like. I screamed when Cycne began to describe with illustrative examples how huge the god's phallus might be, and Perseis threw them out and brought me wine and poppy.

By the time they came to dress me in gold and carry me up to the temple I was in despair.

I don't remember the journey up the hill. They put the litter down and the priest helped me remove my clothes. His touch was like a healer's—he had no interest in my body. I was trying not to have any interest in it either. I called Eleni and could not find him. I did not try again. I was so desolate that I did not even cry.

Then everyone went away and the temple was empty.

The sun streamed in. The walls were of gold and shone so brightly that I closed my eyes.

The touch was light as a feather. A warm finger was laid on my knee and travelled upward, circled my belly, continued up to my face, touched my lips. A body lay down beside me. I could feel warm breath on my shoulder, then on my breast as a mouth kissed and then suckled each nipple, so gently that a breeze might have blown him away. I lay still, awaiting an onslaught which did not come. Instead the mouth continued to suck and kiss, moving down my body and then up again, delicate as flowers. I moved a little, appreciating the caresses, still afraid of the plunging phallus and the pain. Each time the hands followed the movement, withdrawing, exquisitely courteous, if I pulled away.

After a while I did not pull away. The hands and the mouth grew bolder, the caresses deeper. The mouth kissing mine was sweet, but not like honey. It was the distilled essence of a wild taste like dust and strange herbs. I sucked at the mouth, the moving lips, and explored the body on the altar.

He felt like a young man, long limbed and smooth, with strong arms and long curly hair. I felt over the face; high nosed, broad of forehead and chin, so young that there was no scrape of beard. I heard him draw in a long breath as I found the phallus and stroked it gently.

I had never thought that I could please a god.

The fingers entered me and found the opening silky with moisture. The mouth joined them and I felt my back arch as it had when Eleni had found the goddesses' pearl. We were lying flank to flank with our legs intertwined. I knew that I would still not have the courage to lie on my back and await the stabbing thrust. A hand slid down between our bodies, leaving a trail of sparks in its wake.

Then he was inside me, Apollo Archer god, and there was no pain. Each movement, slow and considered, dragged a sigh out of my lungs, filled me with fire, melted my bones. I clasped him close and we began to move faster, harder, his hair mingling with mine on our golden bed. 'Cassandra,' said the god and I opened my eyes.

Beautiful, the Lord Apollo seemed to me, noble and glorious, and he cleaved closer to me than flesh cleaves to bone. I was full of him. Then sunlight exploded and I cried aloud and so did he.

When I could see again I was laying in the arms of a boy on the altar of Apollo, sobbing with joy and relief.

'Cassandra,' he said, leaning up on one elbow, but it was not the voice of a god. It was a youth's voice, husky and uncertain. He had such dark brown eyes that I could not tell what he was thinking. I probed and found that I knew nothing about him. I was intrigued.

'What is your name?' I asked. Then the question seemed funny and we both laughed until he stopped my mouth with a kiss. The kiss was almost as sweet as the god's had been.

'The god gave us to each other,' he observed. 'He called me from the shops. Your brother was annoyed.'

'Hector does not like delays in unloading,' I agreed. 'So Apollo called you?'

'The sky was filled with light and the voice said, "Go to the temple and make love with all your skill to the daughter of Priam," So I came. Did I please you, Princess?'

'Was the god with you all the time?'

'Yes. But I was there, too. I don't really understand, Cassandra, nothing like this has ever happened to me before.'

I stretched luxuriously. I felt wonderful. The nameless boy's hand cupped my breast, the fingers almost touching, sending a little spurt of delight through my body.

'Tell me your name,' I begged, as my hand slid along a wet thigh.

'Dion,' he whispered. 'Dion the fisherman.'

Making love with Dion the fisherman was almost as delightful as making love to the god. He was closer to me, not divine but human, warm as flesh, not fire. He was clumsier and so was I, but we learned fast, I and my well-skilled boy. We reached a climax with a rush.

Apollo had given me a lover. It was a godly gift.

◇◇◇

That was a cold winter, but Dion kept me warm. Eleni was lost to me, apart from occasional glimpses. He had shut his mind and that was a loss as grievous as a missing limb which still itches and pains even though it is gone. Dion's family lived in the lower city and I often went there. I could not marry him but that did not matter when I lay down in the fish-smelling nets to embrace his lithe body, wreathing my arms around his neck, locking my legs around his waist.

The god did not come to us again, but he did not need to. I stopped worrying about my lack of culinary skill when I ate partially roasted fish with Dion. His family were honoured that Apollo had chosen their son. I felt that he had given me new life when I thought I might die of the loss of Eleni.

Dion never reflected on anything. If the sea killed him, then it killed him. If the god called him, he obeyed. He had no interest in the world, did not wish to travel or trade. He was deeply content, calm, beautiful, and loving. He acted on my grief and loss like a marsh-herb poultice on a burn. He healed me.

The freezing gales flayed Troy that winter. I had gone out with the boats when the sky turned black and we cut the nets and drove for shore, battered by great waves. Dion was clinging to a stay. I had wrapped my cloak around me and tied it with a cord and was embracing the mast like a lover, my cheek against the turned wood.

'Row, you pampered sons of Corinth whores!' bellowed the shipmaster, Ethipi. 'Steer inland, fool, or we'll be smashed to kindling on the cliff!'

The wind lashed and howled and the wise-eyed boat groaned in all her timbers as Ethipi strove to keep her head into the wind. The steering oar snapped with a crack and flung Maeles, the navigator overboard. Icy water smashed the side. The sail flapped loose and shredded. My grip was failing.

'Cassandra!' Dion stumbled to me and we bound ourselves together to the mast, 'I love you! Can't you save us?'

I called to my brother but he did not hear. Then I called the god. It was hard to concentrate. The wind was bellowing and each wave landed with a crash like thunder. Our boat whined at this mistreatment and Dion was pinning me so tight that I could not breathe.

I freed my arms from my lover and raised them in the invoking gesture. I did not know how to call the god of the sea, Blue-Haired Poseidon, Earth Shaker, so I used the Apollonian ceremony. What could I offer the god? The words formed themselves in my mouth without any intervention from my distracted wits.

'Lord Poseidon,' I shrieked, 'do not destroy us and we will take you back into our city. I, Cassandra, daughter of Priam, promise this.' I swung and slid as the boat bucked like a horse. Dion secured me and held me fast, his face against my neck. I could feel his wet curls dripping onto my breast and water ran cold down my body. 'Lord Poseidon, I call upon you to hear our prayer,' I cried, contemplating the tripartite invocation. 'Dread Lord Poseidon, save all of us and you shall return in triumph to the city of Dardanus and Laomendon who insulted you. I, Cassandra, swear this by all the gods.'

The sea hit us once more and the boat screamed. I heard the mast, under incredible strain, wail as the wood began to twist under the fist blows of the gale. We staggered across the face of an enormous wave like a drunken fly. We were lost. I began, under my breath, the prayer for the dying. All of us, including me and my beautiful Dion, were going to die when that wave overtoppled. It would smash us under a hammer of water as an ant is crushed under an anvil.

The wind did not fall. It stopped. Dion released me and stepped back, awestruck. Shipmaster Ethipi roared, 'Row, dogs!' and the ship began to move in an eerie calm. I heard each separate splash as the oars entered the sea. Over us towered the thunderheads, meeting the mountain of black water. The god's power had stopped time. We rowed silently through slack water and then we heard a cry.

'Wait!' wailed a voice. Hands slapped the gunwale and the lost navigator pulled himself into the boat and fell dripping and coughing on the deck.

'All of us,' I heard them begin to mutter. 'She said all of us and now we've even got Maeles back! The god is with her. The god is with the princess.'

'Row!' bellowed Ethipi. They rowed.

We beached the boat beside the ruined dock and ran inland. There is only one path up the cliffs, narrow and dangerous. I did not wish to hurry, but Dion dragged me. I wanted to look at the suspended wave. I was sure that the Lord Poseidon would not betray his bargain. We had been reprieved on my promise.

We reached the top of the cliff, joining a crowd of fisherfolk and sailors who had retreated there out of the endangered bay of Troy. Women, children, old and young men, they were all stunned by the violence of the weather. They were all staring out to sea.

As soon as the last foot paced the cliff top, the wave fell. It seemed to roll forward very slowly, then drop on the harbour with a noise like the gods fighting in the sky. Ship's backs snapped. Hector's trading dock was broken like a seashell. Water flooded and clawed at the cliff as foam flew and the hungry sea sucked at the land.

Then it receded and sleet began to blow like daggers.

'Princess,' Shipmaster Ethipi knelt at my feet. I was embarrassed and tugged at him. 'You saved us all,' he said. Then he announced to the crowd, 'She did not just save herself. All of us, she said, all of us. We even got Maeles out of the cauldron of a sea and he should have been dead and drowned deep. She bargained for our lives with the God of the Sea, Poseidon Earth Shaker. Who can doubt his power? We all know and fear it. She is our princess. She is our lady. We are greatly favoured. Why, Apollo even gave her Dion here as a present; one of us.'

I was surrounded by people. They did not touch me, but their eyes were full of awe. I, personally, had not deserved this. I wanted to sit down and I wanted everyone to go away so I could be sick in decent privacy. I was shuddering. My drenched cloak clung to my skin.

'Cassandra is a true princess,' said an old woman. 'This is a great thing and the city must know. But we must care for her now. See, she's fainting.'

I have a vague memory of being borne up in many arms and after that the next thing I recall is being fed salty fish soup by Dion's mother.

'Is everyone all right?' I murmured. 'someone should see to Maeles…' and then I drifted out again.

Perseis came when I did not return home in time, ready to scorch my ears off, and those of my fisherman lover. She did not say that Dion was low born and no fit lover for a princess, but she thought it. She found me in the centre of a pious group of the sea-people. It was a terrible waste of a good scolding. Perseis immediately sent for Tithone.

I had a high fever and was sick and delirious, which was fortunate, because thus it was not me who had to convince my father Priam to bring Poseidon back into Troy.

I was sick for three weeks. There are fragmented memories of Hector's body filling the doorway of the wooden shack, Státhi's lashing tail, and my brother's worried face. The news of my intercession with the Blue-Haired, exiled god had gone all over the city in two watches and Priam had no choice but to re-admit him, though I doubted that he would be pleased with me. It was announced that new priests of Poseidon would be found and the temple would be re-opened.

The new priests of Poseidon, I was told, were Maeles and Dion.

By the time I had recovered enough to walk, the dedication ceremony had taken place. Dion lived in a house which had been built near where Hector was planning his new jetty (on a greatly improved scale, of course). I had made my fisherman a powerful person. He came to his mother's house every morning and night while I was there, bringing me shells and coral and strange things found in shipwrecks and sitting beside me for a watch at a time. He did not talk, but that did not trouble me because talking hurt my head. I lay languidly stroking the net-cuts and the rowing callouses on his broad palms. I found comfort in his regard for my irreparable grief.

All the time that I was ill, Eleni had never come to see me.

◇◇◇

'She melts in the arms of my avatar, myself in mortal form,' gloated Apollo. 'She is mine.'

'But the city of Troy,' commented Poseidon, stretching out a weed-wreathed arm in blessing, 'has accepted me again. I have priests and I have worship. Troy shall not fall.' Salt water dripped onto the creamy marble at his massive sandalled feet.

'You did it on purpose,' accused Apollo. 'You summoned the great wave, you knew she would try to save Dion, my chosen one. You cheated!'

'It is done,' said Aphrodite venomously. 'You made my daughter love you, my Lord Sun God, and on account of that love she has welcomed your rival into the city. Your favourite, Dion, is priest of Poseidon now. Possibly you should not have chosen a fisherman.'

Apollo bared white teeth in a soft red mouth. 'It is she, Cassandra, your darling, that has done this. She will find out what it is to affront a god!'

'Cruel and petty—petty and cruel, these new gods,' observed Demeter the Great Mother. 'You heard the King of Ithaca, Odysseus the Nimble-Witted. What he said was true. You play with these poor mortals for sport. You have no pity. I warned you, Sun God. I support her, this misused princess, if you cheat.'

'You have no power, old woman,' snarled Apollo.

'I have taken over your worship. Your python-priestesses at Delphi are now my oracles. Mortals are forgetting you in the dazzle of my eye, which is the sun. Soon there will be no one who remembers you, crone of the earth, but a few old women who scatter seeds and mumble invocations. You have no power.'

Demeter said nothing.

'Cassandra will suffer for this,' continued Apollo. The fire of his eyes heated the water in the Pool of Mortal Lives, so that steam arose from the surface. 'And I do not forget the insults of Odysseus of Ithaca.'

'The game continues,' said Aphrodite, rolling the golden apple from hand to pearly-perfect hand.

Chapter Twelve

Diomenes

We were saved. The army of suitors were reported still to be sacking the plain of Argos, but the Atreidae and their prisoner Elene were safe within walls.

I saw her as she walked in from the horse litter. She was tired and dusty but not bruised as I had feared. She was dishevelled, dressed in a tunic too big for her and she was beautiful enough to stop my heart.

She looked into the crowd and saw me. She did not smile. The gaze of her trout pool eyes encompassed my whole vision for what seemed like a long time. Then she was hustled into the women's quarters and I knew I would never see her again.

Eumides was behind me. He slid an arm around my waist and drew me out of the press of people.

'Asclepid, I fear that I have lost my heart. You are right. She is the most beautiful woman in the world. Come, we need wine and solitude.'

We were not to get either. Arion was called upon to entertain the Lord of Men and I was taken by my master to tend the temple of Apollo, which was without a priest and had been neglected. I think that the Master Epidavros was making perfectly sure that I was not summoned to the Lady Elene's side if she was unwell from fatigue or fever.

The temple was in disarray, however, and the Lord Apollo, if he had existed, would probably have struck Mycenae with all manner of plagues in his annoyance.

In fact, in view of the lack of any drainage and the number of wells which seemed to be in exactly the wrong places, Apollo might do that in spite of his non-existence.

'Master, look at this.' I had been weeping listlessly and something had made a clinking noise in the dust. 'I would not go to her again, Master.' I added, continuing a different train of thought. 'Such a thing only happens once in one lifetime.'

'Being the brother of Death may have made you wise beyond your years, Chryse. What have you found?'

'A seal, I think.' I polished it on my dusting cloth and held it up to the lamp. 'Very old.'

'Yes, and broken. Probably cast away.' He turned it in his surgeon's fingers. 'By the gods, Chryse. Look at the image!'

I still could not see it until my master crouched and printed the seal in the dust. Then it was clear. The horned ram, Perseus' seal. Perseus, the demigod, first king of Mycenae.

'A very interesting find. Arion must see this. Now we must keep sweeping and see what else may be here.'

It was a poor temple. The Apollo was wooden, much cracked and faded. I dusted him thoroughly and cleaned the stains of old blood from the altar. The offerings with which the temple must have been packed had been looted bit by bit as the worship faded, along with the furniture and the tapestry, which fell to shreds as I touched it. It was an unhappy place and exactly matched my mood.

Zeus was the ruling god of Mycenae, the Father. Heracles came second; the hero. Otherwise they had a rich temple dedicated to the foreigner, Aphrodite of Cyprus, the goddess of love. For the first time it struck me as odd that the Achaeans kept their women confined, punished female adultery with death, and lauded domestic virtue, yet worshipped the goddess of lust and lawless passion.

I have never made much sense out of Achaeans.

My master and I finished the shrine and moved into the body of the temple. There was a roar from the acropolis.

'I think the league has been signed,' I said hopefully, but my master frowned.

'No. That was another sort of noise. Come, Chryse. I have an idea that might be useful if I can get to that rogue of a bard in time. We will have to risk the great hall. She will not be there.'

My life hung on the thread of an Argive woman's word. I did not care.

Glaucus struggled through the crowd and we forced our way into the great hall. The shouting was deafening. Each prince and princeling was proclaiming his own case at the top of his and his captain's voices. I caught sight of Odysseus of Ithaca. He appeared to be carrying on three arguments at once with perfect ease.

Glaucus sighted Arion, shouted 'Catch!' and threw him the broken seal. Arion caught it, examined it, and pulled Odysseus' expensive hem.

The king of Ithaca took the seal and looked at it carefully. Then he smiled.

He walked to the middle of the dais and grabbed both Aias, shook them, and gave them an order. They bellowed 'Silence' in unison.

It worked. Odysseus held up the seal.

'Do you know what I have here?' he asked in a conversational tone which reached me at the back as though he was peaking in my ear. No one interjected. 'This is the seal of a hero. Perseus the demigod left it in the temple of Apollo when he passed through here. Now where,' he continued, walking along the dais, 'do we find heroes now? Here men contend as though there were no gods. Here men bellow and brag as though there were no death. Remember, princes and kings, high-born and proud, there is a destiny for all of us. Perseus' destiny was to be a hero. He was the first king of this palace, of golden-walled Mycenae. Danae's child by Zeus Cloud-Compeller, even the journey in the wooden box and the quest of the Medusa's head was not beyond him. With the gifts of the gods he slew the monster and flew glittering through the skies. He outwitted the graeae, beat the gorgons, though they turned all men to stone. In the kibesis woven of gold he carried the venomous head; by that weapon he rescued wife, fair Andromeda, fairest of all mortal women until Elene was born.'

I heard Arion's lyre chiming behind the words, binding the spell of the king of Ithaca's voice.

'By his own strength and honour and will he conquered the unconquerable, endured the unendurable. What would Perseus, first king of this golden fortress, have said of these babbling boasters that throng his hall, these quarrelling upjumped princes who shriek like market women, who believe that the loudest voice means the strongest arm? He knew that only a great-hearted man, a man of honour whose word is of stone and bronze, can attract the favour of fate. For it is all a matter of fate. It is Menelaus' fate to have Elene and Elene's fate to be his wife.'

Some muttering broke out and I saw Arion lay a strong hand on one man's shoulder.

'If we fight then we shall assuredly die,' continued the king of Ithaca, without raising his voice. 'And that would be a waste. Better we should live, for in life there is hope, joy, wine, and women.' Coarse laughter greeted this remark. 'But in death there is cold, the decay of mirth, the draught of the Styx, and endless unremembering in a dark realm ruled by the rich one. Consider, princes, consider death. It comes to us all, but it need not come soon.'

There was complete silence and attention in the hall as he went on, still in a confidential tone. 'As it will if we do not make this league. Here are princes and kings and men of great worth; here are heroes. When Perseus asked for peace, did he not get it? Partly because he was in a position to enforce it. As am I. I will kill the first man who strikes another.'

He gestured elegantly at the walls. Around them were ranked all the bowmen in the city. Phrygians who spoke no Achaean.

They were Odysseus' own guard. Each bow was drawn; there was an arrow on each string.

'Under the gods we all make our own choices. I choose to swear that Elene's father shall award her to whom he will and we will all defend against anyone who tries to take her away. I swear before all the gods that I will defend Menelaus Prince of Sparta's bride, Elene, from ravishment and capture.'

He made it sound noble, even heroic. I was enchanted by his voice. Glaucus my master was leaning on Arion and listening like a child. The bard was grinning in admiration.

The hall echoed with men repeating after him, 'I swear that I will defend…'

Menelaus sat back in his seat and fanned himself with a fold of his robe. I noticed that Agamemnon had not moved. He was sitting on his throne with his great sword across his knees, like a statue of a god, as he had been while the mob raged at him.

Odysseus completed the oath. 'Heroes and high-born men, tomorrow you ride home,' he said, 'but tonight you feast!' and he drained a cup of wine and smashed it against the wall.

◇◇◇

The next day the army rode, each to their several homes. It took them five hours to leave the city. Master Glaucus, Eumides, and Arion were busy. Eumides returned to our room after noon. He had skinned both sets of knuckles and had a few extra bruises, but he appeared very happy and swapped extremely indecent sea-songs with Arion as I dabbed comfrey lotion on his hands.

My master was in deep converse with an asclepid, a very old man with a profound knowledge of herbs. I found his halting speech and slow tongue tedious to listen to and wandered outside.

I could not even sit on the wall, because everyone in Mycenae seemed to be sweeping. Most of the populace had gone out to the fields to see if anything could be saved of the harvest. The remaining slaves were bad tempered. They would not actually be rude to me because I was an asclepid, but they asked me to move my feet and then myself until finally I wandered right out of the city and sat down on a suitable rock to grieve.

It was time to leave Mycenae. I could not bear to be in the same place as Elene and never touch her. The Achaean women were seldom seen, anyway. They kept to their houses unless they were so poor that they had no slaves to send to market. Even then they hurried along the streets, muffled in veils and unspeaking.

I was summoned back from my sulking rock by a shout from the walls. 'Come, Chryse!' called Eumides, 'your master has work for you!'

I dawdled up the steep road, scuffing my sandals in the grey limestone gravel. I was still chewing my mouthful of mint when Master Glaucus cuffed my ear and bade me follow.

I followed. He seemed to be in a hurry. We puffed down the hill to the poorest streets and I heard moaning as I came.

Little stone houses lined the walls. They were no bigger than shepherd's huts and much dirtier, because all the sewage and rubbish of the acropolis flowed downhill. There seemed to be no gutters and the stench, even on a cold autumn day, was enough to make me choke.

Master Glaucus paused to kilt up his tunic and take off his boots and his healer's gown. I gave my sandals to Eumides, who had accompanied my master. He was looking decidedly green.

'Don't come any further, Trojan,' I said. 'It can only get worse. Does Arion know where we are?'

'Yes,' said Eumides. 'What is happening in that hell-pit?'

'I think we've got plague. If you stay here the master will be able to send messages, which would be very useful. Can you wait at the top of that stair?' I judged that it was out of the dangerous miasma. Healers are protected by Asclepius; we seldom get sick. I did not know if the god was going to protect me, since I did not believe in him, and I was sure that he would not help a Trojan who knew no real gods.

'I do not have to—you are not ordering me?' asked the ex-slave.

'No, of course not, don't be so sensitive! You may go or stay as you wish, but if you go send another to wait on us.'

I did not want to go down into that poisonous fog, but I was going to, and I did not want to delay any more in case I lost my courage altogether.

Eumides sat down on the wall, holding the robes in his arms. The small houses were filled with dead and dying. Master Glaucus was ordering the stronger men to carry them all out into the flat place at the bottom of the stairs. The smell was enough to bleach an African chieftain and I hastily wrapped a length of bandage over my nose and mouth.

'Chryse, go that way and find out how many are sick, bid them all come out, especially the women, take no denial, call the wrath of the gods down on them if they argue. By Apollo Sun Bright himself, this is a dreadful place! Enter every house and mark where there are corpses. We must isolate them somewhere close but out of the city and have this den cleansed or Mycenae will be a graveyard within a week. Hurry, asclepid!'

I picked my way down the filthy street of six houses. This was what Master Glaucus had not allowed me to see in Kokkinades.

The first house was empty. The second contained a dead woman clutching a dead child and a man in the last stages of fever. When I dragged him out, hands passed him down the alley and I drew the sign on the door, breathing the parting prayer to Thanatos, my protector. All in the third house were dead; a woman and three children. I marked the door with a chalk circle. The fourth house contained a recovering woman and her new-born. She was carried out, weeping about shame, since Achaean women who had given birth were strictly forbidden to leave their houses until ten days had passed and the proper cleansing had taken place. I told her that Asclepius would explain to Zeus. The fifth hovel also had no life inside. I was not sickened by the dead—they were gone. What remains is only a shell, a plaster image of someone once beloved. My master need not have kept me apart from them.

When I came to the sixth house I found three dead men and a girl, crouched in the corner, her face blank with shock. The men in this house had not died of the plague. Two had been poisoned and the one lying across the girl's legs had been stabbed. She still had the dagger in her hand.

I crouched next to the girl. She was very young, perhaps younger than me. I heaved aside the corpse and took the knife out of her fingers.

'I am Chryse the healer priest,' I said gently. 'What is your name?'

'Elis,' she faltered. 'They came to rape me. This is a street where whores live, but I am not one of them. They came to drink my mother's wine, for we have no protector. My mother... where...'

'Hush, we will find her.' I hoped that she was not the dark-haired woman in the filthy house. 'Now, are you hurt?'

'No, they did not...they did not have time. I put it in the wine.'

'Yes, what did you put in the wine? That was quick thinking.' I have often found that shocked people will recover better if they have to think about something else. The girl's eyes were dilated black and I was worried that she might have taken poison herself.

'Hecate's leaf,' she said mechanically. 'The lord will exile me and the men of the city will rape me; then they will stone me and I will die!' Her voice rose to a wail. 'Aie! Aie!' Her hands clenched and she began to beat her breast and tear her hair.

'Drink this and do not lament yet,' I urged. I could see what had happened. I could also see the bruises forming on her thighs and arms, and the swollen face. Such a small creature, did they need to beat her in order to rape her? If they had approached her with kind words and presents, they might have had what they wanted without any coercion. But here into this poor and dirty place, they had to come swaggering. They had pinned her like prey in their god-like power and beat her when she dared to protest. Such heroes, to rob a poor maiden of her only pos-session. Such deservedly dead heroes.

I heard my master calling me and said to the men outside the door, 'Carry these out, they are dead, and I will bring the maiden.' They dragged the bodies into the alley and then to the wall, where they threw them over for slaves to pile and burn later.

'You will be silent about this deed,' I said to Elis. 'And I will be silent as well. You did rightly, daughter of Mycenae. If you survive this plague and wish for cleansing, go up into the city to the temple of Hera and there open your heart to the goddess. She is a woman and the guardian of families. She will forgive you. Go, there are other women who are dying. Go to them and help them.'

She went where I pushed her and I came to my master's side.

'The plague-struck must be carried out of the city, before this spreads. They must have clean air. Chryse, establish a camp uphill from Mycenae and see if the goatherds know where there is water. You know the treatment. Now, where is our Trojan friend? I must wash and then I must speak to Agamemnon, Lord of Men.'

Eumides the free man brought water and washed my master down, draped him in his healer's gown, and then said diffidently, 'Can I help you, Chryse?'

'Yes, run and get all the poppy that we have, bring a jar of honey and a big cauldron and come to the camp. Poppy will stop this plague, if it is what my master thinks it is. Do you know where the nearest spring is?'

'Up there,' he pointed. 'That's where the god Pan found his lady giving birth under a tree. They call it the Spring of the Nymph.'

'Is it pure water?'

'The goats like it.'

This was good news. I escorted the trail of sick people on hastily made litters out of the city. We plodded along, whimpering and groaning, until we came to the flat, high grassy Spring of the Nymph and I tasted the water. It seemed clean and had a pleasant tang of snow.

'Lie down, cursed of Apollo,' I ordered. 'You have been struck down by the god and some of you are dead but those still alive may remain alive. You must pray to Apollo the Archer, Sun God and to Asclepius, Master of Healing.'

The crying decreased until only the newborn wailed. She was affronted about being born at all into this disconcerting world. I took the girl-baby from the mother's arms. The woman seemed to have no fever, so I had her carried to the side and she lay down with a sigh of relief. She did not seem to be bleeding from the birth and as her eyes closed in sleep, she told me that the baby was two days old.

I considered the baby. She was beautiful. I rocked her gently until her screams died away to sobs. A tiny hand gripped my finger, all perfect and complete, with little nails like shells. She snuffled at me, burrowing her round hard head into my chest. Finding no suitable breast, she heaved a resigned sigh and went to sleep.

I sat nursing the child. The suppliants were praying, but I had no prayer to offer, and I could not do anything until Eumides arrived with the cauldron. I could see all the way to the sun. The sky was as blue as lapis lazuli and the rounded shoulders of the hills were green-grey with spinifex and goat-thorn. A gentle breeze wafted the smell of sickness away. The air was clean of men; there was nothing here that they had ever smirched with their dirty fingers.

Elis came to kneel beside me. She was still shocked and white, having found her mother's corpse under the wall, but she had recovered her courage, which must have been considerable.

'There are seven women who are very ill,' she whispered, 'and your slave has come with the medicines, Healer.'

'He isn't a slave,' said Eumides. 'He's a free man and this cauldron is heavy.'

'Elis, help him with building a fire. First the poppy, then we will need hot water to wash them in and some sort of cover. It will be cold tonight.'

'You make the fire and I'll go to the herdsmen,' offered Eumides. 'They will have skins and they may have tents if we can pay them.'

'Tell them that Apollo will pay,' I said, meaning the temple. I knew what my master was doing. He was announcing to Agamemnon that the god Apollo had cursed his city, the looted temple being evidence of the city's blasphemy and the plague being proof of the god's displeasure. I knew that the temple would be refurbished and new priests found, and that woven blankets and such food as was to be found in the city would be on the way up the hill, along with whoever else had caught this plague.

Apollo has several plagues at his disposal. One is this dreadful and sudden one, from which no one recovers if untreated. It is as though the insides turn to liquid, so that the victim desiccates fast—in a few days it can reduce a strong man to a skeleton whom his family cannot recognise. I believe that the Egyptians use some caustic purge to clean out a corpse before mummifying it; they call this fever after it, the sarcophagi disease. We call it purging fever. This is the worst of Apollo's arrows.

The second we call the ague. It arises out of swamps and mists. It gives fevers that either kill or return at times for the rest of the sufferer's life. It also makes corkscrews out of the bones and twists fingers into useless knots.

The third brings sneezing and coughing and a high but intermittent fever. Cities especially are prone to this plague in winter. It kills only the old, the sick, and very young children, and there are various herbs which will mollify the heat of the fever. We call it the chill or snow fever.

Apollo is not a god to be insulted lightly.

Elis and I made the fire and melted the honey and poppy. I had just administered a dose to the last patient when men came from the city bearing torches and blankets. They brought fifteen further sufferers who had to be bedded on the grass. It was getting dark when Eumides and his goatherds had erected tents and we had everyone tucked in for the night.

We sat by the fire—the goatherds, Eumides, and me—to eat white cheese, flat bread, and grapes. I took a swallow of hot milk and wine, a drink new to me, and listened as they began to tell stories of their patron, Pan the Ageless, Unborn, Forest Master, Lord of Goats, Titan, Oldest of the Gods.

'This spring,' said the oldest man, a bent grandfather with a face like carved wood, 'is the Nymph's Spring. This was a dry land, this Argos, dry as a desert. Nothing grew here and no one lived here. A pregnant nymph and her husband who were travelling were attacked by bandits just over there,' he pointed to the road, beyond the ring of firelight, 'and the husband was killed. The nymph ran until she fell under this tree. She prayed to the gods of this place, whoever they were, to save the child. Then she swooned, poor maid. When she woke she was bedded with goats, sheltered under their fleece and healed by their warm breath. Goat-God Pan, Lord of Woods and Darkness, had found her and sent his flock. Her babe was born and at her breast; they say she had slept for days. She accepted the god when he revealed himself later—who could refuse Pan, Goat-Foot, Satyr-Lord, the lecherous and joyful? They drank wine here and she stayed until she died an old woman. But it was too dry here for women and goats, so Pan struck this place with his olive-staff and water sprang up. If it was not for the fountains of Pan our Master, there would be no men in Agamemnon's great city.'

They passed the cup around again. I had grown up with men like these.

'I herded goats,' I said, and they laughed. 'Yes,' I insisted, 'I lay in the grass all day and chewed thyme and watched the clouds and thought each sun's journey as long as years. Give me your pipe, Master, and I will show you.'

The old man gave me a shepherd's pipe. It had been a long time since I had played one, but I lifted it to my lips and blew gently down. Music, sweet and breathy. I managed to remember all the calling tunes for the goats and the one I had learned from an old man in my village. At that they sat up.

'Where did you learn that, asclepid?' demanded the old man.

'Pithias, the goatherd who came to the market at Irion,' I said remembering him well, old and gnarled like these herd masters.

'He taught me that tune and another which I cannot recall, and to use honey and verbena for bearing staggers.'

Heads nodded around the circle. 'He was a wise man, your Pithias,' they agreed. 'That is a calling tune, but it is not for a goat—no, not a goat.'

'What, then?'

'For the god of goats,' the oldest man whispered. 'It is a secret.'

'I will keep it,' I vowed. I went to sleep eventually, with the sound of the pipes in my ears, leaning on Eumides' warm bare shoulder.

Chapter Thirteen

Cassandra

I was summoned from Dion's embrace by the elegant Apollo Priest, who came in the middle of the afternoon and told me to wait upon the god at noon the next day. Noon was the sun's highest point and the azimuth of Apollo's power. Mysion seemed distant with me, not pleasant as he had been, but I could not tell in what manner I had offended. It was cold and I had only a light tunic on. I ran back to Dion's bed on rapidly freezing feet and dived into his arms.

'You have done nothing to offend Apollo Priest,' he soothed, taking my cold ankles into his warm hands and defrosting my toes. 'You worry too much, Cassandra, my bright lady. Naturally he is not going to approve of me. There is a new god in the city of Tros and that will unbalance the powers until they get used to it.'

My Dion had acquired a sophisticated taste for politics which I had not anticipated. He was not a simple fisherman any more. He was, however, still gentle and comforting. I leaned back onto his shoulder and pulled at a tress of his kelp-brown hair. He smelt of the sea, tempered with scented oil from Lemnos which had been levied from an Argive ship as tax for passing the Pillars of Heracles. Priam, as an act of devotion to the God of the Sea, had given three months' tolls to the newly erected Temple of

Poseidon. I turned to find his mouth and kissed him. He was after all, Apollo's gift to me, his favoured maiden.

At noon the next day I walked with Perseis to the temple. She was pleased with me, although I had learned no craft. It appeared that she had come from fisherfolk herself and the lack of the Blue-Haired One in Troy had always bothered her.

'Cassandra, you are blooming like a flower,' she said. It was true. My breasts had grown full, my waist slender, my hair long and curly and golden. In the silver mirror my face had rounded and grown beautiful, even to me. 'Dion Poseidon Priest has cherished you. Do you still have bad dreams?'

'No, not at all.' It had been months since I had seen the sea covered in black ships. 'No, I sleep well.'

'There is nothing like a young man to improve a maiden's sleep,' she agreed with a quirk to her mouth. 'Now, here we are, and I will wait for you.'

I went confidently into the temple and knelt before the altar. The golden suns on the walls blazed with the glow and silence of noon.

Then the light struck me. I fell down. There was a roaring in my ears, stronger than a million bees. The voice of the god came, like the striking of bells, and I felt my body quiver. I clawed for support; Eleni's mind was shuttered and I could never reach Dion. A weight pinned me flat and supine under the god.

'Cassandra,' snarled the voice, golden and dangerous as a lion, 'you betrayed me!'

'Never!' I gasped under what felt like paving stones. 'Lord Apollo, ver!'

'I gave you a lover, faithless woman, I gave you Dion, my beloved, for your joy. I lay with you in love. I gave you prophecy, daughter of Priam. All these things I gave you, woman of Troy.'

'Yes!' my spine felt as if it would crack. 'Yes, Lord, you gave me love and great gifts and I am grateful!'

'Traitor,' roared Apollo. Now the weight on me was hot and animal, a beast's weight. Taloned paws held me down, stabbed through thigh and breast. I think I screamed in pain and astonishment. 'You brought my rival Poseidon back into Ilium! You let my own beloved Dion become a priest of Earth-Shaker!'

Teeth closed on my throat. The magnitude of my folly choked me. The jaw shut. I was shaken and dragged by the predator.

Then something opened my lips and the beast's tongue, rank with carrion, licked into my mouth.

'I cannot retrieve my gifts,' the voice blazed, 'but I can make them useless, despised and disgraced of Apollo. You shall never be believed again. You shall know, and you shall hear, and you shall see the fates of all and you will not speak them, Cassandra,' the voice dropped to a hissing purr like smith's charcoal. 'Never until the city falls and you are captive of the Argives will you prophesy again.'

Then he was gone. I felt my body spasm so hard that I thought that my bones would break. I fell into blackness.

I woke with Tithone beside me. I was lying on the stones of the temple steps, where someone had dropped me. The taste in my mouth was so foul that I retched repeatedly.

'I heard,' she said grimly. 'You can walk. Get up.' She seemed very angry. I stumbled to my feet and followed her to her house in the lower city.

'Now,' she said, sitting me down and applying a wound-herb compress to the worst of the bites, 'drink some wine and I will tend to you, daughter of Priam.'

'He said…' I began to weep, 'the god said…'

'Gods!' snorted Tithone. 'Keep still. This jealous god has nearly bitten out your throat.'

The wounds were not deep but they began to hurt. I shut my jaws and tried not to cry out. Tithone was stiff-spined with outrage and I could not bear her displeasure as well as the god's. I put a hand on her arm.

'Don't be angry with me,' I pleaded. 'I can't endure it, Lady.'

'Angry with you? By all the gods excluding one, I am not angry with *you*. I am angry with Apollo. Take back his gift, indeed,' she snorted. 'The Mother gave you that gift, daughter of Priam, not the Sun God. And back to the Mother you will go as soon as I can patch you up enough to walk further without bleeding to death. Mother Gaia is older than any Sun God, older and wiser. The gods ought to behave better than men, Cassandra, but they don't.'

'What should I have done?' I whispered. 'The boat was about to be crushed and we would all have been killed. Me and Maeles and Ethipi and the wise-eyed boat and Dion…It is no use calling for Apollo at sea.'

'I can't for the life of me think of what else you could have done, Cassandra, but that will make no difference to this jealous boy of a god. When Perseis came to fetch me it was known what had happened; the cat-foot priest heard it all. Just when we might need a prophecy, too,' she added in an undertone, 'he has to cripple the pre-eminent seer in Troy. Do not despair, Cassandra. You are not the beloved of a god anymore, but that is a fate shared by most people. There. Now. What else hurts?'

'There is slime in my mouth…' I bent to the drain and vomited the wine.

Tithone gave me water and began to pound herbs in a mortar. I saw mother's leaf, a dried mushroom, and sage beaten into a pulp with salt.

'Scrub your mouth out with this,' she ordered. 'Don't swallow.'

I did as she ordered. My mouth felt numb but the dreadful rotten savour was gone.

'Good. I thought so. The Mother is more powerful,' she said with satisfaction. 'Now you may drink this,' it was a strong infusion of wine, valerian, and all-heal, 'and then you will come with me. The Mother will guard you, my golden daughter. I never did approve of this fashion for male gods,' she added, ushering me out of her house and along the lane. 'Men are not reliable, useful though they may be for certain purposes.' She was still too angry to grin. 'Come along, daughter.'

The force of her personality impelled me along the streets. People who saw me went in and closed their doors. I was hurt by this. Tithone noticed and the next time it happened made such a frightful sign in the air that I wondered that the door did not shatter. I had not previously known that she was a priestess of Hecate Destroyer as well as of Gaia, the nurturing mother.

I was inside the temple and kneeling at the feet of the Pallathi before I was prepared. I had no prayer ready. I was shaking and in pain and all I could think of was to cry, 'I couldn't help it! Mother, have mercy on me!'

I heard nothing from the goddess, but what I saw was the city in flames, beloved Ilium burning. When I tried to speak, my tongue clove to the roof of my mouth and I convulsed. I rolled to the feet of the Pallathi and heard Tithone and another woman conversing over my body. I wondered if I was dead.

'So that is what he has done,' said the Mother's priestess. 'Petty, cruel, and self-involved, that is a male god, except for our Lord Dionysius, of course.'

'Petty and cruel beyond belief, but will she survive it? She has lost her twin and now is likely to lose her reason. I would not have my own dear daughter die on a god's whim.' Tithone spat with fury, like Státhi when someone planted an armoured sandal on his tail.

'We will all die one day,' said the older voice, 'but not yet. She is strong, this daughter of Gaia. She will live. Come, we can lift her.'

'I can hear you!' I tried to cry. I heard my own throat issue a croaking hoise like a marsh frog.

I was lifted and laid in the sanctuary.

◇◇◇

Later that day Perseis came to take me back to the Temple of the Maidens. She was sorry for me, as were my companions. Even Cycne did not comment on the tooth-marks on my throat. They brought me watered wine and talked soothingly of the preparations for Hector's marriage feast, of strange tales and stories brought back by the sea-captains about Achaea and Thrace. Finally I slept.

I was careful of myself for the next seven days, moving as though I was made of terracotta, untrusting of everything, unwilling to speak. I found my voice again with great trepidation.

'They say that the most beautiful woman in the world is now princess of Sparta,' observed Eirene. 'Her name is Elene and her father was the Achaean Father God Zeus.'

'Cloud-Compeller, Master of Storms,' I murmured, finding that I could speak the names of gods without my tongue twisting. We were lying in the cool green water. I had anchored myself to the edge by one toe and was floating. My hair spread around me like a nymph's. I could feel the drag as I turned my head. No one commented on the fact that I had spoken at last, but I felt their attention.

'Her mother was Leda, seduced by the god in the shape of a swan,' scoffed Andromache. 'Beast gods. I do not like the gods of the Argives.'

'They are powerful, nonetheless. Why shouldn't a god be in the form of an animal? Angry Apollo came to Cassandra as a lion,' said Cycne. 'Glug,' she commented as Polyxena dived, grabbed her by the ankles and dragged her under.

'Have you seen Andromache's tunic and cloak for the wedding? Purple of the finest spinning and the gown is of Egyptian gauze. And Hector has sent jewels,' said Eirene quickly. 'There is no need to drown her, Polyxena. Even barbarians learn tact eventually.'

'Not this barbarian,' said Cycne ruefully, wiping her hair out of her eyes. 'Sorry, Cassandra. Tell us about Dion,' she added, compounding her offence. 'Does he still please you? I lay with a fisherman once, but he was rough and hasty and I did not go back to him. Besides, I would not risk the docks,' she shuddered. 'I will not be a slave again.'

'I have not seen him,' I said carefully, waiting for another attack. 'He comes every day to call for me but I have not…I have not dared.'

'We will go to the Temple of Poseidon tomorrow,' announced Perseis. 'Come, maidens, we must send our sister Andromache to her husband with splendour. Cycne, are the wedding pots glazed yet?'

'Yes, Lady, with crimson and saffron flowers, they need another coat of glaze and then will be fired again. They are the best things I have ever made,' said Cycne, climbing out of the pool and wringing her hair into a rope.

'Eirene, how goes the spinning?'

'It is finished and the weavers are working on it now. I think that there will be enough cloth for five chitons. Polyxena has made a fast rose and a very pretty green,' said Eirene, hugging my little sister. 'And Iris had nearly completed the gold brooch; she is looking for the perfect pearl.'

'Good. Cassandra will fill the cosmetic bag when Aia has finished decorating it and Oenone has made rush baskets for the gifts. The wedding is only five days away, daughters of Priam. We must be as industrious as the bees of the Mother. Now, tomorrow we are going, as I said, to Poseidon. You will consider a suitable offering to welcome back our Exiled God. He likes anything blue or green, but if you can't think of anything else a gift of sea shells will do. Cassandra, I believe that you have your perfume to distil.'

'Yes, Lady,' I dragged myself out to the green water. I was feeling better in the undemanding company of my sisters. I had found out my limits. I could not speak a prophecy. I could try, but then I would spasm and choke and no words could be understood. Apollo my god was revealed as a vicious, jealous child and I was crippled. More of me had gone; I felt that only a thin slice remained of the happy Cassandra who had been Eleni's twin and Apollo's favourite.

But with that sliver I was still myself.

I spent the afternoon peacefully distilling the five essences— hawthorn, myrrh, pine, hyacinth, and jasmine—into a perfume of great sweetness for my sister Andromache's marriage to my brother Hector.

I had reason for loving Hector more than ever. He had come to the Palace of the Maidens three days earlier and spoken for a long time to Perseis. Then he had called me and we had walked into the city together.

Although I had grown, my brother Hector was still huge. When I curled a finger into his belt, his arm came around my shoulders and held me close. He said, looking down through the golden beard, 'Now, little sister, I believe that you cannot speak at the moment, but Perseis and Tithone the healer think that this will pass. However, the Lady of Maidens also says that you lack a craft other than healing and I thought I might give you one.'

I could not, or dared not, speak or I would have protested. Hector looked into my eyes and said, 'I will teach you to write, Cassandra. I need a scribe. Now we are going to the guard's house above the city and I will show you how it is arranged.'

Státhi leapt up onto the wall when we reached it. He was always at risk of being stepped on when he kept to the ground, for he did not deign to avoid the feet of mere men. His progress through a crowd was always marked with people hopping and swearing as they were scratched. When he was particularly affronted with humans, he rode on Hector's shoulder, hooking his claws into the warrior's harness. Hardened Phoenician traders had made very advantageous bargains for Troy when confronted with Hector's grey eyes and Státhi's green ones disconcertingly on a level.

'This is my sister Cassandra, Priam's daughter,' said Hector to the guard as we came into the tower above the Scamander Gate. 'She will be my scribe. You will guard her and protect her and her orders are mine.'

There were four men in the tower. I found out later that there are always four men in the Scamander tower. They scanned me briefly, said, 'As the commander orders,' to Hector and returned to looking out over the city and the plain.

'Here, Cassandra, is papyrus and here is ink—do you remember when you spilled it over Pariki's head?' I smiled at the recollection, but did not dare to speak. He sighed. 'Yes. Well, you must listen carefully. Every word has a sound of its own, but it is made up of other sounds which also occur in other words. Consider. This is your name. Ca-sa-nd-ra.' He made four marks on the papyrus. 'And this is mine. He-ct-or.' Three marks. 'If we write the "sa" in Cassandra like this,' he repeated a mark, 'and the "nd" like this, what is the word?'

He had forgotten that I was mute and he was trying with such kindness and patience to help me. I risked the wrath of Apollo. I made a great effort and croaked 'Sand.'

'Good!' he took my hand and pressed it. 'Good. Now, if those three marks are Hector and this one is "ro," what is this word?'

'Hero.' It seemed exceptionally simple. My brother Hector, however, was impressed. He gathered me in his armoured bosom and hugged out all my breath. Hector was never really aware of how strong he was.

'Cassandra, you are a remarkable girl. I have tried to teach that simple set of facts to men who are considered wise and they could not learn it. I will write out the whole syllabry and you can learn it. After that you can copy the signs until the stylus moves easily in your hand and then—why, then, little sister, you will be Hector's scribe. Would that please you?'

I threw myself at him and wrapped both arms around his neck. 'Oh, Hector,' I whispered, 'I would love to be Hector's scribe.'

◇◇◇

The art of writing did not take much effort to learn, though my brother was right. When I exhibited the mystery to the other girls they went blank and could not understand what I was doing. I was too frightened of the wrath of the jealous god to talk much to them anyway.

We went to the Temple of the Blue-Haired One in the morning. It was still cold and I wore two tunics and a cloak. We had brought blue cloth, a green dish painted with fish, and a wooden model of a shop made out of driftwood which Iris had worked on for a month, not knowing (or perhaps foreknowing) that the Sea God would return to Troy. I had nothing but a handful of interesting pebbles, polished by the waves.

Maeles greeted us. It was a small temple, warmed by a fire of salt-soaked timbers which burned with blue and green sparks. We knelt next to the Exiled God and prayed for protection for our city from storm and for our ships from wreck. I felt no presence of any god and I was thankful that no visions came to offend my eyes, knot my tongue, and turn my wits.

Through the temple the sea-wind blew, smelling of weed and salt, and the flames flickered. The ocean pulsed like a heartbeat.

We were leaving when Dion, in his sea-coloured robes, intercepted me at the door. I was afraid of him, as I was afraid of everything since the god had cursed me. He put out his hard hand, cupping my cheek in the gesture that my lost Eleni had used, and I froze. I looked for Perseis and the maidens but they had tactfully withdrawn. I was deserted.

I was abandoned with my own lover in the temple of the god I had brought back into the city. Nevertheless I was trembling and dared not speak.

'Come,' he said gently, and I followed him to kneel down before the altar. 'Apollo has rejected us,' he said as his mouth came down on mine, 'but Poseidon the Powerful has accepted us.'

'No,' I pushed him away. 'Dion, I am afraid!'

'You must trust me,' he said, stroking me with hands that could control a wilful sail or a straying oar. 'You need me, Cassandra my bright Lady, and I need you, and Poseidon needs us and will shelter us. You need only accept.'

'No!' I jerked out of his embrace and sprang to my feet. 'Accept? Accept? All my life I have accepted. I accepted the Lady and she robbed me of my twin, closer than you could ever be, close in my mind, half of myself. He is gone—Ishtar decided that she wanted Eleni and stole him by a vision, so that he loves one he cannot have and has shut his heart to me, his own sister, his twin!'

I could hear my voice rise to a shriek. 'Then I accepted the Lord Dionysius and the stranger with the blue bead violated me and hurt me, intruding into my body. The Lord Apollo gave me you, then stole my tongue because I offended him in saving your life! We are only chess pieces to the gods, they care nothing for us, we are puppets, wooden dolls with no hearts to break, no wounds that bleed. I will not accept. No more. I will accept nothing!'

I screamed at him and all the gods in anger and loathing. Dion was watching me. I turned to run out of the temple but found myself facing him. I raised my arm to strike. He did not turn his face away, but gazed at me with pity and love. He was beautiful; the long curly hair, the kelp-brown eyes, the curve of the as-yet-unshaven jaw, the straight line of the red mouth. I could not sustain my fury and it melted away. I was spent and unsteady on my feet; I felt him carry me to his bed and the warmth as he lay down beside me.

The fingers walked up my hip, delicately, as they had in the temple. I shuddered and pushed the spidery caress away. Dion did not retreat. His hand moved palm down between my thighs, sliding across the pearl, then his mouth sucked hard at the nipples. I grabbed a handful of his hair and clasped the head to my breast, hoping for some strong sensation to fill the agonising hollow in my soul. The slipping fingers were wet now; they made a soft sucking sound. My grasp found the phallus.

I lay as I had never lain since the stranger and it was Dion in my arms. The first thrust hurt, but I thrust back until he was deep in the clutch of my womb, deeper than the god or the stranger, stronger than the sea.

Anger fuelled me; my wave peaked and crashed and peaked again while the sea throbbed in my blood and the Priest of Poseidon thudded between my thighs like the Bull from the Sea.

I lost time. The rhythm was oceanic and there was nothing in the world but the mask of his face and the weight of his body and the phallus moving, sliding, between strangers salty with sweat.

As I felt his seed fountain in my womb, I screamed like a gull in desperate loss and triumph.

◇◇◇

'Tithone—she's one of yours, Demeter. How dare she speak of Apollo so disdainfully? Do you allow your priestesses to blaspheme the Archer, Lord of the Sun, old woman?'

'You have hurt her pupil, closer than daughter,' said the Earth Mother slowly. 'She speaks as she finds. And so do I. Vain and vicious, that is the new rule of these young gods.'

'Old woman, you do not dare to speak so to me! I have given great gifts to men. Medicine and knowledge, herbs to heal and wound, and letters to carve their glories into the walls of their stone cities.'

'And you have taken great worth from them. You strike them with plagues, you snuff the stench of their suffering, you drink in their screams. It is not their own glory you would have them write, but your own.'

'Earth Mother,' Apollo lifted his bow and laid an arrow on the string, 'I will end your blasphemy.'

'Sun God,' Demeter drew her flowery robe about her and laughed, 'you cannot kill me. I am the Earth. I am the force that hammers a fragile grass blade through hard-packed brick. Your temples are stone, Archer; mine are the mountains and the valleys, the streams that thread the flesh of the earth like veins. You breathe the stench of burning flesh; I smell flowers and fruit and wheatfields golden with grain. Princeling, you flatter yourself. No man and no god can destroy me. I was here with my brother, Pan the Ageless, before you Children of Chronos came to vex my peaceful world; and I will be here after you have gone, after the men you tortured have quite forgotten you, and the temples you had them build are worn stones scattered in the grass.'

The arrow left the string, aimed with immortal precision. It flew towards the unprotected breast of Demeter, struck, and sank.

Demeter smiled, opening the robe to reveal milk-heavy breasts unmarked by the passage of the dart. Apollo threw down his bow.

Aphrodite caressed the golden apple and laughed.

Chapter Fourteen

Diomenes

The pestilence took three weeks to pass. All that time I remained on the mountain. I had persuaded my master to leave the plague to me and anyway, I did not want to enter the city of Mycenae again. Ten of my patients died. For a panicky couple of days I thought that they all would die.

Eumides the free man stayed with me. He showed a deft hand with the turning and carrying and no sign of disgust at the cleansing of the sick. On the sixth day, when I felt that I would lose them all, he sat with me as a woman died.

The only mercy showed by the god Apollo in the purging fever is that the dying slip away. Once the moisture is all gone from the body, they are not in pain and they are corpses a day or so before the soul finally departs. This woman had been a big, heavy market trader, whose boast was that she could carry ten flat baskets on her head; now she was so light that the breeze could have blown her away. Her hand did not clasp mine, her fingers were slack, and her breathing barely puffed out the cracked lips. Only her hair was still human, a rich brown, flowing down over the stained chiton. I did not have enough spare clothes to replace the robes of the ones who were going to die.

'Drink this,' Eumides put a wooden cup of broth into my hand, taking my place. 'Does she know that we are here, Asclepid?'

'I don't know. She might. There is nothing else I can do for her.' I sipped at the soup, which was hot and savoury with healing herbs. 'My master says that if all we can do is to sit and watch them die then at least we can do that.' I was so tired that my eyes were closing against my will and so tense that my neck ached.

While he held the woman's hand, she died.

I found myself crying. Eumides helped me to my feet, steadying me in his embrace, and led me to our tent. It was noon and hot inside the goat-smelling darkness. Inexplicable revulsion shoved me away from it.

'No,' I said. 'I cannot go inside.'

'Come up the mountain, then,' he said, putting down my cup and catching up a wine-flask on a thong. 'Elis, we are going higher up,' he called, and she nodded. The once-frightened man-slaying girl had been careful, attentive, and responsible. All evidence of her killing had been burned on the pyre still smouldering below the city. She had not mentioned the incident again and I had promised to be silent. By the time she got back to Mycenae she would be one deserving of the reward which the Lord of Men had offered to those willing to tend the sick. The suppliants trusted her, believing in her virtue; only one protected by the gods would come and voluntarily tend the plague-stricken. It was a pity that her mother was dead, but she grieved quietly, if she grieved at all. I could leave her with them for an hour.

Eumides led me, then when I stumbled he carried me up the steep path. He laid me down on the sharp-scented mountain herbage and sat behind me.

My head was on his chest in the shade of an olive tree, my body began to soak up the sun through my tunic. Eumides' strong fingers began to massage my back and neck. I felt the twang as my jaw unlocked under the clever pressure.

'They are all going to die,' I murmured. 'I have failed, failed utterly.'

'But you are not afraid of death, Chryse,' he answered. 'You have knotted your shoulders like old leather straps. Turn a little to the sun. There. You are not afraid?'

'I'm not, but they are. They are depending on me to save them, I can see it in their eyes, and I can't.' I began to cry again. 'Is there to be no life left in the world?' I said. Strong arms were supporting me. I had been so long without sleep that I was seeing spots in front of my eyes and my body was chilled and fevered by turns. Eumides held me close. Then he kissed me and I slumped forward into his warmth, hungry for life and the pulse of breath.

We were making love before I realised what was happening. His touch was soothing, his mouth sweet, and I thought momentarily of how I must stink, how kind it was of him to comfort me when I smelt of death-sweat and sickness. He was sure and practised, and forgave my clumsiness when I tried to please him. Healer's fingers are trained to be deft and my ability had not entirely deserted me, even though I was tired enough to welcome the return of the black angel. I have always loved to give pleasure. I felt him gasp, his mouth on mine, his inner lip as smooth as wet silk, and I smelt wormwood.

The sun shone like a metal shield in the sky. His mouth was sliding down my chest, the dirty tunic cast aside. I lay naked, encompassed in the scent of rue and sage bruised by our weight. I had been cold, now I burned. I felt my whole body spasm as he found the phallus and when I reached a climax I felt that all my despair and pain had been sucked out of me.

I clung to Eumides, overwhelmed with gratitude. Then I fell asleep as if I had been stunned by a percussive herb of the fourth power.

I woke to a feeling of immense safety. I was lying on his chest, his back against the sacred tree. He had watched over me for three hours, until the sun left his throne and it began to get cold. At some time he had gone down to the camp to fetch me water to wash in and a clean tunic. We were both still naked, wrapped in my healer's cloak, purple and gold, woven of the finest wool.

'Eumides,' I said, jerking awake then relaxing into his warmth. 'Eumides.'

'Chryse,' he murmured. 'It is time to wake. I would love to lie with you all day and night but I can't. We'll freeze.'

'Yes. All right.' I struggled to my feet, feeling more alive than I had since coming to Mycenae of the golden walls. 'Thank you, Trojan. That was a great gift.'

He took my hand and kissed me gently. 'Love is the gift of a free man,' he said, and we washed and dressed and went down the hill to the patients.

No one else had died. No one else did die. The pyre burned itself out. I escorted the survivors back to the city. Master Glaucus told me not to enter Mycenae but to await him at the gate, under the lions. A crowd of women were there as we paced up the path, with offerings for the favoured of the gods who had survived Apollo's arrows. A tall, commanding woman in a gold chiton and crimson cloak caught and fixed me in my place. She had black hair tumbling to her waist, a smooth and olive-coloured complexion and an eye that could have opened seashells. Her daughters stood behind her; I could not see them well, but among them was Elene, hidden under a grey veil. The tall woman had a basket of bread and the daughters had wine and coins to distribute to the suppliants.

'Apollo's temple has been repainted,' observed Eumides. 'They say that the altar is gilded, now. It must have cost Agamemnon several fortunes.'

'Who is that woman?' I asked, fascinated by the basilisk gaze which seemed to contain concentrated horror and despair. She lived with bitter hatred burning out her guts. I could not look away from her regard.

'Ah, that is the queen. Clytemnestra, she is called. Behind her is Iphigenia and Electra. They are beautiful, but more lovely is the girl under the veil who hides from men's eyes.'

'Yes,' I agreed, trying not to think of Elene. 'I fear that queen dislikes me but her life cannot have made her trusting of men. Thank all the gods, here is the master.'

Master Glaucus walked out through the crowd, which parted to allow him passage. He counted the patients as they filed past him.

'You have done well,' he said to me gravely. 'You are now a healer and shall be confirmed at the Temple of Asclepius. Now, leave your patients. We are going to Corinth.'

I saw that he held the reins of Pyla and Banthos. With them was a slave and two other horses, the big raw-boned grey which only Arion could ride and a smaller rather nervous gelding the Mycenae double-axe brand.

'This is Agamemnon's reward for the Trojan Eumides' care of the sick,' he said, giving the rein into the ex-slave's grasp. 'I have had all our belongings packed and we need only mount and ride. Straight to Corinth, I think; perhaps we shall see Argos later. Come,' he added, as Arion paced down the gravel path in his singing robes, 'let us go, if you will, Eumides.'

'With all my heart,' said the Trojan fervently.

I said farewell to Elis. With the reward she would be relatively rich and able to choose a suitable husband. She dropped to the ground and kissed my feet. I was very embarrassed, but raised her, and Master Glaucus gave her a blessing.

Then the saved ones went back into the city. I turned my back on the most beautiful woman in the world and we rode down the path and into the road.

'How far to Corinth?' I called as we picked up speed. It was delightful to be riding again, free on the roads. I saw that Eumides, riding beside me, was weeping and laughing. 'Three years!' he said, coughing, with tears streaming down his face. 'Three years in fetters and now I am free, astride a horse, and on my way home! Thank all the gods!'

'Two days. We shall sleep the night at Klénia or Hiliomodi if the weather turns cold,' said Arion. 'Oh, by the way, asclepid, I have a present for you. I'll give it to you when we stop at noon.'

I teased him about it, but he would tell me nothing, and a bard is not to be pressed too far, especially a bard in possession of a dangerous secret which would make such a good song.

◇◇◇

The Argolid is a flattish, well-watered plain, very easy to ride upon. I swapped the goatherd's tale of Pan with Arion in exchange for the present.

'It is this,' he said, and produced a small package tied with a golden ribbon such as the Argive women wear in their hair. I shook out a veil made of the finest gauze. Burying my face in it, I breathed again the scent of Elene's skin.

'Fold it close and the scent will stay for about a week,' observed the bard. 'She sent it to your master for you when she asked for more poppy syrup.'

'So you did not see her?' I asked, feverishly bundling the precious talisman together and tying it around my neck under the Cyclopes' token.

'No man will see her again if Menelaus can help it. They set out just behind us, Chryse, heading for Sparta, now that the army of suitors has sworn a peace and gone home. Now. That is enough. Have you heard the song I made of the Odyssean peace? I know you haven't because I have just this moment finished it.' He tuned his lyre, glared around to make sure that we were all listening and began to chant

Odysseus of Ithaca, he of the nimble wits,
Sly Odysseus, peace was in his hands,
Spoke thus to the Argives, the high-born captains
We shall have a league…

It was a good song—all his songs were good. I wondered that he had been able to make a peace almost as exciting as a war. He was a bard of immense skill.

◇◇◇

I do not now remember what the village we slept in was called, but it was relatively clean and we refilled our water flasks from the spring. Arion sang a song about it as I drowsed on Eumides' shoulder. Long ago, as the goatherds had said, this was a dry place. Here a nymph out hunting had shot at a satyr by mistake and ran from his justifiable wrath straight into the arms of

Poseidon Blue-Haired, Master of Horses, Earth Shaker. I would
have thought that she might have been better off with the satyr,
Poseidon being the most powerful of gods and rather short
tempered, but he lay with the nymph and was so pleased with
her that as her morning gift he had told her to shoot an arrow
into a rock (presumably the satyr had gone by then). When the
arrow was pulled out a spring gushed forth.

Eumides mumbled something about the truly remarkable
number of nymphs and gods astray on the one small plain. Arion
called him a godless Trojan and I laughed sleepily. I lay that night
in Eumides' arms. He was tender of me and my broken heart.

Corinth seemed small after the great palaces of Mycenae
and Tiryns. We went first to the white stone temple of Apollo
to offer a sacrifice—a lamb out of deference to my memories
of the goatherds—and to explain to the god how we had dealt
with his plague in the city of the golden walls.

Master Glaucus pulled me forward and presented me to
Apollo Sun-Bright. The pained eyes of the statue stared life-
lessly into mine. 'Here is Chryse the Healer, worthy of your son
Asclepius' regard,' he said. 'Accept him and protect him. He is
fearless, tested, and skilled.'

I waited, but no sign came.

We left the temple and wandered into the agora, where we
bought grapes and figs and decided not to purchase fish, because
we were going on to the port of Lechaion the next day to find a
ship for Eumides. There the fish might be a little less way-worn.

'Now, I wonder who that is?' I heard my master mutter. 'An
important person, evidently, but certainly foreign.'

A tall young man was standing at the door of the temple of
Poseidon, leaning against a pillar and surrounded by what was
evidently a trading ship's crew. He had long golden hair which
was confined by a golden fillet, a chiton of rusty red and the belt
and harness of a warrior. He was very well made and handsome
as he stood there in the agora of Corinth and he attracted many
eyes. Arion joined us with Eumides at his shoulder. They had
been talking to shipmasters and had bargained for a passage on

a Kriti ship bound up through the Pillars of Heracles into the Euxine sea, trading in honey and wine.

'The Kriti will skin you in a bargain,' Arion was saying, 'but they keep it once it is made, unlike the Ionians, curse them for pirates. And I speak from experience, Trojan. That is how I got my name, trusting an Ionian. Now who is this superior youth? A prince, by his studied carelessness.'

'A prince indeed,' said Eumides. 'A prince of my own city. That is Alexandratos, called Pariki, a son of Priam and a prince of Troy.'

'You have never told me about him,' I observed.

'There is not much to tell. When he was born there was a curse on him, so they call him city-destroyer. Priam would not have him killed but fostered him with a shepherd—that is an embroidered version of a shepherd's scrip at his immaculate waist. He was accepted back into the court a few years ago. Priam must have sent him trading to Achaea.'

'Do you want to speak to him?' asked my master. Eumides shook his head.

'Not I,' he said hastily. 'He was not liked and I do not want to attract any attention. Pariki never comes to harm himself, but those who accompany him have come to strange fates. I am glad that I am not in his crew.'

I took another look at the languid and beautiful young man with the grey eyes of the god-touched and then followed Eumides to our tavern.

That night, the last night we were to spend together, I turned my head on our shared pillow and said, 'Tell me about Troy.'

'It is a great city, built by Poseidon himself, though he is exiled due to a quarrel between him and Laomendon, the fifth king. It stands on a shallow bay, where the current carrying ships through the Pillars flows in. We levy a toll on such ships. They object to this. What do you want to know?'

'Tell me about the king.'

'I do not know Priam; he is a very old man. I knew Hector, his son, though, a hero, huge as a wall and a great warrior, though gentle enough to children and maids. His sister Cassandra is the most beautiful of the royal daughters, though Andromache runs her close. Cassandra and Eleni, the royal twins. I haven't thought of them in years, Chryse; both golden haired and grey eyed, identical except one is male and one is female. I used to lie in my hut among the fisherfolk and dream of lying with them both at once. That would be wonderful. They must be lovely now. They would be about thirteen or fourteen, I suppose—just the right age. Cassandra and Eleni are God-Possessed; they are prophets, both of them. They share the same mind and heart; they even finish each other's sentences. I remember that they poured a flask of black ink on that same Pariki's head, once. The city laughed for weeks.'

He reached for the wine and poured a cup and we shared it draught for draught.

'I do not want to leave you, Chryse,' he said unexpectedly, in the middle of a highly spiced recitation of the royal twin's exposure of a scandal. 'You are more beautiful than Eleni, Priam's son, and you freed me and gave me back my life. I do not think I would have survived much longer in the kitchens of Mycenae.'

'That is why I freed you,' I said, returning his embrace. 'You have discharged your debt, Eumides. You have nothing to repay. I think that I was pining to death of a broken heart.'

'Elene of Sparta was as fair as the morning,' he began to sing Arion's song under his breath. 'She has possession of your heart, Chryse. Perhaps if she had not, I would not be taking ship on the tide from Lechaion for Troy with a hundred amphorae of Kriti honey. It will take you a long time before you can love again.'

'I will never love again,' I stated. He hugged me and slid a hand along my belly.

'Never is a long day, asclepid,' he said.

◇◇◇

The journey from Lechaion to Epidavros took us three months, for we stopped in every village on the way to repair the temples and restore the oracle of Asclepius. Argos had an outbreak of a stubborn skin itch. When we repassed Mycenae the city was healthy and settling down for a long winter's sleep. We stayed there almost a month, ordering the building of some rudimentary drains and cleansing the lower city. There I saw Elis again. She had joined the Pythiae, the virgin priestesses of Apollo. She seemed happy. She told me that Hera had forgiven her.

I slept every night with my face in Elene's veil and thought that my heart would never truly heal.

◇◇◇

Epidavros was peaceful in the spring sun as we came down the road to the gate. I breathed in the scent of cypress and hyacinth and resolved never to leave it again, for the world was far too painful. I never went with the others to the whores in the village. I was faithful to Elene and to Eumides, who had healed me.

One morning in spring I was applying a hot lychnis poultice to a traveller from the Argive lands. He wanted to talk, to take his mind off the pain of the hot wet cloth and the ulcer underneath. He had traded as far as Egypt and had there picked up an intestinal worm which eats its way out of the body through an ulcer in the leg. I had snared and wound the worm out over a stick; now I was cleansing the sore.

'Great clamour in Sparta,' he commented. 'Are you sure that you got all of the worm?'

'Examine the body if you like; I was very careful. What is happening in Sparta?'

'The princess has been abducted.'

'What, Elene of Sparta?' he winced as I pressed on the poultice.

'Elene, yes, a stranger has taken her. One Pariki, prince of Troy.'

'Nonsense, who could abduct someone out of a palace without waking the guard?' I scoffed.

'Ah, but she went willingly—that's what they are all saying. No one believed for a moment that she liked her husband, though it was her duty to love him.'

I cleansed the small wound carefully and covered the compress with a loose bandage. I doubted that Elene would allow herself to be stolen again, even if she had to kill to prevent it; but she certainly might have run away. And with that very beautiful youth in the rusty-red tunic; well, she had a right to give herself to whomever she pleased.

I loved her still so much that I was not even jealous. I hoped that he would treat her well and strove not to yearn.

◇◇◇

A year later, Arion the bard was visiting my master and said that the heroes of Odysseus' League were preparing for war with Troy. I had heard many songs about war but I had never seen it.

We at Epidavros bound wounds and set bones and repaired the dreadful damage men do to each other in battle. Aren't there enough dangers in the world, without seeking more perils?

I remember when they brought in some injured men from a skirmish between two Mycenaean clans which were in blood feud—the Mycenaeans eat, drink, and breathe war—and I first saw what a sword thrust through the belly can do. It was a young man, perhaps eighteen—I was fifteen myself—and his intestines had been pierced, through all the delicate membranes which hold the organs in place. We are taught to feed such a patient garlic soup, so after an hour a sniff at the wound will tell whether the guts are whole, and the man may live, or they are cut, in which case he will die and no nursing can save him. He was in great pain, groaning, and I could not give him poppy because it delays digestion.

He was sweating, rolling his head on his battle-friend's thigh. A well-made young man with black hair and dark eyes, like most Mycenaeans. His friend was wiping his face with a cloth, holding the hand which groped for comfort. 'Myrses,' he whispered, 'Myrses, my golden one, it will be better soon. Myrses, my dearest friend, my own love, I am here,' and Myrses seemed to hear him and tried not to cry out as I handled him.

I waited the hour and smelt garlic through the wound.

I was not old enough to control my face and the friend knew as soon as he looked at me. But his stroking hand never ceased moving, only hesitated for a second. 'Chryse,' said the older man, his eyes piercing me, 'are you sure?'

'There is something I can try,' I faltered, for they said I had the gift of healing, but I had never tried to consciously invoke it.

'Try,' said the man. 'And I will give you my daughter for wife, my bronze cup, my chariot horse. By my name Palamedes and by all the gods, by Ares and by Zeus, I swear.'

'Not I but the god,' I said ritually. 'Loosen his tunic, I must touch him.'

I knelt next to the bench and saw that Palamedes had unsheathed his bronze knife, sharp as a razor. If I could not cure Myrses, Palamedes his lover would kill him. This is the battle-friend's sworn oath and duty, if there is a wound which cannot be cured. It sometimes takes gut-stabbed men three days to die, always in the greatest agony.

The wound gaped in the young man's belly. The garlic stench flowed from the gap, though there was now not much blood. I laid my palms flat on the wound, covering the *omphalosi*, the navel and centre of all human energy, as Delphi is the omphalosi of the world.

I tried to pray, but I was sickened by the smell composed of blood, fear, sweat, and the oil the Mycenaeans use on their leather. I hesitated and Palamedes' hand gripped my shoulder and shook me gently.

'Have faith, little priest,' he almost grinned, his white teeth showing through his black beard, though tears were running down his face, cutting channels in the dust.

I closed my eyes and called to the god. Thereafter I felt nothing—no sensation of heat or cold and I saw no one and heard no sound. It was as though I, Chryse, had ceased to exist.

The next thing I knew was a man's voice which sounded very loud, demanding in Achaean, 'Palamedes? Where am I?' Someone shoved me and I opened my eyes as I fell. I tried to clamber to my feet but could not manage it. My knees were as stiff as if I had been kneeling for days. Then a rough hand dragged me up and into a close embrace—I felt the bosses on a leather harness dig into my cheek—and someone began to laugh.

Voices called. I was put down dizzy on the bench and realised it was empty. My patient was standing up, turning his bare belly into the light of the oil lamp.

There was an angry red scar, as though he had been healed a week. Palamedes was bellowing, 'A miracle.' The small temple had filled with a press of people and there were a hundred eyes on me. I flinched from their greedy, curious stare. Master Glaucus came and smiled at me. Philostrates of the healing hands was summoned to massage my limbs back to life. My knees were bruised black and I was shivering as though I had been caught in the snows of Parnassus for a week.

When I could stand, Master Glaucus gave me Kriti wine to drink. He asked me so many questions which I could not answer, then conducted us all to the great temple where Myreses the Mycenaean told the assembly of patients and priests what had happened and showed his scar.

I had healed him, through the god, but I went outside as soon as I could and was sick in the bushes next to the temple of Athena Pronaea. I could not eat meat for a month afterwards. They gave me mild and honey to drink and told me that I was a healer. I felt empty and sick. The god's vessel was a poor clay thing, easily smashed and discarded. I felt that I had been used and broken and cast away. I felt violated.

Myrses and Palamedes came later to deliver their offerings. Palamedes told me that I had gone white and still, so still that he feared that I was dead. Myrses had fallen into a light sleep and Palamedes did not want to disturb him so he had sat, supporting his lover, watching, for almost two days.

He said that he had heard the owls of the lady hooting in the cypresses and seen the sunlight arrows of Apollo shooting golden through the open door. Master Glaucus had been called and counselled that I be left alone, a vessel of the god which must not be touched. Palamedes had never left Myrses, although nothing seemed to be happening. He said that he was watching the rise and fall of Myrses' chest when he had seen a bright glow surrounding my hands. Myrses screamed and twisted, crying that someone had filled his guts with burning coals. Palamedes held him fast. Myrses had gripped his lover's hands so hard that there were still bruises there three weeks afterwards.

Myrses said that he had fallen asleep and seen a vision of the god Apollo, who had fired an arrow into his belly, a fire arrow which burned. He said that the sensation of his intestines knitting together was like being crawled over by ten thousand ants. He was worried about me, uneasy in my company, as though I had a gift which set me apart and which I might take back.

'I have brought my daughter,' said Palamedes. 'She is called Chryse, too—Chryseis. Have you any use for a wife, little priest?'

He put my hand into the hand of a girl, perhaps fourteen, a marriageable age. She had hair like chestnut wood but I could not see her eyes. She kept them lowered. Mycenaean maidens are expected to be demure in the presence of men. But her hand felt good in mine, so I kept it. I had not touched a woman in friendship since Elene.

'I have a use for her,' I said, smiling at the big man. 'The gods be with you.'

'And also with you,' Myrses said hastily and left. Palamedes patted his daughter on the shoulder.

'Daughter, I leave you in good hands,' he grinned, kissed me on the cheek, and followed his friend.

'Chryse?' I asked, curiously. She looked at me for the first time. Her eyes were golden, as golden as amber. The small strong hand clenched on mine. She laughed, then covered her mouth.

'Chryse?' she asked, in the same tone. We laughed. Her lips were as sweet as Kriti honey under mine as I kissed her.

Eros does fire arrows randomly though the world. Chryse and I were struck and transfixed on a single shaft.

That is when I changed my name. I became Diomenes again, the name my mother gave me. I am Diomenes the asclepid. A Healer Priest. And I still do not believe in the gods.

Chapter Fifteen

Cassandra

I found out where Eleni had been when I was ill. He was in the Temple of Apollo. He had been confined there since Poseidon Blue-Haired had stilled the wave.

The priests had known what would happen when Dion was made Poseidon Priest and I caused the god to be brought back into Troy. They knew that they had lost me, but they were determined that one of the royal twins should remain Apollo's darling.

Idume, Adonis Priest, told me that they had threatened my twin with divine wrath, had soothed him with food and wine and priestesses of Ishtar, to no avail. He had cried and begged and finally tried to escape from the temple. It was told in the city that I was dying. He wanted to be with me. Finally Apollo's priests had drugged him with hemlock.

He was chained in the shrine. His chains were of gold.

I could not enter the temple of Apollo. I had no god now, except the Mother who guards all women. I bribed Idume with coins and potions to speak to Eleni and tell him that I still loved him.

I tried to reach him with my mind but I could not. Now, more than ever, when we needed to touch, his mind was shuttered, cut off.

The shock of the god's punishment was fading, however. I began to believe that I could live with my twisted tongue.

I was feeling relatively sanguine—my twin had not deserted me after all—and I went for a walk along the harbour. I was leaning on a wall looking out to sea when the man beside me said, 'Look, there's a Thessalian ship,' and pointed, and his hand was all bones—a skeletal hand—and when I looked at his face it was a skull. A death's head was grinning at me, naked, flesh quite gone from the gleaming bones.

'Are you all right, Princess?' said the skull, and I gasped something about the heat and stumbled away.

A market woman gave me a drink of watered wine and I sat in the shade for a moment. Perhaps it had been the sun.

Somehow I did not believe this comforting theory. I had never had a vision like that before. I had seen the past and the future, but never watched someone change in front of me from being alive to being long dead. Was this some new persecution by the god? Was I, perhaps, losing my mind? It was generally thought in the king's council that I was mad, although Hector's trust in me and his stated opinion kept the voices who wished to exclude me down to a mutter.

I looked back but the man had gone. I was secretly pleased that I did not know who he was. If I had just acquired—or been cursed with—the ability to see death, I was in no hurry to perfect it.

◇◇◇

Hector's marriage with Andromache was to be on the day before the Dionysiad began, a propitious time and one in which many people married. I gave bride and groom three days to enjoy one another. During the Feast of Dionysius, it was strictly forbidden to open any door which was shut or pull aside any curtain which was drawn. Maidens, children, and old people stayed indoors, venturing out either side of the noon watch to buy food and transact any absolutely necessary business. Animal-keepers stayed with their charges and women near their time went to lie in Tithone's house in the lower city. For the Three Days of the Dionysiad, Troy was mad.

Perseis, Cycne, Eirene, Iris, and I arrayed Andromache in her wedding finery. She was pale and drew each breath carefully, like a child who has found a wonderful seashell and holds it prayerfully, lest it should shatter in the hand. We turned her around as she was clad, first in the gauze under tunic, then in the cloth-of-gold chiton. Her dark hair was loose and brushed until it shone like burnished bronze. Her sandals were of thrice-treated kid. She wore a wreath made of bay for fidelity, ivy for luxury, spring flowers for beauty, fig-blossom for fertility, and hyssop for health. Perseis dabbed scented oil behind her ears and on her wrists and ankles and navel.

She was solemn as a statue.

'Are you afraid?' asked Cycne, always one to plant a dainty foot right in the middle of thinning ice.

'Afraid?' she gave us a wondering look. 'Afraid? Me? Of Hector?'

We led her up to the palace, with singers all around and dancers leaping. Andromache was as silent and beautiful as the Pallathi herself. She did not smile at the outrageous things the chanters were suggesting, nor did she flinch at the description of Hector as 'the bull,' together with what must have been an exaggerated expectation of his capacity. I have never seen anyone so absolutely, utterly determined and fated as Andromache walking to her wedding with my brother.

We came to the palace doors and they were thrown open. We paraded up the centre of the great hall and came to the thrones, where Andromache knelt beside Hector.

He looked solemn too. He had been dressed in a tunic and cloak of purple of the finest dye and was also crowned with a wreath. His hair flowed like fleece, pale and cloudy. He reached out a hand and Andromache's met it and clasped. To me they seemed perfectly married from that point. I was racked with envy, sick with jealousy, and I hated myself for feeling like that about my dear sister and my dearer brother.

I betook myself and my roiling emotions behind a convenient pillar. There I came nose-to-elbow with a familiar figure. A god-like profile turned, golden hair shifted across a perfectly-moulded shoulder and silvery eyes flashed.

Pariki was back from trading with Sparta. He looked at me and smiled.

'Missing your twin, eh, Cassandra?' he asked with patently false sympathy.

A wave of anger obliterated all base yearnings and I immediately felt better.

'Hector, son of Priam, Cuirass of Troy of the house of Dardanus and Tros, marries Andromache the warrior, daughter of Thebes,' announced my father in his quavering voice. 'This is of their own will and sanctioned by the gods. May they live long and be blessed!'

'Live long and be blessed!' the company cried. Priam filled a cup with wine and gave a mouthful each to Andromache and to Hector. Then he and Hecube the Queen drank the rest and flung the cup to smash against the wall.

Priam was old and his aim was not good. The cup flew wide, breaking against the pillar next to which Pariki and I stood. This was a very bad omen. The crowd murmured. But before the effect could deepen, Hecube cried, 'Feast and rejoice!' and servers filled cups and thrust forward tables on which honey cakes, bean cakes, and gluey confections were heaped.

I had sighted Eleni with the priests of Apollo but I did not approach him. Sorrow deeper than death was gnawing at me, souring the sweetness of the cake I was eating.

Pariki walked gracefully to the front of the hall, followed by a sailor bearing a cage in which something grey lay still. I followed him, drearily sure that there was not going to be anything amusing in this gathering for one cursed of Apollo, and terrified that I would be presented with a vision.

'Brother,' he said to Hector, 'I rejoice in your wedding and I have brought you a present from Egypt.'

He gestured to the crewman, who laid the cage on the floor and drew out a limp furry thing with trailing legs and tail. Hector cupped it in his hands, then put it to his face and breathed gently on it. I saw one ear come up and the little ribcage heave.

'Cassandra,' said Hector, 'bring me warm goat's milk and hurry.'

I was so pleased and honoured by his relying on me that I ran straight out of the hall and chivvied a kitchen hand into warming me a pipkin of milk while she was doing three other things at once and yelling at the boy who turned the spit.

'If it is for the Lord Hector then I will do it,' she declared, 'though what he wants with milk at a wedding I cannot guess. There, now get out of my kitchen, Princess,' and I sped back.

The limp fur was reviving a little in the warmth of Hector's huge hands. He took the milk and began to feed it, drop by drop, to the creature. It put out a little pink tongue and I realised that it was a Státhi, a tiny one, with a black nose and wet silver whiskers. When it was full of milk, Andromache took it from her husband's hands and laid it in her breast, tightening the ceinture to hold its negligible weight. It mewed a little and Státhi himself rose majestically from his seat at the table to sniff at it. He then sat down on Andromache's lap, a thing he had never done before, and began to purr. Andromache bore up under the weight and seemed conscious of the honour.

'I thank you, brother,' said Hector politely, rising to his feet to embrace Pariki. 'You must have travelled far to find another such as Státhi. He will be grateful, too.'

'Travelled far? Yes, indeed,' said Pariki, lounging with one buttock on the table and still contriving to look decorous. 'As far as Sparta, where I took the most beautiful woman in the world for my own as the goddess promised and then to Egypt where she was stolen from me.'

Hector had gone cold and stony in a moment. His voice, was however, calm.

'As the goddess promised? Tell me the tale, brother! All should hear it!' and he shouted for silence. Pariki, delighted by the attention which he considered his due, began not to speak but to sing in his pleasant light voice:

Pariki on Mount Idus, watching the sheep graze,
Saw three women glowing with the sun's fire.
Bearing an apple came Hermes the God,
'Judge between them, most beautiful of shepherds,
Who is Kalliste, the fairest of them all?'

As he sang, I saw them in my mind's eye. The tall and commanding Mother, spindle in hand; the Warrior Maiden, helmeted, bearing aegeis, the goat's skin shield; the sinuous Ishtar, smiling, her hands running down her perfect body. Pariki offered kingdoms and wisdom, and choosing instead, as might have been guessed, the possession of Elene, Princess of Sparta.

His voice chanted on, describing his arrival at the palace, the foolish hospitality of Menelaus—fat, breathless, old and red-faced, hence deserving no courtesy—the stolen moments with almond-eyed, dark-haired Argive Elene, until she agreed to flee with him.

Then the driving of his ship by jealous gods across to Egypt, where the priestesses of Isis took Elene into their temple and refused to let her go. Pariki sang:

… Trojan ships will come,
Red sailed and well found to the delta of the Nile,
To restore Elene of Sparta to her Pariki again.

That was too much for Hector. 'No, they won't,' he roared. 'Fool, fool of a brother. Well do they call you City-Destroyer! What will you tell the Achaeans, boy, when they come knocking at the gates of Troy asking for their princess again? "Sorry, she left me in Egypt?" For she left you, Pariki, she was not stolen. I have been often to Egypt. The priestesses of the Lady of the Pillar do not kidnap women. She fled her husband with you and then she left you because of what you are, Pariki, a graceful, decorated doll with no brains in your head or heart in your chest. A perfect dupe for an unhappy woman. I have heard about the marriage of Elene of Sparta, poor girl. You must have been ideal for her purposes, Pariki. Cruel, discourteous, and stupid. You have brought an army down upon us. What other ingenious things have you done? Did you steal the Státhi as well?'

It was clear from the shocked, sly look on the shepherd's face that Hector had hit upon the truth.

'So we cannot even ask Egypt to give the girl up,' groaned Hector. 'You have insulted them by stealing a divine beast—and nearly killing it. Oh, well done, Pariki. What will you do next? There is still Phrygia and Caria to insult; perhaps you can bring the Hittites into this as well.'

'Come, it may not be as bad as that,' said Priam in his creaking voice. 'I at least am glad to see you, Pariki, safe home and honoured by the goddess.' He stretched out a hand for his son's. Pariki knelt at his feet and stared up into the old man's face.

'Have I done badly, father?' he whispered piteously. Priam stroked the downcast head. Hector snorted.

I was in the grip of so horrible a vision that I bit my knuckle to blood. Black ships and the stench of death and rotting. It rolled over me until I was nearly stifled. Clenching my jaw to keep from speaking, I looked for Eleni and found him sweating and trembling. Apollo Priest bore him up on one side and wiped his face with a cloth. Eleni was still sharing my visions. But he was saying nothing.

With an effort I dragged myself out of the vision. Unlike the skeletal man, I had at least seen this one many times before.

◇◇◇

We sent the newlywed son and daughter of Priam off to their decorated bed. Státhi accompanied them and I hoped that he would not wound Andromache too badly. She walked firmly into the chamber, sat down on the bed, and held out her arms to Hector. Despite bad omens and an impending war, Andromache had no doubts.

I had thousands, but it was not the time to voice them. Perseis took us up to the walls after noon to watch them bring in the bull of Dionysius, Troy's one perfect sacrifice. He was carefully chosen, a black bull with certain white markings, the one under the tongue being the most important; a mark in the shape of a dolphin. A herd of Dionysius cattle had been bred with care and kept apart from the other beasts, so that Troy would always have its Three Days' bull.

The air had turned soft; it was nearly spring. We saw the procession heading across the plain; men and women danced and leapt around the bull, garlanding him with fresh leaves and flowers, kissing his nose. A sacrifice to the Lord Dionysius would not be proper unless it was something that everyone loved and cared for. The Dionysius bull had been gentled and handled since he had been a calf. He had no fear of humans and would not be afraid until the moment that the knife cut his throat; perhaps not even then.

'Spring is early this year,' commented Perseis. 'Clear your forehead of that frown, daughter of Priam,' she chided me. 'Hector is married and the Dionysius bull is mustered. Eleni did not come because he could not; the god Apollo keeps him close.'

'Or his priests do,' I muttered.

'Or his priests, what matter? Was it another vision, Cassandra?' she asked in a low voice. I set my jaw and nodded my head. My hair, unbound for the festival fell forward over my eyes. I waited for the nausea and spasm to jolt me, but it seemed that the god could tolerate gestures.

'The same vision?' persisted Cycen. I nodded again.

'Then there is nothing new to report,' said Perseis cheerfully. 'There—what a fine bull! Look at the way he paws the ground.'

My eyes were blurring. All I could see, overlaid on the glossy coat of the bull and the fluttering, flowery tunics of the dancers were carrion birds, vultures and buzzards and crows, stooping over a battlefield littered with unburied dead. The skeletal bull pawed the ground with a hoof which had been dry for years;

around him danced the merry rout of the dead, corpse-pale and ragged, bones glinting through their cerements. I said nothing.

◇◇◇

Tithone always locked herself in for the Dionysiad. I took leave of her early in the morning. She handed over a basket of medicines and patted me on the cheek.

'If any maid needed to disconnect her wits, my daughter, it is you,' she said. 'Give that to Perseis and tell her not to worry about the virgins. I have looked them all over and none of them have any disease that time will not cure—time even cures maidenhood, eh, my bird? In any case she can summon me in the noon watch if she needs me. Go, Cassandra, drink deep and revel. It is the due of the god and not one of these new male ones either, but the old pulse of the land and the sky. Forget Apollo. The Sun Bright has treated you ill and you need the flesh to comfort you.'

Then she shut her door on me, grumbling to one of the birthing mothers, 'Hush, pretty, hush. It will all be over soon.'

I walked up the steep street to Perseis, wondering how the flesh could disconnect my visions. On the way I looked in on Nyssa. As I neared the door, I heard her talking to a baby.

'Cassandra!' she said. 'How is it with you, my child?'

'I am all right,' I paused at the door. 'Is this your new one, then?'

'Yes, the precious lamb, the first of last year's sacrifice babies. Look at its beautiful eyes!'

'Beautiful,' I agreed, burning with jealousy. I wished fervently that I was a baby again, when I had my twin and I was sure of everything. Nyssa glanced at me, cradling the newborn.

'Eleni loves you,' she said. 'I'm sure that he loves you still.'

'I cannot tell,' I said, and trailed drearily away, though she called to me to come in and sit down and she'd talk to me when she'd fed the baby.

'Dionysius the Lord is the oldest god,' Perseis instructed as Cycne, Eirene, Iris and I sat at her feet in the noon calm. 'He is the god of increase, of maleness, the phallus, wine, music, and madness. For three days in each year his rule of Troy is absolute, as it was in the Island. For those three days any act is sanctioned; no taboo stands. Of course, if any acts take place which the city has forbidden by law—like rape or murder—then they will be investigated later and the offender punished. But Dionysius rages in these three days, so all maids and tenderlings are shut away. These are the rules, young women. If you tire of the mob, or are afraid, you may leave it and come indoors. But you must not bring anyone with you into the Temple of Maidens—do you understand? Dionysius rules in the open, in the plain, and in the streets; he is forbidden to those within doors and you must not bring him with you. Any door will open to your knock, but once inside, you cannot come out again, for the god will have left you. You must behave with courtesy to those who shelter you and they in turn will help and comfort you. Take off the ivy wreath when you go in, leave the thyrsus outside. Old people and children have nothing to do with the youthful god of reckless joy. Every year some people are hurt and occasionally someone is killed, but that is not your concern. Bring or send all those who are injured to Tithone's house. But this is the rule, daughters of Priam: once you have drunk the bull's blood, you can leave the worshippers only once and then for the rest of the festival you cannot rejoin them. Is that understood?'

We nodded. It seemed clear. She looked at us. We had made wreaths out of ivy and each of us had a staff cut of ash-wood, crowned with a pine cone and wound about with white wool— the thyrsus of the Lord Dionysius.

'Come, we must welcome him into Troy,' she said, and we joined the people running down the streets to the Scamander Gate.

The bull was crossing the Place of Strangers' Gods as we lined the top of the gate and cheered him inside. No visions came to cloud my sight. On every side were the citizens of Troy, from market-women to smiths and spinners, all clad in the white tunics demanded of the cult, bare of jewellery or bracelets of rank. I caught sight of the Egyptian woman who had borne the deformed child, with her husband beside her, clad in 'woven air.' They were shadowed with mist; I saw blood on their fine gauze. I shook my head, bewildered for a moment. The visions came and went in the blink of an eye.

My tunic streamed out behind me as I joined hands with Cycne and Iris and we began the long dance which escorts the sacrifice to the topmost point of the city of Tros.

Drummers and pipe players accompanied us as we began to sing the chant which summons our Lord Dionysius. 'Evoë!' we called, and I heard deep voices rumble under and shrill voices carol over the stave I was singing. 'Evoë, evoë! Come Lord Dionysius, Dolphin-Rider, Grape-Crusher, Wine-maker, Joy-Filled, Lord of laughter and of light! Come to thy daughters, fill us with thy wine, sate us with thy love, Phallus Bearer! Evoë! Evoë!'

The hindquarters of the bull flexed as he strode up the cobbled street, winding like the dance around the hill of Troy, his hoofs cleaving prints in the carpet of petals, the air heavy with jasmine and spring flowers. Cycne's hand was strong in mine, Iris' clutched my wrist. I felt the drag of my hair as I shook my head and someone planted a passing kiss on my neck as we surged up, up into the acropolis, with the sky as blue as forget-me-nots and the sun as warm as Apollo's blessing, which I had forfeited.

The bull and the city feasted that night in Priam's palace. All of the furnishings had been packed away. Hector and Andromache were in their bridal chamber with Státhi and the cub. Any virgins and children among the sons and daughters of Priam had been hidden away from the revellers of Dionysius. Wine flowed from the cellars of Priam, though the king and queen were also behind a closed door. As master we had Dionysius' priest, Polites, my brother. We ate too much and I fell asleep with my head pillowed on Iris' hip.

I woke to someone kissing me in the half dark and I kissed him back, assuming it was someone I knew, but when I opened my eyes it was a stranger, a young man with black eyes and swarthy skin, who gathered me into his arms, though not into a full embrace because that was banned until the third day. He was skilled, however, and I relaxed into the caresses.

Then we drank more wine and danced again, the dancers brushing against each other, kissing with open mouths, touching and fumbling under tunics which were crumpled and stained with wine.

The servers who had drawn lots to provide the cold food—for no fire must be lit until the sacrifice fire in honour of the Lord Dionysius—put out more bread and cheese and we ate and sang and slept again. My head was spinning with wine and the closeness of so many people. I drifted in and out of sleep, with kisses landing on lip and breast. Somewhere near me a woman was making the bird-like cries towards climax—ah, ah, ah!—but her breath gusted out in a frustrated sigh as her lover moved away. There must be no consummation until we had drunk the bull's blood and that was a day and this night away.

I slid one hand along a male chest, up over a shoulder, found a mouth and pulled him into my arms. I wanted the weight on my body, the solid humanity anchoring what remained of Cassandra to the flesh which was supposed to give me comfort.

I woke in sunlight, wincing at the glare, shoved the young man away, and crawled up the steps to the bull, who was lying next to the fountain. His gently eyes examined me as I drank deeply and breathed in the sweet hay-scent of his breath. I staggered to my feet and embraced the bull, scratching him on the whorl of hair in the centre of his forehead and he lowed and nudged me.

O perfect bull, perfect sacrifice! The spring water hit what remained of the wine in my insides and I was drunk again and sat down dizzily, leaning my head against the bull's side. I fell asleep.

Two watches later the sun was westering and the Dionysius revellers were waking, groaning, getting to their feet. Polites signalled to the musicians and they began a low drumbeat. The pipers raised their reed-pipe and the voices began, our invocation of the god of wine and madness—'Evoë! Evoë! Lord Dionysius, come!' I was dragged into the dance, up the steps and around the bull, my hands clasped by strangers, the wine fizzing in my head, my wits utterly gone, faster and faster as night began to fall. I found my feet and danced, my ivy wreath slipping, my tunic falling off my shoulder. The drums throbbed like a heart-beat. Strength poured into me like wine into a cup and the palace rang with cries and the god came.

As Polites brought the knife across the patient beast's throat and blood gushed out into the trough, I heard a divine voice laughing, calling, 'Children, Bacchantes, I come, I come!' like a thousand brazen trumpets. The hall echoed and shook. I thrust my thyrsus into the blood, watching as the white wool turned red, gulped at the wine with its rusty tang, and kissed the nearest mouth. Dionysius was with us, in the dark of the temple, in the death of the gentle, wise-eyed bull who had fallen without pain or complaint.

I slipped down and rolled from under the dancer's feet, pulling at a thigh so that a man fell on top of me, kissing a blood-stained mouth and grappling with urgent hands at a shaggy head and a tunic which I tore.

I was splayed under someone and my sheath filled at last; an ache burst into a pain and I screamed and laughed and sucked at a breast while another phallus replaced the fallen one and hands gripped and palpated me.

Under the command of the god I was as flexible as seaweed, soft as clay, absorbing my lovers in the wormwood scent of seam and exhaled wine and blood. We were dragged to our feet by the drums and the wine and we streamed out of the palace like an army, weeping and laughing, hand in hand down the steep streets, crowned with ivy and drunk with Dionysius.

I was seized by strong hands and dropped to my knees, falling over an entwined couple. One man took me from behind as dogs mate, one lay under me sucking at my breasts, I kissed a woman's mouth, climax took me again, and I sank under the blows of the god, weeping with relief and joy. I heard the others howling to Dionysius as I lay on my back grasping at a swarthy stranger's back, his laughing mouth closing on mine, biting at my lips. My fingernails tore a furrow down his face and I sucked his blood and felt his phallus inside me blossom in his pain.

I saw no faces, only mouths, eyes, teeth, hands, bodies. The long string of twisting bodies encircled the acropolis, our scent holding us together in a pack like wolves.

The doors of Troy were shut against us, the revellers under the cold high moon of spring. We were out in the streets and divorced from the sober citizens, intoxicated with wine and the god, free of all bonds and maddened.

I saw women lie with women, men with men. The street was littered with lovers. A boy sniffed the length of my body like a dog and growled as he coupled with me, baring white teeth. I bit into his shoulder as he joined with me, thrusting the sheath down on the phallus, sucking at him.

The god's last gift took my mind in the cool shadows under the Temple of Apollo and I woke there in the morning still joined to a black-haired stranger who had fallen asleep in my arms.

◇◇◇

I washed and anointed my bruises and dressed in a clean chiton. Dionysius had taught me that I could lose my mind and still be alive. That is a valuable lesson.

The next day, Polyxena went out to the Temple of the Pathfinder and the war began.

Chapter Sixteen

Diomenes

I was married to Chryseis, daughter of Palamedes of Mycenae, by my master, who joined our hands and blessed us. Then Itarnes swept me off to drink with the acolytes who boasted of their conquests of maidens as though they had, as Elene said, stolen something or done something clever. I did not want to drink and I found their voices wearisome. The only conquest in my life had been Elene's conquest of me and I could never speak of it. I sang along with their bawdy songs, thankful that Arion Dolphin-Rider was not there. That bard has a fund of lewd songs which would have kept me up all night.

Finally they led me to the small stone house which my master had given me. The wives of other asclepids had anointed my bride with scented oils and draped her in a red veil. She looked very beautiful to me, sitting with her downcast eyes on the floor beside our bed.

For Mycenaean maidens must not presume to use their husband's goods without permission or they will be beaten.

I found myself wondering about my mother, the Carian woman from a country where women are valued and honoured for their skill. How had she come to marry that rough goatherd, my father, and how had she felt, given away in a foreign ceremony to a man she did not know? Had she been afraid?

I took both of my wife's hands and raised her to her feet and into my embrace. My friends cheered as I kissed her, then mercifully they all went away and I could shut and bar the door. There were tears on her face as I folded back the veil.

'Chryseis,' I asked. 'Is this by your will?'

'It would not matter if it was not,' she said in her quiet, clear voice. 'My father has power of life or death over me and he gave me to you. I am yours to do with whatever you will, Master.'

'Do not call me Master!' I held her at arm's length. 'I am your husband, I am Diomenes—call me husband if you like, but not Master.'

'It is by my will, Diomenes, but I am afraid. You will hurt me. The women told me that it will hurt.'

I fervently but silently cursed all women except the one in my arms. 'I will try not to hurt you,' I said. 'I love you, my golden one.'

Her body relaxed into my embrace and a tendril of her hair tickled my nose. I sneezed and she laughed.

'A good omen,' she said. 'Husband.'

I lay down on the sleeping mat and she lay beside me. With as much gentleness as I had and with all the skill I had learned, I began to teach my golden wife about love. I could not forget the eager embrace of Elene as she accepted me into her body. Chryseis was different; her breasts were smaller, higher, and her body hardened with labour. She was too frightened to respond to me that first night. Despite all my care, I hurt her, and she cried. So did I. I kissed away her tears and she kissed away mine and we fell asleep mouth to mouth.

I woke at dawn. Her head was on my shoulder, her glorious hair arrayed across my chest. I felt as though the gods, in whom I did not believe, had awarded me another Diomenes, a female counterpart of myself. She was so close to me that I could not tell which heartbeat I heard, for they pulsed as one. I have never been happier in my life as the morning I woke with Chryseis in my arms and the spring sun shooting arrows under the door.

She was astoundingly beautiful, loving, gentle, with a hard edge of practicality. She was also remarkably unlearned.

The Argives teach their women nothing, no languages or arts, lest they be defiled by contact with the world and lose their maiden purity. Chryseis did not know that the sun was a ball of fire that warmed the earth; that the earth was round, cradled in the River Ocean; that different herbs had been signed for different illnesses. She had never seen a pot made, or wood carved, or fish caught. She had spent all of her fourteen years spinning and weaving and dancing in the women's quarters of her father's house and had hardly poked her well-shaped nose out of doors in dread of the beating she would receive if she did. She had a head stuffed with a staggering array of old wives' tales and superstitions, and her religion consisted of sacrifices to the oldest form of the goddess, Hecate the Dark Mother, drinker of dog's blood.

But let loose in the relatively free atmosphere of Epidavros, where no social distinctions are allowed, she blossomed. She picked up basic Trojan in a month, Carian in two months, and spoke better Egyptian than me by the end of the year. She haunted the craftsmen until someone allowed her to try enamelling and she produced such beautiful butterflies that Master Glaucus asked for one as a cloak brooch. She had been so constrained by violence and threat of social ruin that she had stopped asking questions; now she asked thousands, so that Itarnes begged for mercy. The old men called for her to sit by them in the sun because she listened to them so intelligently.

'The state is a matter of consent,' I heard old Master Tiraes instruct her as she sat at his feet. 'The king and the subjects all agree that one shall rule and others shall be ruled. Decisions taken by a king, therefore, bind his followers, but they cannot be forced too far, because then they will depose the king and seek another, better able to carry out their will.'

Chryseis thought about this, chewing a fingernail.

'I do not recall, Master, that any man ever asked the consent of women to sell or buy them,' she commented. The old man chuckled and patted her head.

'Women and slaves have no minds,' he quoted an old saying. 'All body and no rationality. You are an animal, my dear—though a very clever animal,' he added, as though she had been a performing dog. Chryseis did not take instant offence but seemed deep in thought. She was about to say something which would devastate the old man's calm, so I decided to intervene.

'Come, wife,' I said. 'I would speak with you,' and she farewelled Tiraes and followed me to the grove, where we sat down under a cypress.

'Diomenes, do you believe that women have no minds?'

'No, Chryseis. You are proof of that.'

'Then why did Master Tiraes say so? Is that what all men think?'

I surveyed my acquaintance—even my own master. I nodded.

'That is unfair,' she said. 'Entirely unfair.'

I had to agree. 'But if women ruled,' I began, 'if women ruled…'

'Well, what if they did? There are places where women are kings—Egypt, they say, and there are the Amazon who fight like men.'

'Yes.' Now I thought about it, I had no single reason why women could not rule. It was obviously out of the question but I could not explain why. 'But it's impossible.' I tried to bluster. She did not get angry with me but resumed chewing her fingernail and examining me with her bright eyes. I could never persist in a falsehood under that clear gaze. 'All right, wife, I have to admit it. I don't know why men think that women have no minds. You are right, it is entirely unfair.'

'You admit that I can think?' she asked in Trojan and repeated in Carian, Phrygian, and Egyptian. I nodded. She kissed me.

'As long as you know,' she said, pressing her breasts against my shoulder, 'then the others can think what they like. There is an old saying among the priestesses of Hecate, husband, just as convincing as the ones that old man has been spouting.'

'What is that?' I asked unwisely.

'A man is a fool attached to a phallus,' she said sweetly, and kissed me on the mouth to smother my reply.

◇◇◇

Arion Dolphin-Rider came when Chryseis and I had been married four months. It was winter; that winter was wet and misty, generating rheums and agues and cloaking the temple with fog. I saw him come riding to the suppliant's gate, his singing robes dank with moisture.

I held his horse as he dismounted and wrung out his hair and beard.

'Welcome,' I said. 'Welcome, Master Bard! Come within.' I handed the rein to a slave and took the old man's arm. 'Come and get warm and I shall tell my master that you are here.'

I took him to my house and sent a slave running for Master Glaucus. Chryseis rose from her seat beside the fire to greet him and he grunted with surprise.

'This is Palamedes' daughter, boy, the golden maiden? He underestimated her beauty and I have never known him to do that before, the boaster! Beautiful lady, give me leave to sit down for I am overwhelmed by your presence. I had not thought to find a goddess in a humble asclepid's cell!'

Chryseis laughed and bade him be seated, then warmed wine for him while I took off his boots and thawed his feet.

'You know what your father's been up to, girl?' he asked Chryseis. 'He's caught Odysseus out, that sly one, he of the nimble wits, king of Ithaca. You've heard that they are mounting an expedition against Troy to retrieve Elene of Sparta?' he cocked a bold, dark eye at me and I nodded. 'Well, Diomenes...ah, here is your master. Greetings Glaucus, you old tortoise! Here you've been safe in your shell while I tramped the roads getting older and considerably more way-worn. No, I can't move again to your fine house. Stay here with me and let me refresh my spirit by gazing on the golden Chryseis, Palamedes' daughter, most fair of women since Elene was...er...abducted.'

Master Glaucus grunted with laughter and let himself down onto the sleeping mat. I had finished with the bard's frozen toes and sat next to Chryseis, admiring her grace as she heated wine for our guests. Her wrists looked delicate, but they were strong and muscles moved under the skin of her upper arm as she tilted the pot and poured spiced wine for the bard and Master Glaucus.

'As I was saying, Palamedes went with Agamemnon to persuade the old fox Odysseus to come on this Trojan venture, in the name of that league we saw sworn in Mycenae of the golden walls. There they found the king of Ithaca, completely out of his wits, ploughing with an ox and a goat, sowing salt in his own acres and giggling. They were all taken in but your father, girl. He picked up the king's son, the baby Telemachus, and plumped him down in front of the ploughshare. Of course Odysseus stopped and it was revealed that he wasn't mad after all. So he's going to Troy and I don't think he's happy. Your father should watch his back, my golden maiden. He's got a long memory, the king of Ithaca.'

'Who else is going on this…expedition? They can't really think that the Trojans will keep the Argive woman, can they, not if they arrive on the beaches with an army?'

'This isn't about any woman. Women are two to an obol,' snarled Arion. 'This is about the wealth and position of Troy. Even if they give back adulterous, traitorous Elene to be the sport of the Achaean soldiers, that will not stop Agamemnon. He wants Troy and I expect that he is going to have it, though not as easily as he thinks. There is Hector in Troy, and many good bowmen, and while they have those things Troy will not fall like a ripe fruit into anyone's hand, even if he is Lord of men.'

I winced at his mention of Elene and Chryseis winced at his description of what would happen to her. We embraced to comfort each other as the shadows lengthened. Rain began to fall outside, a soft relentless patter. Our brazier burnt red and hot and the old men's voices went on.

'Once they enlisted Odysseus, however, he obtained Achilles for them. He is the best warrior of our time; greater than Trojan Hector, they say. His father is Zeus and his mother's a sea-nymph—Thetis is her name. She made him invulnerable by dipping him in the Styx. She hid him among the maidens at the court of King Sciros; Odysseus the Sly One came as a peddler and brought jewellery and necklaces and a shield and sword. Naturally Achilles took up the weapons and was revealed. The hero is a strange one; but he is a man. One of the daughters is pregnant. He said that he was just doing as the girls do among themselves and there was this surprising development.' Arion guffawed, 'So there will be a child of Achilles, the hero, even if he meets his fate at Troy. He is called Man Slayer, Grey-Eyed, God-touched, not long to live. But the maid's an aberration. He had drunk from the springs of Salmancis all right; he's a man-lover as well as a man-slayer. He's bringing the ant-warriors, the Myrmidon in brown armour and his adored Patroclus, a man loved by everyone, not just this touchy boy-warrior.'

'Patroclus lived here for two years, learning medicine. He worked with Macaon and might have become a surgeon but he turned to war,' my master sighed and took a sip of wine. 'A waste of a good healer. So, who else, brother bard?'

'Agamemnon, Lord of Men, and Menelaus the injured husband, cuckold Menelaus with the toothy smile—so difficult to flatter him, even in a ballad that has been bought and paid for!—Even a bard has his pride, brother…what was I saying?'

'Who else has joined in this war?' asked my master patiently. 'Diomenes, perhaps you could send for some food.'

'Are you saying that I am drunk, brother?'

'Yes, brother, a little, perhaps,' said Master Glaucus.

I signalled to our only slave to go the master's house and get meat and bread. Old men should not drink on an empty belly. The girl scrambled away from the hearth and was gone into the rainy darkness, letting in a gust of cold air which made Arion swear and shiver.

'That was a breath of death, by Pluton the rich one! I grow old, brother. Too old for heroes. I need a willing girl to warm my old bones and I will loll in the sun and watch the road roll out like a ribbon and never, never take my poor old feet further than the agora.'

'And you will sit under the olive trees and gossip with men who have never left their village,' said Glaucus gently. 'And they will never believe your travels.'

'True,' Arion pulled his cloak tighter around his shoulders. 'Bards need an educated audience. This is an heroic time and who will remember the gallant deaths if there is no song to commemorate them? They would go down into the deeds with unsung, lost forever, spilling their names and their deeds with their blood, and no man would remember them. Men would never say of a fine steed, "That is almost as good as Achilles' chariot horse." Men would never say of a bright-eyed girl, "She is the equal of Argive Elene, the most beautiful woman in the world." There would be no honour to stand by, no great ancestors to comfort the heart when the belly drops and the gorge rises at the sound of men running to battle. No, there must be songs, brother. And I must make them.' He took a deep breath, which bubbled in his chest, and coughed.

'So, who else sails for the sack of Troy? The allies of Mycenae; Tiryns, Corinth, Lacedemon, Kriti, Arcadia, Elis led by Meges the Charioteer, Rhodes with Tlepolemus Kin-Killer. Argos, Hellas, Phylace, Pherae, Methone, Argissa, Cyphus, men even from Pelion and Boeotia—both Aias are there, mighty heroes. Trachis too, and most of the islands. A great army. Do you know if your sons will go?'

'They have spoken to me about it. I am against it. Healers, however, will be needed—how well only Asclepius knows. I expect that they will follow the army, probably with the men of Ithome. There is a question of asking the god. If he gives permission, who am I to withhold it?'

My master's eyes were dark with pain. Arion put out a shaking hand and the two beards mingled in a kiss.

The slave had returned with food and Chryseis laid out a platter for them. She was pale in the red light.

'What is wrong, my wife?' I asked.

'I am very afraid, Diomenes,' she said concisely—Chryseis was always neat. 'I am afraid of battle and war and I fear my own death.'

'You have no reason to fear that,' I whispered into her sweet-scented neck. 'You are young and healthy and the war will not come here.'

'You asked me what was wrong, not if it was reasonable,' she reminded me.

Arion had heard part of what she said. 'Never worry you hear, maiden,' he said coughing again. 'War comes not to peaceful Epidavros. You need not fear death or ravishment here.'

'And the women of Troy?' she asked softly.

'They will suffer if Troy is defeated,' he said. 'It is all a matter of fate. Women's fate runs with men's, for good fortune or ill, Palamedes' daughter.'

Chryseis did not reply. Arion began to cough so hard that Master Glaucus became alarmed and opened the door. The bard walked four paces and collapsed bonelessly into my master's arms.

'You must come with me, old friend,' he said gently. 'Come, Chryse, Lady, we will carry him.'

Together, we heaved the old bard up out of the mud and carried him to the master's house. Chryseis laid his grizzled head down gently on the master's bed.

'He has travelled far,' she commented, observing his battered feet.

'Too far for a foolish old man in this weather,' snapped the master. 'Brew me the pectoral herbs, Chryse, honey but not poppy. And you, Lady,' he was always very polite to Chryseis, 'soak those cloths in boiling water, wring them out, and lay them on his chest. We will be lucky to save him. Old rogue of a bard,' he scolded fondly, 'haven't you, at your advanced age, enough sense to come in out of the rain?'

We sewed the bard into a freshly flayed sheepskin to keep him warm and shared the watch, my master and me. Chryseis sat with me far into the night, talking softly about herbs and stars in various languages while the lamp burned down and the sick man's breathing heaved, laboured, paused for nerve-shattering time then heaved and wheezed again. We were finishing each other's sentences, catching the other's thought, and this was so magical and new that I continually tested it, never accepting, always questioning.

We were talking about gods.

'The Father, that is Zeus, and the Mother is Hera, except that there are several mothers. Even…'

'Aphrodite is a mother,' I said absently, then stared into her amber eyes in the lamplight. 'How did I know what you were going to say?'

'We are one,' she said simply, laying my hand over hers, palm to palm. 'You always know what you are saying to yourself. Well, usually,' she added and laughed. The small flame of the oil-saucer made her glow; a golden woman with hair like sunset cloud and eyes like jewels.

I never felt the need to touch her to know that she was there. Her presence could be felt, like the change in the air if someone comes into a room. She was behind me and about me all the time, close as flesh to bone; her scent pervaded me.

'Goddess,' said Arion, reaching out a wavering hand. She took it in both of her own. I could tell from his touching her that he was still burning like a furnace. 'Goddess, forgive. I never told about Elene and Chryse, never a word, though the secret burned my breast. I will make a song of it for you, the innocent boy and the most beautiful Elene with eyes like pools and a mouth like a red poppy. That will amuse you, Aphrodite, Lady of Love.'

Chryseis held the hand tightly and her expression did not change. I said, 'Arion, Dolphin-Rider, be calm. You are in Epidavros in the master's house and it is Chryse, I am here, and my wife Chryseis.'

'Goddess,' the old man forced himself to sit upright, then fell out of bed and fumbled at Chryseis' knees. 'Forgive your singer. Chryse was scarce a man and we sent him to soothe the woes of your favoured one knowing what might happen. She needed him, Aphrodite, Lady of Doves, and you sent your own sign to approve us. Forgive me now, grown worn in the service of love.'

Chryseis understood in a flash; I saw knowledge and calculation flush her face and she shut her mouth hard on my most dangerous secret. Then she stood up to her full height and cupped Arion's cheek, tilting his head so that he looked up at the column of her body into her eyes. She was as tall as a cryselephantine statue, ivory and gold, and she took my breath away.

'Speak no more, Arion,' Her voice sounded richer, deeper, stronger than Chryseis' own. 'I am the goddess on whom you call and I say to you, be silent. For all you have done and for your sweet songs, Bard, I forgive you and honour you. Be forgiven, I say; my displeasure is assuaged. Arion,' her hand hovered over his head, palm out, then came down solidly, 'you are healed.'

We heaved him back into bed and by the time we had him settled the aura had gone, divinity had departed, and my Chryseis was familiar again, a girl clad in an unbound tunic who was tying back her hair with a piece of string.

'Oh, Chryseis,' I began and she put her finger to my lips.

'Later and when we are alone,' she whispered. 'He can still hear. Look, fool Asclepid, feel his forehead. Is it not cooler? It was hot enough to brand my hands at sunset.'

'Yes,' I said. 'Get me warm cloths and tell the slave to call the master. I think that Arion Dolphin-Rider has been forgiven by the Goddess.'

I tried to explain what I had seen when she drew herself up and declaimed that she was the Lady Aphrodite, but words faltered on my tongue. Perhaps it had been a trick of the light; Chryseis was a clever woman and words came easily to her, the words which would flog Arion like a tired horse over the final hurdle to recovery. Even his sudden movement might have provoked the sweat which broke his fever. She herself had no opinion, considering my quibbles as vapourings from a weary mind. She did not say a word about Elene of Sparta and I could not talk about it. We slept for a long time, woke to dreamily make love, and slept again, and when we emerged into the cool mist we heard Arion demanding wine from the master's house slave, and the full-throated howl of outrage when he was told firmly that he couldn't have any.

'He's better,' said Chryseis, fetching a short sigh. 'I'm glad I'm not that slave. He will have orders to offer him barley broth,' she said, and I added just before a roar and a smash sounded from inside the house. 'And there goes the bowl.'

◇◇◇

Two months later, as the year turned gradually into spring, I saw a line of marching men coming to Epidavros on the road to the sea. The sun glinted off their armour; they seemed like bronze men to me, with greaves and breastplates and helmets wrought like beasts or in the shape of angry faces.

They could not enter the temple—Asclepius has no use for war and utterly rejects those who wound or kill—so they halted outside the suppliant's gate. Dogs barked and Chryseis, at my side, shivered as if she were cold, though she had a thick tunic on and it was a warm day with a gentle breeze.

'Macaon and Polidarius,' demanded the leader, 'the men from Ithome of the terraced hills, from Tricca and from Oechalia of Eurytus, are here to take you to the conquest of Troy.'

Macaon and Palidarius stood at the gate, asclepid priests, both sons of Glaucus. They were tall and clad in armour, carrying spears and swords. Each had a shield and each led a horse loaded down with medical herbs. No horse, I knew, could carry the remedies needed for an army of this size and I wondered where more would come from once these were exhausted. I had helped in the sorting bundling of dried plants; woundleaf and pounded bark for bleeding, remedies for the plagues of Apollo, and the mixed burning herbs for stunning the wounded during surgery. Laurel and hemlock and nightshade, burned in a vessel and inhaled, will produce intoxication of percussive force, strong enough to hold even during an amputation. Such men usually die, however. If not from the smoke, from the shock.

I wondered how many of these strong young men would live to see the next spring or even harvest. Chryseis was holding my hand so tightly that her nails cut into my palm.

'Farewell,' Master Glaucus' voice was steady. 'Seek not glory, for that is death. Survive, my sons, and return.' While they knelt for his blessing, he added with aching sincerity, 'You carry your father's heart with you. Return soon, for I am an old man and need my heart.'

They kissed him and turned away from the cypresses and the walls. Forty men marched away down the white road. I could follow their dust long after they had gone: dust and a glint of bronze.

Master Glaucus went back into the house and closed the door. Chryseis fainted for the first time in her life and I carried her back to our house. When I revived her she held me as tightly as a drowning man clutches a plank.

'Don't let me go!' her voice was shrill and urgent.

'I will hold you forever,' I whispered. 'Why are you afraid? What's the matter, my love, my sweet maiden?'

'I am bearing your child,' she said very quietly, 'and I fear that I will die.'

◇◇◇

'This golden maiden—is she yours now?' Apollo drawled. 'They were your words, Lady of Doves, I know your speech. I gave this child of Palamedes the warrior to my Diomenes of the healing hands, to distract him from your Cassandra. He loves her, Lady. I would have thought you would oppose the girl, not put divine words into her pretty mouth.'

'Ah, but that is my bard, my Arion, who sings my praises all over the known world. I could not let such a man fail under my displeasure,' said Aphrodite. 'But you should look to your puppet maiden, Lord Apollo, she is pregnant. Make your peace with Demeter.'

'Never,' said Apollo.

Chapter Seventeen

Cassandra

I peacefully baited hooks, my feet paddling in the sea, sitting on Hector's new jetty. Dion and Maeles were beside me, repairing a net. It was a cool windy day, at the time of the filling of the marketplace.

I pricked my finger on a hook and Maeles took my hand, exclaiming at the tiny wound.

His bent head was drenched in blood. I could see the fatal wound in his skull which had cloven through the bone, revealing the grey matter of the brain. This vision stayed a little longer, long enough for me to see the sea covered in black ships behind him and the smell of burning.

The god was not just trying to terrify me with dances of bones and pictures of corpses. He was showing me how Maeles would die—how they would all die, the ones I had seen.

He was giving me previsions of death and sealing my tongue. Because I could not speak the glimpses were vivid; I could even smell blood and the bilious stench of relaxed bowels which accompanies death.

I pulled my hand away and the gory head tilted and the white mouth said concernedly, 'Princess?'

I did not scream. I looked away, struck my head violently with both hands, and the vision was gone; Maeles was himself again.

I began to hate the god Apollo then; not only with the expected hurt of a betrayed priestess, but flooded with outrage; how dare he do this to me, to Cassandra the princess, when I had been his favoured maiden, his faithful woman? Was there no gratitude in the gods, no justice?

Behind the bent head of the dead Maeles I had seen something else. I saw a sail, then another. I got to my feet, dropping my line and shading my eyes. More ships and more, black ships with black sails, occupying the horizon, strung out over the calm water like toys. This was no vision. This was real.

Dion grabbed one arm and Maeles the other. We began to run back to the city.

They knew about the ships by the time we arrived, breathless at the Scamander Gate. The trumpets were sounding the alarm, a sharp, staccato sound. Feet were running on the ladders and platforms inside the walls. The Scamander Gate was starting to close as we flung ourselves inside.

I looked over the plain and saw a small figure, then another; girls, by their long tunics, and I shouted to the guard to hold the gate.

'Hector Priam's son says to close it!' yelled the guard. 'There are hundreds of Achaean ships out there, Princess!'

'And they can't arrive in the blink of an eye,' I screamed back. 'Hold onto your manhood and wait. That will give you something to do, anyway,' I added caustically. The soldiers on the wall laughed and the gate, tree trunks sheathed in bronze, tall as three men and immensely heavy, scraped to a halt.

Soon the running figures resolved into women. Foremost was my little sister Polyxena, spattered with red and shrieking, completely out of her mind with terror. Behind her careered a riderless horse, which the other girl finally had the sense to grab and mount, collecting the fleeing Polyxena as she rode. Amazon-trained riders can master any beast in any conditions; I saw that the rider was Andromache.

They skidded into the city in a flurry of hooves and the great gate slammed shut with a sound like thunder. I grabbed the rein and Dion lifted the child down.

At first I thought the blood was hers, but there was too much of it for a living ten-year-old girl. Someone had been slain. I tried to soothe Polyxena, but she was so far gone that I passed her stiffened body to Andromache and Dion led the horse into the city to Tithone the healer.

She caught the child in her arms, shook her, and slapped her across the face.

There was a sudden silence when the screaming stopped and Tithone clasped my sister in a close hug. Polyxena collapsed and began to cry.

'What happened?' Tithone asked Andromache. 'Cassandra, brew the hysteria herbs and don't forget the mistletoe; send one Poseidon priest to stable and care for that poor horse, which I perceive is one from the king's stable, and the other to find Hector, Bulwark of Troy, he must hear this.'

Dion and Maeles did as they were bid. No one argued with Tithone. Polyxena was speechless, but Andromache drank some of my potion and sat perfectly still for ten minutes until she had stopped shaking. Finally she said, 'We went out to the Pathfinder, to offer him flowers, Erecthi came with us. You know how Polyxena has always hated him. We came to the shrine, made the offering. Erecthi was riding and we were walking; taking turns. Then...' she shuddered and took another gulp of the infusion, 'then this...this man ran out from the wood. He chased Erecthi, he caught him, and Erecthi got away and mounted again and then this man ran down the horse, he ran faster, caught our brother and...' she took a deep breath. 'And killed him, but that's not all...I can't...oh, Cassandra...' She did not weep, but shuddered as if she was freezing. Her teeth chattered. I cast my cloak over her shoulders and held her close.

'Tell us,' said Tithone gently.

'He killed him, his blood spilled all over Polyxena, and on me, his eyes, he had grey eyes, like stones, eyes like stones with a cold light in them, his golden hair flowed over his shoulders...not very tall, not much taller than me, he didn't even look strong... he was not interested in us, he did not raise a hand against us...

he let us run away…he cut off Erecthi's head,' she said clearly. 'Cut is off and set it on the altar of Pathfinder…'

She dropped to her knees and vomited into the drain, then sat back on her heels, panting. Hector gathered her up into his arms. I had not heard him come in.

'Achilles,' he said. 'Achilles Stone Heart, Swift Runner, Grey-Eyed, Man Slayer. Achilles has come. Oh, Pariki. I wish my mother had left you to die.'

We said nothing.

Presently Hector set Andromache gently on her feet. 'Sweet love,' he said to her, 'my dearest, I must go. Stay with Tithone until you feel better. Cassandra, bring the writing materials and follow.'

'Hector!' I cried after him. 'Where to?'

'The king's council,' his voice trailed back over his shoulder as he began to walk, very fast, up the steep streets.

I gathered ink and papyrus and three styli in case my favourite one should wear out. Tithone grabbed my arm.

'Walk,' she hissed. 'Saunter. There will be panic if they see you running.' I nodded and paced the alleys until I came to the doors of the palace.

The audience chamber was full of many men and they were all shouting. Hector was standing next to the king, his hand on the old man's shoulder. I threaded through the gathering, getting my ears cuffed by mistake by Anchises, who thought I was a straying hound. I stood on his foot, kicked another's shins, and shoved to the front where I sat down at Hector's feet, laying out my inkpot, my styli, and my roll of papyrus.

Hector looked down through his golden beard. 'Cassandra my sister, are you afraid?'

'No, brother,' I said truthfully. I knew what the end of the city would be. Despair is for those who see the end without hope and I had no hope. But I would die in the death throes of Troy, so why should I be afraid? I was already bereft and cursed. There was not much more that any god, however vengeful, could do to Cassandra.

'Hear all men!' bellowed Hector, putting out a huge hand and drawing me to my feet. 'Here is a maiden worth ten of you! I will not call you women,' he said in a lower tone, 'as the Argives do to insult each other, for to call you women would be a compliment and I do not mean to compliment you. The women of Troy take measures for their defense; just now my own wife is more collected and calm than you, after watching our brother Erecthi slaughtered and mutilated before her eyes.'

I supposed that this description of the wretchedly ill Andromache could count as dramatic licence. It was having some effect on the sons of Priam, anyway. They had stopped yelling and were now muttering. I swallowed to clear my ears.

'Good. How many ships are there?' asked Hector.

'Lord, from the Scaean Gate we counted forty-seven,' reported the guard.

'Any signals? Do we know who they are?'

'Lord, they carry the red sword of Lacedemon and the ram's head of Mycenae.'

'Menelaus wants his wife back,' commented Achises.

'And we haven't got her,' said Polites, glaring at Pariki.

'It would not matter if we had. This is not a war over one woman, but over the wealth of Troy. Make no mistake, brothers, they mean to use this pretext provided by our brother Alexandratos to take our city.' The murmur rose to a howl and Hector continued reassuringly, 'But they shall not succeed. These are Argives and they have few bowmen unless they have hired Scythians. Therefore, as long as there are guards on the wall, they cannot take the city. Polites, call the queen our mother and Myrine the Amazon. Deiphobos, have swift horses prepare. We will need to call our allies and we will have to do it now, before the Argives are at our gates.'

Since Hector had taken command, everyone had relaxed and started quibbling. I sat down again, putting my bare foot—I had not had time to find my sandals—on his foot. He gave me confidence. It seemed impossible that even the gods could stop Hector.

Pandarus, big and strong and with no brains at all, stood to ask, 'Why don't we just take chariots out and fight? We can beat any Achaean scum with our hands tied behind our backs. We're the men of Tros and Dardanus!'

'Someone tie his hands behind his back,' ordered Hector without expression. This got a laugh and he repeated it. The Scaean guard, who were Hector's own men, pinned Pandarus and secured his wrists. 'Bring him here. So, Pandarus, you could fight them all?' the big man nodded foolishly. 'Can you protect your arse?' asked Hector, spinning him around and kicking him soundly, so that he stumbled and fell off the dais. 'If you can't cover you face or your arse, how can you fight?' The audience laughed, a little hysterically.

'But we should fight,' protested Pandarus, face down on the floor. 'We can't just leave them to besiege Troy.'

'Can't we?'

'My son,' said the king, 'some show must be made or they will think that we are all cowards.'

'Who cares what Achaean strangers think?' asked Hector.

'I care,' Pariki put in. 'Let me challenge Menelaus to single combat. I took the old cuckold's wife; let him fight me for her.'

Hector gave him a narrow look. 'You, brother?'

'Me. I'm not just Aphrodite's darling,' said Pariki, baring a muscular arm.

'They must come to parley,' said Anchises. 'Then Pariki should issue his challenge. Either he will kill Menelaus,' the old man's eyes glinted at the thought, 'or Menelaus will kill Pariki.'

Hector thought about this, standing by the king's throne. 'All right, but I am sending for the allies anyway. If the Argives go home, then we shall have a feast for them; if not, we will need them. Lady Mother and Queen of Troy, Keeper of Grain, how much is there in the city?'

He knelt before Hecube, making the sacred gesture to the lady of increase and lifting the hem of her garment to his lips.

'The grainaries are full, my son,' said my mother, touching Hector's forehead in ritual blessing. 'Enough in the queen's store to feed the city a year, maybe more. You know better than any what else is stored, Bulwark of Troy.'

'Amazon, what say you?' Hector asked. Myrine had come in with the queen. She stood tall and scornful, observing the sons of Priam with cold eyes.

'If we fight on the plain, we may be defeated,' she said matter-of-factly. 'Hector is right. If they wish to besiege us, let them. They will waste their valour and miss their own sowing and harvest. What matters it to Troy that there is an army in the fields? Let them sit in the marsh and eat frogs. I would not counsel any battle; not until allies arrive and until there is need. None of you have seen battle; you must be trained. But if they come to parley and this challenge,' she shot Pariki a disbelieving look, 'then we must go out in as great an array as we can; chariots, spears, armour. These Argives judge men by their pretty clothes,' her lip curled. 'And they do not believe that women can fight. It will be interesting to see how long they cherish that opinion after they have met the Amazons.'

'Who will you send to the Amazons?' asked Hector.

'I will go myself. I reckon to be back in three weeks. Give me the sign.'

Hector took a Trojan arrow, painted it the king's colour, purple, and broke it over his knee. Priam flinched at the sound, but the queen sat motionless. Myrine did not bow, but slapped her palm flat against her breast; a warrior's salute. Then she was gone.

Hector broke more arrows, handing them out to the riders who knelt at his feet.

'Lycaon's son Pandus under Mount Idus. Adrestus and Amphius from Apaesus. Go to Asius, son of Hyrtacusin Arisbe. The Pelasgians of Larissa; find Lethus' sons. Perois of the Thracians; the king of the Cicones, Euphemus, son of Troezenus. Go to Axius, the beautiful river, and bring this to the king of the Paoeonians. You will ride to Dytorus, you should find the Paphlagonions there at this time of year; their lord is Pylaemenes. In Mysia speak to Ascanius. Find Tmolus and give him this.

Find the son of Nomion of Caria. Lastly, go to Lydia and find Sarpedon; tell him Hector bids him remember the boar-hunt.

I had noted all the names down in the priest's script as he spoke. Now I drew a black line under the names. Troy had no more allies.

'Brave messengers of Troy, go carefully,' Hector warned. 'Ride around any trouble. No heroic fight you could wage, even if you were as strong as gods, would aid Troy as much as allies. It will wait until you return, I promise.'

They bowed, were blessed, and were gone.

'Now, brothers, who are the gate wards for the next watch?'

Deiphobos, Polites, and Cerasus stepped forward.

'Watch must be kept all the time, brothers,' said Hector. 'They will try to storm the gate one moonless night when they think us asleep. We will not sleep. Regardless of the outcome of this single combat, I do not believe that the Argives, having mounted such an expedition, will tamely go home without plunder. Nor do I believe that we can buy them off. They will return after they have spent our gold and attack again. We do better to keep the money and know where the enemy is.'

He was frowning as he spoke; there was a pair of lines between his brows. His eyes, however, were serene and determined and everyone was listening. His voice was low and commanding. He stood easily, leaning on his heels, with Státhi on his shoulder; the same Hector as he had always been, infinitely to be relied upon. I felt an uprush of relief in the room. Hector would know how to wage this sort of war. He went on in his steady, patient tone.

'Each gate will have four companies of men—you may choose your own. Twenty-five men in each company on two watch shifts. But we do not leave mere soldiers to guard our walls, do we, sons of Priam? Each shift shall have one of us as captain. Each company must have two runners, ten archers, twelve soldiers, and a captain. While this war lasts, sons of the great king, we will live here in the palace. Half of us must always be in armour, ready to repel attack.'

There was some muttering at this but Hector said firmly, 'This must be so. Or we shall see the women of Troy enslaved, our children murdered, and the Achaeans will feast on our city and pick their teeth with our bones. Do you understand?' he bellowed.

I jumped and saved my inkpot by a whisker. Státhi bristled and spat at me.

'The watches will be measured by the fall of sand,' Hector added. 'The alarm signal for each gate as follows; for the Scaean, three short blasts, repeated; for the Dardanian, one long blast and one short blast, repeated; for the Scamander, continuous long blasts. Sons of Priam who are in the palace, wait after the general alarm for the signal, then take your companies to the threatened gate. Now, go and recruit your fighters. Pick the women trained by Myrine for the archers; they are the best in Troy, apart from the eight Scythians. Keep them together; they do not speak Trojan and could not understand the orders if they are separated. You may have any people you need and we can feed them all; but choose tried fighters if you can, not ambitious boys.'

Hector glowed at Pariki, who was posing elegantly by the door where the sunlight fell on his hair, and then Pandarus, who was sitting on the floor, rubbing his wrists.

Hecube walked to the door, taking a knife from me as she passed. She was not really old, I realised, just worn from child-bearing and the weight of authority. She cut into the flesh of her inner arm and cupped her hand to catch the blood which ran down.

Each son of Priam knelt before her at the door and she marked his forehead with her blood.

I had never seen this ritual; it is ancient beyond measure. The Life Giver, the Grain Keeper of the City, was making a sacrifice of herself, marking each of her warriors as her acolytes. I knelt myself as she returned my knife and I felt her thumb press into my skin.

'Cassandra, dear daughter, right hand of Hector, may the goddess protect you,' she said. I gazed up into eyes without hope and shivered. Hecube was not gifted with prophecy, but she knew what was going to happen to Troy. I bound up my mother's arm with a bandage made of a strip of tunic and tried not to shiver.

The priest of Apollo came into the palace as the last of the sons of Priam left. The king, it appeared, had sent for him. Behind him walked my twin, Eleni, dressed in the sun robes of a dedicated priest. He would not look at my face.

'What says Apollo?' asked the king and Eleni closed his eyes.

I shared the vision. A swift grey-eyed murderer, a chariot falling, the crash of men in armour; then the towers burning. I was seized by my bother Hector. He put a hand over my mouth as I started to speak and then to choke. I struggled to retain control of my body.

I felt Eleni's mind for the first time since Poseidon had returned. He saw the same as me; I was sure of it. But what he said as he sweated under the stench of smoke and death was 'Victory'.

'Eleni, no!' I struggled free of Hector. 'Tell the truth! Tell the truth, twin, if you ever loved me! Oh, the reek of burning,' and my voice went, my tongue twisted, and I fell into Hector's arms, convulsing, my mouth full of blood.

Eleni did not look at me. 'Victory,' he repeated, and the Apollo Priest led him away.

Hector carried me to Tithone, who washed out my mouth and found that I had bitten the inside of my cheek. She was grimmer than usual. As I spat salt water into her drain, I asked why.

'You know what we are called, Cassandra?'

'The healers? Yes, Clotho, Lachesis, and Athropos...' I had never thought about this before. 'The spinners, the fates. Clotho the Spinner, Lachesis the Weaver, Athropos who cuts the thread of life.'

'Clotho who deals with births and beginnings. Lachesis who treats those who will live. And Athropos who...'

'Kills?' I sat up, the pain of my twin's betrayal almost banished by the shock. 'We kill?'

She nodded. 'If this war proceeds, Princess, you will see. Forget your twin. He is under the dominion of a vengeful god and maybe Apollo will protect him. We have women's work to do and you must join your brother on the walls as he orders our defence. The riders are gone these three hours and they say that the Argive ships have landed. Go, Cassandra, healer and scribe, and make no more prophecies. They will not be needed.' She shut her mouth with a snap.

I went.

I found Hector on the wall near the Scamander Gate. Státhi was perched on his shoulder, clinging to his leather harness with his back feet while he combed his claws through Hector's hair. I bobbed up at my brother's side and he began to speak, without commenting on either Eleni or me, gently detaching the beast's hold and patting his paw.

'Troy has three gates,' he reminded me. 'Each one looks in a different direction and only Scamander commands the other two; you cannot see Scaean from Dardanian or the other way around. Státhi, you are scratching me; I am sure that you do not wish to do that. Therefore in every tower there are trumpeters or in this case one sleeping trumpeter,' he kicked the musician awake, 'and there is the sand glass which measures the watches.' He pointed out a huge glass pot, poised on another, through which sand was slowly trickling. 'When all the sand is gone into the bottom vessel, the drum sounds for a change of watch. As it will very soon.'

He looked at the trumpeter. The man waited until the last grain of sand had gone, then began to beat a large bronze drum, three beats and then a pause. Feet sounded on the stairs and twelve men came into the tower. They were half-dressed in tunics and assorted armour and seemed out of breath. Behind them came ten women, bows in hand. They selected arrows from the bundles on the tower floor and filed past to line the walls, eight paces apart.

Polites came after them. 'Brother, I have selected my guards,' he said, saluting with one hand on his breast. 'They will be ready soon.'

'I hope the Achaeans don't come first,' said Hector grimly. 'In the future, tell your previous watch that they must not leave the gate unguarded. If your next watch is late, then they must wait. A few broken heads will ensure that it turns up on time. Tell them to take a lesson from these archers. What is your name, Lady?' he asked the woman nearest to him.

'Psyche, Lord Hector.'

'You are skilled with the bow?'

'Myrine the Amazon taught me,' said the woman. 'I go hunting rabbits in the plain to feed my children, Lord. I am still a good shot. And if the Achaeans come, they will find out how Psyche feels about slavery.' She was short and plump and had a mass of dark hair, which she had bound back ruthlessly with a scarf like the market-traders wear. Hector took her bow, looking along it, tested the string, and handed it back.

Instead of speaking, he bowed ceremoniously to the archer, dislodged a talon from his neck from where the Státhi had adjusted his grip, and said, 'Come, Cassandra.'

The inside of the wall, which is of stone and three times as high as a tall man, is lined with platforms and stairs of wood, which extend all the way around and join each tower to the other. I followed Hector's heels and we traversed the lower quarter and came to the Scaean Gate, where the watch had changed and Deiphobos was berating his new soldiers about their lack of gear and lateness.

Hector listened without comment. The archers—including the Scythians—lined the wall. We looked out to sea.

Most of the ships had beached and had been dragged out of the water. Black ships with black sails—I crushed down the vision. Men had landed and were making camp, lighting little fires and fetching water. That was a good sign. The only water they could find would be water from where the Scamander flowed into the swamp and that water produced fever. I wished them all dead. The bay of Troy was empty; all our ships were either still at sea or had been dragged up to lie under the walls.

Straight down to the water the wall went. Just looking down made me dizzy. Troy is built over the river; the Scamander drains the city into the marshes—another reason why they are dangerous—and the wall over the sea is sheer; only a seagull or one of the shipmaster Aegyptus' African monkeys could climb it.

The Scythians' leather breeches offended my nose—Scythians have a religious objection to washing—as we passed them on the way to the Dardanian Gate. This looks out onto the swamps.

'They are least likely to come this way,' said Hector. 'But don't tell the guards that. Swamps and chariots do not mix. I am sorry about Eleni, my sister.'

'He was lying,' I said cautiously.

'Yes, I expect that he was.'

'Why?' the question yowled out of me as though I had been Státhi, who gave me a reproving look and leaned away from my voice.

Hector said very gently, 'What has telling the truth brought you, Cassandra, most unlucky of the daughters of Priam? Eleni is afraid of the god, afraid of the priests, afraid of himself. He must find his own fate, Cassandra,' said my brother, 'and we must find ours.'

'Who goes there?' demanded a harsh voice at that moment, and we stood still until Cerasus came and called off the guard. She was a small woman with a very long spear and for a while it looked as if the Champion of Troy was going to be spitted like a goose by his own defenders. Hector gently put the spear away from his groin.

'You have chosen your soldiers, brother?'

'As you nearly felt, brother.' Cerasus, always the most easy-going of Priam's sons, grinned. 'But am I to keep this gate always, Hector? I do not believe that they will attack on this side.'

'No, this gate will rest the weary ones; I fear that we will grow weary before the Argives go home. We will rotate the watch, Cerasus; you will have excitement enough. Are you well supplied?'

'We need more arrows.'

I made a note that the Dardanian Gate needed more arrows, next to the one which said that no wine was to be supplied hence-forward to the trumpeters.

'Begin your patrols, brother; four soldiers at a time, half a watch between the towers, then they can rest, but in armour, Cerasus. We do not know where the attack will come or when. This is not the sort of war that Agamemnon thinks it will be. He cannot drive a chariot horse full tilt against our stone walls. It would take a year to starve us out, even if we could not supply the city from the sea. Cassandra, make a note; I must talk to the priests of Poseidon and the fishermen and traders; ships will be our lifeline to the outside world, they must be protected. Can you fire arrows straight down from here, Cerasus?'

'Close enough to straight down. I have good archers.'

'Have them bring up oil and boulders; we must discourage any attack on the ships. Torches, too; all of the towers must have a supply of torches.'

I made another note. I looked over the wall out to sea, where the great wave had come. I wondered suddenly if Poseidon had made it to entrap a daughter of Priam into bringing him back into Troy. Poseidon would not care what happened to me—why should he? He was a god and gods have no interest in mortals except when it suits them. I was aghast at how far I had fallen from the Cassandra who was sunnily sure that the gods loved her as Nyssa did, as Eleni did…

I averted my face so that no tears would dilute my ink or blur my carefully constructed syllables. Hector, with Státhi on his shoulder, made an odd and compelling outline as he left the Dardanian tower and walked along the platform, stamping occasionally to check that the flooring was sound. There were a couple of wobbly places and I made another entry on my papyrus roll.

The ordinary noises of the city were reasserting themselves; babies cried, doors closed, chickens clucked, women sang at the loom. I heard hammers beating in the street of smiths and saw a man hanging out cloth at the dyers. I had often climbed the walls and the city looked much the same as it always had, sounded the same, and now, with the coming of dark, it smelt the same—of cooking onions and poured wine and water, which smells different from wine in the flask as it comes from the Island of Kriti, sealed with the goddess' seal. Bread was being taken out of the ashes in flat cakes. Children were being summoned for washing and bed. It all seemed reassuringly normal, everyday, safe.

Yet arrows bristled over our walls and the kings of the Achaeans had come with armies to attack us.

'We will hold the city of Dardanus and Priam,' mused Hector as I scuttled after him back to the Scamander Gate, where we could sight the little fires on the beaches which marked the Argive camp. He stroked Státhi and the cat angled his furry chin to the caress of the strong fingers. 'We will stave off fate yet awhile, Cassandra healer-scribe, my beloved sister.'

◇◇◇

I was sitting in the palace under a vine, later that day, making a list. Hector loved lists. The black marks scuttled over the paper like ants.

'Arrows—Cassandra, we must ensure that we have enough arrows. This war will be fought with darts,' said my brother, and I saw blood gush from a gaping wound in his neck and pour down the armour he wasn't wearing. I stared, refusing to look away—I was not going to blink, I would not give the god so much satisfaction. My insides liquefied. Hector was going to die. Behind the vision I smelt smoke and saw the palace doors broken and meal, smashed crockery, and wine on the tiled floor.

This was my curse which the vengeful Apollo had inflicted on me. To know and not to speak; and the suppression of my voice had sharpened my eyes. I was sick with despair. What would I do without Hector, my dearest brother, my shield against the council, who said I was mad?

Denying the vision would not work—the priestesses had told me that when Eleni and I had cried and begged not to have to watch some dreadful picture. I wanted to hit my head against the wall until the skull split, so that I could let out the sending. Instead, I faltered, and made a blot, bit my thumb until I saw red bruises bloom under my teeth. I needed advice; I could not despair and let the sendings overtake me or I would go mad and then I would have no defence against my visions. With a huge effort, I summoned up what the priestesses had told me about prophecy.

'Allow yourself to be one with the god,' I heard the soothing voices. 'The vision cannot be denied or pushed away or it will return, and when it returns it will be either unclear or much worse. It is not in mere humans to countermand a god. What he sends, you must see.'

'Talk to the carpenters,' Hector said, blood pulsing from his death-wound. 'See if they can substitute different woods for the shafts. We won't be able to go out into the swamp for reeds.'

My fingers wrote in syllables as he spoke to them. My inner voice listened to the priestesses. 'Prophecy cannot affect the future,' the remembered voices said. 'Men turn aside from seeing and fall into a pit. Prophecy is dangerous as a guide to action. It is just a piece cut out of the future. Your heart must not be moved, priestess of Apollo. Your love must not be given to any living thing.'

'And we had better check how much bronze we have—in ingots and in treasure which can be melted down,' said Hector, white as clay, his long hair matted with bright red blood. I dropped the stylus and bent to pick it up.

When I looked again the picture was gone. Resolve was hardening my heart. *Very well, Apollo*, I said in my heart, *I will see what you command. But you will not break Cassandra with visions. I am a princess and woman of Troy and though gods cannot be countermanded they can be defied. I will try and warn those who are about to die. Hector will die in this battle, in the sack of the city which Eleni and I have seen since we were three. Very well then; the city must not fall.*

I threw my anger and outrage at the blue sky, hoping that the god could hear. *Strike me dead, I prayed, strike me dead if you wish, childish, cruel, pitiless Apollo, but I will circumvent you, I will thwart you! I will stare and stare into the smelter's fire of death and I will not be destroyed...*

'Cassandra, did you hear? I said, we must go and check the armour of the next watch. Some of those leather shirts wouldn't keep out a hailstone. Cassandra?' he asked, worried, 'Are you all right?'

'Yes, Hector,' I said and added, 'I love you.'

He held me close and I thrust my face into his neck, kissing the place where the wound would let out his life. I acknowledged it, because a vision denied will poison the seer and not affect the fates. Hector must die; if I could not prevent it, Hector would die.

A priestess' love should not be given to any living thing, but only to the god, who cannot die.

◇◇◇

'The Princess Cassandra has defied you,' said Aphrodite. 'Apart from death there is nothing more that you can do to her, vengeful Apollo. And you may not be able to keep your golden Diomenes from the beaches at Troy.'

'And Troy shall not fall.' Sea-water slick muscles rippled in Poseidon's giant torso as he drew a deep, satisfied breath.

'Troy will fall,' Athene breathed on the water in the Pool of Mortal Lies. *'Men of my cities in Achaea are come, heroes and kings. I shall inspire them.'*

'But not aid them,' said Zeus Cloud-Compeller dryly. *'I will not have gods embroiling themselves in mortal war. That is cheating daughter. Inspire them all you wish, but you may not go down into the battle.'*

'But father,' protested Athene, *'not any of us? Not Apollo?'*

'None of you. This is the urgent petition of Demeter and she is right.'

Poseidon grinned. 'You cannot forbid me my oceans, Lord Father.'

'No. But is this your business, Sea God?'

'It is while the others try and destroy my city.'

'My Diomenes will lie at Epidavros in the arms of his wife and the war will never come near him,' declared Apollo. 'I care nothing for your squabbling over Troy.'

Chapter Eighteen

Diomenes

Spring came. Chryseis' fear never wholly left her. Although she did not speak of it again, I felt her uncertainty. It tainted my dreams, crept into my mind as we lay on the same pillow, as though the thoughts were conducted from head to head.

Her body began to swell, imperceptibly at first, and she was sick every morning, retching so hard that I ransacked the memories of every old man in the temple of Epidavros for remedies. I tried all the anti-nausea herbs; mint and thyme and sage and white-grass, comfrey and vervain and wormwood. Then I tried balm and lavender, poppy, borage, mother's herb, and marshleaf. Finally I happened on an ilex mixture which at least allowed her to retain milk or broth. Master Glaucus told me to devote all my care to her.

Arion sat in the strengthening sun as I brought Chryseis to lie in the shade and he sang quietly to her, regaining his voice. She drowsed in my arms, her head snuggled below my collarbone, while we listened as the rich voice sang, not of battles and death but of Pan and Dionysius, of Aphrodite and the judgement of Pariki, the fate of Hermaphrodita the nymph:

> *I would have him forever,*
> *Mine of me, flesh of my bone.*

Goddess, give me my shepherd,
So that we will never be parted in this world.

The warm light made an aureole of gold around Chryseis, who had turned on the bench to cradle her belly with one arm and embrace me with the other. I brushed a tendril of her hair away from my face.

Swift the Goddess answered, and the bodies melted
Together in truth flowed Hermia and her lover,
Phallus and breasts under the nymph's long hair,
One body, one mind, never to part.
Beware, lovers, how you call on the Powers
Lest you find that you get what you want.

Arion coughed experimentally and patted his chest. 'I was reminded of that song by looking at the pair of you, Diomenes. So similar you might have been twins. It's odd, you know, I find it hard to write songs about happiness. After it is gone, yes; aching ballads of loss are easy; but to say, "I am happy, my wife is beautiful and she loves me and I love her"—somehow the audience never likes it, the rhymes don't come. The muse is a captious creature. How is your beautiful wife, my golden one?'

'She is better than she was,' I stroked the long hair. 'The child is transforming her to suit its own purposes; she is very tired. When this is over she will be my joyful Chryseis again, eh, my bird, my heart?'

She smiled in her sleep and I kissed her.

Arion was looking at me with a wry quirk to his mouth, as though he had bitten a new olive. But he said nothing.

It was a generous spring and when Chryseis grew well enough to be left alone I ranged out with the herb-gatherers, seeking sweet flowers and potent leaves and roots to be preserved in oil or troches or syrups, or to be dried for the bleak days when disease strikes. For my child I cut the sacred herbs for his cradle; basil and vervain for the healer's baby.

I came into my little house one evening and my wife embraced me and sniffed. 'Orchid,' she said delightedly. 'And thyme and sage. You have been on the mountain.'

'I have and I found you this.' It was a stone shaped like a shell, so perfect that you could see the striations, though the sea was three days distant. 'How is it with you, Chryseis my heart?'

'It is well,' she said. 'I feel better than I have since I began to carry this burden. Come, let us be close, husband, come and lie with me, I have been cold without you.'

Very gently, and with trembling care, I caressed the beloved body, stroking down her face to her breasts, kissing the navel which was beginning to protrude. She shivered and pulled me down to lie around her burden, twining her legs with mine. I have always been more delighted with another's pleasure than my own; now I pleased her and she drew me close, closer. For a long time, I could not tell which of us was female and pregnant and which was male and potent; mouth and phallus connected us, exchanged us, like Hermia and her shepherd, Chryseis/Chryse, on creature and glowing with love.

We slept as last, but she cried in Morpheus' embrace. I found a wet patch on my chest in the morning. She said that she did not remember what she had dreamed about.

Arion stayed with us until summer was ripening and the first barley crop was gathered and lay drying in the fields. One morning I heard his voice calling. I left my bed and came to the door barefoot.

'Well, asclepid, I am off,' he announced. 'I am taking the road again. I came to thank you for your care, my golden one, to give you such blessing as the bard has to bestow, and to introduce you to my apprentice.'

Behind him stood a boy of perhaps twelve, laden down with a cloak, a blanket, a provisions bag, a drum, and a lyre. He had brown curly hair and eyes that were almost black. He smiled shyly.

'This is Menon the Egyptian,' said Arion. 'A fine singer and a good flute player. I need some company these days, Chryse, I am getting old.'

'Where are you going, Master Bard?' I asked, yawning and rubbing a hand through my hair. 'Back to Mycenae?'

'Useless, boy. Clytemnestra rules there and she has no ear for music and absolutely no sense of humour. There are naught but children, women, and old men in that city now. I hear that she has admitted Aegisthis, the revenge child, son of Thyestes, into Mycenae. That bodes no good to Agamemnon, no good at all. He should not have sacrificed his daughter Iphigenia to Aeolas for a south-west wind—even though it worked it was unwise. No, I am following the black ships, Diomenes. I am going to Troy.'

'He sacrificed his daughter?' I gasped.

'Yes. Sent Talthybius the herald to bring the girl, telling her mother that she was to marry Achilles; Clytemnestra dressed Iphigenia in all her bridal finery and her red veil and sent her forth with blessings. Then Agamemnon and that scoundrel Calchas, the high priest, took the child to the mountain top and cut her pretty throat on the altar. Such a waste. Queen Clytemnestra has borne a great deal from the Lord of Men; her own baby disposed of like a deformed whelp, her husband slaughtered before her eyes. It is a doomed house, the house of Atreus. I fear some dreadful stroke if the Lord of Mycenae comes home alive to his own city. But I have had news of great deeds. There are songs to be made of the siege of Troy.'

'Is there word? Have you heard of my sons?' asked Glaucus from his own door.

'They are well and doing great deeds; it appears that there has been heavy fighting and many Argives have died. This I heard last night from a Corinth trader—you treated him for pile, respected Master, but did not think to ask him for any news. Are you ready, Menon?'

The boy grinned and hefted the baggage, his foot pawing the ground like a restless horse's hoof in eagerness to be gone. I had been like that once, before I encountered the world. I smiled at him and hoped that the road would bring him happiness like mine.

'Good fortune, then, old friend,' said Glaucus and kissed Arion. 'Take good care of him, Menon.'

I embraced the old man and he kissed me, then looked at me again with that pitying, almost scornful gaze.

'Farewell, Diomenes Chryse God-Touched,' he said, and pushed me away almost roughly. 'I'll see you on the beaches.'

I watched him mount and ride out of the suppliant's gate and into the road.

'Why did he say that, Master?' I asked Glaucus. 'I have no intention of going to Troy.'

'He is an old man and his wits are not what they were,' said my master soothingly. 'How is the lady, your wife?'

'She seems content and is no longer sick,' I said staring after the retreating back of the bard and the boy.

'Good. Come to the temple of surgery this morning, Diomenes. We are to watch an interesting technique for repairing a nerve.'

I returned to my house to find myself some breakfast, thinking of the bright face of Iphigenia with her basket of coins on the steps of Mycenae. Chryseis was still asleep when I left.

◇◇◇

The soldier had been stunned with the anaesthetic smoke. Itarnes had slit his inner arm, between the bones, and was probing the bloody flesh with a silver blade as thin as gold leaf.

'There,' he instructed, 'is the old scar; a sword thrust through the arm. You can see how the hand has begun to wither. He is completely without sensation in the fingers. Here is the nerve, that string—' he pointed out a thread as fine as thin flax. 'And see how it is cloven. Now if I lie this end next to this and this end here,' he did so, delicately capturing the nerves in the pincers, 'and we wrap a little material around them—this is goat bladder, boiled three times and dried in strong sun, then oiled with olive oil and beaten and washed again—now, we will stitch the arm and we will see. It must remain still for a week,' he added, drawing the edges of the wound closed. 'And he must have enough poppy so that he feels nothing and does not try to move his fingers or it may pull the threads out of alignment.'

'Itarnes, do you really think that this will work? Why torture the man?' grumbled Tiraes. 'If the hand is to wither, it will
wither.'

'And he will be no more a man,' said Itarnes crossly. 'He's an
Achaean, they cannot bear mutilation. It is this or leave him to
kill himself—you know what they are like. There. Come back
in a week, brothers, and we shall see whether he is to be alive
or dead.'

The slaves carried the soldier away.

'Ah, Chry...Diomenes,' said Itarnes. 'Stay with me while I
wash my hands. You have the right reflexes—have you thought
of surgery? I would be glad to teach you.'

'I...no, I haven't thought of it,' I watched as he scrubbed
his hands in a lychnis solution and dried them on a piece of
linen. The slave took the bowl away. 'I haven't, but it might be
interesting. Why, Itarnes, are you thinking of going to this war?
Surely it will be over by the time you get there?'

'I don't think it will be over,' he said slowly as we left the
temple. 'I'm not going, no. But I think you'll...never mind.
Come along. First principle of the knife; don't.'

'Don't?'

'If you can avoid cutting into flesh, then avoid it. It is a last
resort. As soon as the skin is breached, all sorts of things can go
wrong. There is inflammation, there is bleeding, there is putre-
faction, swelling, and death. Most of my patients die.'

'Then why do you do it?'

'The rest are snatched out of your favourite Thanatos' arms
as if by a miracle.' He smiled.

'Oh.' I could not think of a useful comment. 'How do we
begin?'

'With the dead,' he said. 'You have been to a dissection, haven't
you? It is a terrible burden and a frightening thing, to take apart
what the gods have designed and the Mother has made. Only
we must understand, Diomenes. Understanding the world is our
purpose in life, the reason why the gods gave us wits and hands.
But it must be done prayerfully, with the breath held in awe.'

We walked to the mortuary. There was only one body there, an old man.

'Now, asclepid, how did he die?' Itarnes asked me. I stripped back the cerements and felt over the body, gently, finding a large lump in the swollen abdomen and smaller ones all over the chest, in both armpits and under the jaw.

'Cancer,' I said. 'The crab killed him. This is the first tumour; the others have multiplied as he weakened.'

'Good. When the priests call us this evening, you will see if you are right.'

I went to the deep pool in the river, put off my tunic, and swam in the cold water for a long time, until I felt cleansed.

◇◇◇

That night, among clouds of incense, it was revealed as Itarnes peeled back the secrets of the old man's body that he had died not of cancer but of the Egyptian worm which makes cysts in the cavities of the belly and the lung. It was his spleen that I had felt.

A week later I watched as the Achaean flexed fingers which had not worked for a month and saw the smile creep over his face of a man reprieved from death.

◇◇◇

After three months I was as accomplished a surgeon as I was going to be, which was only ordinarily skilled, and Chryseis was at her time.

She went into labour at the dead watch, when the stars burn bright and the moon is down. I felt her shift clumsily to lay her head on my shoulder. She was sweating. A whimper escaped her close-tight lips and I awoke fully.

'It is beginning,' she said. 'Stay with me.'

'Always,' I replied. 'Sit up, dear heart.' I pulled her up into my arms so that we were leaning against the wall. 'Keep warm and be brave, sweet maiden.'

She snuggled closer and my arms enfolded her. We lay like that until dawn came.

I sent for the priest of Demeter at noon. He came, an old man with wise eyes and a broken nose, which he always said he got as a present from a birthing mother. He talked to Chryseis, prodded her belly, and waited while one pain ebbed and another one came. 'Soon,' he said, and she sighed. Her eyes closed, those amber eyes which had always enthralled me. Her eyelashes lay ordered and dark on her pale cheek. I had changed her tunic twice. She was drenched in fluids, but she could not swallow.

'Call me again at dusk,' said Demeter's priest. 'Give her milk and honey; I will make some infusions. Talk to her,' he added.

I sat next to my wife and began to talk, not expecting a reply, meandering my way through my travels, from Kokkinades to Tiryns, Tiryns to Midea and the Cyclopes, Midea to Mycenae, where Eumides the freed slave had comforted my broken heart. I wondered where he was, my Trojan. I remembered suddenly the taste of his lips, blood and starvation, as he kissed me in the street of Mycenae. I had not thought of him for a year. He had been afraid of being sacrificed and I assured him that we did not do such things. Now Agamemnon had done it; spilled his daughter's blood for a wind to Troy. Chryseis replied sometimes, asking occasional questions, laughing at the description of the soot-covered smith and the cleaning treatment dictated by Asclepius. Each time she began a sentence, the pain would come again and she would break off and clutch my hand, gasp, and forget what she had been saying. So finally I just babbled, wittering on like an old man in the marketplace, for every pain hurt me, struck like a knife into my vitals, and it took all my hard-earned healer's self-command to make my voice work.

Even as she was, her hair draggling across her shoulders, her body swollen and deformed, her face twisted with anguish, tears flowing from her eyes, she was exceedingly beautiful to me.

At night I called the priest of Demeter again. He listened at her belly, lifted her onto her feet, jolted her so that she screamed, and muttered, 'I'll make another infusion, Diomenes.'

I smelt it when he brought it. Pennyroyal, to expel a dead child.

I did not care about the child. I wished it never conceived. She was getting weaker; the pains were lessening as her strength was exhausted. I could not speak to her now, but I could sing, long, long ballads of gods and maidens, so old that half of the words were incomprehensible.

The night lasted a hundred years. By the oil lamp, I held her twisting body, wracked with agony, and I could do nothing.

Itarnes came at dawn the next day and I screamed at him to go away. I had seen the removal by knife of a child from a living mother. She had died immediately and the child had lived; I remembered a little hand curling up out of the bloody ruin of the womb. Itarnes limped away.

At noon my master came and I crawled out of the little house to his feet, so cramped that I could not walk. I sat down and stared blankly at him.

'You will drink this,' he gave me a cup of undiluted wine. I was so exhausted that I did as I was bid, and blinked. 'You will eat,' he gave me a bowl of suppliant's broth and I drank it. Some force flowed back into me. I stretched. He pulled me to my feet.

'Chryse, she must be taken out of the sacred precinct,' he said gently. I understood slowly, shook my head and cried, 'No! Master, no. Please.'

'It must be,' he said. Slaves carrying a litter went into my little house and I heard a shriek. I dived in and lifted her in my arms, then walked out into the bright sunlight.

I carried my wife to the fountain and sat down with her on the cool grass. Glaucus stood a moment, unspeaking, then went away. No one must die or be born in the tholos of Epidavros. I did not think that anything would be born from this tortured body. At dusk I heard someone coming in. It was Itarnes. 'It is the only hope to save your child,' he urged 'Let me use the knife, Diomenes.'

'The child is dead,' I said dully. 'There is nothing to be done.'

At dawn the next day I felt a change. I had long since ceased to speak or sing. Once I laid her down with her back to the tree, cocooned in my cloak, but she cried after me, so my presence was comforting her. I noticed that several slaves and the priest of Demeter were sitting three paces away from us, waiting. I had nothing to say to them. My throat had contracted too tightly for me to speak.

A cock crowed. The day began to lighten, grey with mist. Chryseis convulsed and screamed; I had never heard such a sound. Her legs flexed, cramped, flexed again. I bore her up as something was born on a gush and pulse of blood. I saw the after-birth delivered; the womb was emptied; her burden was gone.

Someone gathered up the born thing; cloths were brought, and she sipped wine and water, lying in my arms. Blood glued my tunic to my body, warm blood. Chryseis was bleeding to death and no bark would staunch it. The attendants scurried away as I snarled at them to be gone.

I laid both hands on her belly and I called the god.

My cry rose to heaven, my thought ranged; I demanded, I summoned. I cast out my call and there was nothing in the world which would answer me. Heaven was hollow and echo-ing. In my most desperate need I promised I would devote all my life to the sick; I vowed that I believed in the gods. Just give me my Chrysies, Lord Pluton, of all your bounty, you do not need her gentle presence in you dark kingdom. Do not let her wander voiceless with the shades, lost to me forever. Do not take her away from me, or I must follow for I cannot live without her smile. You healed the boys because of his lover; heal my wife because of me! I am Diomenes, God-Touched, Chryse, of the healing hands, your servant, your slave. Apollo, Asclepius, Demeter Protector of Women, all gods, hear and answer me!

There was no sound.

My back hurt, my belly flamed as if a fire had been lit there. I was back on the grass near the fountain, with my wife in my arms. Her body was heavy with escaping life, her limbs loose, her hands which tried to reach up and caress my face were too heavy for the delicate wrists to lift. I stared into the amber eyes as they found mine and the gaze locked.

'Chryse?' she said in that mimic's voice she had used when we first met.

'Chryse,' I whispered. 'I love you.'

'I love you,' she said, 'husband...' Her voice was gone. She breathed her last breath into my mouth as I kissed her.

Her lips grew cold. The golden eyes had glazed. I saw the gods at last, too late, too late! The cloudy angel of death descended with a rustle of feathers, and Chryseis rose, naked and glittering, to lie in his everlasting arms. I saw her turn and snuggle into his downy breast, heave a sigh, and fall asleep. The angel laid one hand for a moment on my head as though he was blessing me and then they were gone.

I was holding an idol resembling Chryseis, a carrion image. She was gone. However, when slaves came and tried to take her out of my embrace, I clung to her and I believe that I fought them.

I do not remember the rest of the summer.

Chapter Nineteen

Cassandra

I was kneeling at the window in the Scamander Gate tower when I saw that the Achaeans, who had buzzed around their camps like a swarm of bees for a week, had suddenly split into groups and I caught a runner and told her to find Hector straight away.

It was a bright morning and I shaded my eyes. The sun shot level shafts along the plain of Troy, dazzling the sight. Through a halo of dust I could see an army marching.

Trumpeters blew the general alarm. I heard feet running and the clang of armour as soldiers scaled the ladders. Soon the wall was lined with watchers.

'They're coming,' breathed Polites from behind me. 'The whole of the Achaean army, I would say. Has Hector been summoned?'

'Hector is here,' said Hector quietly. 'What is moving?'

'The Argive host,' I replied. 'In armour, with chariots.'

'There is a herald.' He pointed out a red horsetail on the helmet of a tall man who rode ahead of the dust cloud. 'A challenge, perhaps? Or a parley?'

Státhi stalked along the wall, interested in the moving, toy-sized chariots, and put out a questing paw to capture a horse and rider. Hector put him down onto the watchtower floor and he sat, wrapping his tail around himself, elaborately unimpressed.

'A parley,' said Polites. 'See, the reversed shield.'

The Achaeans had huge shields, tall as a man, with cross-bindings of bronze in the shape of two fish, tied tail to tail. The red-helmeted one was carrying his shield sideways and had no weapons that we could see. The Argives usually bore a bundle of spears, light and pointed, unlike the Trojans' heavy brazen javelins with their wicked spade-shaped heads. This herald had no spears.

He walked his horse ahead of the army, which had halted in the idle of the plain, trotting right through the Place of Stranger's Gods and stopping under the Scamander watchtower, in front of the firmly closed gate.

'Men of Troy!' he called. 'Is there one listening with the rank to parley with the Atreidae, lords of the land of Pelops, mighty warriors?'

'There is one,' said Hector equably. 'Hector, Son of Priam, Prince of Troy. Your name, Argive?'

'Talthybius, Herald of Agamemnon Lord of Men, Master of Mycenae of the Golden Walls, and of Menelaus his brother, Prince of Sparta.'

'Speak, herald,' said Hector.

Talthybius took a deep breath and announced, 'The Lords of Achaea, Menelaus and Agamemnon, demand the return of Elene, the most beautiful woman in the world, stolen from her husband by Pariki, Prince of Troy.'

'We do not have Elene, Princess of Sparta, as your masters must know,' said Hector. 'She left my brother in Egypt and she is still there. Go seek her, herald, at the delta of the Nile in the temple of Isis.'

'She was taken by your brother, Prince of Troy,' said Talthybius. 'You must return her.'

'We cannot do that,' said Hector patiently. 'News travels fast in the trading ports; they have been laughing for months at Pariki's abandonment by Elene. Ask them in Corinth and in Navplion. This is not the cause of your war, Herald. Have your masters given you anything else to say?'

The herald looked up. His eyes glittered; for a moment I saw his long hands drip with blood and knew it was Trojan blood. I bit my lip and did not speak and the vision washed over me like a wave and was gone. I was becoming skilled in not speaking, but that did not preserve me from knowing.

'I stole her because you stole Hesione, Princess of Troy,' said Pariki's voice from the wall. 'I lost her and you still have Hesione. It seems that the Achaeans have the better of the bargain.'

Hector took two strides and was beside his brother, gagging him with one hand and whispering, 'Say one more word, Pariki, and I will snap your neck.' Pariki paled. Hector released him and he backed away, his hand automatically smoothing his dishevelled hair.

'My masters bid me say that the war against Troy, which has occupied eight years, must be brought to a conclusion,' the herald continued. I raised my eyebrows at Polites. It was news to us that Achaea had been at war with us at all.

Of course, they raided our port occasionally and stole women and goods; and any ship which they captured was looted and the crew enslaved. They continually attacked our coasts and tried to disrupt our trade and had been attempting to plot against us with our allies, Caria and Phrygia, and even with Thrace, but that did not constitute a war, did it? I realised that perhaps, in the Argive mind, it did. We had just assumed that the new king of Mycenae was short of gold and had employed more pirates than usual.

'What conclusion do the Atreidae intend?' asked Hector.

'We have fought bravely,' said the herald, 'sacking many cities and villages in Caria and in Phrygia. Much gold and bronze and many slaves have come to Atreidae as they sat in their magnificent cities.' He paused.

'Well, they are fortunate,' said Hector.

'Now they come to sack the city of Troy. Come out and fight, Hector. We await you in the plain.'

'And you can continue to await me,' said Hector coolly. 'I will not come forth from Dardanus' city of Tros, built by Poseidon, to engage with a lawless host. Attack more undefended villages, I say to the Atreidae, since that is their piratical way; let them exercise their valour on enslaving children; let them go forth and murder more goatherds.'

'Heart of a doe,' taunted the herald. 'Are the men of Troy castrated that they have no courage?'

'You have exceeded your office, Talthybius of the lying tongue,' yelled Polites. 'Return to the Atreidae and tell them what our commander, Hector of the glittering helmet has said.'

'This conference is ended,' Hector said, and moved away from the wall.

'Will they attack?' I asked. Hector was staring at the army as the herald rode back to it. When he reached the Achaean commanders and gave his message, we heard a cry of rage and fury from many throats. I never heard a thousand men cry out at once. It was chilling. I tried not to shiver as I sat on the floor, eye-to-eye with Státhi, who was unconcerned.

'Yes, I think they will,' said Hector. 'Is everyone out of the lower city?'

'No, Lord, there are some who would not come; I went at dawn to order them in, but they refused.' Polites was apologetic. 'I had some of them carried inside. The gates are shut and guarded. It is surely too late to open them.'

'Then they will die,' said Hector. 'Go and call to them over the Dardanian Gate; tell them to look out upon the plain. If they run for the city now, we can save them. Go with him, Cassandra. The people trust you.'

I ran after Polites to the Dardanian Gate and shrieked down to the hovels, 'The Argives have come! The army is marching! Come inside, all who do not wish to be slaughtered!'

'Princess!' A startled man looked up. 'Will they kill us?'

'Yes!' I screamed. It was easy to speak when I did not have to prophesy. 'Thus it will be if you do not come inside now!'

The man paused, sighted along the plain, and then called, 'Cassandra, our princess has prophesied! Come, to the gate, to the gate, wife, come now, mother!'

I do not know his name but he was a good leader. The word spread along the sprawling alleys and people ran, carrying babies and bundles. We must have collected a hundred of the lower city's laggard citizens through the open gate before the Argive army struck the Scamander side and sweating soldiers slammed the portal and barred it with tree trunks.

Even then one young man beat upon it. Polites dropped a rope to him and he clung and began to climb. I saw his death before it came to him.

An Argive spear pierced him and he shrieked and fell. Polites dragged up the rope. 'Archers!' he commanded and ten women stepped forward to the breast-high rampart. 'Wait the signal.'

The noise of the army was deafening. Dust rose from their feet upon the earth and their footsteps rang like drums. They bellowed, 'Eleu, eleu, eleu, leu, leu,' as though they were hunting. Rough music for murder.

I heard screams in the lower city as the huts burst into flame; I saw women dragged out and raped in plain sight, slaughtered and eviscerated. They cut off one man's head and thrust it on a spear for the sake of his long hair. One of the archers clutched her breast and groaned, 'My son!'

She was a brave woman. She did not speak again after her shocked cry but bent her bow as the order came and the Trojan arrows sped like birds to find lodgings in Argive flesh. 'Seek for the joint of the armour,' instructed Psyche, Myrine's pupil. 'Aim for the legs, the armpit, the neck. There,' she said as a yelling man fell dead, pierced through the eye, onto the body of the woman he was attempting to gut like a deer. 'See? Take a deep breath, let it out slowly, and release the arrow; do not pluck at the string like a harpist. One in ten of our arrows will find good lodging.'

I went to Scamander to find Hector. He was standing in the tower, supervising the archers.

'Hold,' he ordered. 'They have fallen back. We must not waste the arrows. Good, archers of Troy, see how many have been felled by your skill!'

The Scamander Gate was piled with dead. I looked down on them without pity; indeed, I seemed to have no emotions and that was a relief. The army had drawn back and were screaming insults at us. 'Come out, Trojan cowards, women, dolls!' they cried. 'Come out and fight like men.'

'Come out and die like fools,' growled Hector. 'Here they come again. Archers, bend your bows. Wait for the signal. Cassandra, go down to the gate and tell them to be on guard. I do not think that the enemy can break it, but they must watch for any Argive who reaches it and tries to climb.'

I ran down the ladder and then the stairs. Fifty soldiers gathered on either side of the massive gate, listening to the screams of the dying outside. If any foe managed to climb he would be shot off the gate by the Scythians, who kept to their group, horn bows ready. Theirs were the only faces which were smiling. Scythians love war.

I myself was not enamoured. Dust was blurring the attack outside and I was glad because I felt no glow of satisfaction at watching anyone die. Neither did the archers, though they drew and loosed with cold efficiency. Hours had flown past. The Argives attacked, were driven off, attacked again. The mound of dead Achaeans under the gate grew. There was a pool of collected blood the size of a lake in the Place of Strangers' Gods. The drum sounded for the change of watch.

'Myrine would be proud of you,' Hector told his soldiers. 'Stay where you are until the one behind can replace you. Go into the watchtower, warriors, and then down into the palace where Priam will give you wine and bread. Songs will be made of your skill.'

The men smiled wearily at that, but a baker said, flexing her tired arms, 'I want no songs, Hector Prince of Troy, but peace and more peace for a thousand years.'

A few Achaean arrows skipped off the walls, slightly wounding one archer and killing a soldier in the tower. An unlucky boy. I found as I came to tend him that it was Sirianthis and he was dying. The arrow had pierced his neck and gone right through his chest. I lifted him in my arms and rested his head against my breast.

'Cassandra,' he said with an effort. 'It's all going dark,' and he died.

I laid him down, but then found that the arrow had arched his body so that he could not lie flat, even in death. I took my knife and sawed through the shaft. The breath left him as I rolled him onto a stretcher to be carried away for burning.

Poor Siri, always clumsy, always unlucky. I noticed as I straightened his body that there was still a callous on the bone in the shoulder joint which I had mended so long ago. At that moment I found out how much I could hate. A dark wave flooded through me. My senses sharpened, my hands began to tremble. Had I had the power of a god, I would have blasted the Achaean army off the face of the earth. I would have laughed while they were atomised and danced on the pieces.

Towards dusk the remains of the Argive army began to retreat. We did not trust them. No soldier left the walls until they were almost out of sight. Night fell. The watches were maintained. We saw their little fires; they would have seen the torches at each tower.

Tithone sent for me at dawn the next day. I had slept, it appeared, though I did not remember doing so. I put on a working tunic and followed the runner to Tithone's house. She was sitting in the street with ten women almost her own age; all healers. One of them was an Egyptian in the characteristic squared headdress and three women from the port.

'Cassandra, we must do something about the dead,' she said harshly. 'When the sun rises they will begin to stink and the city will be infected with the miasma. There must be a way that Hector can arrange to drag them away from the walls, over the river, and into the plain. Do you know anything of the customs of the Argives? How do they dispose of their dead?'

'They bury them,' I answered, ransacking my memory for sailor's tales. 'They won't be able to do that here.'

'No; that plain is hard earth and solid stone one spade's breadth down.'

'Tithone, Mistress, come up on the walls,' I urged. 'There are too many for us to bury or burn; it is a massacre outside Scamander Gate. The Argives must come for their own dead, though what they will do with them I do not know or care. Of our own; maybe thirty were murdered. We can burn that many. I will go and ask Hector and then I will come with you.'

'No, Cassandra, my daughter, we will deal with them. You are too young, maiden, to carry the dead. That is the crone's task, Athrope's duty. I do not doubt your courage,' she added, 'but this is the way of it; old women know death and cannot be sickened of life by any horror. We have clung to it this long; we are intimate with despair. You, my daughter, Healer Scribe have borne no child and it is forbidden for you to do this. Ask your brother, Cassandra, what he means to do about the corpses. We will await you here.'

I found Hector in the palace, eating bread dipped in olive oil and drinking not wine but water. Andromache was with him. I did not have to touch her to know that she was pregnant, though possibly she did not know this yet. I could not speak of my message in the hearing of an expectant mother so I stroked Státhi and offered him a piece of dried fish. He considered it for a moment, then snatched it out of my grasp, missing my fingers with his sharp white teeth only because I pulled them back. I had fed Státhi before. He could not be tamed.

The Státhi cub, however, was still reposing in Andromache's bosom, being fed on goat's milk. It purred and suckled at her ear while she winced and giggled, and it did not scratch her once, proving that it was entirely domesticated. Andromache allowed me to hold it, a tiny thing with a cold black nose and blue eyes which fitted neatly into the palm of my hand and had a delightful, absurd, triangular tail.

'Is it female?' I asked, and Andromache nodded. 'Státhi will be pleased,' I added. 'Can I borrow Hector for a moment, sister?'

Hector came three paces with me and I explained about the dead. He frowned.

'We will have to wait and see what the Achaeans do today. We have beaten back their first assault with great loss; they will be surprised and shocked. If they attack again, anyone caught on the plain will be killed. It is too risky, Cassandra, until I have some words from those pirates tell Tithone to wait. If they have not come by tomorrow, I will send a herald to their camp, a Trojan less haughty than their Talthybius. Deiphobos, I think. Three days will not render the dead so offensive that they cannot be handled.'

As I walked back down the steep streets, I reflected that three days made stinking carrion out of any corpse, especially in summer. For an eye blink everyone I saw was dead. There was a woman with the marks of the strangler's hands on her throat; a man with a wound in the belly out of which his entrails bulged. The wine-seller walking ahead of me had an arrow in his back; a woman carrying a basket was drowned, her hair flowing like seaweed, her face swollen with water.

'Apollo,' I spoke aloud. 'I defy you!' the corpses' gummy eyes turned on me and I flung myself aside into the cool, paved entrance of the temple of the Mother.

'Gaia,' I began the ritual prayer automatically. 'Look down on your children. Mother,' I screamed, 'I can't bear it!' and I fell flat and began to beat my head against the floor, babbling and crying. Acid burned in my breast.

Someone said, 'Cassandra.'

The woman sitting in the shrine was draped in green garments. When I lifted my head I saw that they were living plants. The Earth Mother, ever nurturing, ever patient, the most tolerant of goddesses until she becomes angry, and then she is death, drought or flood or fire and famine on the plains.

'Daughter,' she said, 'your sight is sharp. You would not have seen me before Apollo cursed you.'

'Mother,' I rose to my knees, 'help me. Take this burden from me.'

'Cassandra,' her voice was a caress. 'You must know and not speak and you must live. From this curse you have gained eyes brighter than any other's. You are strong. You will bear this and you will endure; just as I endure, as the earth endures. Stone is strong but can be cracked in fire; metal must be your heart, daughter; to see and know and not speak you must be as flexible as metal. Time will melt you and re-cast you and then you will be shining.'

'Mother, it's not fair, it's not just!'

'Justice?' she seemed amused, though I could not see her face under the fold of her jasmine veil. 'What have the gods to do with justice?'

'How shall I bear it?' I wailed. A hand stroked my cheek.

'You will bear it,' she said. 'You have already begun.'

Then she was gone and the shrine was empty. I touched my face where the goddess' hand had lingered and smelt a fragrance divinely sweet, divinely strong.

Then I walked into the market place and the traders were all alive. The smoke from the citadel caught my throat. The priests of Apollo were burning Sirianthis.

Mid-morning brought Talthybius, less insulting of tongue, requesting a truce to bury the dead. This Hector granted, and a long string of horses were brought to drag the dead Argives away. The trail of led animals and their burdens stretched all the way from the city to the Achaean camp. We heard them wailing as they went, calling the names of the dead as though they could answer, weeping for their lovers and their comrades.

Tithone took her women out into the devastated ruins of the lower city after noon. They had a wagon drawn by two horses and twenty soldiers.

I was leaning on the wall, looking down into the plain, when I saw the old women hunting among the fallen huts and the remains of little houses. I saw Tithone drag out a man with both legs crushed who still cried pitifully. She examined him, then knelt next to him, talking; I could not hear what she said. He nodded.

Then I saw a healer's knife flash, the head fall to one side as the throat was stabbed through. The whimpering ceased.

The soldiers who had been sent with the Athropeae were tearing the huts apart for wood and building a pyre between Scamander and the plain. Twenty cartloads of summer-dried wood went into the foundation; then they began to lay out bodies with consideration and respect; I sighted the eviscerated woman and the baby I had not seen which the rapists had smothered under her. Twenty-five corpses were laid out before they started the fire.

The Place of Strangers' Gods was soaked in blood; flies buzzed there. The crones directed that the wagon should be used to carry sand from the river bank to cover the ground. Then they stayed to tend their fire as the convulsing dead took flame at last and burned brightly. When it had died down they beat the embers with spades to smash all the remaining bones, carried the ashes to the Scamander, and gave them to the river.

I had never thought that Tithone the Healer could kill. I came down to the gate to meet her as she returned.

'There are three alive,' she said wearily. 'They are your charge, Cassandra. We go to be purified by the Mother.'

There was a child, who had been under a fallen hut, so horrified by something she had seen that she had not cried. There was a woman in the rags of a tunic and a young man with a dented head and broken arm. I brought them all to Tithone's house, the only Trojans saved of the massacre of the lower city.

The child was shocked, not hurt; she began to wail as soon as she knew that she was safe. I examined her carefully and could find no wound and gave her into the arms of an enameller who had lost her baby. She held the girl safely but not too tightly and carried her away to be fed. The young man had been struck by a falling house-beam. There was a depression in his skull, but he could see and hear and complained only of the pain of his broken arm. I washed him, fed him poppy and comfrey, and set the arm and splinted it. It was a clean break. I sent him to the palace to sleep off the drug. He would either not wake again because of some injury to his head or be all right in the morning. My vision said that he would not live.

The young woman did not react until I cut off the remains of her filthy tunic and began to wash her. Polyxena, my sister, who had come to help me pointed to a series of bruises which told their own tale; on her shoulders, her wrists, and the inside of her thighs, where she had clamped legs over her assailants hip-bones to resist his invasion of her body.

She shuddered as the cool water and soap-leaf sluice away blood and slime. 'I was a maiden,' she whispered.

'Yes, you were,' I agreed. 'You are not badly hurt.'

'That's why they didn't kill me,' she said, beginning to sob and laugh. 'They said that they had dishonoured Troy by mating with me; they left me alive to tell the Trojans that this will be the fate of all their virgins. They are mad, they are all mad, Cassandra. I was going to the god; will he still accept me?'

'Of course,' I said soothingly. 'You have made your sacrifice. You belong to the Lord Dionysius and the Mother now. Go and talk to the priestesses of Gaia; they will consecrate you.'

'They thought that they had done something lawless and daring,' she stopped laughing. 'I've been lying out there all night, wondering about them. I'm alright, Cassandra, there were only two of them and it was over in a moment. It was not their phalluses I was afraid of, but their spears. They killed Lani, though. I heard them kill her. Is the baby…'

'The baby is dead.'

'They are monsters,' she said, and began to weep.

I treated her bruises and sent Polyxena to lead her to the temple of Gaia. The Mother's priestesses would comfort her.

Polyxena came back, her face dark with thought. I asked her if she was afraid.

'No. But I cannot get his face out of my mind.'

'Whose face?' I was not paying attention to my sister. I was counting pots of ointment and wondering where I would get fresh comfrey for the wounded.

'*His* face, the swift runner, Achilles.'

That engaged my notice. I swung towards her and said 'Polyxena, you cannot fall in love with a murdering Achaean.'

'I am not in love with him,' she flashed. 'But I can't get him out of my head…the grey eyes and the golden hair of Achilles.'

I dosed her with a strong infusion of hyssop and mistletoe and took her back to the Maidens.

Perseis had decided that her maidens should be usefully occupied. She had sent them on a vigorous rummage through the linens for old cloth, and was supervising the making of bandages. This is a tedious, fiddly process, for each cloth has to be washed and dried in the sun, then torn, soaked in salt water, dried again, and rolled. There were enough old tunics in the pile to last us for years—or so I thought—and the process would take the maidens some days. I delivered Polyxena to the Mistress of Maidens, mentioning that she was not well—anyone who had fallen in love with Achilles was definitely ill. While I was there, I collected some clean tunics and my washing things from my little room. It seemed like years since I had danced in the grip of Dionysius. I patted my fresco affectionately—I had always liked those fish. Even the octopus seemed less menacing when the Argive army was massing outside.

Iris was telling a long story about the founding of Troy, accompanied by Cycne on the lap harp. She laid it aside as I came in. I was looking briefly at every person I saw, just raising my eyes for a flashing glance, in case they were dead. If they were I stared if I could endure it. Luckily, the maidens of Troy looked as alive as they usually did. This time.

'Tell us,' she begged. 'What is happening? I am too slow for a runner and too tall for an archer. Hector sent me back because I was too visible over the wall.'

'The assault has been beaten off and they are licking their wounds like dogs.' I leaned against a pillar, longing for a bath and a dark place with no gods, but knowing that I would not get it. 'Hector says that the walls will hold.' There was a sigh of relief. Everyone trusted Hector's opinion. 'But he says they will come again and I have to get back to him. Eirene, can you get me some more ink?' She nodded and took my ink-pot.

'What of the lower city?' asked Iris. 'We heard the…screams.'

'Most were saved, twenty-five are dead. So is Siri, poor Siri. An arrow; luckily these Achaeans have few archers and we have many.'

'Will they take the city?' asked Cycne. 'Because I will not be a slave again.' She showed me a thick knife, worn inside her tunic. I shook my head.

'They will not take the city today,' I hazarded. 'Or tomorrow. I have to go.'

'Dion was looking for you,' said Cycne. 'What shall we tell him?'

I had completely forgotten him. 'Where is he?'

'Down by the Scaean Gate, protecting the ships. He and Maeles have set up the temple of Poseidon there. I saw them when we went to fetch sea water for the bandages.'

'Tell him I will find him if I have time.' I heard the alarm sound, flat short blasts on the trumpets of the Scaean and the Scamander towers. Gathering my clean chiton and my ink and medicines, I picked up my robe and ran.

I climbed to the Scamander Gate and looked across the plain. Hector and Deiphobos stood side by side and gaped.

'Surely they do not mean to try this frontal assault again,' whispered Deiphobos, son of Priam. 'Not after the damage we did to them! More than a hundred must have been killed by arrows alone.'

'They are fools who wish to die,' grunted Hector. 'Or, no, that is unfair. They think that the city should have fallen; they are trying to bash down the walls with their heads. Are the archers ready?'

We had drawn the Scythians as well as the usual soldiers. Eight of them lined our part of the wall, grinning. I did not like to be in close proximity to them because they stank, being desert people and unused to water. (Tithone said that they and water would repel each other and that was why Scythians could not drown.) Nevertheless they were efficient. Their horn bows were twice the length of ours. They shot heavier arrows, bolts as long as my arm, with stone heads. They were encouraging each other in guttural tones, nudging elbow to rib and chuckling.

'The fools come straight on,' commented one, 'as though there were no gods in Troy.'

'Not only do we have gods, we have bowmen as well,' said another and they laughed aloud. I wished that I did not understand Scythian.

No challenge came from the approaching army. They had left their chariots behind—there is no use for chariots in a siege, they can hardly batter our walls with their horse's heads. Instead, they were riding in a great circle around the city. I wondered how they would manage in the marsh when the alarm came from the Dardanian Gate. Cerasus was about to see some fighting.

The elite guard, twenty-five of Priam's sons, came hurtling down to the Dardanian Gate from the palace. I ran with Hector around the walls as arrows skipped across the stones. Behind me I heard the deeper twang of the Scythian bow and the congratulatory cries as the wielders counted fallen foes. 'One, two, three—no brother, that was only the horse. Nonsense, brother, the man fell under the horse, he must be dead. No, you are right, he's getting up, but he will be dead soon.' The bow sang. 'There, you owe me a bottle of wine, brother, I have drawn first blood. And another bottle for the horse.'

Their voices faded behind me, arguing about whether a half bottle was the price for a horse since horses were admitted to be half as intelligent as men. I did not have time to be sick.

Cerasus had organised his archers. As we came up he gave the order to fire. The Dardanian Gate is smaller than the others. Around it stretch the marshes and swamps into which the Scamander drains, splitting into a thousand little streams. I used to gather marsh-leaf there, sovereign for all inflammations, and the children of Troy caught fish and eels in the muddy waters. The city's sewers, in times of high tide, back up into the swamp, and it is an unhealthy place; no one lives there because of the fever in the water. Scamander splits into two streams at Troy; one runs under the city and into the bay and one meanders sadly into this soggy place.

It was no place for horses. The fine steeds floundered and neighed their complaints. I saw one of them bore the king's brand; they had raided our own herds, the pirates. Some had thrown their captors and were splashing through the shallows; some, under the weight of armoured riders, were mired to the belly and unable to move.

The infantry were no better off. Cerasus ordered another volley and thirty men were cast screaming into the swamp, where unless they were instantly rescued they were going to drown under the weight of breastplate and helmet.

'This is slaughter,' said our brother into Hector's ear. 'Shall I continue?'

'Better they be slaughtered than us,' said the warrior grimly. 'I think this is a diversion. Guard your gate, brother, and pick off the men, try and spare the horses. It is not their fault. Aha,' he added as the alarm sounded for the Scamander Gate. 'What did I say? Cassandra, take Státhi. Follow and keep down.'

We paced the city again, high up above the houses. Státhi did not want to be held and scratched me until I clasped him under one arm and seized hold of all four taloned feet. I heard a hub-bub on the wall and a large stone smashed and splinted on the breastwork.

'Slingers!' exclaimed Deiphobos. 'Brother, there are catapults.'

Moving like a tortoise, a wall of shields locked side to side was shuffling towards Troy. Behind it were men with leather slings and many men with spears.

'Yes. Move the soldiers back; keep only the ones small enough to just see over the wall. They cannot bring down Poseidon's work with little rocks, but they can damage us.'

A flight of spears hit the wall and fell back; the next went over our heads to stick in the wooden scaffolding. Some fell into the city and I heard a scream.

'Lay shields behind you to stop those spears getting through,' ordered Hector. 'Gather them; they may be returned to their

owners. Keep your heads down. What is their plan, Cassandra?'
he seemed puzzled. 'Throwing stones is not going to work. Boy,
run to Cerasus, son of Priam, and bring him Hector's greetings
and ask him what is happening with him.' The runner sped
away. He was about eight and no spear would catch him; he
was a good span smaller than the wall. 'Deiphobos, what do
you think?' said Hector.

Deiphobos was rattled but preserving him calm. 'It is a
diversion?'

'Possibly, but for what?'

The Scythian commented and I translated, 'They may be carrying a ram. In which case I think that we should demonstrate
what Scythian bows will do before they get close to the gate.'

'Do so,' said Deiphobos at Hector's nod.

The Scythians were the best bowmen in the world. Perhaps
because each missed mark was paid for by a slash across the chest
by their master when they were learning, they seldom missed.
They wore leather breeches, leather caps, and a lot of golden
jewellery, and their chests were bare and scarred. Although they
were taller than the wall, they never stayed visible long enough
for a catapult to hit them.

Hector and I crouched at the watchtower window which
commanded the plain and saw the Argives fall; I had never
realised that a Scythian arrow could go through a shield. They
pinned the shields to the men behind, through seven layers of
ox-hide, through leather helmets and through the chinks in
bronze armour. One after another they reaped the attackers
as with a scythe; the Argives fell in their formation, in a neat
horse-shoe shape, with stone-tipped bolts through them. Their
battering ram lay draped in corpses.

It took one of them all watch to die. He cried for his mother.

At dusk Hector ordered the Scythians to kill him. They were
unwilling; they relished the sound of their enemy's cries, saying
that it pleased their bloodthirsty gods. But Hector insisted, the
bow twanged and the cries ceased.

I hated the Scythians, at that moment, more than I loathed the Achaean army.

◇◇◇

Pan threw aside his pipes. The shapely, long-fingered hand clenched into a fist. He seized a cup of nectar and drained it in a gulp, flinging it aside so that it smashed. Shards of red terracotta decorated with dancing maidens scattered across the stones of Olympus with a sound like dry leaves.

'Warriors and ships,' he snorted. 'Siege and death! Mortals are frail and easily broken. Why have you begun this slaughter? I see gods here—powerful gods, Children of Time and Chaos. What are you doing to this earth which Demeter made?'

'Goat-God,' sneered Apollo. 'Your worship is dying and your devotees can't even write your name. What call have you to meddle in our game?'

'You play an evil game, one stinking of murder,' Pan stamped goat feet on the smooth floor. 'Death is final to these mortals. They have little life as it is. How will they breed more men if you kill them like flies? The race will die out. That is not good husbandry. You offend the old gods, Demeter called Gaia, Dionysius God of Wine and Madness and me, God of Forests and Darkness. We were here before any of you came to trouble the woods, where men innocently coupled, danced, and bred, slept and died under the leaves, in Arcadia before the Titans warred in Heaven. Humans call on us for justice. What shall we say, Sun Bright? What will you say when the smoke rises from their altars and mortals beg for mercy?'

'Mercy?' mused Apollo. 'Mercy for mortals?' The undying afternoon gilded his perfect face into a bronze mask, distant, unchanging, beautiful. 'I do not know the meaning of that word.'

Chapter Twenty

Diomenes

I had been mad for a time—I do not know how long. I remembered, vaguely, the voices of priests; I recalled weeping until I could not see; I could hear my own voice calling on the gods, cursing them as if I believed in them.

After three days of agony I had stolen a flask of poppy and wine and drunk it all, trying to die, calling on Thanatos to come, because I now longed for death. Instead, in black dreams I saw the angel turn away from me. Even death had rejected me and Chryseis was gone.

Every expression on her face, the curl of her hair, the scent of her skin, they all bloomed in my darkened mind to torment me. No one now would finish my sentences or draw me close to her bright countenance and kiss my mouth with a taste of flowers. No dearest wife would lie beside me and warm my chest with her sweet breath. I lay in the tholos and howled for Chryseis. I heard the echo of her name and the murmur as it died.

There was no sunset or morning in the night of the gods, but I woke hearing a movement, and someone embraced me. I felt a body, smooth and female and young. She wore the mask of Aphrodite, dimly visible in the light of a small oil lamp set against the wall.

'Chryse Diomenes, it is time to return,' she said. 'You have despaired long enough.'

'I know these tricks,' I snarled. 'Take off the mask, slave woman. There are no gods.'

She took off the golden face of the goddess and revealed her own; a slender girl, perhaps sixteen years old, with dark hair and bright eyes. She bent over me and kissed me. 'You have wandered in the dark for long enough; so the priests say,' she said simply. 'They sent me here to bring you back. If I fail I will be beaten. Chryse, I knew Chryseis; I mourned for her too.'

'They sent you here because they have not succeeded in making me forget her,' I said, lying back in her arms. She stroked me gently, turning my face into her breast.

'I know you cannot forget her. They are fools if they think that you will lose your pain, Diomenes the Healer. But pain can be borne,' she said, her hands finding my tunic hem and drawing it up. 'I did not want to be a slave and tried to die, but I live now and will continue to live.'

Her kiss was sweet, her touch deft. Her body received me and some of my agony lessened in her embrace. I let her lead me to the surface; I would not have her beaten on my account. I had tried to die and failed. Now I would have to try and live.

I went back to my house and found that it had been cleaned. All trace of Chryseis had gone. My master waited at my door and told me gently, 'It is all in this box, Diomenes. When you feel strong enough, you may open it. There are bodies to be healed, my dear son, people need you; you cannot waste yourself.'

'Then I will go to Troy,' I said dully. 'There the need must be greatest and I cannot stay here where…' I choked and regained command of my voice, 'where I have taken an incurable wound.'

'A ship sails from Navplion, Diomenes, before the middle of the season; after that it is dangerous to try the wide seas and Boreas blows all the time; so the shipmasters tell me. You have a week to prepare; I am sending a load of medicines to Troy, you can take them to my sons. Now you must come with me.'

'Master,' I said, and trailed at his heels. We came into his house where a slave woman was nursing two children. It was cruel to make me see them; I was about to appeal to my master's mercy when he said, 'These are your children, Diomenes. I have named them and the god has accepted them. Chryse and Chryseis; they are twins.'

I staggered to a seat on the bench beside the woman. Small faces, golden skin, and blue eyes. A little hand clutched one of my fingers in a firm grasp. I stared at them and then detached the grip roughly, making the baby cry.

'I cannot bear them,' I managed to stutter. 'I wish they had died. They killed their mother.'

My master sent the nurse out of the room, clucking indignantly.

'I will care for them nonetheless,' he observed. 'Take some bread and meat, my Diomenes, and I will tell you of your voyage. You have survived tragedy, my son, and now you must learn to love again. If not another wife, then humanity as a whole. Men need your love to be healed. You more than others will understand pain now, just as you will understand madness, having been mad.'

I stopped shaking with loathing and took some wine. He was right. I had been a child, playing games with my Chryseis in the sunlight. Now I was a man and I wished with all my heart that it was not so.

I attended more demonstrations of surgery, I checked and packed and re-packed the herbs which the master was sending to Polidarius and the razor-sharp bronze knives for Macaon. I ate and I slept, falling into the routine of the temple as though I had never railed on death in the tholos' darkness.

I did not forget, but I was doomed to live.

On the night before I set out for Troy I took the box and opened it. Not much to show for her short life, my own golden one. Just three tunics, the white shell-shaped stone I had given her, a string of amber beads which matched her eyes, a golden coin and seven copper ones, a pair of sandals worn through the heels. Her red wedding gauze was there as well. Tears poured from my eyes. I wiped them impatiently away lest they spot the fabric.

I folded Elene's veil and Chryseis' together, tying the bundle to the necklace, which I looped over my head. Then I added to the box my best tunic, embroidered with gold, twenty gold coins of Mycenae and eleven of the Phrygian trading currency, a chunk of rock with a garnet in it and a set of instruments given to me by my master when I had been made an asclepid. I took the box to the master's house and gave it into his hands.

'For my...for the children,' I said, and he folded me in a close hug, kissed me, and blessed me.

The journey to Navplion was uneventful. There were bandits on the roads, but they would not attack an asclepid. Indeed, I attended to various wounds, including a serious compound fracture, for three robber chiefs along the way and received safe conduct from one to the other. This might have amused me once. Now I was so solemn that my fellow travellers accorded me great respect as one favoured with a god's attention and possibly under an interesting curse.

I saw my face in a clear pool as I was drinking from another spring of the nymph. I was amazed to find that I looked much the same; hazel eyes, golden hair falling straight to my shoulders, no lines on my forehead, no brand that said 'tragedy.' My eyes showed no sign of all the tears I had shed. But my face was still, unmoving, like a mask.

I was sixteen years old.

The ship was called the *Ram* and had a ram's head for Mycenae on her single sail. I had never sailed before and I was almost interested. She was about twenty-five paces long, had benches for twenty rowers, and a little space fore and aft for gear and passengers, one of which was me. I saw the precious herbs stowed in the bow and greeted the shipmaster. He was short, stocky, black-bearded, and gruff.

'It is late for a voyage to Troy,' he said. 'It may take longer than you expect, asclepid. Have you ever been in a boat before?'

'No, never.'

'Then if there is any trouble, you will stay in your place, hang on tight and don't talk,' he ordered. 'If you please, asclepid,' he added hurriedly, 'she's a well-found ship. See, here, the way she is put together.' I saw little pegs hammered into the hull as he pointed. 'Mortice and tenon,' he said proudly. 'Every peg marks a locking joint.' He demonstrated with his fingers a tongue-and-groove arrangement. 'Every plank is locked to another plank like dogs in heat and she takes the sea like a swan. The crew is all here, now that I have retrieved them, the lazy drunken rogues, so if you are ready, asclepid, we will catch this tide.'

I scrambled to my place at the stern, next to the man handling two steering oars, and they shoved us off into the channel. Oars shot out and they began to row, hauling at the thick, unbending wood. We did not slip into the sea, but trudged like old women carrying burdens, out of the channel and into the Aegean. The land slid past slowly, grey cliffs and pebbly beaches. I was leaving behind all that I had ever known.

I was spared any further grief. I was sick and I stayed sick for days. The sea did not agree with me and I racked my brains, between bouts of vomiting, to wonder whether I had offended Poseidon by refusing to believe in him.

Each night we found anchorage and rowed ashore, or swam ashore if it was not too far. I had learned to swim in a river; the ocean was different. It was colder, to begin with, and it kept slapping me in the face, so that I arrived on shore spluttering, to various comments about land-dwelling beasts. I had already failed to appreciate them telling me that the only cure for sea-sickness was to sit under a tree. I had retorted that the other cure was death and they left me alone after that.

From Navplion to Idra; Idra to Salamis; Salamis to Skiathos; Skiathos to Skioni, the journey took two weeks, most of it rowing. The shipmaster said that he hoped to catch a south-west wind which would take us across the Aegean to Lemnos, then into the bay of Troy to the beaches where the Argive army dwelt.

'Troy still stands,' he said. 'The armies have not made a dent in it and they are dying in hundreds. I reckon that there were more than a thousand men with the Atreidae; forty-seven hollow ships, maybe forty men in each, not to mention the light, fast beaked ones like the *Ram*. The Trojans won't come out and we can't get in and they have bowmen. Agamemnon waits as we do, asclepid, for a change of wind. Can you have a look at my steersman's hands? He says they're sore, the scoundrel, and that's why he heeled her over so hard that we all got wet today.'

I examined the sailor's hands and was amazed that he could use them. They were like goatskin mittens, the palms as hard as the sole of a foot, but cracked and blistered beyond belief. There were new blisters rising under the old ones, the whole hand was raw and must have been very painful.

'You see, asclepid,' said the man shyly, 'they get nice and calloused, then they get wet and the salt water softens them, and they blister again.'

I made him a poultice of thyme and vervain, and gave him a pot of sheep's grease to rub into the insulted flesh. Then I made a new infusion to try and cure my seasickness, which I would try out tomorrow, and went to sleep in green silence with the stars blazing overhead.

Dawn brought the south-west wind and we ran into the sea and climbed aboard the *Ram* as she rocked and swayed at her mooring. The anchor hauled up, the sail filled and bellied, the halyards were tied down and we were off. Oars were shipped and the steersman laughed.

'No more rowing, mates,' he cried.

'No,' agreed the shipmaster. 'Time to grease the oar-straps and make good the gear.'

A ball of white mutton fat was produced and they began to anoint the leathers, while two stood at the nine light ropes which anchored and manoeuvred the sail, in case the notoriously fickle wind should change or drop.

'She's running like a horse,' reported the steersman. 'Sweetly she goes!'

I had drunk the infusion I had given to Chryseis and for the first time I was not sick. I had leisure to look around and the sea was wide and blue. Distant creatures broke the surface. They leapt curbing into the air, landing to splash and turn. We were close enough to see the smiles on their beaked faces.

'What are they?' I asked. The shipmaster grinned. 'Dolphins, asclepid, Dionysius' darlings. There was a bard once, I heard, rode one of them to Tarentum. What was his name, now?'

'Arion,' I said, smiling. 'Arion Dolphin-Rider. He's at Troy. I know him well.'

'Has he taught you any songs?' asked the steersman. 'We've sung all of ours.'

Much to my surprise, I found myself chanting the story of Elene, the most beautiful woman in the world, and the league of suitors at Mycenae.

I wondered what had happened to Odysseus.

The wind took us across the Aegean, unfailing, and we did not stop for darkness that day or the next. As the sun came up the shipmaster yelled, 'Out the oars! Take up the sail!'

Lemnos was approaching at a rapid rate. The oars hit the water together; the men grunted as they took the strain until the sail was furled up to the masthead. Then we rowed gently into the arms of the island where the women had slaughtered all their men. The only men on Lemnos were Thracian settlers, who had a rather haunted look, and the children engendered by the Argonauts when Jason had landed here.

We slept the night in a fishing village, as our shipmaster did not want to waste the heaven-sent south wind. I remember that I ate good roasted fish there, though the sailors grumbled, wanting meat. Then they vanished for the night, taken in by the Lemnos women who, it appeared, were still short of children.

Dawn brought red-eyed rowers, exhaling wine, to crew the benches of the *Ram* as we hoisted sail, skirted the island, and sailed along dreadful cliffs. The current, the shipmaster said, was ordinarily adverse, the headwaters of the Euxine sea spilling with great force through the Pillars of Heracles and down the coast of Phrygia and Caria. However, it appeared that the non-existent Poseidon had forgiven me for whatever it was I had done to offend him and we skimmed along like a landing bird.

The bay of Troy was wide and shallow. At its head was the city, walled with grey stone, with three gate towers. It seemed tall and ominous. Dusk was falling as we rowed to the beaches, where hundreds of small fires twinkled in night. Troy was lit by torches in each tower.

'The eyes of Troy never sleep,' commented the shipmaster.

The *Ram* was hauled onto the shore and I splashed down with my load of herbs into the Atreidae's war.

I slept on the beach that night, as it was too late to find the sons of Glaucus in the interlocking lines of clans and dialects. I was tired but uncomfortable among so many strangers. Towards dawn I was woken by a hand fumbling over my throat and I grabbed for the wrist and my knife. A startled soldier dragged me upright as he backed and I clung to him.

'Sorry, asclepid,' he said hurriedly. 'I thought…'

'That I was a sailor who wouldn't mind having his throat cut in order that you should have his valuables?' I asked, and three men laughed.

'Your timing always was terrible, Thersites,' one commented. 'Trying to rob an asclepid, you'll be in trouble now if you are wounded.'

The man snarled an extremely indelicate reply. I released him and sheathed my knife. 'You can carry the herbs, Thersites,' I ordered. 'Take me to Macaon and Polidarius, the sons of Asclepius.'

He led the way, staggering under the weight of the medicines, through a hundred small encampments towards a row of tents.

Macaon was asleep, but Polidarius embraced me and took me and the bale of herbs joyfully inside.

'Greetings, little brother, you are welcome, doubly welcome if you have some comfrey and more vervain.'

'I have all of those and more; I carry your respected father's greetings and his love; how is it with you?'

'If I had known what war was like, little brother, I would not have come; but I am here and there is no going back,' said Polidarius. 'Come out and we will light a fire and warm some wine.'

We looked at each other in the cool light. He was taller than me, my master's son, with dark hair and brown eyes. He had been careless and jovial, but now there were streaks of grey in the chestnut hair and new lines around his mouth. I realised that he was examining me just as narrowly.

'What happened to you, Chryse?' he asked in a physician's voice. 'Have you been very ill?'

'Yes, in that ship, and before that. I ran mad when Chryseis died.' I had managed the sentence without a quaver in my voice; I was proud of myself. He nodded.

'Arion Dolphin-Rider said it would be so,' he said, stooping to blow on the embers of his cooking fire. 'Hand me some kindling.'

'How did he know, that old man?' I cried.

'Because you were too happy,' grumbled a voice like a bear's, awoken from a winter's sleep at half-past January. 'The gods do not allow men to taste pure happiness for long, Chryse. I told you—songs of loss are easy to write. That is because losing is more common than finding, finding more common than keeping. Is there any wine for an old man, Polidarius Asclepid Priest?'

'You do not need wine, but an infusion, which I shall presently prepare, against over-indulgence,' said Polidarius primly. The old man sat down on a driftwood plank and blinked, like the bear to which I had compared him. His beard and hair were liberally greased with animal fat and he had certainly slept in his clothes.

'Where is your apprentice, Arion, he should be looking after you—at least enough to keep your beard out of the dish,' I exclaimed, sitting down next to him. He grinned, that slow and irresistible grin which seemed to take you into a gleeful conspiracy with him. 'Aren't men fools?' the grin said. 'And aren't they *funny*?' I found my mouth moving in sympathy.

'The boy has found that he has no head for wine. Menelaus gave him too much and the whelp is sleeping yet. I am amusing the kings, Chryse, and that is no laughing matter. Especially,' he whispered, nearly knocking me down with the wine on his breath, 'since Troy, despite all efforts, had not fallen and we are not, it seems, feasting in the ruins of the towers. They are not happy and neither is this army—but your fellow asclepids can tell you about that. I am glad to see you, Chryse Diomenes, Death's Little Brother.'

'I am glad to see you too,' I said, realising that it was true. 'I saw dolphins on the voyage—Arion, did you really ride one?'

'It is all true,' he spread his hands on his knees. 'Strange as it seems, I did not improve that story at all.'

I smelt mint; Polidarius had prepared the infusion and I drank some too. He produced bread and oil and we ate, the bard complaining bitterly that a mixture of mint and oil would collide catastrophically with the wine in his insides and it would be all our fault if he could not sing that night. Polidarius bore this prospect philosophically. It was evidently a ritual argument.

Men were waking and cooking breakfast on the beaches. Macaon came out of the tent and said 'Chryse! So it was true then. I mean, a fellow surgeon, how delightful.' He looked even older than his brother, worn and stooped. His hands were red with scrubbing.

I did not ask how the war was going. Troy loomed up, a stony block on its hill. The gate I could see was fast shut and there was a flicker of movement on the walls; people pacing to and fro. Without the power of Poseidon Blue-Haired, Earth Shaker, I could not see how an army could get in, if there were men on the walls. Macaon followed my gaze and said quietly, 'Indeed. You see the problem. They won't come out—why should they?—and we can't get in.'

'How many are dead trying?' asked Arion rhetorically. 'Uncounted—there must be hundreds. Pierced through with Trojan arrows, bitter darts—they have some Scythians there, or my name's not Arion, famous bard, great singer of the Achaeans.'

'Which, of course, it is, therefore they have Scythians,' agreed Macaon. 'Those arrows can go through ox-hide like butter and they never miss.'

'What of the wounded?' I asked.

'They die,' said Macaon wearily. 'I am officiating over the slaughter of all the young men in the world. By the time I get to them they have bled out their lives. The smallest wound is inflamed in hours and they die of blood-poisoning in days. Not to mention the number who die on the plain before another truce is arranged to bring back the dead. Some survive. It has been better since I have been boiling the sea water to wash the wounds, but there is no hiding this, Chryse; only one out of about fifty can be saved.'

'Then we shall save that one,' I said, putting down my empty cup. 'If that is all we can do then we will do that, as my master says.'

The brothers laughed. 'I can hear him saying it,' declared Polidarius. 'Yes. We can do that. Come, Chryse, there is a council this morning; come with us and we will introduce you to Agamemnon and the captains.'

'We've met,' I said, finding that my fear of Elene's secret being disclosed had quite left me. 'But we shall meet again. I wonder if he remembers me?' For I had grown since I had last encountered the Atreidae and learned a great deal since I had lain in Elene's arms.

The meeting was held in a cleared circle where chariots turned around. There was Menelaus of the cold smile, Palamedes and his lover Myrses, Agamemnon as huge as a mountain, the elegant red-headed Odysseus, holding a staff of office next to an old man with silver hair who was, Polidarius informed me, Nestor, son of the Nyleus of Pylos, who had sailed with Jason on the Argo a generation ago. Someone was missing, however, and I asked Arion about him.

'Achilles the Swift Runner, ah yes. The great hero is sulking in his tent about a girl captured in some village that this gallant army sacked; Agamemnon claimed her, Achilles wanted her, though what he wanted with her is another matter. He's a strange one, a hero; but it is well known that he loves only one person, and that is Patroclus; that's him, over there.'

A tall handsome man was hovering on the edge of the gathering. He turned his head and looked into me. Dark eyes full of compassion, dark hair which curled over a marble brow. Patroclus was as beautiful as a statue, princely and gentle. I could understand Achilles' feelings.

Agamemnon was speaking into Odysseus' ear, arguing. It appeared that the king was urging something with which the prince of Ithaca disagreed. Finally Odysseus shrugged, hefted his sceptre, which was of olive wood, as long as a staff and bound with silver, and drifted unobtrusively towards the sea-side of the gathering.

The men on the beaches had come up and were standing in a series of concentric rings around the commanders. There must have been eight hundred soldiers there; I have never seen so many men in one place before.

'Gallant friends and men-at-arms,' announced Agamemnon in a great voice, 'we have failed. Zeus, Son of Chronos, has cheated me. He told me that Troy would fall into my hand like a ripe fig; it has not. The walls repel us and we die under the arrows of Ilium. Some powerful god protects them. More of us die every day. The timbers of our ships are rotting in the water and our rigging has perished. Our wives and children sit and wait for us in vain. Therefore I say; board ships and let us go home. Troy with the broad streets will never fall to us.'

This was astonishing. Macaon grinned with relief, but Arion was solemn and did not speak or react.

There was a roar and a rush of feet as the whole army ran for the ships. It was like corn in a tumbled field when the west wind bends the ears or the stirring of the sea when Boreas howls in winter. The whole host flowed down to the beaches, leaving the king's council and the healers and one bard standing alone in a waste of trampled ground.

With an unexpected speed, the king of Ithaca was before them, swinging his sceptre and talking, talking, to the captains and the men as the chocks were taken out from under the beaked ships and launchways were cleared in the sand. Out of curiosity,

I followed him and heard him say to one chieftain, 'I am sure that you do not mean to fall in with this retreat, Lord; this is a test and Agamemnon will be angry if you show yourselves cowards. A clever man like you would not be taken in.' Next he brought the staff across the face of a rower, who fell back with a cry. 'Idiot! Are you making decisions now for the Lord of men? Get back on the beach and tremble under the wrath of the Atreidae!' This is a test and I'm afraid that the soldiers may be punished for it,' he murmured to another man in an embroidered tunic. 'I am sure that you are just examining your boat for damage in last night's blow, but you wouldn't want Agamemnon to misunderstand, would you? Best to get back to the council before he is offended,' and he swished the staff again so that five sailors ducked.

No one has ever been as ingenious and persuasive of tongue as Odysseus of Ithaca, great-grandson of Hermes, grandson of Autolycus the thief. I dogged his heels the length of the beach, as ship after ship fell to his words and the men trudged back to the stained and stinking beaches. He had turned the purpose of the mob, who had seemed strong enough to trample all before them. They flocked back from the ships, except for three that had launched and rowed off, to be caught up by the Hellespontine current and whirled towards Lesbos. Even if they wanted to get back to the war, I reflected, they would not be able to return against that current and the north wind.

I wished them well.

Meanwhile the troops had settled like a flock of disturbed pigeons. Only one still stood—Thersites, the thief who had tried to rob me of my amber necklace. He was ugly; bow-legged, snaggle-toothed, bald, and bad-tempered. But he had a fine line in invective and yelled to Agamemnon, 'My Lord, what more do you want? You have had the pick of the plunder; you can't get into your hut for gold and bronze and you've more women that you can lie with. And you, women of the Achaeans—I can't call you men, drivelling followers of the Atreidae on this doomed beach—why do you trust him? He's even quarrelled with Achilles, swift runner, great hero—who might be able to win his war for him. All over a girl when he's got more girls than I've had all my life—luckily Achilles is craven too, or he'd have wiped out the insult in blood.'

'Very interesting, Thersites,' said Odysseus, swinging his staff. 'Your arguments would be more persuasive if you weren't such a coward yourself. We'll test it, shall we? Sit down and shut your mouth or I'll break your head.'

Thersites looked around for support, found none, and sat down. The army laughed. Odysseus began to speak. It was impossible not to listen to him.

'Kings and lords of men, your army is worthless. They all promised to stay; when you tested them they all ran away. They whimper like cowards when asked to endure a little hardship; they fret and complain like babies. It would be a shame to us and to our children's children if we come away from Ilium empty handed. Calchas the seer told us it would take ten years to reduce Troy; we have already fought eight and a half years. If it takes another little time, what of it? Are we not stored with the loot of many villages and towns? Soldiers, are you not ashamed? Can you not wait a little time more to feast on the riches of Ilium?'

There was a shout of approval from the men. Nestor, the old man, commented, 'Any man who leaves before he has captured a Trojan woman and loaded himself with gold is a fool. Now, Agamemnon, I have some advice. Let us sacrifice and then if the omens are right, go forth to a challenge and a parley. Let us shame these city-hugging maidens into coming out to fight like men.'

Calchas the High Priest, with his blood-streaked robes and hungry eyes, cut the throat of a lamb and flayed it, wrapping chunks from the thighs in fat and burning them on a hot fire. He announced that the omens were excellent for bringing the Trojans to battle.

Then Agamemnon knelt before the gods and I heard his prayer: 'Most glorious Zeus, Thunderer, grant that the sun may not set before I bring down the palace of Priam, burn the gates and slaughter the men of Troy, and rip the breast of Hector's tunic with bronze; Lord of High Heaven, let this be.' Sunlight spilled over his bearded head, turning his profile to gold. Men murmured at this sign of favour.

I went back to the tent of the healers to prepare bandages and splints, boil sea water, and whet surgical knives.

Chapter Twenty-one

Cassandra

The allies started to arrive, first from Caria, then Phrygia and Thrace, and finally the Amazons led by Myrine.

I saw them swoop in from the west and at first I thought that they were a mob of wild unmounted horses, so low did the riders crouch and so magnificently did they blend with their steeds. They came to the Dardanian Gate with much splashing and were admitted; I ran down to welcome them.

'Myrine,' I said, 'welcome and thrice welcome for the help you bring.'

'Cassandra, here is my lady; Penthesileia our queen and Charis my sister; twelve were all of our people I could find. We do not dwell in cities and our virtue is that it is very hard to locate us.'

The lady of the Amazons was tall, thin, dark-eyed, and strong. She wore goatskin breeches even more noisome than those of the Scythians and she laughed when she saw my nose wrinkle.

'Yes, a bath, I think—where shall we lie? Myrine, we are going to need a wash before we encounter those who live in cities. Princess, I greet you. Where is Hector? How goes the siege? We met some of those Achaean pirates raiding a seaside village as we rode in, so we took a long way, first removing them from troubling the world, of course.'

I bowed to her. 'Lady, lodge, if you will, with Myrine and Eris. I shall call Hector when you are bathed and rested. The Argive army has not stirred from their camp for a week and we will be warned if they move.' I explained the trumpet signals and the sequence of watches as they led their horses to the stables. The Amazon's mounts were remarkably tame. Charis could lift hoofs and pull back tails without the suggestion of a snap or kick, though both the Amazons and the horses seemed dirty, worn and underfed.

When they were quite certain that the horses were comfortable, they followed me to the Amazon's chamber next to the Temple of the Maiden. There they stripped and scrubbed themselves with oatmeal and soap-leaf. I had never seen women like them. The women of Troy were strong and skilled, but rarely did I see the peasants who tilled fields; Trojan women stayed out of the direct sun. The Amazons, whatever their stature, were tanned in the same places; throat and half the face which the helmet did not cover, arms where the armoured shirt did not shade. Their legs were pale; patchwork women with alert, wary eyes and the crowsfeet of those who stare over long distances.

They were also diverse. Eris of the dark scowl had a head cropped close as a ball, the flat scar where her breast had been removed, and the strings of enemy's teeth around her neck; the picture which most of us had of an Amazon who fights like a man, or as Eris would say, much better than a man. Myrine was a small, light woman, with long brown hair which she was proud of and combed as carefully as her horse's tail; a good archer whom I had sighted in the Dionysiad, hunting men through the mob. Charis was beautiful; her thighs and arms were long muscled and straight, her body was ivory patched with gold and her black hair was cut raggedly at shoulder level, long enough to pad her helmet. Her body bore no marks of childbearing, but she did not touch her comrades in the same way as did Myrine and Eris, or the horse-lady Hippia and her lover Aigleia.

These two kissed cordially when they had washed. Aigleia commented, 'Well, there was a face under all that mud! Welcome back, my love!' Therefore I was more surprised when one of Hippia's bundles moved and let out a small cry.

She unearthed the bag and removed a baby; perhaps three months old, but plump and well cared for, if filthy. Hippia took the baby and her lover into the pool of the Maiden once they had been cleansed and they lay together in a close embrace, luxuriating in the clean water. I was puzzled.

'Do not be concerned, daughter of Priam,' said Myrine. 'We are the only free women and we live as we please. We bear children, such of us who either like or can endure men, for we need new Amazons to replace us.'

'And do you really expose the male babies, as the Achaeans say?'

She snorted. 'There is no truth in the Argive pirates, you should know that. We give the boy-children back to their fathers; in some places we have almost settled down, though never quite; an Amazon may sleep under a roof, but she must not even be buried in a city. We lie with the men of a certain village at the Dionysiad, then bring or send them the male offspring. The villagers like this—they value sons more than daughters, the fools. Thus everyone is happy. And for us—our lady is a dedicated Maiden, I like men, some like women and men, Tydia and her lovers only like women. The only pure Amazon is Charis. She doesn't want anyone—or rather, she is complete in herself.' Charis grinned, sluicing down her indescribably filthy breeches and flinging them to soak in a tub along with the others. Penthesileia dropped her tunic and walked into the pool, laying her head back against someone's breast with a sigh. 'Ah, water; it is nice to visit civilisation occasionally.' She dipped her head under and sat up, wiping her long black hair out of her eyes. 'So,' she said, 'you have seen fighting. The battles, Princess Cassandra. Tell us.'

I sat down on the tiles and dabbled my feet in the water, soaking my ink-stained hands, and told the tale of three attacks on the city and how they had been driven off. As I described the defences of the city and the rules made by Hector, the lady of the Amazons nodded approvingly.

'This is a good prince—almost as intelligent as an Amazon, though you need not tell him I said that. Sit in the marsh and eat frogs, Myrine, indeed! You were quite right. While they squat on the plain and the gates are shut they could wait outside the city until their hair turns grey. What is the estimate of the army—about nine hundred? Hmm. Too many for open battle, especially if there are many chariots. However, there was some mutiny in their camp this morning—so that bandit said before I killed him. Well, sisters, we have until the noon watch to lie around and imitate concubines, after which we must dress and call on the lord of the city. Myrine, can you clothe us?'

'Hector is a generous prince,' said Myrine. 'I have breeches for all of us.'

As I withdrew my feet and dried them, I saw the queen of the Amazons with a spear in her breast.

I had found that if I stared at the visions hard enough they went away. I gazed at Penthesileia and she looked into my eyes; her hair falling, her joints loosening, lying back to die as if she were sleeping. I said in my heart, 'I acknowledge that she will die,' and the sending dissolved. They never faded; they came and went.

'I must go—I have to see the arrow-makers,' I said shakily, finding my papyrus list of tasks, my inkpot, and my stylus. 'I'll see you at noon.'

I left them laughing and splashing in the pool of the Maiden and went off to argue with the arrow-makers, who were complaining about not being able to go into the marsh to harvest reeds and about a lack of arrowheads, which sent me to have another argument with the bronzesmiths who said that the arrow-makers wanted impossible precision and returned three out of every five heads, saying that they were misshapen.

This took me a whole watch to sort out. The city was nervous, tempers were fraying. Once I had persuaded the fletchers to accept that a little sanding and paring would perfect most of the heads and the smiths to be a little more careful with cleaning their moulds, I was tired and irritated, but I had the promise of more arrows. Then I had three soldiers demanding to be excused because their wives were giving birth and I had to engage the priestess of Gaia in a theological debate about the extent to which the goddess would allow her rites to be ignored in a city under siege. Finally she agreed to ask the goddess about it and I sent the soldiers back to their places. In a narrow alley near the Scaean Gate I found Dion.

He was wearing Poseidon's robes, the green and blue of the sea, and he smelt of kelp. I glanced sidelong at him, but there was no vision. I walked into his arms and rested my flushed face against his shoulder.

'Cassandra,' he drew me into the little temple which he and Maeles had built. 'I have not seen you for so long I was wondering if I had imagined you.'

'There is the defence of Troy,' I said stiffly, but he did not mean to chide me. Instead he kissed me and I lay down in his arms.

A different vision came as I held him close and felt his caresses loosen my joints; Dion and several goats huddled together in hollow ship; a small vessel on a vast sea, sailing on until it was a black dot which was swallowed up by the distance.

I said nothing, but held him tighter. I was going to lose all that I had; Dion, as well.

◇◇◇

At noon, the Amazons came to the king's council, were introduced to Priam and Hecube, and had just begun to discuss the situation when a trumpet called from Scamander Gate and a runner came for Hector.

He went, with Státhi on his shoulder and me scuttling at his heels. It was Talthybius again, his deep voice echoing off the walls.

'Hector, Prince of Troy, I bring an offer of parley and truce from the most mighty Atreidae,' he said, more politely than usual. 'Assemble with your army and allies and all your champions on the plain to meet with Menelaus and Agamemnon. What is your reply?'

'I must consult with the Lords of my city,' said Hector. 'Return for my answer before night falls.'

We went back to the council and reported the Argive terms to the king and his counsellors.

'I say we ignore them,' said Hector. 'If they want a truce let them declare it to the walls. They are trying to tempt us into open battle; as the Amazon says, there are too many of them for us to safely join on the plain.'

'Safety!' mocked Pariki. 'Always you speak of safety, my brother! I will offer single combat. Then I will kill Menelaus and they will go home.'

'And if Menelaus kills you,' growled Hector, while Státhi rose on his shoulder and hissed, 'will you surrender the city and all the people we have sworn to guard?'

'Yet there might be some use in a parley,' mused the old man, Anchises. A lightning bolt had scarred and twisted him, but once he had been so beautiful that the goddess Ishtar had borne him a son—Aeneas the handsome, fully as beautiful as Pariki and a gentle character as well. 'As you say, Prince Hector, they will not go home without some sort of ceremony. We may be able to persuade them that it is late for sailing to Pelops' land and that they do not want to endure a winter here.'

'They will not endure it here—they will go and raid Caria or Mysia for warm lodging,' said Polites. 'They are ravaging the coasts, drawing off our allies to fight the raiders. We have to reach some arrangement with them, though we cannot risk open battle.'

'Cannot risk! Are we men?' sneered Pariki, and Pandarus added, 'Just let us fight them, without all these words such as old men and children use! The people will laugh at me if I do not strike a blow in anger.'

'I hope so,' said Hector. 'I prefer them laughing to weeping in Argive chains.'

'Enough,' said Priam wearily. 'If they want a parley with an army, then we will go out, tomorrow, at noon, in as much array as we can. Chariots and riding horses, every soldier armoured and with as many weapons as is proper. Hector, you will decide which gate we shall issue from and where we will take our stand. Midway between the city and the camp, perhaps, with Scamander at our backs.'

'Father, no, I do not think that wise. Armoured men cannot swim and the Scamander is treacherous…'

'Arrange it as you will, my son,' said the king. 'But tomorrow I walk out to speak to the Atreidae, alone, if I have to.'

Hector bowed and the king waved a hand to show that the audience was ended.

For some reason Hector then collected all the spearsmen he could find and they marched the palace roof for two watches, practising a three-rank advance, bristling with bronze.

◇◇◇

The next morning the army of Troy issued forth from the Scamander Gate and walked into position in the plain between the river and the city. In tunic and gambeson I walked behind Hector, as his right hand. I had a bow and a quiver of arrows; the heavy helmet hid my face and was cushioned by my hair. On the flanks skirmished the Amazons, while the allies marched under their own captains in groups in the middle, and before us all went three ranks of spearsmen.

I had not been out of the city since the siege began. The plain seemed terribly big and flat, stretching all the way to the sea. Over the miles between the Achaeans were marching. A dust cloud rolled over them, blurring the details on banners and shields. By the bigger shadows in the middle, I guessed that the Atreidae were riding in chariots to this parley. We stopped when Hector gave the order and sat down in our places.

The sun grew hotter and the sweat dripping down under my helmet made my scalp itch. I wished I had thought to bring more water. I wondered if I was waiting to be killed.

The Argives came within a bowshot of us, making a noise like a storm. Uncouth cries like birds rose clamouring from our allies, the Mysians and Carians, who hated the Argives fiercely for the damage they had done to their villages. The Achaeans made no sound or reply. We stood up. Priam tottered forward, hands open, Polites at his elbow ready to support him.

'We have come to your parley,' he said. 'I am Priam, King of holy Ilium. Who will speak to us?'

A stout black-bearded man and a mountain of muscle climbed down out of their chariots and walked towards the king.

'I am Menelaus, King of Sparta, and this is my brother Agamemnon, King of Mycenae,' said the black-bearded one.

'Challenge,' called Pariki, emerging from the sons of Priam and waving two bronzed spears. 'I challenge you to single combat, Cuckold Prince! I stole your wife, Menelaus, she came with me willingly, as amorous as a doe at rutting season. I stole her because the goddess promised, and for the sake of Hesione, Princess of Troy, abducted by Telamon.' His voice was failing as he watched Menelaus, his beard splitting in a mirthless grin, reach for and draw a long sword.

'Come then, little princeling of a dishonoured city,' hissed Menelaus. 'Come and be spitted for your theft!'

He lunged and Pariki ducked away, hiding himself among the ranks. This was too much for Hector.

'Come forth, doll, painted thing, pretty boy!' he bellowed. 'Pariki, City Destroyer, I wish you had never been born! You come from a courageous family; why are you the only coward; why are your limbs loose with fear—why should you escape the revenge of the one you have wronged? You wanted a single combat—here it is.'

'You are tireless and brave,' quavered Pariki's voice, 'indomitable Hector! But the goddess who gave me deathless beauty did not think I would need courage. However, if I must fight, I must. Clear a space between the armies; these are the terms. If I fall, all my goods will go to Menelaus; if he falls, all his to me.'

'Are these terms acceptable, my Lords?' asked Priam.

'Listen to me,' said Menelaus to his army. 'We cannot recover Elene, but Trojan gold is not to be despised. Either Pariki or I must die—we are fated. Therefore, bring a black ewe from Troy and I will send to the ships for a white ram. We will sacrifice to the gods for favour, then we will fight, and no one must intervene. Lord Priam will hold the oaths; old men consider carefully, and think of the future as well as the past.'

Hector sent an Amazon riding back to Troy for a black ewe and an Argive rode to the ships for a ram. Meanwhile the armies sat down and looked at each other. Thus I saw first the elegant Odysseus, who had stripped off his armour and was walking among the ranks, talking to the soldiers, who seemed less imposing now that I could see their faces. They were merely men, some better looking than others, nursing helmets in their laps. Some were chewing what I judged to be dried meat; one was drinking water from a flask.

The Amazon and the Argive brought the sacrifices and both kings rose and washed their hands in wine. Then the beasts were killed—a barbaric custom—and wine and blood was spilled upon the baked earth.

We all prayed with King Priam, 'Witness our oath, most high and holy, Lord of Light and of the silver bow, Apollo; let us all be cursed if we break this oath.' Then Priam drew back, wiping a hand over his brow.

'I return to the city,' he said. 'I cannot look on this contest.' His chariot was turned and Antenor, his driver, whistled to the horses.

Hector rose to meet with Odysseus and they paced out the ground, walking side by side. It struck me that they might have been friends in another place or time. They agreed amicably on the number of paces to be cleared, and the watching armies drew apart to allow the combatants space. 'Let there be peace,' I heard Polites praying under his breath, and the whisper of the same prayer wafted over both armies. 'Let the false one die and rot and let there be peace between us.'

They were arming Pariki in the best we could provide; Lycaon's breastplate and greaves, a helmet with a horse-hair crest which belonged to Polites. Finally he took up his own sword, with the hilt studded with silver, and a Trojan spear with a bronze head.

Menelaus was also equipped in full armour. Both of them clanked as they moved, with a creaking of leather straps; neither face could be seen. The mask on Pariki's helmet was of a snarling panther while Menelaus' helmet was undecorated, with no crevice where a spear could lodge; he had a featureless metal face, like the bronze giant made by Hephaestus.

They drew lots. Menelaus was to cast the first spear.

He flung it. Pariki dodged, so that it struck the round shield, glanced off and tore his tunic but did not touch his skin. Menelaus drew his sword and brought it down on Pariki's helmet. The crowd hissed. The sword broke into half a dozen pieces. I saw a glitter, then a shadow; I focused my inner eyes and saw a golden lady in front of Pariki, her slender arms around his neck; the sword had broken on the misty billows of her hair. Ishtar/Aphrodite was protecting her darling. I heard him chuckle and he brushed off fragments of sword. Menelaus swore by Zeus and hurled himself at Pariki, grabbing him by the throat and beginning to strangle him. When this did not work he seized the chin strap and swung Pariki off his feet, spinning him around so that he began to choke.

The golden lady reached up with slim fingers and snapped the strap. Menelaus was left holding the helmet and Pariki was slung into the Trojan ranks. Menelaus dived after him, kicking up dust, roaring like a wounded lion, 'Where is he? Where is the misbegotten son of Troy?'

He was gone. I had seen the Goddess of Love lift my trouble-making brother in her arms and whisk him away towards Troy in a rosy cloud, attended by doves.

I could not tell anyone and this was probably lucky, because Hector would have been utterly disgusted.

Menelaus prowled through the ranks of Trojans, who were well trained and puzzled enough not to laugh; but Prince Pariki was not to be found and the Achaeans must have known enough about how well Pariki was liked to feel sure that we were not hiding him out of love.

Finally, tiring of this and feeling faintly ridiculous, Menelaus left our ranks and announced that he had won.

Hector rose to agree that he had indeed driven his opponent from the field when there was a lightning flash out of a clear sky. While everyone was rubbing their eyes, I saw a bright woman in a glittering helmet and breastplate breathe something into Pandarus' ear, and before I could do anything—indeed I could not speak, but I would have tried—the god-beguiled fool grinned, bent his bow, and shot Menelaus in the belly.

There was a howl and everyone leapt to their feet. Menelaus was standing, shocked, with blood flowing out through the joints of his armour and running down his war-skirt to his feet. His bare legs were patterned with blood, little rivulets of bright red against the olive skin. I fought off the vision of Athene diverting the arrow, standing somehow at Pandarus' back and in front of his target simultaneously. Goddesses can do that. I backed with the army as Agamemnon knelt by his brother and cried aloud that if he died Troy would be destroyed to the last man, even to the last baby in the womb.

I did not think that Menelaus was going to die—if he had been badly injured he would not still have been standing on his feet, however bloodstained—but I was fairly sure that I was, and my brothers, and the Trojan army with us.

We had covered almost a hundred paces when we heard the cry, 'Attack!' and we turned to fight.

I had a bow and my healer's knife and I was determined to die with Hector, so I kept close to him as he walked to the chariots and secured a horse. He dragged me up behind him. Poor Hector, he always had pets; at least Státhi had agreed to stay behind. But we had practised this manoeuvre in the careless days when we had frolicked on the plain with Eleni and me clinging onto him; the rider behind can protect the foremost rider's back, and I twisted around and put an arrow to the string, as the horse moved uneasily beneath us. I was not used to being draped in a blanket jingling with bronze plates, although the armoured cloth gave me the purchase to balance behind my brother. Hector's battle array was simple; he had his three ranks of spearmen, the chariots in the middle, the Amazons and the Mysian cavalry on the flanks, and two-thirds of the number of the Achaeans under their own commanders ranged across the plain.

'Troy!' he bellowed, and the ranks answered, 'Troy!'

The enemy advanced at a run, but we did not run to meet them. Dust blanketed my sight; all I saw for an uncounted time were the looming bodies and bared teeth of Achaeans as I shot them off Hector's back while he rode up and down and across the line of battle. There was a clanging like bronze bells as the armour collided; I heard dreadful screams in the dust; but I had no time to be afraid. I sighted along my arrows for the attackers and I shot them as they came.

I know how many I hit, for I had twenty arrows, and I only missed once. A spear clanged off my helmet and Hector reached around to hold me as I slipped, but I recovered quickly; it was a good helmet. I saw that a shield was cloven and a man pinned behind it; someone was stripping a dead man of his armour when he was struck with a spear in turn and died with a gurgle. A wheel crunched over a living man, the horses running wild, the driver draped bonelessly over the wicker. A rock fell among our ranks and crushed a Trojan helmet.

Then the chariots came. Hector forced his mare at a gallop into the front rank and screamed an order; I heard an ordered clank of metal and the thud as spear butts grounded. The three ranks stood, each spear at a different angle, bristling like a hedgehog, as the chariots of the Achaeans rumbled towards us.

I could not shut my eyes. They came slowly, it seemed to me, the horses cantering like racers, manes braided and tails flowing, beautiful and deadly. They were close enough for me to see the metal men's eyes when they ran themselves onto the spear wall with a heaven-splitting shriek and fine steeds were so much carrion flesh and agonised kicking hoofs and the Trojans retreated again, foot by foot, keeping to their ranks.

Someone was crying aloud to the goddess Athene; I heard an Argive say that it was Diomedes of the loud war-cry. The goddess was with him, whispering in his ear. I saw him fell two brothers together with one sweep of his sword, then he raged on ahead of his comrades, along a battle line which strained and wavered and never quite broke, though the ground was soaked in blood and the noise was more than I could bear. I drew and loosed as Hector's horse battered her way through the ranks, and his sword moved like a reaping hook; he did not tire. He was moving us closer to this Diomedes, who was god-possessed and battle-mad. A chariot drew up with Pandarus and Aeneas, the son of Aphrodite. We lost sight of them as the tide of battle rolled us like wrack; then I saw Pandarus launch his spear, which bounced off a shield and slew someone else. Diomedes had torn off his helmet; surely even Pandarus could not miss him. But the armoured goddess was beside the Argive, smiling; and he threw before Pandarus could draw his sword.

We were quite close to him when a spear pierced his eye and sliced through his chin. The chariot was pulled up. Pandarus toppled dead onto the ground in a flash of burnished bronze. A cast stone felled Aeneas as he knelt beside Pandarus; I think it broke his legs, but his mother came for him, Aphrodite in a scented mist, and carried him away, depositing him in a Trojan chariot with the other wounded.

Then I saw such an amazing thing that I grasped Hector in shock. The battle-mad Diomedes, thwarted of Aeneas, was thrusting his spear at the goddess, at Aphrodite herself; he wounded her on the hand and she fled.

This was not enough for him, for another god came, Ares, the Butcher of men in bloody armour, and Diomedes pounced on him and hacked and slashed.

'He is mad,' commented Hector. 'He is fighting the air,' but I could see blows landing on immortal flesh and ichor staining a tunic woven by the graces. Diomedes actually fought Ares off to get to Aeneas.

Sarpedon came and many Trojans, and there was fierce battle around the body; I did not think that Aeneas was dead. I leaned down as we passed and grabbed a quiver off the body of a dead archer, for all my arrows were gone.

I heard a Carian war cry and we were swept aside by their advance; then Hector leapt down and drew his sword, attacking the men who sought to gain Aeneas until they were driven back.

Then suddenly we heard a trumpet. The Achaeans were behind us. We had been outflanked.

Hector wheeled the horse and put the reins into my hands. Beside us, our brother Cerasus fell, speared through the belly. Hector cried to me, 'Go into the city, tell the queen to sacrifice her richest garment to the Lady,' he yelled, 'and bring me a fresh horse.'

◇◇◇

I tumbled off the mare at the Dardanian Gate. Someone took her and led her away. I gasped that I needed a fresh mount and ran up the streets to the palace, stumbling and bloodstained. I fell at the feet of Hecube my mother and delivered Hector's message.

'We can see what is happening,' she said slowly. 'I will do as my son says. Must you go back, Cassandra?'

'Hector needs me,' I gasped. Tithone caught me and made me drink a measure of wine, water, and barley meal, which tasted revolting, before she allowed me to mount again and ride back.

The noise struck me afresh. And there was that goddess, the lady of the glittering helmet, moving among the ranks, whispering, touching. In her wake the Argives were refreshed; her harvest was the bodies of my brothers. I cried upon Hecate, drinker of dog's blood, destroying mother, to banish her. There was a flapping of wings as some new god descended between me and Athene and I thought I saw the Maiden's eyes turn on me, narrowing. Hecate Destroyer had come, although I did not know if she was responding to my call. Hecate was blood-drenched, slippery with gore, and I was glad that I could not see her face. She carried fear of death with her like a cloud. Her presence shielded us from the worst of the Argive advance, chilling Achaean hearts, dimming their eyes.

I found Hector and he climbed onto the horse. I settled myself behind him.

We crossed the Scamander by wading; it was not too deep and the tide was out. We dragged such of the wounded as could move after us and we clove our way to the Scamander Gate and into the city of Troy.

Chapter Twenty-two

Diomenes

I had never seen a battle so I tried to watch, but dust foiled my eyes. It sounded like a hundred smithies all beating hammers together; there were shrieks from men and horses. Some of them were war cries, I gathered; some were just the usual despair and pain.

'Come, you cannot see anything through the dust,' said Macaon. 'It will be hours yet before they start to come back. I have to go and set a bone for the Myrmidons; would you like to meet Achilles the God-Touched?'

I nodded, fell in beside him, and we traced a path across the tumbled and filthy sands.

'So why isn't he fighting? Some quarrel about a girl, Arion said?'

'Yes. Briseis, that's her name; as beautiful as Aphrodite, they say. She was captured below the city, in the bay; she's a Trojan. Agamemnon wanted her and what the Lord of Men wants, he takes. That's the ostensible reason, although I don't know what he'd want with the girl or any girl. He isn't afraid of war, nor has he been idle. Achilles has been raiding up and down the coast, he and his ant-warriors, attacking as far as a league inland. No city is safe. Thousands must have died since the man-slayer came. He has no pity,' remarked Macaon. 'His heart is of flint, and the hard flint they use to make arrowheads at that. When they come upon anyone—shepherd, goatherd, fisherman, trader—they steal all that he has and kill him and leave the corpse to be found by the terrified villagers. I believe that Ponticha in Caria surrendered, hoping to save some lives; but he killed them all anyway, as they stood in the agora, and burned the town around them. Not only men, women, and children are slaughtered, but goats and dogs; nothing alive is left in a village after Achilles has called. Nothing alive will be there ever again, either, for he sows the acres with salt if he has time.'

'Is he a monster, then?' I asked, imagining a man bigger than Agamemnon or the Aias, with griping hands and a snarling face.

'Oh yes, he's a monster,' said Macaon softly. 'Hail, Prince Achilles, hail Myrmidons! Macaon the healer and Chryse the Asclepid are here; you asked me to come.' He added in a whisper. 'Always announce yourself in a loud voice, even if they have begged you to visit. They're touchy. Two Argive messengers have been speared before they could get their message out.'

I stood beside him as three armed warriors prodded us with stabbing swords into the camp. They had come up behind us and I had not heard a footstep.

Achilles was sitting on a throne—the spoil of some city—outside a wooden hut such as fishermen make. He did not look like a monster. He was slender, the same height as me, with soft golden hair falling to his waist, smooth cheeks which were still too young to shave, and delicate, even features. Patroclus was standing behind him, holding a spear. He smiled at us and Achilles turned to look at us.

His eyes were remarkable, as grey as the sea before a storm, and as hard and polished as the granite pebbles in the pool at Epidavros where I had played as a boy. They were eyes which held the object of his regard for as long as he wished. Perfectly self-contained eyes; painted eyes on a heartless, perfect, marble Kouros, and underneath them quirked the unchanging immortal's smile.

I had always been comfortable with Thanatos who was Death; I knew I had nothing to fear from what he might do to me;

indeed I had sought him most diligently when I had been mad. This was a man who sought death too, but who worshipped him as a god and a desirable end for all things; this was a Titan from giants; this was a son of Chaos, who wanted nothing but death, fire, ruin, and waste, to the end of the world, in the triumph of strife and night. This was one whose touch evoked dead children, barren fields, slaughtered herds, pestilence, and the sterile wind which stirred the plain of dust in the underworld.

I shook off the influence. I am a healer, I reminded myself, and this beautiful young man is mad, quite mad.

I knew about madness, having been mad myself.

Macaon endured the stare of Achilles badly; he flinched and shook himself as a horse does when tormented by flies. 'You called us to attend one of your comrades,' he reminded Achilles. The hero smiled and gestured with one strong hand and a man was brought to us. He had a fracture of the right arm.

Macaon sat him down on the sand and began to test his reflexes, pricking the palm of the hand with a silver pin. There was no jerk or twitch. The physician looked at me and I shook my head. The arm had been broken across both bones and it was clear that the nerve was severed. Heavy inflammation purpled and swelled leaking tissues. It must have been very painful, but the soldier did not flinch as we turned his arm one way and another.

'Come,' said Achilles to me, and Patroclus added, 'If you please, Asclepid Priest.'

I left the Myrmidon as Macaon began to flush the wound with boiled sea water, hoping to reduce the swelling so he could gauge if the arm would recover. I stood before the hero and looked again into his disturbing eyes.

'You are not afraid of death,' he said. His voice was light and clear.

'No, Lord.'

'Macaon is afraid.'

'So are most men, Lord.'

'Why are you not afraid of me? I could have you killed. I could have you speared through—now. What would happen then?'

The point of the spear was at my throat. As an asclepid, I wore no armour. I was, I found, genuinely not afraid. I moved the spearhead down my body to illustrate my points as I spoke in a demonstrator's voice, as I had heard back in the temple when my master was explaining anatomy.

'Lord, if you strike here I will die in a few moments; if here in an hour, depending on whether you puncture the heart or the lung; if here it may take me three days to die in agony, but I will die; if here and you will rupture the great vessel in the groin, a gnat's life and I will be dead; in any case the dark angel will come for me, gentle as a mother, and carry me in his arms to my Chryseis who waits this side of the Styx, thirsting for me to come.'

I waited for his response, wondering if he was going to kill me. There was no way of knowing or even guessing from the stone-grey eyes. I did not look away, but that would not have stopped him. My life hung on a thread, a whisker, a single hair.

He laughed, a child's laugh, golden and unequivocal, and Patroclus took back his spear.

'So Thanatos will come, eh? How do you know?'

'Lord, I have seen him. He nursed me as a child and later he came and carried my Chryseis away.' I spoke simply, as one does to the mad, and he seemed impressed.

'You believe this?' he asked evenly.

'Lord, I have no need for belief; I know. Thanatos is as real as you are, Lord, or the sea, or this beach.'

'Perhaps we might ask the asclepid to sit down,' said Patroclus. 'If you mean to talk to him, he might like some wine.' Achilles nodded and I was supplied with a chair and a goblet encrusted with pearls. The wine was winter mead, made of honey and grapes; the fruit of some village's cellar, stored against the bitter blasts of winter. Well, they would not need it now. Not after Achilles had called.

'How goes the battle?' he asked, lounging back in his throne.

Patroclus said, 'I cannot see, my heart; there is too much dust, but they have not gained the city.'

'And they will not, without me,' said the hero with satisfaction. 'They do not appreciate me, Patroclus. Agamemnon took Briseis; I wanted her, I won her, it was my men who captured her, and he already had the maiden Araiea, when I went to all the trouble of killing her father and both of her bothers and her husband to get her. No, this coastal raiding is amusing, Agamemnon's army is lessening and sickening by the day, wasted in these battles; it will break against the walls of Troy. When he is at wit's end he will beg me on his knees and I will refuse until he has given me treasure and the woman I want; then I shall issue forth and slay until the city is gutted and I return home with Priam's old head on a spear, his white hair my banner as I sail home in triumph. They made a prophecy about me, asclepid.'

'Lord?' I was being careful of what I said; the less the better.

'You can live long in peace and obscurity, or a short time in glory. I chose the glory, asclepid—what is your name?'

'Chryse, Lord.' I do not know why I did not tell him that my name was Diomenes; perhaps it was a remnant of the old superstition that to tell such a man gives him power over you. In any case I had decided to go back to my childhood name; that was how the sons of Asclepius knew me, and every time it was spoken it reminded me of my twin-wife. There was a Diomedes in the Argive army; I did not want to be confused with him.

'Golden,' mused Achilles. 'A lucky name. Are you lucky?' he demanded.

'Yes, Lord. It is lucky to be alive—and lucky to be dead too. All life is a gift.'

He leapt to his feet, light as a deer, and I wondered if I was about to be doubly fortunate if I escaped back to the Argive lines with any breath in my body or pulse in my blood. Patroclus put a hand on the bare, smooth shoulder.

'Sweet Lord,' he said soothingly, 'Achilles, my heart.'

'Fortunately for you, asclepid, I agree with you. Life has a value all of itself; and I garner more of it every day,' said Achilles. 'Well, Macaon, Asclepius' son, how is my Myrmidon?' he got up and walked lightly down the sands to where the soldier sat at the healer's feet.

'There is nothing I can do,' confessed Macaon. 'He will be crippled.'

Achilles drew faster than thought, made a sideways slash with his sword, and the soldier lay decapitated on the sand. His comrades wrapped the body in a sailcloth and carried it away without wailing or comment.

After that there was not much to say and Macaon and I were dismissed from the presence and escorted to the edge of the camp by Patroclus.

'Come again, Chryse,' he said, holding my hand in both of his. 'He likes to talk to you. There are few whose conversation does not irritate him.'

'Why do you bear it?' I asked, though it was an impertinent and dangerous question to ask a stranger. The lips parted over white teeth as Patroclus smiled sadly. 'I am the only person in the world that Achilles loves,' he said. 'It would be a mercy and a blessing if you would share my burden.'

I nodded. Macaon and I walked away. Macaon was shaking and stopped to wipe his brow.

'That is the most dangerous man in the world,' he said.

◇◇◇

Before dusk we heard them coming. Wailing the names and titles of the life-bereft, the exhausted Argives staggered into camp, their wounded and dead dragged behind them.

I heard some of what had happened as I flooded wounds with salt water. In ten minutes my red tunic was stiff with gore. Surgeons wear a red tunic so that the blood will not show and terrify the patients. Macaon was right; one in fifty might be saved.

There were crush wounds from stones and hoofs and chariot wheels; all of them would die. There were broken bones from cast stones; most of them would live. There were head wounds, who might retain their wits; there were innumerable arrow and dart puncture injuries and they, too, would wait for Thanatos.

Once the skin was breached, inflammation and death were sure to stalk along the dirty beaches where we laid the wounded.

Polidarius had made barley broth loaded with poppy to nourish and sedate them and he walked the camp of groaning men, dipping his ladle and filling small bowls for the battle-friends to feed their wounded lovers.

Bronze knives cured all that we could not relieve as men, sobbing or stone-faced, performed the last act of mercy and love. The dead were wrapped in their cloaks and carried away. The pile of bodies in the small valley which the Achaeans had taken for sepulture grew higher every day. The stench was unbelievable and the vultures feasted there.

Perhaps one hundred and thirty men had been killed; another two hundred were injured. Of those most would die.

'The enemy got back to Troy,' one soldier complained as I set his friend's broken leg. 'Will he live?'

'It is a closed, clean break; yes, he will recover if you care for him. Come for soup every day, do not let him drink wine, and here is poppy for the pain. He must not move for a least two weeks; let him not even try to stand.'

I had drawn the heels down until they were even and bound the legs to a splint at ankle and knee. 'Unless he wants to limp for the rest of his life, he must not put any weight on that leg until it is healed. The muscles will contract and try to pull the leg up; you must gently pull it down and re-tie the bindings. If you are diligent he will owe you his leg, as well as his life. So, they escaped back into the city?'

'Yes, asclepid, although the god-like Diomedes hewed like a man cutting trees; he says he wounded Aphrodite, and fought Ares, Butcher of Men, off the Trojan Aeneas, yet he could not take him; they have more archers, and Mysian cavalry besides, and one of the Lacemedonians says some of the cavalry are women, Amazons—they ride like centaurs and cannot be caught. They drove us to one side after we had got behind them, between Scamander and the plain; many of us drowned trying to follow, they say Poseidon is on their side; the river came up and a wave took many men. Come, my dear,' he lifted his friend and began to carry him down the beach. 'Come, my heart, it will be better soon. I am here.'

I watched as a man killed his best-beloved, weeping like a fountain as the knife went home. I bandaged endless wounds which were already beginning to suppurate as I watched.

We worked all night, the three healers, and gradually, towards dawn, when the torches burned pale, the groaning had died down; the dead had been carried away, the ones we had been able to treat were sleeping with their friends. The camp was silent except for the sobbing of men in the arms of Morpheus, who exhibited again in his mercy the events that they could not bear to review when awake. We sat down for the first time in ten hours, drank wine, and blinked reddened eyes. When the sun rose we walked down to the sea to wash.

'We have to find a clean place to work,' I said, my words stumbling over my tongue. 'They are rotting before they come to us; hold me, Polidarius, I think I am fainting.'

The water was cold with dawn chill and he let me down into it, holding my wrists in a firm grip. I lay under the water for a while, watching the blood bloom in clouds out of my tunic and my hair. I had been dipped in blood like a sacrifice.

I surfaced. The water was foul with excrement and floating debris. I made a disgusted exclamation. Bathing had actually made me dirtier.

'Apollo will strike them with his arrows,' commented Polidarius. 'That is what Master Glaucus would say. I have not been thinking, Chryse; the emergencies have come so quickly that I have forgotten my first principles. This coast is not flushed by the tidal race outside, the current that pours out of the Pillars of Heracles. The waters lie idle and are shallow. Only a great storm will cleanse this sea. I must look at the way the water goes—it may be that over there it is cleaner.' He hauled me to my feet and we waded back. 'I have brine boiling over my fire. Come ashore and we will wash off our bath with that. Yes. I must have a look at the lie of the land nearer to the Pillars, over that way.'

'Over there is Achilles' camp,' said Macaon. 'Be careful, brother.'

We slept for five hours, lying close together. The Macaon went to report to the king and I went with Polidarius to survey the beaches.

The Myrmidon guard stopped us, examined us narrowly, and then let us go on, round Achilles' encampment and onto the rocky escarpment which enclosed the bay. Here the air was clean and the thin strip of sand untouched; but the water we waded out was just as tainted. It was the custom to anoint steering oars with olive oil so that they clove the water more cleanly; this practise had led to the formation of slicks which trapped and held the nauseating detritus of the army. Even the sea stank.

'How have you endured this, my brother?' I asked as we picked our way to the top of the cliff and breathed new air. 'This is stockyard slaughter, not medicine.'

'We do what we must,' he said. 'What we must, little brother.'

We stared for a while straight across the Pillars of Heracles to the land beyond.

'When do you think that the arrows will strike?' I asked.

'Apollo has no patience with the impious,' Macaon said wryly. 'He has even less patience with the impious who buy their water at four obols a bucket from those who draw it from the River Scamander where it pours into the bay, after it drains the city of Troy. Those who insist that their crew trudge, complaining, a long way upstream to collect it (such as the elegant Odysseus), and who mainly live on their ships anchored out to sea (which Odysseus does), and those who always dilute their drinking water not with honey but with terebinthate wine (as, it happens, does Odysseus)—those men alone may hope to escape the god's wrath.'

'How long?'

'Not long now, little brother.'

We found a rainwater-fed stream which ran down the rocks. After washing our tunics and ourselves, we caught a bucket full and went back to camp.

◇◇◇

The attack had damaged the army, both in men, weapons and horses, and morale. After a sickening morning cauterising putrescent wounds and watching young men die, I ran out of the camp, deciding that I needed to look at the other side of the bay, or I might burst into tears, steal a boat, and flee home to Epidavros like a coward.

I ran full tilt into a fine tunic and someone grabbed me by the shoulder and shook me. I threw up an arm to cover my head in case it was a Myrmidon and looked into the face of red-headed Odysseus.

'My apologies,' he said mildly. 'I seem to have got in your way, asclepid.'

'Lord Odysseus, how clumsy of me,' I faltered. 'I am…I have been…I was going…'

'Then we shall go together.' He took my arm and we began to walk along the plain of Troy like old friends. 'I intended to send for you, Chryse Diomenes, about now. You came early.'

'Lord, I had reason.'

He did not ask me what reason, but patted me gently on the shoulder. I think that he knew—Odysseus usually did, which might have been why he was giving me a choice of names.

'Call me Chryse, Lord. There is a Diomedes in this army and I would not be confused with him.'

'You wouldn't be. I won't ask you to call me Kokkinos or Phyrre.' Both were terms referring to his red hair. 'But you need not call me Lord. I am just Odysseus, Chryse Asclepid Priest. So. How do you like war?'

'Not at all, Odysseus.'

'No, who could?'

'Achilles the Hero likes it well enough.'

'Achilles wants to destroy the world; slaughter makes him happy. I think that the story is true that he is the son of Thetis and Zeus; Zeus is a Titan, the son of Chronos.' This so agreed with my own thought that I gaped at the king of Ithaca and he smiled and tipped my chin, closing my mouth with his forefinger.

'They are heroes, Chryse; as I said to you once, the world is different for heroes, they like killing and plunder.'

'But on your small and poverty-stricken island…' I quoted him.

He laughed. '…we cannot afford heroes. Yes. These heroes have generous gods, Asclepid—"Compulsion" and "Power" are their names, or you could call them "Oh, but you must" and "Hand it over." My Ithaca is barren and rocky and ruled by "Poverty" and "Hardship"—"Not an obol to spare" and "Sorry, I can't."'

I laughed at his conceit, wondering how long it had been since I had laughed.

'There, that is better. I did not bring you here to die of despair, asclepid. Now, what were you looking for here in the plain?'

'I wanted to get away, Odysseus, but I also wanted to have a look at the coast. The camp of the Argives is dirty and flies are breeding among the dead; the men have lice and ticks and the ones in the swamp are being bitten to pieces by mosquitoes and they all have dysentery. It augurs badly.'

'Apollo will not be pleased,' he agreed. 'Well, here we are. Keep moving; there are archers on the walls and Scythians who can shoot near enough to straight down.'

The army was getting its water from the broad Scamander as it rushed out from under the city of Troy and into the bay. A set of barred arches let the water out while making entry to the city through its sewers difficult. A hail from the Scaean Gate, mounted high on the cliff, told us that we were not unobserved. As I watched, a Trojan ship set off into the bay, rowing hard.

'We used to attack them,' observed Odysseus. 'Now they are allowed to come and go. The Argive ships off Lemnos may catch them; it depends on the current.'

Scamander's water was dirty as it went into the bay; Polidarius had been right. If the army were drinking this it was no wonder that they had dysentery. As we walked away from the walls, I realised that I had a question to ask the red-headed king of Ithaca.

'Lord,' I ventured, 'why did you come to Troy?'

'Because of the league, Asclepid. Words must hold and law must rule or there is an end to civilisation and order. And because against my will, they made me come.'

'But this has loosed the Achaean hordes on the unprotected villages of the whole coast,' I protested. 'What order is in that?'

'I am a small king,' he said stonily. 'These villages are in Thessaly, in Thrace, in Caria and Mysia and Phrygia. They all have one thing in common.'

'What?'

'They are not in Ithaca.'

We walked half of the way back to the beaches in silence while I thought about it. I considered the death rate among the soldiers and the probable result of a plague if the army stayed for the winter.

'And the heroes?' I asked. Odysseus smiled a completely charming smile. 'I told you before, Chryse my dear, Asclepid Priest, Thanatos-Blessed, Little Brother of Death. I do not admire heroes. Troy will fall to us eventually; I know how it can be conquered. But what have I against Troy and why should I allow these heroes to go home and ravage Pelops' land and endanger my own people? When the Argives are no longer a threat; when even if they return home alive they will not have sufficient young men for three generations to wage any war at all; then I reveal the plan for the defeat of this harmless city. I am a king, you know,' he added as I stared at him once more. 'A king must defend his kingdom.'

I left him without another word and went back to my wounded.

◇◇◇

Autumn had set in and the gales were beginning, before the army was sent again to the shut-fast gates of Troy. I saw them creep forth armed with a massive tree-trunk which they had been sheathing in bronze for a week. My wounded had recovered or died; I had nothing to do, so I went with the army. Macaon walked beside me, carrying a bundle of bandages.

'We may be able to treat them as they lie on the plain,' he said, a vertical line dividing his brows. 'Fewer may die.'

I was worried about him. Although he was healthy he seemed to have shrunk. His face was wrinkled like that of an old man's and his eyes were dull with fatigue. He would not eat, saying that he had no appetite, and when Polidarius had produced some roasted goat he had pushed it away with a gasp of 'Not more blood!'

I was afraid that if we had to run, I might have to carry him, and I did not know if I could. He was leaning on my shoulder. I took the bag from him and he walked more easily for a while.

All round us the attacking company was marching. Their bronze armour had been greased with fat so that it would not clink. They moved as silently as men can, with only the occasional whispered word, though we were still beyond the Scamander and could not have been heard in the city. There was just enough moonlight to see the ground, though we would wait until Selene departed before attacking.

My master's son took my hand and smiled sadly—that was the only time the gentle Macaon had smiled since I had come to Troy.

'Courage,' he murmured.

'Courage,' I replied.

Chapter Twenty-three

Cassandra

Tithone found a wound in my skull; a big bruise where the helmet had foiled the spear. The salvaged army of Troy was crammed into the alleys of the lower city, stepping on each other's feet, being kicked by exhausted horses and weeping, in some case, with relief at being inside again with a stout wall between us and the god-possessed warriors of the Achaeans. Hector gave orders; the horses were led away to be tended, the undamaged soldiers flowed up into the palace to be comforted and fed, and only the wounded remained with Tithone and her sisters.

Polyxena was there, steadying my head as Tithone wound a bandage around it, scolding me all the while about fighting when I should be healing. The Argives were beating on the gate and screaming at us to come out and be killed. I laughed shakily. It would require something very compelling to make my cautious brother leave the walls of Troy again.

'There,' Tithone completed her binding. My head felt like a wooden ball. 'Cassandra, you must take this infusion of wound-herb, marsh-leaf, and comfrey, then you must go back to the Maidens and allow Perseis to care for you, fool-hardy daughter of Priam.'

I drank the concoction. It tasted good, which meant that I needed it.

Penthesileia was passing and told us that all the Amazons were alive and uninjured. 'No spear thrown by those clumsy Argives can find a mark in us,' she laughed. 'We are faster than the wind; she is our sister. Come, lean on my arm and I will conduct you. You fought well, Princess, very well for a novice. It is the noise, chiefly, which disconcerts a new Amazon. You shot quite well, too, for someone unused to the back of a moving horse. Did you see that Argive fighting the air? He might have managed to kill Aeneas, if he had not gone distracted.'

'Aeneas is alive?'

'I brought him in myself; a stone hit him on the hip and leg, but Tithone does not think the bones broken, just bent and the flesh flattened. He was standing when the stone struck; fatal crush injuries usually happen when the body is between a hard place and the missile. His condition was not improved by that mad gallop across the front of my horse, but there it is. No one will be found alive on the plain now that the army have possession it,' she said matter-of-factly.

The noise was indeed dying down outside, muted by the walls. It seemed that the Achaeans were retreating after their request to open the gate had been greeted with stones and darts. She was right. No wounded cried outside. I even heard the wind again, the constant companion of Ilium. I swallowed and blinked.

'Yes, your ears have come back into use. Good. Your eyes can focus and you are walking in a straight line. I think that you will recover, daughter of Priam. Here is the Palace of the Maidens. Mistress,' she called, 'here is a soldier returned from battle.'

Perseis came to the door. I saw in my accentuated sight a woman damaged beyond recognition; as though a stone club had broken her face into ruin. I could not imagine what could produce such damage. One eye looked blankly at me out of the skull smashed like fruit. I sobbed, stared, blinked, and the vision went. She took me inside and laid me down on my own bed. I slept until the evening of the next day. No Argive ghosts gibbered in black dark and I was grateful.

◇◇◇

I took the bandage off after I had eaten, bathed and dressed in my moss-green tunic. The bruise was purple but not soggy or hot; I judged myself very lucky and resolved to find the smith and tell her that I could recommend her helmets.

But first I was going to find Eleni, my brother. He had sent me a message from the Temple of Apollo by Idume Adonis Priest, who did not care for the Apollonian worship and, if I knew Idume, he had been substantially bribed. I rummaged in my belongings and found a gold coin in case he needed bribing twice.

I did not know what I was going to say to Eleni.

The king's council was called for the fourth watch. I did not have much time. I hurried up the winding path behind the temples, from courtyard to courtyard. I was hailed in the Temple of the Mother by an old woman who looked vaguely familiar. She was sitting on the cobbles, trying to coax something out from an earthenware pot. She was holding a dead mouse by the tail but whatever it was did not rise to this bait.

'Cassandra, help me with the new one; it has coiled around the inside of this pot and they can't stay in terracotta; it's too hot and it will die,' she called. I came, because it is not wise to disobey a priestess and I had offended enough gods as it was. I crouched down next to her.

'What sort is it?' I asked, 'Take away the mouse, it's clearly not hungry.'

'It's the green viper, the puffed-tail African one. Tithone needs its venom to treat the locked jaw; she has several cases of it.'

I nodded. We used snake venom for several healing purposes, though it was so dangerous a therapy we only tried it as a last resort. The locked jaw was the first symptom of an affliction of those who had taken deep puncture wounds which had not been cleansed immediately. The jaw locked, then the spine; they died in a couple of days in agony of dreadful spasms and cramps. Those bitten by the green viper, on the other hand, lost all sensation in their muscles; they died because they lacked the strength to breathe. Thus the locked-jaw patients were treated with a drop of venom, rubbed into a shallow scratch in the skin. If the convulsions could be controlled they recovered. Any miscalculation and they either spasmed to death or died of poisoning.

'We can break the pot, in which case the viper will be angry and might be injured,' I said, 'or I can put in my hand and try to pull it out. In which case it may strike and I will be dead.'

'The god protects you,' she said hopefully.

'The god has rejected me,' I rejoined. 'I'll try.' I took a deep breath, tried not to remember how the snakebite victims died, sent a respectful appeal to the goddess—after all, it was her creature—and slid my hand into the pot. The snake had coiled itself tightly around the inside. I felt very slowly for the head, expecting the sting which meant death, found it, and tightened my grip very slowly. It wriggled, then was trapped.

I drew it slowly out of the pot, my fingers grasping it behind the ugly, spade-shaped head. A fine healthy viper, it seemed. Venom dripped from the fangs in the hissing open mouth, which would be diluted eighteen times before it would be used on humans.

The priestess produced a straw-filled sack and I lowered the snake carefully inside, pushing the head down hard as she drew up the strings and tied them in a knot. I examined my hands for any mark or graze, washed them in a basin of water and only then let out the breath I had been holding.

After that I got to my feet and continued to prowl behind the temples. For some reason, I was shaking.

I was still doing so when a trembling twin enfolded me in a rib-breaking hug and breathed into my hair, 'Oh, Cassandra, you should not handle snakes!'

'You knew,' I said into the heavy golden embroidery. 'Eleni, you are still with me, you knew.' I leaned back to look into his face and demanded, 'Why did you lie? You lied when you said "Victory"—you lied and you have shut your mind to me all this time when you could still find me; I needed you and called for you, I begged for you and you did not come.'

He kissed my forehead over the great bruise. 'Yes, I lied. The priests said they'd kill me if I told the truth—they said the god would shoot me with his arrows. They have poisons and purpose of their own; they hope to deal with the Achaeans, knowing that they respect the gods. I am in their power.'

He kissed me and I responded, wrapped in the scent of his skin, the taste of his mouth.

'Twin, I must escape,' he groaned. 'Mysion Apollo Priest uses me for his purposes, which he says are the god's. But it has been so long that I shut myself off from your pain and your love I cannot find you—I tried when you were ill and they chained me in the temple; I did try, but there was a cloud. I wandered on the dark plain and could not find the spark that was you, sister, you must believe me.' He was crying, tears running down his cheeks. 'Twin, I love you, I love you.'

I embraced him as closely as flesh would allow. 'I love you,' I murmured, catching sight of Idume Adonis Priest grinning unpleasantly at the courtyard door. 'Come with me, twin, come to our brother and he will protect you. Hector is stronger than any priest. Come now. Oh, Eleni, I love you. Come.'

He pulled away from me and leaned his head on the wall. His hair curled at the nape of his neck exactly as it had always done. The sight hurt me.

'If I leave then Apollo will curse me,' he faltered into my neck. 'If he curses me I will not have…her.'

I was struck dumb. It was, of course, true. Apollo would not take his gifts back but he could modify them; he had changed mine so that I would know and could not speak; he would change Eleni's so that he would have Andromache, perhaps, but she would hate him. A mean, niggardly, cruel god was Shining Apollo. He was going to take my twin away, again and forever.

'From the city, then,' I said at last. His eyes shone, grey eyes just like mine.

'From the city,' he agreed, stroking my hair.

'Because you know what will happen to Troy,' I insisted.

'I know and so do you. I will not leave the god, Cassandra. I must leave the temple.'

He was in my mind now, curling into an accustomed hollow which ached unbearably when it was empty and would ache again when he was gone.

'Stay with me; stay in my soul until I can contrive something,' I said. 'I will get you out, twin. Until then, try not to make more prophecies of false hope.'

'Why do you strive against the god?' he asked as he released my hands. 'Troy must be sacked; why do you beat your fists against fate?'

'I don't know,' I confessed, kissing him again. His mouth was sweet enough to make me faint. 'Trust me, twin; search my mind. I will help you. Now, I must go; you are watched.'

He turned in a panicky swirl of robes and ran. Idume smiled crookedly and held out a cupped hand. I folded his fingers over the coin and said quietly, 'If this meeting is known, I prophesy confidently that you will die, Adonis Priest. A little viper venom in the cup and you will sleep and not wake.'

'I am faithful,' he protested. I left the temple courtyard, having purchased a little faith, a scarce and expensive commodity in Troy during the siege.

I probed my own mind a hundred times that day and Eleni was still with me. I felt renewed. I saw twelve dead ones in the street, but the young man that I had seen as a fleshless grinning skeleton passed me without a mark on him. He had been in the battle and had not died.

So I did not know anything; not when, just eventually. I could not warn anyone; it was not specific to a time or place before the city fell, as it had repeatedly done in our visions. Even if I could have spoken, all I could have said was, 'You will die' and everyone knows that.

Telling someone 'You will be skewered by an arrow' or 'You will drown' would be of interest, but not helpful. I did not hope that what I was seeing was untrue. Too many of the dead ones had just died and in the way I had foreseen. But Apollo's most malicious wish was that I should see useless visions; sent only to torture me.

Eleni was puzzled; he saw the sendings but did not understand them and he recoiled. I realised that I had grown in strength beyond my twin. He blocked off the seeing, which he could do because they were not his torment. But I felt his love in my mind; his sympathy, which I had missed like a missing tooth.

Hector reported to the king's council, Státhi on his shoulder. Forty had been killed, twenty-six wounded retrieved, of whom eighteen would die and three were already dead.

'Small loss considering that a whole army was against us,' he added. 'The Amazons and the cavalry drove them off when they encircled us; otherwise we should not have been able to get back. Are you satisfied, Father, with war on the plain?'

'It might have been peace on the plain,' retorted the old man, 'if Pandarus had not fired at Menelaus. Pandarus has paid for his folly. He is dead. It is too much to hope that Menelaus is also.'

'I doubt it,' I said as Hector consulted me with a glance. 'He was standing and bleeding, not even knocked over; the arrow was deflected by his armour,' and the goddess, I did not add. 'He will probably recover, Lord.'

'Then we have lost nearly sixty Trojans for Pandarus' folly,' growled Anchises. 'And no more must fall. Let them swelter on the plain and freeze in the winter gales. I would not counsel that we ever fight on the plain again.'

'You are wise, Anchises,' agreed Hector. 'I presume that Pariki has slaked his thirst for single combat.' He looked for Pariki and found him lounging against a pillar, not a hair out of place, but pale and not smiling. 'Come, brother, tell us. How did you get back to the city so quickly? Did you tunnel? Or did you just outrun a rabbit?'

'The goddess brought me, bright Ishtar,' he muttered sullenly. 'In a mist she carried me and I found myself before the open gate and wafted inside on a scent of roses.'

'Ah,' said Hector dryly. 'I was wafted through the gate myself on a stench of panic and flung spears, but I am not protected by any powerful deities.'

Even if I could have told my elder brother that Pariki was telling the truth, I would not have. The affronted Pariki came forward and knelt next to Priam. The old hand caressed him. He was still Priam's favourite son. The king did not love Hector, bulwark and warrior, anything like he favoured this worthless boy. I bit my lip and did not speak; neither did Hector comment.

'So, we lick our wounds and Agamemnon licks his and we wait,' said Anchises, watching Priam and Hector without expression. 'Hector, beloved Prince and Cuirass of Troy, there are refuge-seekers come from the villages who wish to speak with you. Will you hear them?'

'Yes, of course,' said Hector, sitting down. 'Cassandra, have you that list of villages? I have been trying to map the depredations of the Achaeans to see how seaworthy they are and how long it takes them to circle the Aegean and get back to Troy. I am hoping that they will be dragged down below Kriti by the current and have to row their way back; twenty days, thirty perhaps, in which time they are not resupplying Agamemnon or killing Trojans.'

The king nodded. From the floor of the hall a female voice ragged with pain added, 'They are not killing Trojans, perhaps, but they are killing us. All of my village are dead; murdered in the agora as they tried to bargain with Achilles.'

'Achilles again,' sighed Hector. There were thirty-nine names on my list of villages which had been sacked and ruined. Achilles' name was attached to twenty-eight of them and he was probably responsible for the ones left so devoid of life that there was no survivor left to tell who had brought death upon them.

'Death came in three beaked ships from the sea,' said the woman. 'I was herding goats away from the shore; I saw them coming and I ran. I did not stop to warn Ponticha; it would not have helped. Slim and golden haired and pretty as a girl is Achilles; yet he directed them, I saw him from the tree I had climbed. He waved his hand and they all died, even the children, even the dogs of Ponticha are slaughtered. You are the great prince!' she shrieked into Hector's face, spattering him with spittle. 'Save us! Kill these invaders before they murder us all! You sit safely in your great city behind your walls, while the farmers and herdsmen are sacrificed to feed Achilles till he gluts on our blood! Your brother's folly brought the Achaean pirates here—send them home or kill them before we are all dead. It is the fault of your house, Trojan prince—you must mend it. Kill them! Kill them! Kill them!'

Hector took no offence, but held her close until she stopped screaming, her bitterness smothered against his chest. Then he held her at arm's length and said, 'Lady, I understand. Now you have delivered your message to Hector and you can rest. Go with my wife and she will take you to the healers. You are hurt.' The woman felt dazedly at a splotch of blood which gummed her veil to her head. Andromache led her away.

Hector was disturbed. 'What she says is true. Achilles must die.'

'The priest of Apollo, Eleni, has made a prophecy,' said Polites with a doubtful glance at me.

'What is it?'

'That neither you nor Achilles will survive each other by three days.'

I sought my twin and found him doubtful and wary, but it was a true sending and from the god. Eleni was trying to avoid false hope, but in this he had an interest. If he was to marry Andromache, then Hector must die.

I was so shocked by this realisation that I almost thrust my twin out of my head, except that he seemed as horrified by the prospect as me. I was also finding it hard to resume the old knowledge. His mind felt alien to me now and mine to him. We had grown a long way apart while he had hung in chains in Apollo's temple.

And how was I to get him safe out of the city?

This was my concern as I went to sleep and eat before the night watch. God-tortured eyes are sharp in the dark and not so easily confused by the phantoms which drift across the unfocused eye and cause so many innocent and non-Argive shadows to be pierced by Trojan arrows fired by nervous sentries. Hector and I usually took the first night watch together. Státhi saw well in the dark and liked to hunt the moths which danced around the torches.

I could smuggle Eleni out of any gate; all the gate-guards knew me. The question was, where should he go after that? Inland, that was one possibility; there were plenty of little villages a safe distance from the sea and maybe five days ride distant. He could reach all the internal towns of Phrygia, Caria, and then go on to Egypt by sea or even to wander into the Hittite kingdoms.

No, going to Egypt he would run the risk of encountering the People of the Sea, who were Achaeans. Then again, in Hittite territory there were rumoured to be wandering tribes of cannibals, head hunters, and even monsters. He could reach Africa, but he would be known as an absconding Apollo Priest in the small Trojan communities who lived there for trade; beside it was fever-ridden and unhealthy and Argives and Thessalians had settled there. Not Africa. Lemnos was a possibility; the women of that island had a short way with annoying men and needed husbands; there he would at least be close to me. No, I was being selfish; Lemnos was too close and could be raided at any time by Agamemnon. Inland, perhaps. Or, better; he could cross the Pillars of Heracles; it could be done, further up past Mount Idus; thence into the kingdoms beyond or across into Thrace. Yes, that would be best. Now, I would need to steal a horse, some gear, and food. I was not going to take anyone into this conspiracy, not even my brother Hector, whom I would unfailingly trust with Eleni's life. I knew the power of the gods.

I wondered afresh why the Maiden whom the Achaeans call Athene, Goddess of Battles, she of the Glittering Helmet, would be taking their side against her faithful city of Troy. Our lady queen had sacrificed to that goddess in the heat of the battle, but this might have been cancelled out by the curse I had invoked against the gleaming lady while she was supporting Diomedes. I wondered if the gods were on anyone's side but their own. I decided that their ways were unfathomable and climbed the steps and then the ladder to the Scamander tower as the drum sounded for the night watch.

I sat down knee-to-knee with Hector as we stared out across the darkening plain.

He sighed. 'Cassandra, that woman of Caria was right.'

'What do you mean?'

'That it is our fault that the Achaeans are here; our fault that they are raiding the coast and our most irreparable fault that Achilles Man Slayer has come.'

'My lord brother,' I said soothingly, 'it is not. Do not say so.'

'My lady sister,' he responded in courtesy, 'it is. Pariki stole Elene and this is the harvest.'

'Is this the brother who lectured me about the Atreidae making war on us for years, raiding our ships, enslaving our crews, because of sheer greed for our wealth and position?' I asked rhetorically. Hector nodded.

'Yes, this is the same brother,' he agreed. 'But I feel responsible, nonetheless.'

'That is your burden along with the heavy bundle of all the lives in Troy,' I said, copying Tithone's manner. 'You must balance one load against the other, Hector.'

'And that's true too,' he agreed. We watched Státhi, hunting moths in silence for a long time. He always caught them. He would crouch in what seemed like an unlikely position, until the moth fluttered close. Then a clawed paw thudded down on it and it was extinguished.

Then, being Státhi, he ripped it wing from airy wing and ate it.

We were surrounded with the litter of little lives when Státhi paused, chewing, swallowed, pricked his ears, and leapt onto the wall in front of Hector.

He stared down into the dark under the gate, interested.

'Can you see anything?' asked Hector. By now the moon was down and it was black dark, but I listened and thought I heard something breathing.

'A straying horse, perhaps,' I said, but Hector had walked away from the gate and was calling his archers to the wall.

He lit a torch and ripped it down into the space under the Scamander Gate.

It gleamed on helmets and breastplates as it fell.

'Alarm,' called Hector and the trumpet blew, first the general alarm and then the signal for the Scamander Gate. I heard voices in the palace as the sons of Priam stumbled down the street, half asleep, but by now so used to the calls that Deiphobos said he could reach his own gate with his eyes still shut.

I was kindling torches to provide light for the archers to aim at. Lighting three, I tossed them high and wide. Before they were crushed out under mailed feet I estimated a hundred men and a battering ram slung between them.

I seized my bow. A runner flashed past me, carrying orders for oil and torches. A line on a hook, such as sailors use for climbing cliffs, snaked up and shook under the weight of a climbing man. I dropped the bow and drew my knife, calling for an axe. Another runner leapt down the ladder returned with four battle-axes such as had not been used for generations. They had come, she said, from the temple of Dionysius. By then I had sawed through the rope, but the man was clinging to the wall with both hands. For a moment I stared right into his face; just an ordinary man. He had brown eyes.

I stabbed down with the knife into his throat. He cried out and fell, indicating that I had missed the great blood vessel I had been aiming for.

Now grapnels clanked and the defence grew confusing. I helped three staggering men with a cauldron of pitch and oil. We man-handled it up to the tower and emptied it with a swish and wallop, then rained down torches. The ram was metal sheathed, but the handlers were of flesh. They screamed as they burned.

Hector had sheathed his sword and had taken an axe. He clove the ropes as they attached and the attackers fell howling into the fire below.

The smoke was thick; it was impossible to see. A runner screamed and I grabbed her; I felt along the little body and found the wound; a hook had gone right through the shoulder joint and out through the other side. She was caught like a fish on a line.

Hector's axe flashed. He cut the rope and I carried the child to the bottom of the ladder, passing her to someone below.

By torchlight and our pitch fire, I saw them retreat, but only a little way, a bowshot from the gate. There a young man in a red tunic was tending the wounded. He scraped up Scamander mud and applied it in gooey handfuls to the burns. This was a good treatment and I approved. The Amazon Eris, standing at my side, bent her bow.

'No,' I said quickly. 'No, Eris, he is not a soldier and he is the only one left standing—see, the others have run away. Don't kill him.'

I was interested. He had treated all the burns; now he was encouraging the wounded to walk and drag the others back toward the Argive camp. I heard horses whinnying; it seemed that someone was bringing some transport.

The dying pitch-fire gleamed off the young man's golden hair, the only Achaean I had not instantly tried to kill. He was tall and slender and he was handling the wounded with tenderness and skill. Most of his patients were moving away, now, out of our sight. As he searched among the slain for any who might not be dead, he heaved away the pile of fallen climbers, testing each one by the pulse-point below the jaw and passing on as he found no life within.

Then he found a body in a red robe stuck through with an arrow, and knelt over it, his head bent. I thought that he might be weeping.

'He's one of mine,' said the lady of the Amazons. 'Had I known that you were a protector of healers, Princess, I might have spared him. Or I might not,' she added with a snap of teeth. 'For those who comfort our enemies are our enemies also. If he values his life, he had better get out of range.'

I leaned over the wall to call to him. 'Healer,' I yelled. 'I cannot restrain my allies. Go back. Your friend is dead.'

He lifted his wet face. He was handsome and young. 'You have done good work for Troy tonight,' he called bitterly. 'This is—this was Macaon the surgeon, son of Asclepius.'

'I'm sorry, but in a night attack it is hard to distinguish between healer and hurter. Get away, now, or the Amazons will kill you like they killed Macaon.'

'What is your name, Lady?' he said, laying the dead man's head gently on the ground. 'To whom do I owe my life?'

'Cassandra, Princess of Troy,' I replied. He paused in plain view of all those archers and bowed to me, hands on breast before he followed the wounded out of sight.

I found that the things that had crunched and slipped under my sandals were detached Argive fingers and I was sick.

Next morning, when we went out to take in the cooling battering ram for the sake of its bronze, I had the body of Macaon the healer carried to our own citadel, to be burned in honour, not left to rot.

◇◇◇

Aphrodite huddled at the feet of Demeter, whimpering. Her wounded hand was wrapped in a fold of tunic. Ichor, the blood of the gods, had dripped down the front of her white chiton.

'No one has ever hurt her before,' said Zeus, stroking her hair. 'Poor lady, made only for love, attacked by a mad Argive! Go no more into such forays of desperate mortals, sweet Aphrodite. For the rest of you, you have disobeyed me. Did I not order you to refrain from the battle? You were all there, even the Lady of Doves.'

'Divine Father, I went to rescue Aphrodite,' protested Ares, dangling his helmet and plume. 'I broke no word.'

Zeus nodded and went on, his great voice echoing, so that the birds of Aphrodite rose in a panic of silver wings.

'You, daughter Athene, and you, son Apollo, you are forsworn.'

'Lord, there is a wager,' argued Apollo. 'Mortals must dance to our piping—otherwise we are not gods. I say that the city must fall, as does my sister, in support of the men who give us worship. We

will fade, Lord Zeus, if they forget us. Must I starve for the scent of the burning sacrifice? The altars will be ashen cold if we do not manifest our power to men.'

'I will take a hand myself,' threatened Zeus, 'if this continues. Do you pit your strength and will against me, children?'

He drew himself up. Lightning forked from his hands and the corner of the balustrade broke and fell. The air was offended with the stench of burned stone.

'Lord, I do not oppose you,' Apollo argued. 'Consider the state of these mortals. My favourite is brought to Troy when Demeter kills his wife.'

'I did not kill her,' Demeter said slowly. 'She died.'

'You did not save her, then, old woman. Diomenes has met the daughter of Priam, my ex-priestess Cassandra—and as I said, he is not stricken. I am so close, Father, so close to winning the golden apple that is rightfully mine. Let the wager run a little longer, Father. It would be just.'

'Just?' objected Aphrodite tearfully. 'What is just? You interfere in the life of my darling, tear all her loves away from her, though I have given her back her twin to keep her from despair. You have tormented her with visions and she is drenched in death. You fly into the battle with Ares at your side to turn the Trojan flank.'

'I cannot keep you out of this war, it seems,' mused Zeus. 'And your point about mortals is well made. Who will fear us, if we are not seen to be powerful? Very well. I give the armies and the city of Troy into your hands. More battles I will give you, children—more chances to settle this wager. But if you may join the battle, all may join. We will see who rules Olympus,' said Cloud-Compelling Zeus, and walked away.

Chapter Twenty-four

Diomenes

I went with the soldiers when they dragged away the slain from the walls of Troy, but I could not find the body of my master's son Macaon. The Trojans had taken it; there could be no other explanation. So I waited until the Argives had loaded their cart and led it away, then I walked to the Scamander Gate, with my hands out and empty and called up to the watch, 'I would speak with the Princess Cassandra.'

'Go away, Argive,' said a man's voice. I thanked Heaven that it was not one of those implacable Amazons; they would not have wasted time talking to me.

'I wish to speak to the Princess Cassandra. I am alone and I am unarmed. Tell her that it is the healer Chryse.' There was a silence, then I heard the voice repeat my request to someone he called 'Lord.'

'What do you want with my sister? It is Polites, son of Priam, who asks.' It was a cultured voice speaking very good Achaean.

'I wish to thank her for saving my life and to ask her what has happened to my brother Macaon's body.'

'Macaon? The Argive in the red tunic?'

Bitterness flooded into my heart, but I answered, 'Yes, he wore a red tunic, as I do.'

'Cassandra is a healer herself. She restrained the watch from killing you; she feared that the Achaeans would not come for the bodies before they putrefied and she ordered the healer to be taken in honour to the citadel to be burned with our dead. She has a gentle heart, for all that she is cursed by the god. Stay where you are, healer, in plain sight, and I will send for her. You are greatly honoured, enemy,' he added.

I was fighting down a mixture of emotions—outrage at this mistreatment of Macaon, who deserved to be buried in his own grave at Epidavros with his brother Asclepids; wonder that the Trojan woman had been so bold and had the power to order such things to be done; a desire to see her closer, who was to me only a voice over the battlements and the shadow of a face.

'I am not your enemy,' I said quietly.

They did not reply, but I heard some orders given and feet moving on wooden steps. I stood in clear sight and range of the archers for some time; long enough for the wind to chill me through the tunic which was my only garment. Some sort of argument was going on at ground level in front of me. I could not hear the words but one was a female voice and one a deeper male voice. It was a short dispute, but fierce.

Then a voice hailed me. 'Healer, we are opening the gate. You will not move. The archers have you in their sight.'

I stood still. The gate creaked a little open and two figures came out. One was a huge man, bigger even than Agamemnon. He wore full bronze armour but no helmet. A grey furry creature was clinging to his harness; the mou or cat which Eumides the ex-slave had once told me was Egyptian and the constant companion of…oh, of course. This must be Hector, the Prince of Ilium, Cuirass of the Trojans. He had long golden hair, plaited on either side of a big, broad face and a jutting wiry beard. His sword was in his massive hand and he looked at me coolly, up and down, checking that my hands were empty and that I had no weapons concealed under the tunic.

Behind him, bearing a casket in her hands, was a girl with a great bruise staining one side of her face, from temple to cheekbone. She had grey eyes alive with concern in a pale, beautiful face and the same hair as her brother, unbound and flowing over her dark green tunic. She wore horsemen's boots, lacing up her shin. Her arms were bare and tanned, her hands strong. She bore no weapons, not even a knife.

'Healer?' she said gently. 'I don't know your title.'

'I am Chryse God-Touched, Lady, the Asclepius Priest, healer of Epidavros. How shall I speak of you?'

'As you find me.' She almost smiled. 'I am Cassandra God-Cursed, once priestess of Apollo, now healer of the holy city of Tros. My brother Prince Hector has accompanied me.'

I bowed and the great warrior moved his sword to salute across his armoured breast. The mou shifted a little out of the way of the point, perfectly at home on the giant's shoulder. Both sets of eyes, green and grey, considered me dispassionately.

'Here,' the princess said, offering me the wooden box. 'I feared that your comrades might not come in time. It is a terrible thing to allow a body to rot; his spirit cannot reach heaven without special ceremony, but will wander and become a wailing ghost. He was brave and he did no harm to us; I did not think it right to leave him among the soldiers.'

I moved closer to take the chest and I heard the creak as the archers above me bent their bows. I took the ashes, although burning was considered by the Achaeans as a terrible insult to the dead, only done with slaves and people who had died of some plague, cursed by the gods; or, of course, kings on their way to becoming demigods. However, Macaon would not mind, being dead, and Cassandra was not to know of the customs of Achaea. She had meant it as an honour. And it was going to be much easier to send him home like this.

'That was gently done,' I said. She was close to me, red tunic against green. She smelt of healing herbs, olive and amber oils. I reached out very carefully and touched the bruise.

'Have you been treated for that, Lady of the Trojans?'

'Yes; a comfrey poultice. The bone is not damaged.'

'What did it? A fall? A stone over the walls?'

'An Argive spear when I rode behind my brother.'

I was taken aback. I had no idea that a princess of Troy would have been in the battle. I did not know what to say.

'The women of Troy have a part in their own defence,' she told me. 'It is our city too.' She touched my hand. 'Don't come under our walls with the fighters again, Asclepid Priest; we cannot tell if you are a healer in the dust of battle. Wait for the wounded out of bowshot. Fare well,' and she bowed to me like a soldier or a man, both hands crossed on her undefended breast.

'Wait, Lady…shall I speak to you again?'

She raised her eyebrow, looking at her brother. A smile was turning up the corners of the warrior's mouth.

Hector's deep voice was the one I had heard behind the wall. 'As you wish, sister, but you must have an escort. I have no time to spare for supervising conferences between healers. And we cannot let him in. He may be honourable,' he smiled at me, 'but Agamemnon needs to know about our defences and the healer's allegiance is with the Atreidae who, might I remind you, sister, are here to kill us and sack our city.'

'My allegiance is to Epidavros, to Asclepius, and to Apollo,' I said. 'I came to heal, not to fight. Let me come to the walls, Lord of the Trojans, and speak to your sister again. I bear no weapon.'

'That is for her to decide,' he was definitely smiling now. 'Women own themselves in Troy, Asclepid, and their society is their own to dispose of. Speak to Cassandra the princess, not to me, or you will make her angry.'

I was confused. Did the unmarried maiden not belong to her father and brother in this strange city? But I did not want to offend a fellow healer and I very much wanted to talk to Cassandra again.

'I beg your pardon, Lady. I am an ignorant Carian and know nothing of Trojan manners. May I speak with you again?'

'Yes,' she decided. 'But the prince is right, we cannot let you into the city. Come to the Dardanian Gate and ask for me. Make sure you keep out of bowshot and in clear view as your circle the walls and I will talk to you.'

I bowed low; when I looked up the princess and the warrior were gone and the gate was creaking shut.

◇◇◇

'You must go home,' I insisted to Polidarius. 'My master cannot lose both his sons. You must take Macaon to your father.'

'But Chryse, how will you manage?'

'Surgery is not your field anyway, brother, and there is not much scope in this slaughterhouse for medicine. I will recruit some helpers from the mature men who have lost their friends; their hearts are broken and cannot be further wounded, and they will be gentle with the injured. I will manage, Polidarius. Now, there is a boat waiting, Macaon's ashes are here, and your bundle is here.' I shoved his rolled cloak into his arms. 'There will not be many ships into this harbour now that the autumn gales have begun. Go now; it would break your father's heart if both of his sons died.'

I pushed him out of the hut and led him down the beach to a hollow ship of Corinth with its complement of forty rowers. They were anxious to leave while the south wind lasted.

He was still protesting that he could not leave me when the ship gave a wriggle and a rush, slid down the launching gouge in the sand into the water, and was rowed away towards the mouth of the bay of Troy.

I walked back through the encampment to my hut and sat down, listening to the men wailing for Macaon. 'One thousand and one the Amazon killed,' I heard a voice chanting:

The one slain which was the man
And the thousand he might have saved.
Alas, our grief for Asclepius' son,
Macaon son of Glaucus, peerless among surgeons,
Healer of battle-wounds, comforter of the dying…

Arion stumped into my hut and gave his lyre to Menon, who sat at his feet.

'So the Trojans burned him, hmm?' he commented. 'How do you feel about that, Chryse?'

'It was intended to be an honour,' I answered. 'I took it as such. Macaon has not said a word about it.'

Arion laughed grimly. The bard had aged. His hair was almost all white now and his face was lined like carved wood.

'And you have sent Polidarius home,' he added. 'That was wise, Healer, and kind. But what of yourself?'

'I will continue,' I said.

I realised that I was telling the truth. Chryseis' memory had faded. I could remember her vividly, even painfully, but I had been so exhausted by the many who had died under my hands, by the problems presented to me every day of healing the helpless, that my pain had joined with theirs and I was not seeking death any more. Chryseis was faithful; she would wait for me.

'Yes, in a sea of agony, one small spark is quickly drowned,' commented Arion, reading my thoughts. 'I hear that you conferred with the Princess Cassandra. Is she as beautiful as they say?'

'She is golden haired and grey eyed, though marred with a bruise from an Achaean spear; she was in the battle, riding behind her brother Hector. There is a warrior for your song, Arion, bigger even than Agamemnon, tall as a tree, broad as a shield.'

Arion grinned at me. 'Not a song for the Atreidae, asclepid. They had rather Hector was feeble, cowering behind his walls.'

'But the brother and sister are gentle, even indulgent with each other; it was interesting to see them together. He told me to ask her if she wanted to speak to me again. She said that I could come. I need another healer to talk to.'

'Unless you want Agamemnon to send you to spy on the defences I would not tell anyone else that,' Arion warned. 'Tell him, my dear Chryse, that you went to claim your brother the healer's corpse; he must know that you have been there. No, better still, tell him about the arrangement. Agamemnon will be informed if you visit the city and he has a short way with people he thinks are traitors. Already the Trojan traders are setting out, the last ships before winter closes the port. The idea that you might find a way inside the city will please the king.'

'I will not…' I began hotly and he put a hand over my mouth, whispering, 'Of course not, asclepid, but the king doesn't know that. He needs something to cheer him. Achilles is still sulking and doors of Troy are still shut.'

Arion's advice was always sound. Accordingly, I reported to Agamemnon that I had reclaimed the body of my brother Macaon from the Princess Cassandra and that I had arranged to meet her again.

'Asclepid, can you find a way into the city?'

'Lord,' I said, mentally asking the gods if there were any to forgive my mendacity, 'I will try. But it is a strong city, Lord, and they will not let me inside.'

'Try,' he urged, his face close to mine. 'I will load you with gold, asclepid; a ship-load of gold if you can worm out of this girl a breach in their defences. She will not be able to resist you, golden one, most beautiful of Asclepius' sons. Aphrodite has been busy and Eros her son shoots many bolts. This princess fell in love with you as soon as she saw you; that is why she bade the Amazons, those hell-borne bitches, those furies, hold their bows. Flatter her, Chryse, take her presents and beg her to open the gate and she will yield. She is only a maiden, after all. Here,' he dipped his hand into a barrel and it came up gleaming with gold, 'take this fillet, these chains of gold and these bracelets. There is no woman's heart that's averse to jewels. No maiden exists that cannot be seduced with manly beauty and gold and lies. Promise her love, asclepid, promise her golden children and she will fall into your arms.'

I did not think this at all likely; few princesses would exchange power and position in a great city for Argive chains, even if they were of gold. But I said nothing and I took the jewels. Odysseus came to the conference as Agamemnon dismissed me. I passed him on the way out of the wooden hut.

'Do you think that you can find a way into Troy?' he asked me in a low voice. When I did not reply, he nodded. 'Sometimes even silence is packed with information, Chryse,' he said, then added in a louder tone, 'Hail, Lord Agamemnon! You summoned me?'

'Yes, the winter is setting in. We need wood for fires. I sent a wood-cutting party into the hills yesterday but they have not returned. Your pirates are healthy still, my Lord of Ithaca. Send after them, find out what has happened and bring in the wood.'

'Lord,' suggested Odysseus, 'the shepherds might have killed them. The men of Mount Idus are strong and fast and incredibly hard to capture. They strike and fade back into the woods. It might be them. I will go and see.'

I went out to ask among the Argives for those who were willing to learn the craft of surgeon. After some enquiries, I recruited three of the older men who had steady hands, had lost someone, and who could be spared by their captains. I took them to my hut and began to teach them the rudiments of the healer's art.

Odysseus came back the next day to report that he had found the seven woodcutters dead without a mark on them. However, he had completed their work and brought the load of trees back. He had also brought a dead woodcutter for me to examine.

I cleansed the body and stripped it with the help of my three apprentices, then examined it carefully from head to toe. I even parted the hair and then shaved the scalp, in case a cunning knife had pierced his skull, but I found no mark. I questioned the remains of that company and found that the dead man had been listless, not ill but not well, ever since he had been in the detachment which lay in the Dardanian marshes. Otherwise there was nothing to report of him, poor corpse, until he had been found struck dead in his tent on the mountain.

I did not know how he had died. I burned incense and prayed, then opened the body.

The spleen was swollen and hard and the liver was knobbed. Nothing else was noticeable until I found his brain flooded with blood, his eyes suffused, and his ears and sinuses blocked. He had died of a cerebral haemorrhage.

This was a diagnosis but I had no idea of the cause. I sewed the body together and gave it to the vultures. Then I reported to Agamemnon that the dead man had been struck down with a new disease and that the mountain was clearly dangerous to his army.

Calchas the Apollo Priest conducted a ritual and declared that the mountain was ruled by the Fates and must be avoided in darkness. Thereafter the foresters went out in daylight and hacked wildly, rolling the timber down the slope and retreating before night fell. No more of them died.

◇◇◇

Achilles Man Slayer sent for me the next day. I approached him as one approaches a wild beast; gently and with circumspection, careful to make no sudden move or loud noise. He was sitting on his throne, Patroclus at his side, sipping from a decorated goblet and considering several maidens.

They knelt in the sand in front of him, frightened women in thin tunics which the wind was pulling and flicking. It was cold and they were shivering.

'Spoil,' he said, indicating the women, 'from a small village called—what was it called?'

'Ponticha, my Lord,' said Patroclus evenly. There was a line between his brows and he was composing his voice with care.

'I caught them on the shore—there is no one alive in Ponticha now,' explained the hero. 'I brought you to examine them, Healer—tell me which ones will bear a long sea journey. I am minded to send them as a present to a certain king.'

'As you say, Lord, but let me take them inside, out of this cold wind.'

He slammed a fist down on the arm of the throne. 'No! If you need to strip them then do so here.'

'In the view of all, Lord?' I asked. I knew I was trying his patience but I would not be party, if I could help it, to exposing a lot of captured maidens to death by cold.

'Come, now, my dearest,' soothed Patroclus. 'They will die out here and then they will be of no value. There is no value in death.' Achilles thought about it, his face set like metal, one long hand toying with the ringlets of his beautiful hair. Then he turned a dazzling smile on Patroclus and said, 'If you wish it, sweet Prince, it shall be so.'

'Come inside,' I whispered to the women. 'Now,' and they hurried after me.

There were four of them, one visibly pregnant. All had the white, still faces of those who had seen such dreadful things that they do not dare to think or speak, in case a word jolts them with some unbearable memory. I made a pretence of examining them but there was no chance that I would certify them unfit. If I did, Achilles would order them killed.

After a few minutes and as many soothing words as I could think of, I allowed them to sit down and returned to Achilles' side. I knelt in the tumbled sand and said, 'They are all fit, Lord, for a journey.'

'Do not kneel, Chryse. Come, sit beside me,' he said affably, with genuine charm. 'Have some wine. They say that you go to Troy to speak to a princess,' I nodded. 'Well, Healer, if you can point her out to me in the battle, I'll try not to kill her.'

This was a great concession and I said, 'I thank you, Lord Achilles.'

'I am not a monster,' he said, not sadly but as though he were making a statement. 'I am god-touched and sometimes am god-possessed, and the gods have made a stone out of my heart. Have you a cure for that, healer?'

'No, Lord,' I said, and Patroclus stroked the gold-thread hair of the downcast head.

Achilles was weeping for his stony heart.

◇◇◇

Winter came suddenly. I woke one morning and found the camp white with snow. The sea was as flat as a plate and the colour of lead, as was the sky.

'Snow and more snow coming,' said Arion, crunching over frozen sand, 'I wish I were at home in sunny Thessaly or looking out from my own house in the morning while slaves blow on the cooking fire and bring me warm wine.'

'I wish I was back at Epidavros with the suppliants coming down the road and my master's cook baking barley cakes,' I replied. 'But here we are.'

'So we are.' He sighed and pointed seaward. 'Achilles' ship. Back from looting another village. There is no glory nor any song to sing in the slaughter of goatherds, Asclepid. But that is not what I came to tell you. Put on your cloak and come and see who Menelaus has caught. He is hurt and valuable.'

I cursed Arion for a babbling old man, delaying so long someone might have been bleeding to death, then followed him to the Atreidae's camp. A young man was lying on the snowy ground at the kin's feet. A sword had sliced his scalp and possibly his skull. I knelt to examine him but Menelaus grabbed my arm.

'Asclepid, you must heal this one, or at least bring him back to his senses so he can talk. He must be important; his tunic was embroidered and his gear is of the finest. We caught him entirely by chance. He had left the city in darkness and ought to have been away, but his horse stumbled in the snow and threw him, and while he was stunned the Achaeans caught him.'

'After a struggle,' I said, observing the red patches on his bare arms and back. 'After they kicked him. If you will release me, my Lord, I will see what I can do, but if you want him alive you had better have him carried to my hut, where I can get him thawed. If you leave him here he will die of cold before anyone can treat him and then he will say nothing at all.'

Menelaus scowled but gave the order. Two Mycenaeans lifted the man and bore him to my hut where they dumped him on the floor.

'Out,' I said to their shins as I turned the body over. 'There is not enough room in here for you and me both.'

'We are sworn not to let him escape,' they said stolidly.

'He is not going anywhere. You have beaten him to a pulp and the Lord Menelaus is going to be very angry if he dies. Now out. You can stand guard outside.'

They hesitated, then went. I shut the door of my wooden shack to exclude the snowy chill and unrolled a sheepskin rug.

My brazier burned hot and the air in the little house gradually warmed. I shed my own cloak and lit the sweet incense which Polidarius had brought. It was used at home to perfume the healer's chambers, to bring peace to the asclepid's mind, and to cover the frightening smells of metal and blood. I had not used it before in the mire of agony in which I had been dipped like a sheep at the shearing. But this prisoner had to recover; must recover.

I laid the prisoner down on the red cloak and washed blood away from the battered face, patching the shallow sword-cut with a comfrey compress and feeling over the back for broken bones. I had known who it was as soon as I had seen the curve of the cheek and the golden hair, though I did not know how I was going to hide this from Menelaus.

He had captured the Princess Cassandra.

Chapter Twenty-five

Cassandra

Knowing that my visions were not false, because my twin shared them, gave me courage. I still could not speak but there were things I could do. The walking dead still horrified me, but I could endure them—just. Hector gave me the first pretext.

He came one day down to the temple of Poseidon and said to Dion, 'Priest, I have a task for you to do. It is dangerous and only you can do it. Will you venture?'

'Ask and I shall obey,' said Dion. 'What does Hector the Prince require of Poseidon's priest?'

'It is late for a journey,' said Hector, 'but Poseidon is your ally, you are his faithful one. Dion, I want you to go to Egypt. Pariki stole the cat-cub from the temple of Basht; I would return her. Before it is too late, both Státhi and his wife must go home.' I stared at my brother. I had never thought that he would part with Státhi. Dion, who knew the deep attachment between the two, faltered, 'Lord, it is a perilous journey but I will undertake it. What should I do?'

'Wait for the wind. I will send you Státhi. The carpenter is making me a cage. Keep them warm, Dion, they cannot bear great cold and they must not get wet. Feed them on goat's flesh and water. Do not release them until you are at the temple of Bubastis in the Nile delta or he might try to swim back to me, my determined friend Státhi. Once he is there, he will accustom himself. Any Egyptian will help you, because you are carrying sacred beasts. Avoid the People of the Sea; they live on the left banks of the river and the current will not carry you there. Go soon, Dion, and do not return; that is all I can say.'

Hector left, stroking the grey creature which was his dearest friend. I was shocked and thinking hard.

Dion hugged me. 'He does not want me to come back to Troy,' he whispered. 'He fears some dreadful stroke of fate. Come with me, Cassandra.'

I shook my head. 'No, Dion, stay in Egypt, you will like it there, or find another home. You have been sweet,' I kissed him hard. 'Very sweet your love has been, Dion, and I cannot bear that you should...' I stopped as the vision rose and thrust it firmly down. I lay down with him, relishing his touch. Then I rose and went to confer with my sisters.

'Dion is going to Egypt,' I announced. 'Will any of you go with him?'

'To Egypt?' said Iris. 'No, why should we want to?'

There was no death mark on her or on Eirene. It was doomed Cycne who caught on and said, 'You want me to go with Dion?' I nodded. 'Because of a vision?' I nodded again. 'But I can't swim and I don't like the sea and I don't like sailors, not your Dion either, even if he is a priest. They are rough and I don't like them.'

I could see the blood fountaining from her breast and I tried to speak. This brought the usual attack; I suffered through it, but Cycne was not convinced. She declined to leave the city of Ilium. 'I'm a Trojan now,' she said mulishly. 'I feel safe behind these walls.'

When the wind changed a day later, Hector brought Státhi, yowling with outrage, and his slim, delicate wife in a large wooden cage. Dion's boat was ready, sail furled, oars out.

'Be careful of them,' he said to Dion as he handed the cage into the priest's steady grasp. Státhi scrabbled at the bars and gave Hector one parting scratch. Then he sat down on his paws, wrapping his tail around himself, and Hector kissed his nose.

'Sail well, little brother,' he whispered. 'Come safe to the temple. There you shall lie all day on the marble steps in the sun, waiting for the priests to bring you fish netted fresh from the Nile.' Hector was weeping. So was Dion.

We heard a shout from the Scaean Gate; the Argives were coming. Dion shoved off, leapt in, and the boat rowed out into the bay.

Hector and I ran for the ladder and climbed amid a hail of misdirected arrows. When we gained the top, the little boat was out to sea and my eyes were so blurred with tears that I did not see it dip over the horizon. I resolved, henceforward, that my heart would be of metal.

I stole a horse and suitable gear and ransacked Priam's treasury for gold, for it was unwise to steal from the temple of any god. Eleni met me under Idume's sardonic gaze. However, the Adonis Priest accepted a cup of strong honeyed wine from me, which was foolish of him. Though it was not poisoned, it was certainly drugged. I did not look at him but waited for the thud as he crumpled. Then I cloaked Eleni in a veil and hood and led him down to the Dardanian Gate. It was a chill morning, presaging snow.

'Ride straight but not too fast,' I instructed. 'My love, my dear.'

'My love, my sister,' said Eleni, and kissed me for the last time. Then I cried to the sentries, 'Open!' and they shoved the gate just wide enough for the rider to go out. He leaned down and kissed me again, then the hoofs kicked up the half-frozen swamp water and he was gone as well.

One by one, my loves were falling from me like leaves from a tree.

◇◇◇

Hector was spending most of his time with Andromache, who was more pregnant every day, uneasy and full of fears. Tithone said that there was nothing wrong with her. I was sitting on the window ledge later in the day that Eleni escaped when a black thump absorbed me and I slumped into a faint.

I woke with the dreadful certainty that something had happened to my twin, but I could not tell what. I could not see through his eyes any more, as we had done as children. He was not dead. I would have known that. I was lifted against Hector's chest and heard him say, 'Cassandra, my sister, I am full of foreboding. This is not the god but your brother. What have you done?'

Leaning into his chest, I told him. He gave me into his wife's arms and began to pace the marble floor, thinking aloud, his voice soft and furious.

'That was a foolish thing and we will rue it greatly. He is not dead you say? Then he is probably captured. Gods, if it was not bad enough having Pariki for a brother, I must have Cassandra and Eleni as well.'

I winced, but I had probably deserved this. I should have told Hector. But if I had, he would have sent my twin forth with the knowledge of Mysion Apollo Priest, who was, Eleni said, making some deal with the Achaeans.

I told Hector this as well and he stopped kicking the furniture. 'Ah. That makes more sense, sister. I thought that you were just acting out of childish secrecy. Apollo Priest has always been proud and a man of deep plots. Now, I see why you acted as you have, though I wish you had told me, Cassandra. It is possible that Eleni is not captured, but merely thrown by the horse.'

'Yes,' I agreed, though my head felt as though someone had hit it.

'If he is a prisoner, what then? They will torture him if he does not cooperate, but we will know that, because you will feel it too, Cassandra. Your twin is fluent and clever; he may be able to hide his identity, and even if discovered he may be able to persuade them that he is valuable. Will they ransom him, I wonder? Or do they want him to prophesy for them?'

'Eleni will give no false prophecies,' I said, clutching my head. 'There is something which the god has promised him which he dearly wants; more than life, perhaps. He will tell them the truth about Troy.'

'The truth cannot harm us,' said Hector. 'Cassandra, my sister, you must trust me. If you compromise the safety of Troy again

I will set you outside the walls to bargain with the Argives.' He sounded serious.

I nodded and regretted it immediately.

'I have a plan of my own,' he added, 'which is happening even now. Each day more people leave the city. Long ago Dardanus prophesised, and so did the priestess of the Mother fifteen years ago, that there would be a new city inland from here, Troas, child of Troy. I have sent people there after dark along the line of the Simöes, where the confluence of the rivers covers even a hoof-beat. The priestesses have gone to establish a temple; some from every god except, as it happens, Apollo. Troas is high in the mountains, on the Pillars of Heracles itself. So far they have not seen any Achaeans. The enemy are avoiding the mountains because they fear them. Hundreds have left, traders and makers. Even if Troy falls we shall not be lost; not our skills or our language or our gods. Now you know Hector's secret, little sister; keep it close. There must not be panic. And now the snow has come, we must wait for thaw before any more can leave. Even Achaeans cannot miss trails in the snow.'

I had a vision of the new city, high above the channel; torches gleamed on stone walls and within there was a noise of children playing a counting game and of a man laughing. I smelt wine; I knew that laugh. Dionysius the Dancer was in Troas and pleased. I smiled against my will, for not only did my head hurt but my ribs ached fiercely.

◇◇◇

We heard no more of Eleni's fate for a long time. I was occupied with Tithone, in treating a plague of sneezing and fever which had broken out among the children. It brought a red rash with weakness after it and some of them went blind. After the first, we learned to keep them in a dark room.

There were fewer people in the city every day. Nyssa, my nurse, had gone, weeping and blessing me, carrying the latest of Priam's children. My favourite smith had taken a cart with all of her tools and her husband and children. The city of Troy did not gush people, but it leaked ceaselessly. Hector's pilgrims trudged out in twenties and tens every night when there was no betraying snow, like a patient slowly bleeding to death.

Troy was still great and populous, however. Troas could not be the city that Ilium was. Two generations had lived and died in Troy.

Towards the middle of winter, for some reason, the Achaean ships sailed out in great numbers, leaving only a few men on the beaches I sighted Odysseus' flag and Agamemnon's. The city said, 'They are gone,' but I did not believe it and neither did Hector.

More people left. With the thinned-out guard we could move wagons by day instead of people by night. Troas would be well supplied; we sent seed-wheat and barley, tools and instruments, and towards the second week of this migration Tithone came to me and said, 'Child, I am going to Troas.'

'Oh, Mistress,' I hugged her. 'I…' I was about to beg her not to leave me, then collected myself and said, 'I will miss you.'

'They need me in the new city,' she said. 'Ten healers will stay. Athropiads, as well as those concerned with birth and growth. Fare well, Cassandra. May the fates be kind to you. You have learned well, my daughter, I am proud of you. You are the Healer of Troy now.'

I watched the overladen carts groan out of the Dardanian Gate, pulled by four horses, carrying children and treasure and bundles of medicinal herbs. A child of the Pallathi went to protect Troas, a painted statue rocking her rope cradle.

The Achaeans must have seen us go. They must have noticed a stream of people marching across the plain between the two rivers, leaving Troy, but they did nothing. Indeed we heard no sound from the beaches until a man in a red tunic came to the Dardanian Gate, after all who were leaving had safely gone, and called for Cassandra. I came down to the gate and slipped out, covered by archers, my brother Polites with me as Hector had ordered.

'Princess,' said Chryse the Healer. 'I have bad news for you.'

Chapter Twenty-six

Diomenes

He was a man, I discovered as I washed down the body; a young man so like my Lady Cassandra that he must have been her twin. His scalp was cut but his skull was sound; his many bruises had been inflicted with feet and fists but they had broken no bones. He opened his eyes and registered where he was, then remembered how he had come there.

He moaned, in frustration and grief but not fear, and struggled against my embrace. I said soothingly, 'Hush, I am a friend, I am Chryse the Healer. Lie still now; you are not badly hurt but you are captive. Tell me, how many fingers do you see?'

'Five,' he said. 'How many do you have?' His voice was like hers, too, decisive and sweet.

'Good. They have left your head intact. Don't move or you will bleed again.'

His hand wavered up to touch the bandage, then fell open on my shoulder.

'Chryse?' he whispered. 'Chryse, yes, "Golden" in Achaean, I've heard the name. My sister talked to you—the healer, they said, the Achaean healer priest.'

'I am Chryse the asclepid, but I am only half-Achaean. The other half is Carian and I am wholly your friend.'

'Why?'

'Your sister saved my life,' I said absently, wondering why I was so instantly moved to take the part of this foolish youth who was now a hostage of Agamemnon.

'Kill me,' he begged, grabbing my wrist. 'Once Agamemnon learns who I am, he will hold me hostage for the city.'

'Would the city surrender for the life of one prince?' I was dabbing vervain ointment on the bruises. He thought about it, moving as I requested.

'No, you are right. Well, get it over with,' he said, sitting up and trying to draw the rents in his tunic together. 'Tell the kings.'

'I will tell the kings nothing until you are healed,' I said quietly. 'All you need to do is be witless and unremembering until your scalp wound knits. Now, drink this.'

I wrapped his fingers around a wooden cup filled with an infusion of honey, vervain, and poppy. He did not drink but looked at me narrowly. I had seen just such an expression on his sister's face. Then the eyes grew abstracted as though he was listening. The dark brows drew in, the full lip was caught by the upper teeth.

'I would not poison you,' I said.

He smiled at me. He was beautiful when he smiled. 'It would not matter if it was poisoned. I am trying to find her, to find Cassandra. We share the same sort of mind,' he explained. 'She would have felt the blow that struck me down. But we were parted for a long time and grew away from each other. I only found her again when she stuck her hand into an adder's mouth and almost scared me to death. Oh, my sister, my honey, my heart,' he whispered under his breath, then seemed to give up. 'I cannot find her. Poor Cassandra. Hector will be angry with her! She smuggled me out of Troy without asking his leave.'

I had heard of the bond between twins. Apollo was clearly still with this one, even though his sister said that she was cursed. I wondered very much how that had come about.

My patient drank the infusion and lay down to sleep. I covered him, dropping a fold of cloak artlessly across his face, then went to the door and said to the guards, 'He sleeps and is wandering in his wits. What came to you to hit him so hard?

You are lucky that he is still alive, but so he is, barely. He must have rest to repair his addled brain.'

'He struggled and the Lord of Men told us to secure any person leaving the city,' mumbled one sullenly. 'He should not have fought us so fiercely. Ten against one, how could he hope to win? What will you tell Agamemnon?'

'What I have said; that he fell hard from the horse and needs time to recover; he could not even tell me his name. One of you go and tell him that it may be several days before the Lord of Men can question this prisoner. And bring me Arion the Bard; I want to soothe the suppliant with music.' The guard grasped instantly that my message was meant to exonerate him from mishandling the valuable captive and he was off before I could change my mind.

I went back inside. It was freezing.

Princess Cassandra's twin was sleeping. I listened to his breathing, which was slightly ragged, and ransacked my memory for pectoral herbs, though the wheezing was probably produced by damage to his ribs.

Arion came in through the door like a snowstorm. He apologised, stepped back, and shook his cloak outside, then tiptoed past the sleeper and sat down on a bench next to the brazier, warming his hands. Menon, his shadow, sat down on the floor.

'What have we here?' asked the old man. 'I've seen that face before. Beautiful as Aphrodite. It is…' I waved at him and he lowered his voice, 'Eleni, Prince of Troy, true son of Priam and Hecube the Queen. Twin of the lady Cassandra.'

I pointed at Menon and the old man rumbled, 'He is my apprentice and my trusted follower, asclepid, he keeps secrets as well as I, and I can keep them well, as you know. Is the boy badly hurt?'

'No, but his wits are shaken by a blow on the head. I want you to sing to him. Or perhaps Menon can play the lyre, while we talk.' I wanted some suitable noise to cover the silence and occupy the sentry's ears. Menon caught on, took the lyre, and leaned against the door, tuning it, before he began to play a loud, twanging, discordant dance.

'The music of Caria,' observed Arion. 'It should make you feel at home.'

'I am only half-Carian, so half of me thinks it barbaric. This is a prophet, Arion, a priest in favour with Apollo. The god may want to save the Argive army. All will die if it stays here.'

'What can a prophet do?' asked Arion, rubbing his hands.

'Why, prophesy,' I said. 'If these beaches are swept clean by the winter waves then they will not all die come spring. But if they are not, then the corpses will mount so high that there will not be enough Argives left alive to bury them.'

'Apollo?' asked Arion.

'Or someone. Polidarius foresaw it. It will be like a village I once saw in the Argolid. Almost everyone died there. I would not see that again.'

'I can prophesy if you wish,' said Eleni sleepily. 'But it will be a true sending. My sister offended the god when she brought Poseidon back into the city of Ilium. I would not risk that. She suffers still under the displeasure of Apollo; she knows, but cannot speak. Visions of death haunt her all the time. She is in constant pain, but she cannot tell. He tongue cleaves to the roof of her mouth and she falls and convulses.'

This sounded less like the anger of a god than the falling sickness to me, but I did not want to interrupt him.

'So, what says Apollo?' asked Arion as Menon began to howl some uncouth chorus about sheep-stealing. Eleni closed his clear grey eyes, so unlike Achilles' and said, 'There are three things which must be done to bring about the fall of Troy; to steal the Pallathi of the Maiden from the temple of the Mother; to bring an archer who is abandoned somewhere on an island; to sacrifice to Apollo in the temple in Tauris called the Temple of Doomed Things and Fates.'

'The third is simple; to Tauris the whole host must go. Does an archer marooned on an island mean anything to you, Arion?' I asked.

'Philoctetes, poor beast. He was stung in the heel by a snake and gangrene set in. He stank so much that the men of his ship could not endure his company and they left him on a little island off Lesbos. He is, or was—surely he cannot still be alive—a great bowman, one of the few that can draw the Scythian bow.'

'The Lord Apollo says that he is still alive,' said the priest. 'therefore he is alive. That is all I can see, apart from my own city in flames.'

'And that, later in the winter, is what you will say to Agamemnon,' I said. 'For now you must lie warm, remember that you are witless, and recover.'

'Beware Calchas,' whispered Arion. 'High Priest, he calls himself, an arrogant and dangerous man. He has someone in the city who sends him a message to come to the Scaean Gate; I do not know who it is.'

'Mysion, the priest of Apollo,' said the prisoner wearily. 'He may even have betrayed me to the Argives. He is a proud man and Hector gave him no voice at the king's council. He hates my sister especially, because she brought a new god into the city which threatens his power. Hopeless. Soon he will have no power.'

'Boy, have you no wish to save your city?' hissed Arion.

'I would save it if I could, but I cannot. Troy will fall.' His eyes closed, long lashes lying on an unlined cheek. 'The gods have spoken.'

◇◇◇

The fever came. They called it the arrows of Apollo. It spread quickly among the groups which sheltered together in the tents and who lay close embraced against the cold around the fires.

The plague of Apollo kills seven out of every ten who catch it. There is a high fever, delirium, madness, and collapse. The nights were made hideous by soldiers who rose up to fight and slay their visions, who had to be restrained. Sweating did not help them, nor any herb. They killed themselves or were killed by their friends.

One morning I saw the spotted rash on the chest of the prince of Troy.

He had been playing at being witless; now he was witless indeed. In the cold, I lay close by him to keep his covers on, for a fever patient chills into coma and death very quickly. When

I could not stay, I deputed Menon, who had suffered an attack of this fever before and would not catch it again. Like lightning, Apollo's most lethal arrow never strikes the same person twice.

The Atreidae were so concerned for their army that they paid no attention to the prisoner. Arion was immune; he stayed with me, playing the lyre, sleeping on the bench in the corner. He said he was too old to go forth into the cold, so I left him slumbering like an old badger while I brewed potions to bring down fevers and tended the one patient I had to save.

Of all of them, I desperately wanted to save Eleni.

One night, fourteen days after the onset, I had to hold him down, so fierce were his struggles. He cried on the god, moaning, 'Burning, burning—the city is burning. Oh Ilium. Oh my sister, my sister...' until I hushed him into my arms and I fell asleep with his head on my breast.

I did not think he would live to see Eos trail her garment over the horizon. I wondered how I would tell the woman who waited in the shut fast city that her brother was dead.

I woke wet with sweat. The face in the small light was as smooth as a child's. I thought he might have gone, so I moved, and he embraced me tighter, his mouth seeking mine. 'Oh Cassandra,' he murmured. 'Cassandra my sister, my love,' and I returned his kiss, feeling warmth flow into my veins, and long-abandoned feelings made my skin glow.

I heard myself gasp and I shuddered. My seed had spilled in his fingers. It had been so long since anyone had touched me in love. I remembered Eumides the Trojan and his body and his love; but I could not allow my own lust to exhaust this prince of Ilium when he seemed to have recovered. His god had saved him; I would not kill him in my embrace. 'Sleep,' I said, freeing my mouth and stroking his hair. 'Sleep, my...my dear, my brother.'

Arion had heard all of this; he lay down on the other side of the prince of Ilium and took my hand.

'Chryse, you are healing yourself,' was all he said, then we fell asleep again. The next morning I went and called to the daughter of Priam and told her that her brother was a captive.

She was so beautiful. Her hair and the shape of her face, the delicate bones and the full mouth, were identical to her brother's. But her eyes—her eyes were deep, wise with knowledge too great for a mortal to endure. She had the lines between her brows and the set of jaw seen in patients in constant, chronic pain. Taking my hand under the threat of the archers, she said, 'Is he well?'

'Lady, he has been ill, but he is recovering.'

'What was it?'

'The spotted fever.'

'No,' she said, her strong fingers clenching hard. 'They do not recover from the spotted fever. Yet he is not dead; I would know that. I know many things I would rather not know. The god has no reason to spare me.'

'Fourteen days he lay delirious, Lady, and then he fell into a sleep and the fever broke. You must have seen this, Healer of Troy.'

'Yes, but rarely,' she said. The wise eyes searched me; she needed to see into my soul. I knew that I could hide nothing from this golden-haired lady and I straightened under her gaze. She held me with her eyes, then nodded and sighed with relief. Her face softened. She and her brother had the same enchanting smile.

'Yes, you are telling the truth. I thank you for your care of my twin, Priest of Asclepius,' and she leaned forward and kissed me on the cheek, as is the custom with Trojan maidens. Her breath was warm. For a moment I felt the soft curve of her breast against my arm and I trembled.

Then she was gone. I pondered my fate, bitterly. What point was there in falling in love with the princess of Troy, Cassandra the cursed, who looked like a goddess and who was the Achaean's chief prize and spoil when the city fell? No share of loot would come to me; she would be allotted to one of the kings.

Yet I loved her. And she could never love me. I was an enemy. I went back to care for Eleni and tried not to think of her.

Agamemnon sent for him two days later. In the diminished circle of fever-struck, dull and bright-eyed Achaeans, he declaimed his prophecy. Surprisingly, Calchas the High Priest agreed.

'There is need of persuasion in the matter of Philoctetes, who may feel that he has been abandoned,' said Menelaus. 'Therefore you must go there, Odysseus; you of the nimble wits and the golden tongue. If the priests of Apollo have spoken a true sending of the god's, and not some utterance of policy—' he glared at Calchas, then at Eleni, 'then I will sacrifice in Tauris and my army with me; my brother will do the same. But who can get into the city of Troy and steal the Pallathi?'

'That I can do,' said Odysseus quickly, before the gaze could rest on Eleni. 'Leave theft to me; was not my grandfather Autolycus, who named me Odysseus, "surrounded by hatred?" You shall have the Pallathi before you sail.'

He went that night with Diomedes, presumably for his muscle as he was not the brightest of warriors. I do not know how they had got into the city until I saw them return, or rather smelt them. Their path must have led through the sewers.

'Stand upwind, asclepid, and fetch me boiling water,' said Odysseus, filthy beyond recognition.

I poured hot lychnis solution and sea water over his head— fresh water had gone up to nine obols a bucket—and sluiced off the scum. It took eight buckets before he was clean, and eleven for Diomedes, who was bigger. Then we washed a small image, a maiden with an apple in her hand.

'That is the Pallathi,' Odysseus grinned, pulling on a clean tunic and a cloak. 'It was in a temple crammed with copies, large and small, metal and wood, carved and painted and draped.'

'It was the smallest and the plainest. Is this the image, Apollo Priest?'

'It is,' Eleni whispered and bowed to the Maiden.

'Then we said tomorrow,' affirmed Odysseus. Diomedes, once disinfected, had already gone to the kings. He and the elegant thief did not seem to be friends anymore. I wondered what Odysseus had done to him.

The ships set out; the army to Tauris, Odysseus; three ships to the island of the marooned archer. I gave him clean salt, several infusions, and soothing ointment for Philoctetes. It is possible to live for a long time with gangrene, if the diet is spare and the living conditions not too harsh. But, of course, if the flesh is dead no treatment can re-animate it.

Arion, Menon, and Eleni were taken with Agamemnon's host. I fear that the Atreidae did not entirely trust me.

Once they had left, I moved all the remaining men off the beaches and onto the lowest slopes of Mount Idus. I did not want to risk the mysterious sickness which had killed that first woodcutter, but I had to get them off those infected sands. Then I ordered the building of huts, the digging of drains, the collection of clean water, and the systematic burning of the dead. The bodies in the burial pit had fallen mostly to bones; they had been keeping the local vultures fed all winter, but no more would be laid there. I used the authority of the god freely and soon the number of deaths diminished.

Because more of them now lived than died, the soldiers began to trust me.

'The commander ought to have ordered a watch on the city,' commented one, flexing a hand which I had nursed back into use. 'They could come forth and massacre us; there are only about four hundred of us until the kings return and that won't be for at least a month with the winds as they are.'

'Why should the Trojans do that?' I asked. 'Can you feel this finger, now?'

'Ouch, yes. Why shouldn't they, healer? The men of Ilium have reason to hate us. Our tents are full of gold and captives. Achilles raids up and down this coast and his camp is full of weeping maidens. That reminds me, Asclepid. The Lord Achilles has sent you a gift. It's outside. I'll get it.'

I had treated the myrmidons for injuries sustained in practice or inflicted by some maddened goatherd trying to defend his flock and their captain Achilles had occasionally sent me presents of looted wine or dried fruit.

I had gone when he wanted to talk to me, which was rarely. He spent most of his time staring out to sea. Once he had revealed his philosophy. 'Beware how you give your heart to

a man, Chryse,' he had mused, 'lest you change love for hate.'
He had been holding Patroclus' hand as he spoke and the other
man gave no sign that he had heard.

What gift would the Lord of the Myrmidons have sent to a
healer? More figs? More wine? It was to be a different present,
however. The soldier pushed a girl into my house, a bundle of
ripped tunic, torn hair and damaged flesh, said 'Enjoy yourself,'
and went out, closing the door.

Chapter Twenty-seven

Cassandra

Andromache bore a male child, efficiently and for the most part in silence. She had always been healthy, and though despondent during pregnancy, she had decided to give birth as bravely as she could.

I laid the child on her belly, cut the cord, and bestowed the blessing of the Mother. Then I said to the boy-priest waiting outside, 'Go tell Hector that he has a son and a living wife; tell the goddess that there is another man in Troy,' and the footsteps sped away.

Andromache stroked the baby as it grasped with its little hands for the nipple, found it, and bit. She was too tired to flinch.

It was nursing strongly when Hector arrived. He took Andromache's hand and they looked at each other with eyes so full of love and pride that I excused myself and went up onto the wall.

For I was alone. Eleni was with Agamemnon, seasick; Dion was gone to Egypt; even Nyssa and Tithone had deserted me.

Then again, Hector had also sent Státhi away and missed him. Half a dozen times a day he looked for his shadow or put up a hand to stroke a furry body which no longer balanced on his shoulder. Loss came to everyone. It could only be endured.

I went to the Temple of the Mother to burn flowers for the new baby; it was too cold for fresh petals, so I lit the papery dried ones and prayed for the child. The priestess of the Mother was hovering, wanting to tell me something but not wanting to intrude. This annoyed me.

'Well, Lady?' I asked coldly.

'Princess, come into the sanctuary.'

When I followed her it all looked as it usually did—torchlit and echoing, lined and relined with representations of the Pallathi.

'Can you see anything different?'

'No…rather, yes, one of the Pallathi is missing. A little one, she stood over there. Old, made of wood.'

'Yes,' whispered the woman. 'Very old.'

An awful suspicion was dawning on me. 'You mean…the oldest?' She nodded. 'The first?' She nodded again. 'Lord Dionysius protect us, you mean the Pallathi herself?' She stared at me, tears filling her eyes. I knew the prophecy—everyone in the city of Ilium knew it. The city will not fall if the Pallathi is in her place. Now she was gone and I could not account for it. 'But it can't be anyone from outside who stole it,' I protested. 'It must be someone in Troy. How could an Achaean get inside? Ridiculous.'

'If it is not an Argive, how did they dare? Have we a traitor?' she quavered.

I thought it very likely. Any population must have a few traitors. But a traitor who knew which was the real Pallathi, and who had a way of getting her out of the city—well, that was another matter. The cat-foot Priest of Apollo, Mysion of the arrogant countenance and the political purposes, leapt to the head of my list.

I told the priestess to keep the vanishing of the Lady secret and went to talk to Maeles at the Temple of Poseidon. He might have heard news of Dion and besides, I intended to search every temple in Troy before I declared the Pallathi lost. I might as well begin with the little ones.

Maeles was distantly pleased to see me—he was taking his elevation to sole priest of Poseidon to heart—and told me that

Dion was safe and in Egypt. I did not believe this until he told me that the female cat was pregnant, which was something that only Hector and I knew. So Dion was safe. I was heartened.

As I was leaving, a sailor touched my shoulder.

'Lady, would you spare me some words? I am Eumides who was a slave in Achaea and I also know the asclepid, the healer you talked to over the wall.'

'Chryse? Yes, come with me—come into the tavern and talk to me.' I was glad to have something else to think about. 'Let me buy you some wine, Eumides. Don't I know you?'

He was swarthy, with a tangle of dark curls, brown eyes, and white teeth. His hand slid down my shoulder for a fleeting touch and I remembered. He had fallen asleep in my arms at the Dionysiad; he had been my last lover on the third night of wine and blood. I recalled his love, it was passionate and skilled. I remembered with hallucinatory clarity his mouth on my breast. He smiled a wicked smile and I felt myself shiver pleasantly.

However, it was not proper to speak of what had happened in the rites of that god. The hand cupped my breast for a moment, then was removed. I drew a breath.

'Where did you meet the asclepid?'

'In Mycenae, Lady.'

His voice was rich and deep, a honeyed voice. I bought a flask of the old mead at an outrageous price and he tasted it respectfully. He was good looking, this sailor, though a little battered around the face. His hands were blistered with rowing and his eyes had the alertness seen in sailors, hunters and Amazons.

'He bought me; I promised him stories and he freed me. He was grave, lady, a solemn boy, responsible and learned beyond his years, with a sweet kiss and skilled hands to heal and love. I lay with him on the mountain and we were lovers all the way to Corinth, where I took ship for Troy again. He was a child then. He speaks Trojan well. He was a good singer—we used to sing together. But something has happened to him, some great loss. The spark of joy in him, which was never great, is quenched. Lady—did you see—did you see anything of his mind?'

'A little. What do you want to know?'

'I want to know if he still loves me.'

'I saw no vision, Eumides.'

I took the oarsman's hand in both of mine. His fingers were still sensitive despite the hard work; he stroked the inside of my wrist gently as I spoke.

'You know I am cursed; if I saw, I could not tell you what I saw, but I saw nothing. For his mind, he had been bereaved of someone he greatly loved. I do not know who or any more about it.'

'Poor Chryse. You know, he stood up to the Atreidae when we were in that city. He plunged down into a plague pit, when all the house of Pluton would not have dragged me there, and tended the stricken. He is the bravest person I know. What could have happened to my own golden one, my Chryse?'

'Death has happened to him,' I said, taking a sip of the mead.

'But he is Thanatos-touched,' protested Eumides.

This puzzled me and I made him explain.

'He is the Little Brother of the Dark Angel and he is truly not afraid of death. I held his knife to his throat and he smiled at me. I was half-mad with fear that the barbarians were going to sacrifice me but he simply told me to strike if I did not believe him. He is beautiful and sad—so sad, now, Princess. It must be something more than the lost love who carried his heart away when I knew him.'

I was warming to Chryse, I was interested in him. The fleeting touch of his self, his concern, as he tended Eleni had been cool and emollient, very grateful to my scarified emotions. Not passionate, the asclepid, but close and loving and scarred, badly scarred by an irreparable loss. I felt pity, when I had not known I could still feel pity. I noticed that I was thinking about someone other than myself for the first time since the god had cursed me. This may also have had something to do with the magnetically attractive sailor who was stroking my hand and the memory of his embrace.

I sat with him until the night watch, learning about the Asclepid Priest Chryse Diomenes, little brother of Death.

'Lady, you should make a plan,' Eumides said, laying his hard hand on my arm. 'A plan to escape this city.'

'No, I will be here until the end, whatever the end may be, and after that I will not need to escape, because I will be dead.'

'But if you are not dead,' he said softly, 'if you do not die, Lady, you will be a slave. I have been a slave; you must not endure such pain. If Chryse was here, he would say the same. He freed me because he knew I would die in the kitchens of Mycenae. Even to die as a slave is different from dying as a free man.'

'I do not think I will survive, but if I do? What is your plan?'

'You will be spoil for one king or another, Lady. I will know. I can mingle with the Achaean boats and they will not mark me; I have done so already.'

'And then?'

'Slip overboard, Lady, and I will find you.' Eumides was in earnest. It would do no harm to indulge his fantasy. I took his hand and he kissed me.

'If this happens, Eumides, that I am a slave, then I will do as you say and you can net me like a fish.'

◇◇◇

Chryse remained in my thoughts; the golden one, the healer, the only Achaean who made no profession out of slaughter. The refuge-seekers came in day after day, in broken boats and through the marshes, and we sent them on to Troas when they could bear the journey. They all told the same tale, death and ruin out of the sea from the hands of Achilles, grey-eyed. Each one told their tale to Hector while he listened silently.

The turning point, the overburden, came when I was called to the Dardanian Gate. Chryse waited there and he handed over a girl wrapped in his own cloak.

'I brought her to you, Lady,' he said, distressed. 'She cannot bear a man's touch and I can understand that.'

'She is one of many,' I rejoined and he flinched. Instantly I was sorry for hurting him. It was not his fault.

'Achilles gave her to me as a present.' he said through his teeth. 'I do not know whether she will live.'

'Chryse,' someone called from the wall and he said, 'Eumides,' in such a tender, glad voice that I was jealous. 'Oh, Eumides, my friend, you're here?'

'Where else should I be, asclepid? I am a Trojan,' laughed the sailor. 'Have you forgotten me, Chryse?'

'Never. I was thinking of you only last night, wondering if you were here.'

'We'll meet again,' he said. 'Little Brother of Thanatos, we will meet again.'

I took the girl and had her carried inside. Polites bowed to Chryse and so did I.

'The king will be back soon,' he said slowly. 'They will have done the three things needed to bring about the fall of Troy, for the Pallathi is with Agamemnon.'

'It is, indeed.' I mentally withdrew my accusation against all the other priests and decided that Mysion had stolen it. But Chryse had a different tale to tell.

'Odysseus got in through your drains,' he said. 'Take care that no one else does, Lady.'

It was not possible to keep the loss a secret any longer. The Pallathi was gone and Hector's pilgrims increased in number and daring, crossing the plain in broad daylight.

◇◇◇

I took the girl to Tithone's house, where I was living. Most of the maidens of Troy now lived with Perseis, along with some of the wives, since the watchers lived in the palace. Food was getting short, though we still had plenty of grain. I wondered when we would be able to sow a new crop.

The girl was shocked into rigidity; Polyxena and I had to pry her jaw open to spill the hysteria infusion in wine carefully down her throat. She clung so close to the rags of her chiton that we let her keep it, covering her with a new gown and washing underneath it. When I found the red thread bound round her waist I realised that someone had plundered the Temple of the Holy Maiden, the strictly virginal priestesses who love only women and are never in the society of men.

This poor one had been in the society of beasts and was maiden no longer.

She had bled and the torn veil had been rubbed by so many assaults that it was one large sore, weeping plasma. We applied styptics and soothing ointments, then treated the bruises of rape. In all that time she had not spoken or uttered one sound.

Nor did she, until the middle of the night, when the potion wore off enough for her to scream. She screamed for hours and we could not stop her. Occasionally there were names; once she said clearly, 'Achilles!' but mostly a wordless, tormented wail ripped at her throat and horrified all who heard it.

Hector came down to the healer's house, sent by Andromache. He was armed and carrying his sword unsheathed.

'What is happening here?' he demanded. Polyxena looked up as we were attempting to drip poppy syrup past the drawn-back lips.

'This is Achilles' work,' she said, my strange, doomed Polyxena. 'That name again, the one I cannot forget.'

'What has happened to her?' asked Hector as the voice failed at last and the cry died to a whimper.

'Rape, multiple rape,' I said. 'She was a virgin priestess and she was raped by half the Achaean army. Go away, Hector, there is nothing you can do here.'

He reached out to touch the injured woman's cheek and she winced away from his hand. She died about an hour later. Hector stood quite still and said, 'This cannot be borne,' and then he went away.

◇◇◇

When the Achaeans came again to the beaches with the spring, Hector stood at the king's council and announced, 'They must be attacked and the greater part of this army must be killed. I have a plan which will do this. It is risky but it may work. If it does not there are still the walls.'

He crouched to draw on the marble floor with a piece of charcoal.

'Here is the Achaean camp; they have built a wooden wall around their ships. Here are we; here is the Scamander and the bay. Now; if we send half the army here,' he drew a circle around the plain in front of the Scamander Gate, 'and the rest of us attack the ships here,' he drew a line towards the sea, 'then we may take the ships and burn them. If we can do that, they will be stranded and they will all die. Achilles is still refusing to take part in the battle, but Achilles, more than any of them, must die.'

'Prince Hector, what of the prophecy?' sneered Pariki. 'You will not outlive him more than three days.'

'So be it,' said Hector calmly. 'Do you understand?' The captains nodded.

Penthesileia added, 'If you put your cavalry and the chariots on the edges, they will have room to move, and us further out, as scouts and skirmishers.'

'Very well,' Hector said. 'The Argives must raid the coast no longer; they are a plague, like locusts or flies, and they must die. We attack tomorrow. And Achilles, if he enters the battle, is mine.'

There were no dissenting voices. I made three copies of the map for the captains and then I spent an instructive watch explaining very carefully in Scythian that the guards must stay on the Scamander Gate and protect the walls and that they could hunt for heads later.

◇◇◇

Feet raced, hoofs were cleaned, gear was oiled, bronze was polished. I spent a day among the armourers, watching the balancing of chariot wheels, talking to the arrow-makers, and consoling the guards who were to be left behind on the walls.

When the army went forth, I was with them. Hector had no Státhi now to sit on his shoulder, but he still had a sister to protect his back. We waited on the plain for the Argives to arm and stream forth in battle order. As soon as they had all left their camp and begun to run towards us, Hector's wing began to move slowly, sideways.

It was as before; the screaming and the dust, the clash of bronze weapons; I shot steadily as the enemy hunted my brother and the horse laboured under our weight. Hector had reached the edge of the plain when a huge man challenged him and he slid off our horse, leaving me to control the nervous beast.

Hector gripped his spear in the middle and used it to stab. It was a heavy spear but well balanced. It went into the armour at the belly and out the other side. Hector had to trip the body and put a foot on it to retrieve his spear. I do not know who he killed, but he stripped off the armour and flung it aside, as is our custom.

Then we were off again, fighting hard now that we came on the bulk of the Argives. I was deafened by the noise, my eyes running in the smoke of watchfires which we were trampling. We swept aside the defence and threw torches into the ships; several burst into flame. But the wall was defended and moreover it was wet and would not take flame.

Then the ant-warriors came.

They wear brown armour and their helmet is round, so that with only a thin gorget at the neck and the wide, flat curves of the shoulder-pieces, they look like insects. Myrmidons, they are and they move like ants, heedless of loss. Hector said, 'Achilles,' and spurred straight for the leader.

That was a fierce fight. I fell off and watched it from a nearby rock, where I picked off Achaeans until all my arrows were gone. Hector charged straight for Achilles in his decorated armour, calling on him to stand, and the champion stopped his chariot and leapt down.

Then they began to strike each other tirelessly. The first blow was aimed at Hector's throat, but he parried and slashed at the head. Achilles blocked the blow with a screech of blades and then made a long stab for Hector's groin, which he evaded.

Neither could tire out the other; they were equals as swordsmen. The Myrmidons waited, as did the Trojans for the outcome of this single combat.

Hector and Achilles cut, slashed, and parried. At last, with a lucky stroke, Hector backed and turned and with tremendous strength, cut through the gorget, and into his opponent's throat.

He cried aloud in triumph, 'We are saved!' and undid the chinstrap.

Then he stared. Uncovered was a curling dark head. He had killed Patroclus.

The Myrmidons advanced with a scream of rage but we fought back. The wooden walls would not take fire, and arrows came from behind them, including stone-tipped arrows from a Scythian bow. We fell back towards Troy; Hector's expedition had failed.

Night caught us outside the city, with foes behind and all around us. The skirmishing Amazons kept the enemy back, and Simöes gave us water. I tended such of the wounded as I could find. We lit no fires. All around us, I heard men breathing in the dark.

Then a great ululation went up from the beaches, a wail of terrible grief.

'Achilles has lost his only love,' said Hector.

◇◇◇

Morning saw us fighting our way back to the city. Arrows showered around us, men quivered and died under the deadly hail. We heard a great commotion and something clove through the press like a wild fire.

'Achilles,' whispered Hector. 'Find another mount, sister. I must face him alone.' I slipped off the horse and caught a straying one by the bridle.

Then I saw something so singular that, instead of turning my mount and fleeing, I stayed stock still.

A man in gold-inlaid armour, more beautiful than anything I had ever seen, was kneeling, clutching the body of Penthesileia in his arms. The Amazon queen was quite dead, struck through the heart, bleeding her life away into the dust. But he was crying. Achilles the Hero, Sift Runner, Grey-Eyed, Son of Zeus, not long to live, was weeping into the Amazon's pierced breast. I stood close enough to hear what he was murmuring to her as he took off her helmet and stroked her hair.

'Oh my brave one,' he said, tears pouring down his cheeks. 'Oh my brave love.'

He rocked her as though she had been a child—Achilles Stone Heart, Man Slayer.

Then an ugly, bow-legged man laughed jeeringly and Achilles laid the Amazon's body down, rose to his feet, and punched the man so hard that he must have been dead before he hit the ground. Someone in the Argive ranks yelled, 'That was Thersites' last joke!'

Before I joined jesting Thersites in death, I raced my mount for Troy and rode in through the Scamander Gate. I mounted the steps to the tower to see what Hector was doing, panting with fear.

There was a confused mess of struggling men all over the field; it was hard to see what was going on, but all of it was frightful. Several chariots were still duelling; smoke arose from the ships, but not nearly enough; and Achilles' path could be traced through the plain by the hacked corpses who fell in his wake.

'I think we're dead men,' said the Scythian next to me, and I agreed with him.

But we were not, at least, not that day. Most of the army got back in through the gates and they were shut; the Argives returned to their camp and only Achilles remained, alone, as soaked in blood as though he had been wading in it.

'Hector!' he yelled. 'Hector, come out and fight!'

'Tomorrow,' Hector said gravely. 'Tomorrow I will come.'

'Single combat,' called the grey-eyed one and Hector replied, 'Single combat.'

'Hector, no!' I cried. 'Oh, Hector,' I said, seeing that he knew everything I was going to say, agreed with my conclusions and was nevertheless going to do it. 'Oh, Hector, everyone else has left me. Don't you leave me too.'

'I must,' he said, and went to talk to Andromache.

I do not know what was said in that conference but I heard no tears or screams. Hector came forth in the morning and Andromache kissed him and smiled; such a smile as is seen on the face of a poisoned corpse.

Achilles was armoured all in bronze with gold inlay; I could not see his face for he wore a decorated helmet with the mask of a snarling face.

'Come on,' he said. 'Meet your destiny.'

'It lies on the knees of the gods,' said Hector. 'No man can evade his fate. If it is your fate to kill me, then I will die. If yours, then I will kill you.'

He cast his spear; Achilles dodged and it passed him. There was that eye-twisting aura around the fighters which meant that the gods were with us. Brightness fell from the air. There was that goddess again, the glittering lady. She was with Achilles Man Slayer and not with Hector, who stood alone. Achilles did not throw his spear but stabbed with it. Hector ducked and cut at Achilles with his sword.

We were lining the walls; Polites was next to me and next to him Andromache, white as linen and chewing her knuckle. Hector slashed, Achilles danced aside, thrust and parried. The Achaeans cheered.

Hector drove him back three paces with a furious attack. Achilles replied with an equally ferocious advance and regained his ground. Always that goddess was with Achilles, shielding him with her body so that Hector's strokes went astray. Once the sword hit the very centre of Achilles' shield, but it rebounded. I called on Hecate, but there was no rustle of leathery wings. The gods were no longer listening to Cassandra God-Cursed.

The battle went on for almost a watch. I was faint with fear but dared not look away. As the drums were sounding for the change of guard, the gleaming goddess made a fist and threw something to one side. Hector took his eyes off Achilles for an eye blink and Achilles' spear took him in the neck, in the joint of the armour.

I had seen enough of those wounds to know it was a fatal blow. Andromache slid down the wall. I had seen all this before in my vision. I did not speak.

Hector stood for a moment, a puzzled expression on his face, then fell with a clang of armour.

'You killed him,' howled Achilles. 'You killed the only thing I loved. You murdered Patroclus. Why does your death not satisfy me? Why is your blood not enough?' He yelled an order and someone brought forward his chariot. Polites breathed, 'He can't…' as the hero slit Hector's heels like a rabbit's, threaded a rope through, and tied it to the axle.

Then he leapt in and flourished a whip over the horses. The body of my beloved Hector, my dearest brother, bounced behind the chariot in the dust.

I was about to scream aloud when Hector said in my ear, 'Ah. So that's what it's like, being dead.'

'Yes,' I breathed. 'Oh, Hector, how can you leave me?'

'He will die too,' he said with satisfaction. He looked just as I had seen him, but clean and unmarked and in his favourite pale yellow tunic. 'Three days, Cassandra, and he will be dead and the city might be saved. But even if it is not, the pirate and man slayer, the rapist will be dead.'

'Yes, but so are you,' I felt my voice waver. 'Hector, I will only be able to see you until your body is burned and then you will be gone and I'll never see you again and I can't bear it, I can't bear it!'

'Don't cry,' he tried to touch me but his hand went through my shoulder. 'Cassandra, at least you can see me. Don't let them do anything rash about my body. If it pleases that madman to mistreat a husk of Hector, let him. There is no need for you to watch, however. Get them to take Andromache to her chamber. If she can't feel my presence then I fear that this will break her heart.'

'Hearts do not break,' I said bitterly. 'They are only bent and mutilated.'

'Cassandra, we'll meet again. I'll come when you die; I'll be waiting for you.'

The city murmured about my hard heart while I escorted the bearers of Andromache to her rooms. I did not weep.

I could not weep when Hector was walking beside me. It seemed absurd.

Andromache slept at last. She could not see Hector but she believed me when I told her that he was there and relayed what he asked me to say.

Achilles had dragged the body of my brother into his own camp. There was a great wailing and a bonfire showed them to be weeping for the dead. I wept for my own dead, for my brother, and for my lost comrades as I bandaged wounds and set bones, with Polyxena crying beside me for lost Hector.

◇◇◇

Someone left the city the next night; I only knew because Polyxena woke me, tripping over my feet in the dark.

'We have brought Hector home,' she said.

'Who has?'

'My father and I went to bargain with Achilles.'

'What did it cost?'

'A cartload of gold and my maidenhood,' and she fell asleep with her head on my pillow.

Chapter Twenty-eight

Diomenes

I had taken the maiden, whom I judged wounded to death, and given her into the care of the Lady Cassandra. That dusk, still shaken, I was walking past the boats when someone fluted a bird call to me. I knew that whistle.

'Chryse!'

I came to a small boat upturned on the beach and sitting under it was Eumides the ex-slave. I embraced him. He smelt of tar.

'Just repairing the *Far Seer*,' he indicated a little boat, which at a pinch might have carried six people. 'She's mine.'

'A very pretty craft,' I said. 'You should not be here, it is too dangerous.'

'Not for me, I speak excellent kitchen Achaean now and who is to know? Have you missed me, my golden one?' I kissed him and he whispered into my ear, 'I am going back into Troy, to speak to the Lady Cassandra. Even if the city is lost, she must not be.'

'No,' I agreed. 'She is beautiful. Besides she is a healer and the world is going to need healers.'

'A cool statement, Chryse, but I have seen the way you look at her. I will wait with *Far Seer* if she is taken. She likes you—will you come with us?'

'Where to?'

'Who cares?' he laughed. I laughed too, my spirits suddenly lightening. Anywhere, I thought, as long as it was away from Troy.

'All right,' I said, 'but be careful, my sailor.'

That night, it appeared, there was a great council of war. I did not attend it. Arion told me that the captains decided to risk battle if it was offered.

And, miraculously, it was. The Trojan army came forth and challenges were cried and trumpets rang out.

I went back to my hut to make infusions and tear bandages.

◇◇◇

The battle raged all day, then all night. Wounded were conveyed back to me and they seemed excited, as though the war was about to conclude; as though the city had lost its walls. I could see the archers still on guard and a mass of roiling cloud in the middle of the plain. Three ships were burning; the plain was carpeted with dead.

By noon the next day the Trojans had retreated and we were mourning Patroclus. Something like a whirlwind, flashing bronze, had erupted out of Achilles' camp when the body was brought in, and sliced through the Trojan ranks with slaughter; I swear that his sword moved faster than sight, men fell slashed and bleeding without knowing where the blow had come from; and the Myrmidons hunted after him, killing the wounded and following in his swathe like gleaners after a mower.

He stood at the gate and called Hector to fight, and Hector came.

I did not see the combat. I only heard the shriek from the city when the champion fell. Then I heard a disbelieving moan from both armies as Achilles dragged the body round the walls of Troy at the heels of his chariot.

He was mad. I had always thought so.

We were badly damaged and so were the Trojans and the gates were shut again.

That night I was sitting with my three healers and Arion, so tired that I could hardly keep my eyes open, when the old man started, got up, and taking me with him walked silently through the encampment to Achilles' tent.

No Myrmidon stopped us. Beside the tent stood a cart loaded with something that glittered and chinked. The horse was head down, grazing. Arion stood at the door of the tent and beckoned for me to come forward but I would not.

I heard voices within; an old man and a very young girl. 'I will give you a wagon load of treasure if you will give me my son,' said the old voice.

'Why should I do that?' The hero sounded a thousand miles away. 'He killed the only person I loved. Why should I ransom him?'

'For gold,' said the old man wearily. There was a pause.

'For gold and that girl.'

I heard a gasp, then the old man said, 'She is too young, Lord, she is only twelve!'

'You, girl. If I surrender your brother Hector's body, will you give yourself to me?'

Perfectly self-assured, the child's voice said, 'Yes, Lord.'

'Come then. Now.' There was a rustle and a creak of leather bed-straps. I heard no cry from the girl and no sound from the hero. Arion, who could see, widened his eyes.

'Where is the gold?' asked Achilles.

'Outside, Lord.'

Arion and I walked to the other side of the tent as three Myrmidons unpacked the wagon and carried the contents inside. Then they dragged out the piece of meat which had once been Hector, champion of Troy, and threw him into the cart.

The old man and the girl climbed up and the horse moved away towards the city. Inside the tent I heard Achilles talking to Patroclus as though he was there.

'Do you recall how we walked by the waterside, sweet prince, heart's delight?' he said piteously. 'How can you leave me, my golden one, my dearest, my love? I have lain in your arms all night a hundred times. Your breast was ever a pillow for my head. Through all my short life you have loved me and guided me;

without you where shall I go? What shall I do? Oh, Patroclus, how could you leave me?'

'Well, what did you see?' I demanded, as Arion dragged me away.

'You do not want to know,' he rejoined. This was not the case.

'What?' I pulled at his sleeve. 'Tell me or you will have no more of that Kriti wine.'

Arion hesitated, then said reluctantly, 'Achilles stripped off the girl's tunic, lay down on top of her, and kissed her.'

'Yes, and?'

'He took the end of a spear and pushed it inside her, just a little way. That's all.'

'You are joking. Did you know…? Did I tell you about the poor maiden that he gave me as a gift?'

'That was the Myrmidons, not their captain, evidently.'

'Well, well.' I took the bard back to my hut and plied him with good wine, but he swore that was all he had seen. Eventually, I had to believe him.

◇◇◇

The three things were done which presaged the fall of Troy and Eleni Apollo Priest affirmed that it would fall within the month. Odysseus, Eleni said, held the key and must be wooed. The king of Ithaca had taken offence, it seemed, and was sulking aboard his boat. Agamemnon had sent Briseis back to Achilles, swearing that she was untouched, but this had made no difference to the hero. He was still talking to dead Patroclus and Odysseus was refusing to speak to anyone.

I went back to my wounded and listened to Arion composing a song about the fall of the heroes in the great battle of the ships.

Not Epeigeus of Bedeion to his fair home returned,
Nor Prothenor son of Arielycus,
Pomachus, Archesilaus, Stichius,
Palamedes drowned by his beaked ship,
The Boeotian Medon and Iasus of Athens,
Of Phylace Echius and Clonius,

Deiochus slain by Pariki the Abductor,
Patroclus, loved one of Achilles,
Slain in error by the Champion of Ilium,
Soul devouring death took them all,
Death fell before their eyes,
They chewed the dust of the plain.
Illustrious Lycophron, son of Mastor,
Periphetes of Mycenae killed by Hector…

The list of dead went on for ten minutes until I begged him to either stop or to practise elsewhere.

Then he took umbrage too. There was a lot of offence being taken outside Troy that spring.

Chapter Twenty-nine

Cassandra

We laid Hector's damaged body on the pyre and wept, and as the flames mounted we danced. I thought of all he had been to me—brother and comforter and protector, always kind and gentle and reliable—and tore my face with my nails, poured the unsifted ashes over my head, and wept until I was almost blind because his ghost, which had kept me company for days, was gone, gone irretrievably. Andromache, white and silent, nursed her baby; Hecube danced and cried with us, as did soldiers and traders. On his breast I had put his inkpot and papyrus and his favourite stylus, his short sword and a spear and a bracelet I had woven out of Státhi's fur. I was glad that the grey creature had not seen the death of Hector. He would have attacked Achilles and been killed as well.

Andromache's bridal veil covered the body. It flamed and we danced until we stumbled with fatigue and fell asleep in the ashes.

Before I slept I thought of the last conversation I had had with my dead brother.

'Hector, do you know the future?'

'I don't know why everyone assumes that the dead know anything,' he had complained. 'It is difficult being dead; the past and the future is all one; it is hard to explain, my sister. Fate summons me, Cassandra. But I do not think I will see you soon; many others but not you. But I will be waiting, remember; I will come for you, dearest Cassandra.'

In my sleep I saw him again and held him close, but he kept looking over my shoulder, as though he was watching for someone.

When I woke I went to find Polyxena and demanded to know what the murderer had done to her. She told me: a symbolic rape which had not even hurt. Then the vision came; she would die of a cut throat. A clean cut, made with a sword or a very sharp knife. I glared the vision into blinking out. Polyxena had always carried doom with her, my small and solemn sister.

'I can't get his face out of my mind,' she repeated. 'I hate him but I can't forget him.'

'You will meet him again,' I told her grimly. 'Send a message to the Argive camp, say that you will wait for him at the oak tree outside the Scaean Gate.'

'What do you mean to do?'

'Cure you,' I said.

She sent the message by one of the traders who went down to the Argives, selling wine and barley meal. At the first night watch the hero would meet her by the tree. I smiled and left Polyxena counting bandages.

I had something to do in the temple of the Mother.

That day we heard that Achilles had sacrificed twelve Trojan prisoners on the pyre of his only friend. We could see the burning as I climbed down with my little sister from the Scaean Gate. I scaled the tree, Polyxena stood beside it, quivering with tension. Finally he came; a slim young man with long golden hair, not much taller than me. He took her hand and said, 'Maiden, what do you want of me?'

'Your love,' said Polyxena with what sounded like perfect truth. Achilles laughed bitterly. 'I have no love to waste on women,' he said. 'My body you can have; it has not long to live anyway.'

She accepted him into her arms and they lay down. I shot my little bolt, a bird bolt no longer than my hand, and it struck him in the heel.

He twitched and sprang away from her; his reflexes were amazingly quick. When he saw me in the tree, a scarecrow woman with cinder hair and red eyes, he cried, 'Aleko!' by which he meant I was one of the Furies. Then he fell bonelessly into Polyxena's embrace.

There she held him to her unformed breast and there he died about an hour later. Just before the venom of the green viper robbed him of speech, he smiled beautifully, so that his whole face was transformed and said, 'Patroclus!'

He tried to stretch out his hand but he had no control over the muscles. His head dropped, his heart laboured, and then he breathed a long sigh, relaxing him into death.

Polyxena rolled him over and laid him out neatly, with his arms by his side. He was beautiful; his face still unlined, his jaw never shaved. My sister took her small knife and cut a strand of his long hair and wound it around her throat.

My eyes fogged and cleared. A gleaming woman, sea-green and sea-blue wrapped the dead Achilles in her hair and dropped tears like pearls into his smooth brow. Thetis had come for her son. I did not mention her to Polyxena.

We climbed the ladder in the dark. She did not speak of the hero again.

When it was known in the city that Achilles Man Slayer was dead, my brother Pariki modestly informed the council that he had shot him from the Scaean wall with an Amazon bow. Polyxena said nothing. I did not wish our part in Achilles' death to be revealed, so I allowed my brother, the city destroyer, to enjoy his fraudulent glory.

Chapter Thirty

Diomenes

They found Achilles dead that evening with a little puncture wound in his heel. The pyre of Patroclus, so loaded with wine and dead horses and shamefully murdered Trojan boys that it was almost unburnable, was relit for the hero.

I had never been so glad to see someone dead.

Agamemnon ordered the funeral to be impressive but not too expensive and Arion sang a remarkably restrained ode for the hero, omitting mention of having girls raped to death. The remaining troops feasted and drank themselves insensible and Odysseus, as though he had been waiting for this moment, decided that a load of treasure would assuage his injured pride and came to the kings one night, when all of the carrion on the plain had been burned and the smoke had almost dissipated.

'We must dig a firepit and forge a bronze horse, a beautiful offering to the god Apollo, who is master of horses,' he said. In this he was inaccurate, as Poseidon is the master of horses, but I did not mention this. 'Then we will get into our ships and sail to the other side of Tenedos and wait. On the first day, they will keep the watch; on the second day, they will slacken but still be there, but in three days, now that Hector is dead, they will be round at their favourite woman's taking off their armour, I guarantee,' he said. 'The gates will be opened and the city will be ours.'

'How will the gates be opened?' asked Menelaus.

Odysseus shared a glance with Calchas and said suavely, 'They will be opened, Lord,' and Menelaus did not press him.

I took Eleni and Arion to watch while the army found enough skilled craftsmen to make the clay model and then the shell, in order to hollow-cast the horse in the sands of the beaches. Only Mycenaeans had this skill. It was much wondered at in the world, because bronze is too heavy to make solid statues more than about two hands high. Some Mycenaean genius had found that a thin shell of bronze is enough to support a large sculpture, the size of a human.

The smith's fires burned to charcoal all night. It took them three days to make the model and then another two days to pour and cool the mould enough to break it and free the image.

It was remarkable, a full-sized bronze horse with mane and tail flowing, one hoof raised as if about to gallop.

Then we packed up everyone, the wounded and the sick, and sailed off to lie off Tenedos. I was seasick again. Among the flotilla I sighted a little boat with a dark-haired sailor and a crew of three. Eumides was sailing with the fleet.

Chapter Thirty-one

Cassandra

It took Troy a day to believe that the Achaeans had gone. When we finally ventured onto the sands, all we found was a marvellous bronze horse with the inscription: 'To the Sun Bright; a splendid offering by the Achaeans.'

We took it inside. I felt the vision wash over me and crash, tying my tongue: Troy burning. The city I could see was populated with the dead, grotesque, bloody, and still talking.

I woke in the Temple of the Mother and the priestess told me that the Achaeans had gone for good, discouraged now that Achilles was dead.

The watch did not sleep on the walls that night. The king held a council and I went. He was doddering and old beyond belief; he could no longer stand alone. Pariki was at his side all the time, whispering.

'They are gone and now we must dismiss our allies,' said the old man. 'Scythians, you have done nobly; here is your reward,' he loaded them with gold necklaces and decorated belts, adding 'and there are horses for you at the gates.'

The Scythians bowed, took the gold, regretted that they had not collected many heads, and left. The Carians and Mysians were also thanked and went. The Amazons were called and rewarded with more gold than the others. Priam also gave them seventeen of the Trojan horses whose sires and dams were from Olympus. They kissed me cordially, saddened by the death of their lady. I noticed that Eris' chest was now loaded with numberless strings of Argive teeth.

By midnight, all our allies were gone. I wanted to scream, 'No, we need these people, do not let them go!' but no one would listen to Cassandra, who was known to be mad, now that her brother Hector was dead, even if I could have spoken.

More of the people left for Troas. Boats set out into the empty seas, carrying people and livestock. The city was loosening, settling, relaxing. I saw it all and could not say a word.

The first night, the gates were kept shut. The second night, the watch was still there, hanging on although the rest of the city was reverting to normal.

On the third night I received a message from Eleni, mind-to-mind; a warning so strong that it startled me out of my dreary misery and I went into the streets and up onto the Scamander Gate. No one was guarding the walls. I was about to beat the drum for the alarm; I had the drum stick in my hand, when someone threw a bag over my head and I was tossed over a shoulder.

I kicked and struggled until someone held a nauseating cloth over my mouth. It made me dizzy—I think it was compounded of henbane and a certain mushroom, and I could not prevent myself being thrown down onto a stone floor in the dark. Someone hissed, 'Lie there until they come to ravish you, Princess!' It was Mysion, the Priest of Apollo.

I heard a door thud shut.

I tore at the bag until I managed to release myself. I was in the dark. I felt around until I encountered a smooth face, then another, and realised that I was in the Temple of the Pallathi. I knew what was going to happen. I could not save the city. But I could do some damage to the attackers.

The sanctuary leads into the inner chamber of the Mother, where Eleni and I had been taken when we were children and the vicious god had given us the poisoned gift of prophecy. I did not expect to be able to call the spectral snakes, the divine serpents, but I could call the others.

I made the high whistle that meant food and scattered their supply of dead mice across the floor. They came. I heard the rustle of scales on the floor.

Then lightning flashed, thunder struck, and I heard screams and the shattering of wood.

The gates were down.

I arranged myself at the foot of the Pallathi, the biggest one, which was unsteady on its plinth, and waited for the Argives to find me.

◇◇◇

It must have been dusk when the door burst open. A huge man shouldered aside the shards of broken wood, saw me, and grabbed my ankles, fumbling with his tunic. This was not unexpected. I waited until the light from the burning, the red light of my own city burning, could fall on me and let my potential rapist see what he was attacking.

I was wreathed in snakes. They were harmless brown ones, who have no poison, but my huge attacker did not know that. I parted my legs, and the golden one that had been lying along my thighs was dislodged, rearing up and hissing.

The Argive went grey and scrambled to his feet. I pulled my rope.

The falling statue, regrettably, missed him and shattered to lumps of rock on the floor.

'Come with me,' he said through numb lips, 'Lady.'

'Take me to Agamemnon,' I said haughtily.

I began to unwind the snakes, cropping them carefully near the entrance to the lower pit whence they had burrows into the outside earth. If they were not cooked by Troy burning overhead they might gain their freedom, as I had just lost mine.

I retained one, as decoration, and I had other resources.

'What is your name?' I asked the monstrous Achaean and he said, 'Aias, Lady.'

Outside the Temple of Apollo lay Mysion, who had betrayed the city. He had been tortured to death, doubtless to make him reveal the hiding places of all the temple's treasures. They had almost burned his feet off at the ankle. I stepped over him, avoiding the Achaeans who were carrying loads of the Sun Bright's temple furnishing down the stairs. Vengefully I reminded Apollo that this was all his own doing.

As a soldier tried to grab my arm my captor roared, 'She is mine!' and the man let go, falling back as my snake hissed at him.

I followed Aias, son of Telamon, through Troy and I could not close my eyes. In the Palace of the King Polites, Deiphobos and Priam lay slaughtered on the floor, lying as they had fallen from their benches. A girl screamed monotonously as she was raped; until the scream was cut off abruptly. I heard a shriek and saw Perseis thrown from the top of the Palace of Maidens. She died broken on the stones. Her hair tore out of its comb as it always had and flowed over her mutilated face, fine as mist. I understood that the injuries I had seen on her in my vision were produced by the steep streets of Troy.

I heard Achaeans laughing and a girl crying, 'No!' I thought it might be Eirene. Men fought in the streets and alleys, unarmoured, barely awake. They were cut down, crushed under stone casts, slashed, and decapitated. Maeles lolled over his temple railing with his head almost cloven in two. Blood wet the cobbles and everywhere was the stench of smoke.

As we stepped down the streets to the lower city, I saw drunken men dancing in fine tunics, hung about with jewels of the queen of Troy. Barley meal, blood, and wine were spilled into the gutters.

Lying in the street was the body of a girl, a knife standing upright in her left breast. Aias spurned the corpse with his foot as he strode before me. Blood spilled as she was rolled over. It was Cycne, who could not bear to be a slave again.

Along the way my captor met other Argives leading women and they brought us finally into the Place of Stranger's Gods. We were loot; the spoils of Troy. I saw Hecube there, Iris and

Eirene and Andromache with the baby; perhaps three hundred women, mostly unharmed, for we were valuable, not plunder to be wasted. We were the well-skilled women of Troy.

Behind us, as in the vision which had haunted me since childhood, the city burned. The wooden scaffolding that ran along the gates took fire and belched smoke; the Scamander Gate tower flamed and collapsed. It was so familiar that I was not affected as I might have been; it was almost a relief. Ash spilled on us as we were hurried away. Agamemnon did not want his captives damaged.

I heard the other women comforting each other as the soldiers drove us on; not unkindly, but firmly. We were cattle now.

'It's all right, don't cry, at least we're alive,' I heard a linen-spinner tell her sister. 'Even being a slave is better than being dead.'

'I shall tend some man's house,' said Hecube. 'I shall carry water and kindle the fire. Aie! Aie! Ah, my grief! My sons, my sons are all dead!'

I was not so sure about that. Eleni was alive. I knew this because I could feel him. His horror echoed my own as we watched aghast. The vision which had woken us from a sweet sleep when we were three became reality in front of our eyes. My death-visions, the special curse of Apollo on Cassandra, had almost ceased; most of them had already come true. For a flash, I saw the soldiers as skeletons; most of this army was going to die when or before it got home. Only the glowing healer, Chryse, was fleshed in this bony multitude. Only he had life and breath in this bodiless wilderness.

I stumbled, then dragged myself upright. Evidently I was going to live. I must endure.

Chapter Thirty-two

Diomenes

The plan worked. Odysseus' plans always worked. By the middle of the third day the city was taken.

I saw them bring the captives down to the beach, weeping as the city burned behind them. A boy had come in the night, Neoptolemus, saying that he was the son of Achilles, and Agamemnon had accepted this. There was some argument about Achilles' armour; no one seemed to know what had happened to it.

I saw dreadful things on the beaches.

I saw a very pretty youth arguing with a soldier, something about the precedence due to a prince. The soldier lost patience, a sword flashed, and the youth lay with his entrails spilled into the dust.

It seems that he was Pariki, Alexandratos, Prince of Troy.

Then there was a discussion with a woman pale as wool, clutching a baby. They spoke to her and she wailed in heart-rending grief while the other captives tried to comfort her. She tore off her veil and threw sand on her hair; she writhed in agony. It was pitiful to watch her.

Then she kissed the baby, said, 'Go to your father,' and gave it to the son of Achilles.

He went away with it. I later heard that he had thrown it over a cliff. It was the son of Hector, Astyanax.

After that a young man came, carrying an old man on his back. He was one of the captives and Agamemnon said to him, 'What is your name, Trojan?'

'Aeneas, and this is my father Anchises.'

'Put me down, boy, and run. Burdened with me you can never escape,' wailed the crippled old man.

Agamemnon grunted, then said, 'Hear all men! This is an example of filial piety. Let Aeneas and his household pass; give them a ship.'

The young man came to the captives and took two women out of the herd; an old woman and a child. They cried after the others as the young man Aeneas took them away toward the Trojan port. He did not run, but walked proudly. I hoped that he would survive.

The army was breaking into groups with their spoil. The wife of Hector and the Apollo Priest Eleni were allotted to Neoptelemus. Hecube the queen, in ragged garments, her hair torn from its binding, was given to Odysseus who took her arm courteously, as if she had not been the defeated queen of a sacked city. She snarled at him, showing all her teeth, but he spoke soothingly to her and she suffered him to lead her away. The other women were sent here and there across the encampments, pulled apart from their friends, not even given time to say goodbye. My heart was moved; I was close to tears.

Then I saw her, Cassandra the Princess. Her hair was stuck into bunches with ash which the rain was rendering into mud and her cheeks were furrowed with parallel scratches. There was a golden snake around her neck. She looked like Hecate the Destroyer and she had evidently scared her escort half to death, for the Telamonian Aias instantly declined when he was offered the Princess Cassandra as a prize.

Finally Agamemnon ordered her into his own boat and she went with a grim smile. I packed my medicinal gear and a considerable treasure, which I had been given in gratitude by my patients. Wrapping them in a rolled cloak, I humped them to the shore, where I sat down on the bundle.

The wind changed just on dark. I found the little boat and hid inside. Eumides hugged me and said, 'That is the king's ship. I can't afford to row; we'll have to rely on drift. Keep your eyes on the masthead. There is a little of the fire of gods in the air and it glows. There, see?'

All round were rocking ships, men talking and laughing. I heard the occasional splash as someone overbalanced under too much looted wine and fell in, to be hauled aboard again with laughter and curses.

I loathed them all, all of them. The tall city was burning still; the reek of smoke was in my face.

And I had forgotten my infusion for seasickness.

Chapter Thirty-three

Cassandra

My courage was not wearing well. I had not expected them to murder Hector's son. And they had led Polyxena away, saying that she was the bride of Achilles. I saw the red gash in her throat and remembered Iphigenia, daughter of Agamemnon. She did not cling to me but walked calmly after the tall high priest, my doomed little sister, my lamb to the sacrifice.

Extreme hatred is as weakening as extreme joy. I leaned on Agamemnon's arm when he ordered me aboard his ship and looked into his face.

He was tall and strong, broad of bones, obstinate beyond belief. Behind him I saw a vision of a city with high walls and a black-haired woman waiting by an open door with a double axe in her hands.

The axe came down on his neck as I watched, almost decapitating him, smashing the spine with a crunch of broken bone. The tiled floor of a bathroom swam with blood; it smelt like a slaughterhouse. For once, I enjoyed the curse of Apollo. I revelled in the details—his embroidered robe splashed with gore, the red sticky tide creeping to the woman's feet, her laughter echoing in the bathchamber, the scented water pinkening as the blood coloured it. He would die, violently, very soon. I smiled.

Agamemnon saw something of this in my eyes, for he shuddered. He lifted me half off my feet and threw me into the hollow ship.

From somewhere nearby, I suddenly caught a wave of joy from Eleni, half-guilty joy. Bereaved and heart-broken Andromache had put her hand in his.

That carried me for a while. We were lying at anchor in the dark. At the bow, someone was being raped. The shop rocked like a cradle and I heard half-smothered cries of pain and outrage. It might be my turn next. I felt down over my body to oil it so that I would not be too badly injured, but I felt cold and alone and close to despair. Opening my scrip, I took out a flask and prepared to drink it. To die and join Hector sooner than he had expected; to die and sink into the cool dark, where I would see nothing ever again; to go out like the flame of a candle—it really was seductive.

Then I remembered Eumides the Trojan and his fantasy of escape.

I was not chained; they had not so far dared to touch me. Someone shoved a jug of looted harvest wine into my hands and I emptied the whole flask of poppy and honey, with a measured dose of henbane to ensure sleep. I had meant to use it to kill myself, but I suddenly could not believe that all my suffering led only down into the dark. There must be a reason for agony or humans could not bear life. I had become strong in the god's torments and I would not throw it all away if I could manage it. I tasted the wine, and found that the infusion was not noticeable. There was not enough to kill more than one person in it. But I might put the boat's crew to sleep.

The wine went around and I heard people drinking. The woman next to me was already drowsing when the jug came past again. I waited with my breath held until I heard the crock drop and smash. When no voice was raised to complain about clumsy sailors, I rolled to the side, avoided an oar, and slid down into the sea.

The water was cold. I lay on my back, waiting for the cry which would mean my escape had been discovered. Small waves flowed over me, cool and delightful. The serpent writhed off my neck, disgusted by the chill, and swam towards the shore. The mud and ash of mourning melted and sluiced out of my hair. Even the smell of burning began to dissolve.

I turned over and swam one stroke, two. The tide lapped against the rowlocks of the boats, making a soft noise, and I tried to make no louder sound. The king's ship was silent. I was flooded with a strange joy; I had now lost everything; brothers, lover, family, city. There was nothing more that I could mourn for and I floated free in the forgiving water, princess and priestess no longer, loosed of all bonds. I think that I might have laughed.

Then I heard a whisper in Achaean, 'Shall fish be netted, Chryse?' and I touched the steering oar of a small boat and said, 'Net me.'

They lifted me out of the water with hardly a sound. Eumides' arms were clasped around me and Chryse's mouth was on mine.

I had been the city's and the god's since I was three. Now I was no one's but my own.

Epilogue

'Children, I gave the city into your hands,' said Zeus disgustedly. 'Look what ruin you have made. What worship will come to us from fallen Ilium, the Holy City? It is burned and the walls are broken. The people are scattered. The temples are sacked—even your temple, Apollo Sun Bright. Is this desolation the only result of your quarrel?'

'Achilles is dead,' mourned Athena. 'Though his mother has him safe. So many heroes gone, so few ships return on the sea of the great fleet that came.'

'One shall not return,' vowed Apollo, blowing one little black keel far out of its way. 'Odysseus shall wander far before he returns to Ithaca and his dreary, virtuous wife. He'll need all of his nimble wits to get home again. Come, Father, be comforted. What is the loss of a temple to such as us? Men know our power, they fear us, and men always worship what they fear.'

'That is so,' replied Zeus.

'You are makers of ruin,' Demeter moved away. 'Young and pitiless. You will deserve oblivion when it comes. The kindly earth shall cover your temples and grass will grow on your altars. To kill the harmless mortals for so cruel a reason—they will say the gods have no justice and they will be right. Such despair will drive them away from any worship. They will offer no prayers to a cold and empty heaven.'

'Men need gods,' snapped Apollo. 'Even Diomenes needs the idea of gods.'

'*I know nothing about these great matters, but I have won my wager. Cassandra did not die of despair, even when she had lost everything,' gloated Aphrodite. 'She lives yet and she lies in the arms of your favourite Diomenes, who loves her. I have won.'* She tossed the golden apple into the air and laughed like a peal of golden bells.

Apollo snatched it as it fell and balanced it, glowing, on the palm of his unlined immortal hand.

'*You have not won yet,*' he said.

Afterword

Yes, yes, I know. The Trojan War lasted ten years. Sparta wasn't there in 1350 BC, not by that name. The lions at Mycenae are newer than the Trojan War. No one knows the names of the little towns between Epidavros and Mycenae. Everyone knows that Cassandra was killed at Mycenae and everyone knows that she was making clear prophecies and was not believed.

Where Troy once stood is now called the hill of Hissarlik. At least ten Troys are there, each new city being built on the ruins of the old. Although Schliemann, the father of modern archaeology, thought that he had discovered the ruins of Priam's city half way down, it is now generally agreed that Troy VIIb is probably the Ilium of the Trojan War. There isn't a lot left of Troy VIIb, mostly a layer of charcoal. We are talking about a very long time ago, before the Classic Age which everyone associates with Greek civilisation, before Greece was Greece and its people were called Greeks. After (or possibly before, but I have assumed after) Troy fell, so did all of the cities in Achaea, and the Dark Age, lasting 300 years, began with the Dorian invasion (though an enterprising trader in Achaea was still selling posts with fake Greek inscriptions to the Etruscans throughout, which is cheering). I have assumed that Troy fell first, then weakened Mycenae-Argos-Tiryns could not resist the invaders.

Age of the City Of Troy

People moved around a lot in ancient times, as John Boardman in *The Greeks Overseas* demonstrates. It was not unusual to uproot a whole community in response to an oracle and move it to another place, quite often having to fight the locals. This seems to have happened with Troy; Dardanus followed his cow to the hill of Até and his descendants spent several generations fighting for the place before they could begin the building of Troy. The present city was built by Poseidon for Laomedon, who called it Ilium and also Troy in memory of Tros, his father. It was then partially ruined by Heracles, who built it again. Laomedon was the father of Priam, the present king. Note also that there was extensive trading all over the known world, possibly even to America and certainly to England, Herodutus' 'Tin Isles,' for an essential component of bronze.

I have read the book which suggests that Troy was in North America and I do not find it convincing.

Cassandra

Aeschylus in Agamemnon says that Cassandra died in Mycenae, killed by Clytemnestra. I have decided that she didn't.

Customs of Troy and Achaea

The Trojans do not seem to have had animal sacrifice; Hector runs back to the city in a moment of greatest danger and tells his mother to sacrifice her best garment to the Lady. The Achaeans routinely sacrifice an animal for any religious purpose and to divine omens. According to Homer, the Trojans burn their dead and the Achaeans bury them.

Helen

Herodotus says that Troy would have handed her over if they had her and I have to agree. Various other sources support this, suggesting that the Elene in Troy was only an image made by

Aphrodite to protect her darling. The plays, however, are not to be relied upon for history; *Iphigenia in Tauris* by Euripides suggests that the sacrificed Iphigenia survived by divine intervention and officiated at a human-sacrificing temple of Athene in Tauris, being later rescued by her older brother Orestes and his friend Pylades. Note also that Eleni (Helenus) and Cassandra were twins, not Cassandra and Pariki (Paris) as was suggested in Marion Zimmer Bradley's *The Firebrand*.

Homer

Homer's *Iliad* is inconsistent; there are for instance three separate descriptions of how one person is killed. He even kills Aeneas with a stone-cast quite early on, which is tough on Virgil, who followed Aeneas to the founding of Rome. I have used the version which fits in with my story and I am sure that Homer would approve, whoever she, he (or they) was (or were). Please also note that the *Iliad* only occupies a few days at the end of the war; it is actually called 'The Wrath of Achilles' and loses interest when Achilles is slain. It ends with the funerals of Hector and Achilles and is basically concerned with the clash between heroes. I am not especially concerned with heroes. My opinion of them wavers between that of Arion and that of Diomenes.

Homeric Epithets

The epithets—'Argos where horses graze,' 'the bright-eyed lady,' and 'the fish-delighting sea, devourer of ships' are mostly from Homer. Since they remind me strongly of Norse kennings, I have invented some in a similar vein and lifted some from actual Old Norse.

Homosexuality

'An army of lovers shall not fail.' There seems to have been no stigma attached to homosexuality. Indeed, it was inevitable if one drank from the spring of Salmancis. I have set my characters free to find their own sexual partners.

Invented Characters

I have made up Diomenes out of whole cloth, because when casting around for an Achaean voice and finding myself becoming alarmingly anti-Argive, I could not find a hero I liked who survived the *Iliad*, much less the war. So I found Diomenes of the healing hands. I also needed an outsider to describe a battle. As many soldiers have told me, when you are in a battle you cannot see anything but the opponent who is trying to kill you and when the dust dies down you are concerned with rescuing your comrades and staying alive. Diomenes watches the battle from the outside. Homer flies on eagles' wings to view the whole battle; I and my characters are down in the blanketing dust with the soldiers. The temple at Epidavros is as described but the healers are all invented, though most of the patients come from the votive tablets. However, Arion Dolphin-Rider is in Herodotus and did dedicate a dolphin to Dionysius at Tarentum. In the same way all the minor characters in Troy are invented, except the sons of Priam, the Amazons, the royal family, and the priests.

Language

I have assumed that the Trojans spoke a different language, because Cassandra in *Agamemnon* makes her prophecy of murder at Mycenae and remarks, 'I thought you could understand me; I speak good Achaean.' Homer says that the goddess Iris tells Hector to keep the allies together because they all speak different languages. Certainly Hittite was entirely distinct, so was Egyptian, and the others may have been dialects, though anyone trying to speak Swedish to a Dane will soon find that dialect differences can render one completely incomprehensible.

Medicine

I have consulted Hippocrates, Dioscorides (who was a Greek doctor with the Roman army and the ancient herbalist whose descriptions I can actually recognise) via Culpepper's *Complete*

Herbal and English Physician. I have also consulted various old textbooks, especially the medical volume in *The Times History of the War* and *Leaves from a Surgeon's Casebook* by Dr James Harpole.

It is generally agreed that the Greeks knew a lot about medicine, even before the split between the Islands of Cos and Cnidus. I have deduced the practice of hypnotism from the presence of two Gods of Sleep, Morpheus and Hypnos. I may be entirely wrong. However, hypnotism is only useful on the susceptible, so I have added the percussive smoke. Note that at the same time the Chinese had perfectly reliable acupuncture anaesthesia. Old medical books have been used to describe medicine before sulfamioniades and penicillin; many diseases which killed thousands are now almost entirely extinct (tuberculosis, tetanus, smallpox, various fevers). However, Dr Harpole reports that malignant malaria killed a detachment of British soldiers as late as 1935. Having moved from a low-lying malarial swamp to a high mountain, half of them died of cerebral haemorrhage—the authentic Sennarcharib 'breath of the Lord.' Tetanus treatment with snake venom is described by Dr Harpole. The description of the Gaboon or Russell's viper is from Gerald Durrell.

Siege of Troy

Modern experience with the series of wars which have disfigured the twentieth century suggests that people revert to normal very quickly under siege. 'You can get used to anything,' said one old lady about London during the Blitz, and T.S. Eliot adds, 'Habit is a great deadener.'

Troas and Novum Ilium

I found a mention of 'Troas, child of Troy' in Sir Thomas Browne's essay 'Of Troas.' Browne refers to the Roman historian Strabo, who states that Troas was established before the fall of Troy and by the people of that city. Contemporary Roman maps referred to it as 'Novum Ilium,' that is, new Troy. It seems to have survived the Dark Ages when the Argive civilisation fell into ruin, to feature in the Acts of the Apostles and the Epistles of St Paul.

Troy as a Minoan City

The Minoan Kingdom was destroyed by earthquake and invasion about 1300BC. The script Linear B reveals that Crete or Kriti was occupied by someone who spoke early Greek. Minoan (Linear A) has not been deciphered. It was a civilisation with plumbing and no walls. The paintings and artifacts reveal a sunny, delightful, relaxed society in which women had position and power. I have made the bold assumption that the Minoans who spoke Linear A went to Troy. According to various sources the city is only two generations old when the Achaeans come. That makes Troy Minoan, with the wine-loving phallic dancer Dionysius and the Mother, Mistress of Animals and ruler of everything else, as their main gods. This fundamentally sensible arrangement—an irresponsible but powerful male deity and the responsible Mother—is not reflected in Achaea, where they have the stern Father Zeus, his wife Hera, and his squabbling children. It is agreed that the oldest god is Pan; even Herodotus says so.

This book has caused me nightmares; I have never considered what a war would really be like. It may be the first time someone as fervently anti-war as me has tried to take on a siege and the destruction of a city. I felt like a murderer the whole time I was writing it. However, having been fascinated with Greece since I was a child, met my best friend Themetrula Georgovasilopoulos and was made an honorary Greek, and with Ancient Greece since I found Herodotus in an op. shop at the age of twelve, I have attempted it. I have travelled most of the roads I describe on my own feet.

Bibliography

Primary Sources

Aeschylus, *The Oresteia, The Suppliant Maidens, The Persians* and *Seven Against Thebes*, Penguin, London, 1987.

Euripides, *Ion, The Trojan Women, Iphigenia in Tauris, Alcestis, Hippolytus* and *Electra* (I prefer Gilbert Murray's translations), Penguin, London, 1962.

Herodotus, *The Histories* (translation by Aubrey de Selincourt), Penguin, London, 1935.

Hesiod, *Collected Works*, Penguin, London, 1962.

Homer, *The Iliad* and *The Odyssey*, Penguin, London, 1964.

Sophocles, *Antigone, Oedipus the King, Electra, Philoctetes* and *Oedipus at Colonus*, Penguin, London, 1985.

Thucydides, *The History of the Peloponnesian War*, Penguin, London, 1987.

Virgil, *The Aeneid* (translation by John Dryden), Pelican, London, 1971.

Secondary Sources

Boardman, John, *The Greeks Overseas*, Pelican, London, 1964.

Brooks, Iris, *Costume in Greek Classic Drama*, Methuen, London, 1962.

Browne, Sir Thomas, *Miscellaneous Writings* (ed. G. Keynes), Faber and Faber, London, 1931.

Chadwick, John, *The Decipherment of Linear B*, Pelican, London, 1961. Contains Michael Ventris' decoding of this language, proving it be an early form of Greek.

Calpepper, *Complete Herbal and English Physician*, reprinted Harvey Sales, London, 1981. He quotes Dioscorides, the ancient Greek, extensively.

Durrell, Dr James, *Leaves from a Surgeon's Casebook*, Cassell, London, 1942.

Laver, James, *Costume in Antiquity*, Thames and Hudson, London, 1964.

Severin, Tim, *The Jason Voyage* and *The Ulysses Voyage*, Arrow Books, London, 1987. Contain all you need to know about navigating a Bronze Age boat. Severin's remarkable endurance and courage in building Argo was an inspiration to me, as well as providing me with authentic details and maps.

General Sources

I have used votive tablets at Epidavros and Pergamon for medical triumphs, Jung for the psychiatric practice, and archaeological record for the weapons, chariots, and horses. Especially useful were traveller's guidebooks produced by the Greek government, and studies by Woolley, Wheeler, and Cottrell.

To receive a free catalog of Poisoned Pen Press titles, please contact us in one of the following ways:

Phone: 1-800-421-3976
Facsimile: 1-480-949-1707
Email: info@poisonedpenpress.com
Website: www.poisonedpenpress.com

Poisoned Pen Press
6962 E. First Ave. Ste 103
Scottsdale, AZ 85251